REMEMBERING
JONAS

A Novel

By Robert L. Brown

Published by Robert L. Brown, Tucson Arizona

Yodel Day Books

ISBN: 978-0-9861124-0-9
Library of Congress Control Number: 2015904903

Printed in the United States of America

*I dedicate this story
to abandoned children
May their hearts be loved
and their dreams be lived*

A thanks to my creator
For the life that I have
All the old good times
At all the old places
I got my memories
What more can I ask
And thanks to you too
Mom and Dad

Contents

Foreword

I think most everyone would like to look back upon their lives with a worthwhile degree of satisfaction in regards to the choices they've made. Most of us all came from simple and modest backgrounds as did Jonas Miles, the main character of my story. Whether you like the name Jonas or not, I wanted to give my main character an uncommon name. I have not come across any person with the name Jonas in my life, but I know there are many Jonas's out there and I mean that in a good way. There are things in life we have no control over. If we should find ourselves unsatisfied about something in life then it's up to ourselves to change it. Jonas started out as another lost teenage soul where finding his futures path or committing himself to the usual vocational professions seemed a bit difficult. Remembering Jonas', is a multifaceted story of many things that will take the reader through a journey of emotions and perhaps some childhood comparisons. The story remains true to its primary focus and that is anyone who really tries hard enough to make it somewhere, can and will'. It's what we leave behind when were gone that becomes our legacy. It's the things we said and did that will be remembered. 'Remembering Jonas', is a story of the human side with enough built in fantasy that includes some important icons of the times as Jonas Miles takes us through his life's 20th century journey.

ONE

Shoo Birds

The flashing surface of the ocean was alive in constant movement as the momentum of waves came forth steadily as they released their crashing energy upon the sandy beach. The blue sky and warm seventy five degree air temperature could be so typical of a late summer's southern California day. The afternoon sun had once again been victorious in burning off the remnants of any leftover morning fog. Just inside the shallow tidal zone of the spent waves dozens of scurrying feet of beach goers paced themselves up and down the wet firm sand. The place was Santa Monica, a popular beach hang out for many people who lived in Los Angeles.

There within eye shot of a life guard's watching eye a group of girls were trying to beach a rubber raft that they all had been sharing. Once they beached the raft a young girl barely in her teens seemed to be leading three younger girls. These younger girls followed the older one like team work as they all came up on a loose run doing somersaults. All their motions upon the beach had been captured by their chaperone as she filmed them with an 8mm movie camera. The younger ones were quite excited and vocal in expressing their enjoyment of the moment. They each performed a few end over end flips before landing near or on a large black inflated inner tube. Once upon the tube they stared into the camera grinning. One of the young girls sitting on the tube began bouncing up and down until she fell over backwards to the great humor of anyone who might have witnessed it.

There lying on the beach watching the amusing spectacle was twenty seven year old Tom Miles with his wife Sonia. They had only been there a short while and like many Californians enjoyed being down by the sea as often as they could. It was Tom's day off as a manager of a large retail outlet. Unbeknownst to the Miles couple a homeless man was approaching from behind.

"Sir, could you spare some change?" the man asked. The man looked in need and his composure convincingly sincere. Tommy looked at his wife because he had left his wallet in the car. Sonia looked in her purse, took out a dollar bill and handed it to Tom.

"Here you go, guy," Tom said as he handed the note to the man.

"I'm John J, but most just call me JJ," said the man.

"Well here you go, JJ."

"Thank You, thanks, I really appreciate it. Hey, what's your name?" asked the homeless man.

"What's my name?" asked Tommy with a surprised look.

"Yeah," said the man. Tom responded in a somewhat uninspired manner.

"My name is Tom."

"OK, thank you Tom," said the ragged looking man seeming more personal than most pan handlers, offering an air of sincerity as he walked off. Jonas and his wife looked at each other and then looked at JJ as he walked away, his feet churning away at the thick sand.

"Sure, JJ" replied Tommy.

Watching the girls go back into the water Tom's mind turned to other thoughts. Though his eyes were focused upon the seas horizon his mind was thinking about a man named Jonas who had passed away. Jonas Miles was the man who had adopted Tom and given him his last name. As time went by, Tom, or Tommy as his wife called him sat on his sun lounger for quite some time without saying a word. She looked at him and it seemed he was in deep thought.

"What are you thinking?" she asked.

With tears in his eyes he quickly looked at her for a second before returning his gaze back out on the ocean.

"Oh, I was just thinking of Jonas and about all the things we did together," he responded, before grabbing his suntan oil to rub onto his skin.

Meanwhile there was a congregation of gulls that seemed to be sitting amongst the sand and scattered seaweed that was strewn about on the beach. There were a good number of them as they seemed to be observing any activity or just clumsily meandering about amongst the humans. They seemed to be watching just about anything that caught their eye. Suddenly some gibberish seemed to begin, or squawking, whatever you called sea gull talk. It went back and forth for awhile and then suddenly a large number of them took to the air. The onshore breeze caught their outstretched wings and so effortlessly beating their feathered appendages they seemed to ascend aloft with little effort.

These gulls for the time being didn't seem to have any intention of hanging around as most of them ascended in silence, while a few continued their method of screeching gibberish. Soon the flock of gulls soared high above the sea and sandy white coastline. It wasn't uncommon for such groups of birds to wander away from the sea's edge as if exploring any new opportunities that might be found. These sea loving birds occasionally congregated in flocks that could be seen soaring much higher than their typical low paths over tidal zones. Their medium length bodies having long stretched out wings allowed them to quickly move through the air. The onshore breeze as it went along gave them an even greater boost in speed amongst the small scattered creamy cloud's, that too were propelled along by the cool ocean breeze. They were moving in an easterly direction from the ocean's edge where their vantage now offered a spectacular view of the busy city. Certainly in many places down below traffic came to a crawl whilst at ground level there was the robust and fast paced economy of a nineteen nineties Los Angeles. As the gulls flew, one business after another passed beneath their outstretched wings. One was 'Ken's Image Studio', where rolls of cardboard shot out onto large die presses that stamped out life sized figures of Hollywood celebrities. Stacked in neat piles along the floors edge were such figures as Clark Gable, John Wayne, Bette Davis, Greta Garbo, Cary Grant, Gary Cooper, and Marilyn Monroe. God knows for what reasons they were bought. One might place the Duke in a western bar setting or find Gable as Rhet Butler in someone's parlor. The real Hollywood, with all its rich history such as, 'Grauman's Theater,' where movie stars placed their hands and feet into the wet cement of its outdoor foyer was only a short distance away.

Anyone who has lived in California for any length of time knows one can find gulls in the craziest of places. They have even been seen pillaging dump sites in the outlying deserts where it would seem no sign of water was around. Now these gulls that had been traveling in an easterly direction have caught the sight of something. For whatever reason it seems that these winged scavengers have discovered that often where humans are gathered food can be found, even if it's just occasional offerings by picnickers.

The gulls had begun their decent into an area of Hollywood not far from the boulevard that carries its name and all its famous cross streets. From a distance it would appear their target was a large home, however, by some standards this home wouldn't be big enough to measure up to the homes of many celebrities. Behind the home there was a large span of yard as the gulls came in upon set wings. Before these landing birds were many picnic tables and smoking barbecues with children scrambling about. There were children throwing baseballs back and forth as well as a myriad of other games in progress as one would imagine children to play. Hamburgers and hot dogs seemed to be what was on the menu with chips and various sides. This small flock of white washed gliders would crash this party and take anything they could get.

This home was not really a regular home as most of us know homes to be. It was a solid and stout building that had thus far stood its place in time. It sat on North El Centro Avenue in Hollywood. It was the Los Angeles Orphans Home. Through time, the pathway that led to its front door was witness to many a child's emotions. Initially, all feared the doors up ahead that led into some unknown reality but easily imagined misery. There were some children who pleadingly fought every step of the way toward those who brought them there. Some cried while some just approached solemnly. Some went quietly brave as if they had simply mentally prepared themselves to such things as they were used to. There just was no other option for most of them. At least that was the most common given reason to be told.

Most assumed that such children were simply the unfortunate results of impersonal flings or hopeful love rendezvous that rendered the undesirable results of pregnancy. For some, the unwanted results were the aftermath of bad places, bad decisions and bad things. For others it was all about the desire to not be alone, to love and feel loved, and ironically the results of such would deny love to their very own. Herein, lived the children born from such and it would always be the neglected child that had to pay the price. The reasons were many, unknown parents, only one parent, parents deceased, economic failure, parent incarcerated, drug abuse, child abuse, or parents who just thought of them as a burden they couldn't bear.

These children were referred to in many different ways but mostly with acronyms that suggested pity. Pity is something that one does and not what one is. How could one not reason that a given life is at least a gift unto themselves, or even a gift to the world. And so it was and how it was with the children that lived at the orphanage. Childhood of course is the most important time of a human beings life. It's during this period of the psychological development of one's self that will dictate how a person as an individual grows into maturity. Just as important, from very early on it will be the good and bad experiences of a child's life that they will draw from in their adulthood. And in time, surely as the years go by each will arrive at some decision as to their directions in life, or is it as some believe that fate is the chooser.

At the very least it is hoped that they will assume within their biological makeup the desire to believe in themselves, a most worthy and valuable virtue. To some it might be all they would ever have. Fortunately, most of us will never know that feeling of lonely conscience that haunts one's soul through the journey of parentless life. One could assume that such feelings of faultless or deliberate abandonment by a child's parents must occupy a time in ones thoughts. These individuals sometimes find it difficult to realize a born identity. Some are emotionally tougher than others and have what it takes to succeed, while others are obviously reluctant to trust anyone. Perhaps, some of these children may come to possess a host of false identities and personalities that have been affected to them, but such is the way of the world. And in the orphanage as in all homes people would strive to address their needs, to care for them and make them feel loved, or at least the illusion of such. All humans need to be cared about by someone even if only imagined.

So the walls of the home became familiar to many faces, many names, many moods and emotions. For most it was just a passing journey in slow motion. The home served to address their needs, was not unkind, and gave them hope to become responsible citizens in a sometimes crazy and unapologetic world. All of the children who went through the home left worth more, having more knowledge about life. All of the children who grew older and left the home came to know and understand each other better as little or as great as it was. They worked together, helped each other, and hurt each other in comment and deed. Yes, just like normal childhoods outside of such homes.

Most of the kids who left the home could be said to have found a worthwhile and befitting place in life. As they grew old enough to enter the work force some became nurses, some teachers, some cab drivers, and some helped to design and manufacture the needed planes and ships for the defense of their country. Some of the residents became famous, even movie stars. During the decades that followed perhaps some of these children were blessed with kind people who at first didn't seem a beacon of light, but came to them as a dim candle. Like life, a candle has a limited amount of time to glow and shine its light on the world. A candle can come to glow bright as candles glow and perhaps light the way for others, so that someday their light will shine on the world too.

The seagulls were becoming quite obnoxious. Some of the adults tried to shoo the birds away. After all, it was not so uncommon for such birds to commence bombing runs that could result in dirtied clothing or contaminated food containers. The seagulls scurried around tables, flopped about and did some low level glides across the melee of activity. They managed to get a few bites. However, the bounty and effort apparently wasn't worth their time. After a half hour or so a stiff breeze stirred and these busy birds once again took to the air to only go who knows where.

TWO

A Very Good Year

The year was 1962 and there was a cold bite to the air on a cloudy February afternoon at Glendale High School in California. Class had just gotten out for the day. At least it did for seniors Jonas Miles and his friend Derek Means. The two had just gotten into Jonas's two-tone 1956 Chevy Bel Air and in seconds they were pulling out of the school parking lot onto East Broadway. From under the hood a well tuned small block V-8 engine rumbled as it accelerated down the boulevard. Jonas Miles first name was Jonathan but ever since he was a young boy everyone called him Jonas. Jonas was giving his classmate Derek a ride home. The two were on the school varsity baseball team. They both were unusually quiet as the car purred down the road. Then Jonas turned down a residential street and a baseball came rolling out in front of the car as Jonas braked to a sudden stop. Two kids walking home had been tossing a ball around and it had gotten away from them. The Kid got his ball and Jonas started to continue on for the four miles it would take to get Derek home. The runaway ball aroused a thought in Derek's head.

"Wow, wasn't that one heck of a game?" remarked Derek.

"What game?" asked Jonas.

"That last game of the season when we played the Wildcats," responded Derek.

It had been about three weeks since the big game between Glendale and University High. Glendale had beaten Los Angeles by one run. Jonas was one of Glendale's Highs star players and had been voted the most valuable player in baseball that year.

"Yeah, it sure was," responded Jonas, as the remark induced him to reminisce back to that day, particularly the last part of that game. As Jonas drove, the car's occupants remained silent each thinking their own thoughts leaving only the engine talking.

So Jonas was at bat. Glendale was behind one point in the bottom of the ninth inning. The game was nearly over and the score was one to nothing with

University ahead at a home game. Glendale had men on first and second. It was very windy that day and often strong gusts came unexpectedly. The wind was right at the pitchers back and sometimes it came on like the devil. The only home run up to that point had been from the opposing team, the University Wildcats and that hit barely cleared the right field fence. Now it was one out and Jonas was up at the batter's box.

Dume LaCross was University Highs pitcher. He was a southpaw who frequently got his picture published and name mentioned in the local sports edition. He was good enough that the college scouts were paying attention, just like they had been watching Jonas. Dume had a killer fast ball and a fatal slider pitch. Whether it was the wind or just skill his curves were going right around home plate and right into the strike pocket. Occasionally the wind would push the ball past the plate like it had afterburners.

What spectators really liked to see was Dume's so called 'Slinky Shot'. He would wind up with his left arm and make a follow through look so normal, then suddenly as if his left arm became disjointed sling the ball to first base and beat the runner back for an out. So now Dume was winding up for a pitch and Jonas knew that it was important to swing at the right ball if there would be one. No pitch that was going to produce a grounder or a line drive was probably going to win this game. He needed a home run and a miracle. The miracle could be the wind stopping for a few seconds at the right moment. So Dume wound up as he raised his right leg high into the air and launched his streaking rocket toward Jonas.

"Strike!" yelled the umpire.

It was too low and inside for a decent hit. The count was one and one. The home team bleachers were full. People were yelling and doing everything they could to distract Jonas. Again the windup and then the ball came loose from Dume's hand and a blast of wind pushed the ball by like a rocket.

"Ball," was the call.

This time when Dume wound up for the pitch a home school fan had a message for Dume, as he yelled out onto the field.

"Let's get this game over Dume. Burn one in."

Jonas was waiting for the pitch. Again up went the pitchers right leg high into the air and as his arm was coming forward it seemed to disjoint and hurl the ball at first base like a bullet. It beat the runner's scramble back to the base.

"You're out!" yelled the first base official as the home team spectators roared in delight.

"Go Dume! Go Slinky!" came a cheer from the crowd.

"Another one bites the dust," shouted another.

"L.A. rules, pack it up Glendale," followed the vocal jabs.

Now there was only a man on second. Dume seemed to have that little pompous grin like he always did when he pulled off one of his so called slink shots. He wound up again and hurled the ball at high speed right down the center. It was right about where Jonas wanted it as he placed all his power for a full follow through swing, but he popped the ball up and behind for a foul. The count was now two and two. Dume just needed one more strike and the game would be over.

It was one of those times in sports that it happens to every player more often than not, the outcome of a game resting on one's shoulders. The catcher was giving his signals, Dume shook his head, no, no, no, and then yes. It was going to be a breaking ball on the inside. A pitch that if successful would drop inside and low leaving little chance of Jonas getting a decent hit and Los Angeles would go home the victor. It was perfect, the wind calmed for Dume as he looked right at Jonas with his familiar grin.

Dume's father Lonny, always showed up at the games. It was like father like son. To Jonas they were two peas in a pod. Dume's father was one of those people who never shut up always saying things to parents that suggested more insult then complement. Things like,

"Gee, your kid just might make a real ball player some day."

Then of course he would go on and practically rant about how good his kid was. Lonny worked as a bakery truck driver. He spent most of his time hanging around the visiting team's bleachers and he somehow knew which sons had which fathers. He would bet the fathers that their son would never get a hit off his son, Dume. Then if they didn't want to bet he would give them such odds that they either were forced to bet or be shamed. Either way it was a major embarrassment and insult for the father who could not even afford to lose five bucks. Money was tight and twenty bucks went a long ways. So this day there was Dume's father making out like an opportunistic vulture, looking to make some easy money. Before Jonas even came up to bat the senior LaCross already had a visit with Jonas's dad, George. The deal was made.

"Hey there, isn't Jonas Miles your son?" asked Lonny LaCross.

"That's right," responded George. He knew what was going to transpire with the visit because everyone knew about Dume's dad.

"I've got ten bucks that says your son can't get a hit off my boy," stated the elder LaCross with a brazen look.

"I don't know Mr. LaCross, everyone knows how good your boy is. I don't usually put myself in the position of giving away free money. I can see why you have a lot of confidence in him."

"Yeah, ain't he a natural?" responded Lonny grinning.

"Will you give me some odds, like two to one?" asked George.

"Yeah sure, that's the usual" replied the conceited elder LaCross.

"Do you got a hundred bucks on yuh?" asked George Miles.

"A hundred bucks, what for?" asked Lonny with a puzzled look.

"Because I want to bet you fifty bucks and when I win I'll need to get that hundred now," stated George Miles with a serious look.

"Well, I don't know, a hundred bucks?" Lonny stammered, doing some thinking.

"Okay, Yeah sure, but I don't have a hundred, maybe fifty," offered LaCross.

"Well okay, I'll bet you twenty five and if my boy gets a hit then I get fifty. Is it a deal?" asked George Miles, Jonas's father.

There wasn't much Lonny could do. He already offered two to one. Besides he was sure his son would strike out Jonas, Georges boy.

"Yeah, sure it's a deal," grinned Lonny.

At least that was the way the plan went down unbeknownst to Jonas. At the time fifty bucks was about a half weeks pay for many workers so whoever won the pot it would be a nice bonus.

So now Dume was ready for his kill. Many things went through his head in those few seconds prior to his pitch. All the games he had won for his team. The extra money he made for his Dad on the sidelines. Was he just lucky or was he really that good. Unquestionably he was that good. It didn't seem fair for a young man with such a disposition nor such arrogance and conceit to be allowed to walk the face of the earth. Like father like son they say. All the girls hung on his arms like Christmas tree ornaments. It was sickening.

Now the wind was steady at Dume's side and he would propel his pitch with all the planned trajectory of an Apollo space mission. So came that familiar wind up, the right leg high into the air and the follow through with the deadly left arm. Then, just as the ball left his hand as sudden as hell fury the wind changed direction. The strong wind was now coming right down the plate instead of across it. The ball was airborne and just like anything that is in flight it becomes affected by the forces against it. So the ball which was to meet home plate on the inside would now arrive somewhere other than as planned. It would come in low and down center over the plate. So that sudden change in the wind gust had played against the fast moving knuckle sized meteor. Jonas knew this had to be the one. With all his might he swung and the bat and ball met that sweet spot like they were the couple of the century.

All that could be heard was the loud crack of a solid hit as the ball sailed skyward toward center field climbing through the wind. The roaring sound of the home team bleachers went silent as everyone watched the ball climb high and far. Once the ball cleared the fence the visiting team spectators came to life with a renewed crescendo of cheers. As Jonas was running toward first he knew he had hit a homer with plenty of room to spare. He and the man on second came in to score and win the game by one run. Jonas's dad collected his fifty bucks from a reluctant and poorer pitcher's father who was never seen again taking bets for the rest of the year. Suddenly Jonas's daydream was shaken by a voice.

"Hey man, you just passed my house. Where you going?" asked Derek.

"Oh, sorry my mind was somewhere else I guess," responded Jonas.

"Give me some of that stuff," replied Derek with a grin.

Jonas turned the car around and dropped Derek off at his house on North Louise St.

"Anyhow, thanks for the lift. Watch you're speed, this area is like a motorcycle cop hangout," mentioned Derek.

"Yeah, sure, thanks for the warning," responded Jonas as he drove off toward home..

The Miles residence was a clean middleclass four bedroom home off of Wilson Avenue. George A Miles together with his wife Ariane, daughter Elizabeth, and son Jonas, lived within a short drive of the busy hub of Los Angeles and California's popular beaches.

From a darkened den a portable black and white 19 inch TV set was turned on as Ariane listened in. She was peeling carrots and potatoes in the kitchen for the preparation of her savory beef stew. The news was all ablaze with John Glenn's historic blast off from a Gemini Rocket as he made it to earth's orbit. He would complete three successful revolutions before returning home. Ariane heard the front door close.

"Is that you Jonas?"

"Yeah mom."

"How was school?"

"Oh, it's still there."

"What did you say?"

"Great. It was great mom."

"Were having stew tonight," said Ariane.

"Sound's good. It's cold out."

"What Hun?" asked Ariane, no longer able to hear him as he disappeared into his room.

It seemed a challenging time in a period of U.S. history where there was much going on. President Kennedy had his hands full with Cuba and the Soviet Union. Martin Luther King was building his freedom and equal rights movement. Federal troops were sent to make sure a certain black student by the name of James Meredith could register at the University of Mississippi. Race riots with burning buildings and looting would one day soon be a common scene on the evening news. America was a much divided nation with many fiercely challenging change, and others advocating it with the latter having the support of the executive branch.

Jonas Miles had just turned eighteen. He was the oldest with Elizabeth three years behind. Jonas was an average looking boy who was no more self conscious about his body than the next growing child. Now at eighteen Jonas was well muscle toned. He was a typical American mutt. His mother was of western Mediterranean blood and his father's roots came from Germanic, French, and Scottish ancestries.

In high school Jonas tried his hand in several sports. He joined the wrestling team his freshman year but being stuck to straining heavily perspiring bodies wasn't to his liking. Besides, it was at odds with his claustrophobic mania. He liked basketball but was lucky if he even hit a third of his shots. In baseball it was entirely another story for it was there that he found his talent could prosper. In that sport, that was once so commonly referred to as the 'Nations National Pastime,' he excelled, whether in the outfield or standing beside home plate waiting for the next pitch.

In regards to being given advice about choices in life Jonas didn't ask many questions so he was seldom privileged with the offerings of others suggestions. He had always been pretty much on his own. That was just the way it was. It was a typical family with the typical problems. George and Ariane often had their plates full in regard to raising a family and putting food on the table. Times were tough, but times were always tough for a lot of Americans.

"You better go to college or dig ditches," was the only basic advice that George Miles offered his children.

Of course, there were always the discussions at the dinner table that could have been about any number of topics. Things like the gaudy color the neighbors had just painted their house or who was the best candidate for president. At the Miles residence vocational guidance in life was practically nonexistent. Certainly across America some parents may have reasoned based on their own lives they were in no position to give advice. Especially that is if some were not particularly that happy with their own stature in the world.

While in high school Jonas began to realize there was a difference between baseball and football. In baseball everyone was eligible for the glory. A coach can only put you in or take you out. Once you're in the game your achievements at scoring are not limited by the position you play. Everyone gets a chance to hit a home run, catch a fly ball and become the hero of the game. And it's more than just that when you consider how one's ability at running, catching, and throwing is just as important for each player no matter the position one plays. So baseball wasn't a sport where only a few got all the glory, it was all for the taking for anyone who was good enough. In baseball Jonas was more than good enough. As a varsity team member in his junior year no one expected him to be the high caliber baseball player he turned out to be. Having helped bring the school team to first place with his powerful throwing arm, excellent batting average and speed at stealing bases.

Jonas's dad George was a foreman in the commercial printing division of the local newspaper. To be fair, there were some things that George did teach Jonas and that was how to enjoy the great outdoors. Whatever interest in sports Jonas had, most certainly it must have begun with his father's desire in exposing his boy to the manly things of life. So Jonas learned how to hunt, fish, and be part of the world of athletics. It started with George taking Jonas at age nine to watch local junior college baseball games. They also went to watch the Los Angeles Angels play at Wrigley field which was not far from their home in Glendale. Jonas grew up in a time in California where it was very common for the father of a family to raise his boys to become involved not in just athletic sports, but hunting and fishing as well. The Miles had a Jeep that they would drive up into the outlying foothills and hunt game birds such as quail, pheasant, or dove. In the winter they would hunt waterfowl or antlered game in the mountains. Jonas took to his father's passion for almost all things pertinent to the outdoors.

When Jonas entered his teen years he took a course in sailing and started off in very small sailing craft in the harbor. After making friends with people who belonged to some of the more prestigious sailing clubs Jonas was able to get a lot of experience in sailing larger vessels. Often times he would be a part of a sailing team that sailed in off shore yacht races while only a junior in High School.

Though George brought Jonas up to enjoy the same things in life as he, personality wise they seemed as dissimilar as night and day. George was very social, outgoing, extroverted, and always looking at life optimistically with a smile. Jonas had a different nature, introverted, cautious, somewhat sensitive, shy and overly modest. He strangely did not seem to favor praise. Jonas tended to do some things too fast and other things too slow. He drove fast, walked fast, and talked fast. On the flip side he ate, read, and absorbed things slowly. He became easily distracted with his own thinking, his thoughts always running off into different directions. When contemplating anything he always considered all the variables. He was very calculating.

When Jonas was a boy he never had any problems interacting with girls, but years later while gaining some maturity he never quite knew what to make of them. They seemed to have certain things on their minds and it seemed he always had something else on his. He seemed to have an uncanny knack to say the wrong things when he really meant to give a girl a compliment. Much of the time though he didn't have much to say because he was often too far and away in thought. Just like many young people he had at least a few close friends. If you could bring up the right topic you would find Jonas had lots to say, but he was more of a listener then a talker. Jonas's mind always seemed to be in some constant analytical introspective process.

Personally shy as he entered young adulthood after a few beers or drinks the aggressive and confident side of Jonas would come out. It also served to show a side of him that was more like his father. Of course it was a popular consensus that males having aggressive inflated egos always had more success getting a girls attention than those who were timid and reclusive. In the ordinary sober world of Jonas's teenage years securing the females that he was attracted to was quite competitive and difficult.

Even though Jonas was an athlete in significant standing at the school, the girls simply referred to him as the mannequin in the letterman's jacket. The fact was that physically Jonas was completely confident in himself to handle any situation, but in the world of social intercourse he was not so at ease. But in time he would grow out of the shyness of his teen years.

In his senior year in High School Jonas was the third strongest weight lifter even though his body had little bulk. There were talents that Jonas didn't give much thought to such as his voice. He could hum a hymn if he had to which went for singing as well. And his mind was a creative one with attention for detail. He had a profound yet undiscovered artistic ability besides a potent sense of humor when he chose to use it. Jonas did cherish his few good friends and some of them had all the personality traits that Jonas lacked and he having those they lacked. Jonas and his friends seemed to fit together like a jigsaw puzzle. Some had a touch of egotism, some were non-stop talkers, and some just went around all the time like their clock just got wound up. Then there was always the wise cracks between them. If you couldn't take those then it was time to find another planet. Besides, that was part of the fun of hanging around with friends. Wise cracks sometimes referred to as, 'Cutting Down' or 'Chopping' each other could be a pastime. They would go cruising in their tuned up, hopped up cars, however they were referred, whether GM, Ford, or Chrysler products. Once fitted with aftermarket equipment and accessories such as dual feed high risers, headers, and big cams they found their machines could make quite a throaty statement. Sometimes on weekends they would ride down to San Diego where the sailors hung out and go into the nightclub strip joints. Behind the tough talk, lip dangling cigarettes and the rumble of V-8's down the freeway they were just kids most never having yet had any real sex. A time in a teenager's life where there is no place to call one's own and the only offering of a lounge to a young lady is in the back seat of a car.

"Hey gang, dinner is ready," shouted Ariane.

Jonas arrived first, then his father and finally Elizabeth after her mother told her to get off the phone. And then the last family member, 'Bogie' the family Basset Hound showed up. It was not an approved form of generosity feeding the dog at the table.

"Jonas, Fred and I are going up in the mountains Saturday if you want to go?" asked George.

"Gee thanks Dad, but I think I might be getting in late Friday night," he replied.

"Jonas, I hope you guys don't stay out too late. There are so many drunks out there. I hope you guys are not drinking and smoking that stuff the Hippies use," responded his mother, Ariane.

"Ah, don't worry mom. Do I look like a Hippie?"

"I just don't want any cops coming to our door with bad news. Okay!

"Liz, who was that on the phone." asked her mother.

"Her name is Pam," answered her daughter.

"I haven't heard you mention her before," responded her mom.

"I just met her at school."

At dinner the discussion of several topics ensued then the conversation focused on the space program and John Glenn's accomplishments. America was behind after the Soviets had already beaten them with a successful launch to orbit. John Kennedy's challenge to American ingenuity to be the first to place a man on the moon would become reality. It was a time when small hand held transistor radios were very popular with kids and such songs that came out of the air waves were, 'Blue Moon', 'Big Bad John', 'Will You Love Me Tomorrow', and the, 'Duke of Earl'.

A few weeks later on a late Monday afternoon the phone rang at the Miles residence. Elizabeth answered.

"Hey Jonas, its Tim," shouted Elizabeth.

Jonas picked up the phone.

"Hey, what's up?"

"We're going cruising tonight. You're not working at the station, right?" Jonas worked part time at a local gas station.

"No, Yeah sure, I guess we can cruise. Nothing else planned. So who is we?" asked Jonas.

"Who is we? Who is we? Well who do you think? Oscar, Dean, and I, the Super Dude."

"Whose car?" queried Jonas.

"How much gas you got?" responded Tim.

"I'm about out, but...," Jonas was cut off.

"Let's take yours. Don't worry, we'll chip in for gas," said Tim.

Jonas was proud of his 56 Chevy, a custom two tone dark Blue and white sedan with mag's and slicks on the rear. Three hours later they were cruising the boulevards, with cold tall beers stuck between their legs and a few, 'Boones Berry Farms,' wine coolers still in their respective paper bags. Under aged customers knew which liquor stores would sell to minors without carding. There was a lot of traffic on the road for a Monday night. Cars were moving slowly on Hollywood Boulevard and it was thick with pedestrian traffic. It was the kind that young male teenagers liked to see with flowing skirts and candy apple lips. It was a place where slow moving cars were filled with young and horny occupant's that were driven to say daring things compelled by bursting dosages of testosterone and alcohol. Others were just plain bad news, punks brazen and dangerous from the ingestion of too many hard core substances.

Soon the boys found themselves driving by the Beverly Hilton where cop cars were everywhere and bystanders were lining a roped off runway.

"Hey, I forgot, isn't this the Golden Globe gig?" asked Oscar.

"Yeah, it's the Golden Globes." said Dean.

"Let's park and check it out." responded Tim.

"Park where? Florida might be as close as I can get," said Jonas.

"Hey, that car's leaving right there!" blurted Tim.

"Yeah, I've got it."

Another car coming from the other way also had an eye on the spot and stopped to wait. Fortunately for the boys they were able to slide right in.

"All right finish the beer and dump the cans in the trash." "Yeah, sure Joni," replied Dean.

Some friends called Jonas, 'Joni'. When you were a kid you got use to being called just about anything. It could become a lifelong attachment.

The sidewalks were crowded with people. Bright lights blazed along the foot paths, the celebrities walkways were roped off and police were everywhere.

"Get your celebrity photos! Get your celebrity photos!" Such offering's from sidewalk vendors was a common chant as many bystanders were hoping to get their favorite celebrities autograph but rarely succeeded. Many of the stars quickly made their way inside while others were expected to make a few comments about their careers or react to remarks about what they were wearing.

Limousines were busy pulling up and as the boys were walking toward the event they could make out many of the celebrities. Some of the stars spotted were Shirley McLaine, Hayley Mills, Tony Randall, Warren Beatty, Sidney Poitier, and Natalie Wood. As the boys made their way up close to the runway they eventually were successful in getting right on the ropes. The stars were dressed looking as special as ever for the film awards. The boys stood and watched the limos drive up and drop off the stars one by one as they made their way along into the Beverly Hilton. The fans were shouting in a gleeful manner at the celebrities who reacted with hand waves and smiles. Other huge stars that were seen that night passing by were Paul Newman, Audrey Hepburn, Bette Davis, George C Scott, Montgomery Cliff, Jackie Gleason, Marlene Dietrich, Bob Hope, Fred McMurray, Geraldine Page, and Ann Margaret.

Some of the actresses were fortunate with their dress designers who had tastefully cloaked them with class, while others did not fare so well. Considerable time had passed. When it seemed like all the attendees had arrived the boys were about to leave. Then another vehicle pulled up. The windows were dark and an unrecognizable somewhat attractive male was let out of the rear driver side of the limo. As the curb side door was opened by an event attendant a pair of shapely heeled legs set foot on the pavement. Out came a very curvy woman wearing a tight emerald dress with very blonde hair. It only took Jonas a moment to realize it was Marilyn Monroe. She was accompanied by someone he was totally unfamiliar with. She had a white stole around her shoulders and as she got out of the vehicle the young man with her escorted her toward the roped off walkway. Suddenly it was no longer a place of moderate light bulb flashes in succession, but suddenly the place was transformed into what looked like a D-Day beachhead firefight as cameras were blazing everywhere. She looked stunningly beautiful as she made her way slowly up the walkway waving to the crowds. Her young escort looked slightly nervous as he followed along beside her. The breeze was brisk that early March evening and it was quite cool. She would only be yards from the boys as were all the stars that had walked along that same path. Jonas was watching her closely and was asking himself when he ever saw anyone so beautiful, anyone so famously commanding. It was hard to take your eyes off of her.

"Get your celebrity photos! Get Your Photos!" yelled out another vendor who was selling pictures just alongside of Jonas.

"Yeah, give me a Monroe," shouted Jonas as his friends looked on in an amused fashion.

As there is always something different about every human being there were things different about Jonas. Nobody that knew him would have recognized the distinct characteristic that lived in his persona. Perhaps it was just concentration or pure desire that took over that gave Jonas that edge he needed and desperately wanted at a moment's notice. To recognize exactly what it was that made Jonas different wouldn't have been easy even for himself. His mind could be complicated however practical it was. Though like many in their youth who dreamed of lofty goals his essential cognitive senses went largely unused or recognized. He was the tragic and sometimes typical example of those who have so much potential to be great but live in an environment void of encouragement and attention. Jonas was the product of a childhood upbringing left to his own immature mental faculties. He grew up void of experienced and proper intellectual attention and yet he was intelligent, powerfully agile and creatively talented. He was likeable, good looking and just like in the Wizard of Oz you sensed he was missing a virtue. The one that should have taken him out of the world of his ordinary life into one that would have been befitting a celebrity. His few friends saw it in him, somehow unconsciously envisioned him in some bigger and better place.

Yet remarkably, Jonas had this uncanny dexterous method of addressing his sense of urgency, especially an urgency that demanded immediate results. These were things he pulled from out of inside himself. It didn't matter if they be words or actions, he seemed to possess a magical gift to get what he needed at a moment's notice. Whether it was truthful or whimsical, complimentary or rascality, all that mattered at such times as these was that he would succeed at that thing he intensely desired. So when Jonas saw Marilyn Monroe walking along only yards in front of him he knew this would be his only chance in the world to have any eye contact from her, to be noticed, to talk to her, even if it were only one word. Jonas had his beers and the Mister Hyde was out.

The crowds were calling out to Marilyn as she walked slowly along looking left and right as she waved. She wasn't really in the mood to stop for autographs this night. As of lately she had more things requiring her attention and things she required the attention of. Also, she was being escorted by someone unknown to most, a new guy from Mexico. As always she would not fail this night. She would deliver herself to her comrades and fans as the film star Marilyn Monroe, that name that everyone was so familiar with.

"Hey Marilyn, I Love You Babe!" came one.

"I love your dress, Marilyn", yelled others.

"Please, your autograph, Marilyn," shouted lots of others as she smiled and made friendly gestures, but continued to walk.

Now she was almost abreast of Jonas and his friends. The statement that came out of Jonas's mouth was not something that anyone would ordinarily say, nor did it sound respectful. It even shocked his friends.

"Hey Turkey Foot!" he jovially yelled out as she was walking by. Everyone who heard him stared at him in disbelief. To some, they simply didn't hear him right. A sense of agitation showed in many faces of the fans. A seriousness and confrontational look came upon the faces of security and the police. Jonas became a focus of attention and certainly Marilyn wouldn't pay any attention as she walked, but she did become curious. After all, it would seem that not only might this person be a threat with such an ill begotten remark, he had just insulted one of the biggest stars of the century, or did he?

Even the faces of his friends took on a complete look of shock. And still while most stars would have shrugged it off and kept going, Marilyn's walk noticeably slowed almost coming to a complete halt as she looked in the direction from which she heard the remark. Her eyes easily found Jonas because everyone was staring either at him, or her.

"Marilyn", shouted Jonas again.

"Andre said that you might sign my photo, that is if I could ever get your attention," exclaimed Jonas in a purely congenial manner.

For whatever reason, Marilyn turned and walked directly toward Jonas as his friends and crowd looked on in disbelief. She might have even surprised herself with the effort. Her turning and movement seemed to bind her to a commitment in motion. Besides, someone said something to her that was out of her past. As insulting as the comment might have seemed to the crowds it did have some significance to her like a key that had been turned that could open something.

"Andre who?" responded Marilyn, as she arrived near Jonas.

"deDienes," stated Jonas.

"I thought that was who you meant," she answered.

"I've been trying to get your autograph for a long time," answered Jonas. The comment was not really true.

"And I probably will never get another chance." She only had a few months left.

"Sure," she said in that so familiar softened girlish voice that was so characteristic of her.

"What is your name?" she asked.

"Jonas, Jonas Miles," he answered as he looked straight into her eyes and her breath taking presence.

"Could you write something special?" he asked.

At the request she seemed to look at him for a moment, as if she were trying to get a feel for his character in one long gaze. Jonas handed Marilyn the picture that the vendor sold him. It was a photo of her when she was singing a song as a dance hall girl in, 'River of No Return.' As Marilyn was writing she said a few words to him.

"You seem kinda young to know Andre,"

"Honestly, I don't know him. I overheard him at an art show talking to a customer about when you two were on a photo shoot. That's how I knew about, 'Turkey Foot'," responded Jonas.

"Oh, so he's been telling that silly story?" she said with a smile.

"Sorry, but I didn't know how else to get your attention. I am sorry if I embarrassed you," answered Jonas.

"Well, what does it matter? It worked didn't it?" replied Marilyn, still smiling.

"Can I ask you for one more thing?" asked Jonas.

"What's that?" she asked.

'Would you please kiss me on the forehead?" Jonas didn't really believe that part of his request would be fulfilled.

"Well, I never kiss on a first date," said Marilyn, with a kid like voice and a mesmerizing smile.

"OK then, could you kiss the picture," asked Jonas. With that Marilyn kissed his picture leaving a lipstick mark then totally surprising him she leaned over and kissed his forehead. Cameras were flashing everywhere and the next day a photo of Jonas being kissed by Marilyn made it to newspapers across America with the headline.

'LUCKY FAN GETS KISS FROM MARILYN MONROE.'

Marilyn smiled and signed a few more autographs for her fans and then she was gone. That was the last time Jonas and most that were there that night would ever see of Marilyn Monroe in person again. In just a few more short months the mortal in the flesh Marilyn would be gone from her present world.

Minutes later Jonas and his friends were back in his car on the road headed toward Santa Monica.

"Hey, get a few beers in Joni and he's Mr. Don Juan, huh. What was that 'Turkey Foot' thing? That was like an insult dude. Why did you call her 'Turkey Foot', and then she walks over. Go figure," asked Dean.

"Well like I told her, I overheard Andre deDienes, an early photographer of hers talking to a customer about when he took her on a cross country photo shoot way before she was a star. They were up in the mountains somewhere in the snow. Her feet got so cold they turned purple, so he kept calling her 'Turkey Foot'. I guess she never forgot it. I thought if I called out something unusual enough it might get her attention."

"Well I guess? I would have never shouted out to her what you did. That blew my mind," said Tim.

"Yeah, I hear that! Unbelievably awesome," said Oscar.

"Let me see that photo," interjected Dean.

"Seriously, anybody smudges that thing up I will shove their dead bodies out of the car and repeatedly run over them," interjected Jonas.

"And look at Jonas's forehead! Her kiss is on your forehead dude! You know you can't shower for a week," said Dean.

"I'm already ahead of you guys on that one. I will be going to school tomorrow with Marilyn's lips pasted on my forehead, you bet!" said Jonas as they all let out shrieking laughs.

"You're not sleeping tonight?" asked Oscar.

"Yeah, but I'm going to grab some of my dad's sand bags and place them so I can't turn my head," Again, they all laughed.

They each took a turn looking at the photo and what she wrote.

'To Someone Very Special, Love & Kisses, Your friend, signed Marilyn Monroe'. There boldly in red was her kiss in the right hand corner. Jonas didn't think about it but in years to come that photo protected in a rigid glass case would come to be worth thousands of dollars. She wrote the perfect thing for the photo to increase in value, a nameless personalized autograph. It would be one of only a few Marilyn signed photos in existence with a kiss and in this case backed up with a news clipping. Years later, following Marilyn's death Jonas was offered considerable sums of money for the picture but he would never sell it.

When Jonas returned to school on Monday there were two and a half months left in his senior year. During this time several things seemed to occur that would affect Jonas. One change was it seemed his classmates had now looked at him a little differently, the females because he got something more than they could ever give, a kiss from Marilyn Monroe and the males because such attention from such a star was something they were never likely to get. They all knew about the event because Jonas made the front page of local morning paper being kissed by Marilyn Monroe.

Another thing that affected Jonas was the beginning of an enormous conflict that was brewing in Southeast Asia. It was a place where thousands of young Americans barely out of high school would not survive their youth. Soon, Jonas would register for the draft but he would fatefully be spared his presence in that controversial conflict, but sadly many of the nation's youth would not.

THREE

Miles Number One

Geeorge Miles was in bed by nine thirty every work night. He awoke at 4:30am to the alarm on his night stand. He performed the usual morning ritual of filling his percolator coffee maker with water and his favorite grind. Afterward, he showered, dressed, and drank a quick cup of coffee before pouring the rest in his thermos. Then heading off to work he bid Bogie the dog a farewell before heading out the door. Then George got into his chocolate two door 1953 Chevy Bel Air. The car was twelve years old with faded paint and it had a silver dollar size hole in the middle of the floorboard, between the driver and the passenger. You could watch the pavement go by through that hole if you got bored but it wasn't very entertaining to do so. Other than that it was a good solid specimen of a car. It had a nice soft beige velour roof interior and a metal dash that carried a shine.

On weekends that car served for what George and his buddies called their 'Slob'n Car.' They called it that name because that was what George's wife had called the car when she had become frustrated with her husband's weekend jaunts to the outdoors with his hunting pals. Most of George's buddies had their own so called, 'Slob'n Cars,' and they often took turns in their use. It was amazing where such a car could go with a couple of Firestone Mud & Snow,' treads on the rear. With such tires and a little old fashioned grunt force facilitated by 'pushing buddies', the old Chevy never seemed to have a problem going anywhere. Jonas's mother drove the other family car, a white 1959 Chevy Nomad wagon.

Three years had passed since Jonas and his friends were at the Golden Globes. It was 1965 and a lot had happened since that night. For one, Marilyn Monroe suffered a mysterious death in 1962, and John F Kennedy had been assassinated in 63. Lyndon Johnson was President and Jonas's father, George, still worked as a foreman for 'Supra- Consolidated Printing'. It was a subsidiary of the region's newspaper. The building had a typical industrial layout as buildings go with metal bay doors and large windows that faced Pico Boulevard. It was also not far from the beach. The walnut paneled lobby in the front of the building had several plush chairs for customers. The two office workers were seated at a couple of aged heavy oak desks that sat on a blood red carpet. A receptionist was seated at one desk and a secretary at the other. Upon the edge of each desk were heavy Smith Corona typewriters. There was really nothing fancy about the place. Behind the desks was a double doorway that led to the rear of the building where the three full time skilled printing tradesmen worked, George included.

On the other side of the receptionist wall there was a small break room with a soda machine. You had your choice of Coke, Hires root beer, 7up, or Grape Crush all dispensed in returnable bottles. The north wall of the building was mostly large view windows and the south side on the alley had roll up bay doors. It was a considerable distance behind the front offices where all the printing machinery was located. Often the workers would open up the two big bay doors to let in light and the cool breeze.

Jonas was not much older than ten when his father used to bring him and his friends down to the shop when school was out for the summer. George would give his son a five dollar bill so they could enjoy their day. Five bucks was enough to rent a surf rider, buy lunch and purchase live bait on the pier for fishing. At least if Jonas caught enough fish for dinner George would get something for his money.

Meanwhile, several thousand miles across the pacific others were not having a good time. Viet Nam was a hot bed of casualties both on the ground and in the air as F-105 Thunder Chief attack jets, and B-52 bombers hammered the Ho Chi Minh trail. Soon the McDonnell Douglas F-4 fighter aircraft designated the 'Phantom', would be the most coveted fighter jet in Americas arsenal. Huey helicopters couldn't be built fast enough to replace the ones that got shot down. If you finished high school, could count to twenty while standing on one foot while chewing gum then you could you qualify as a warrant officer for chopper pilot training. The defense industries were making a killing off the war. In the United States employment was up. Meanwhile, the youth of America was in rebellion against the establishment. The establishment was the D.C. politicians and the big defense industries. Someone decided to call these young Americans 'Hippies.' Whatever you called it, hemp, cannabis, marijuana, the dried flower tops of the plant began to be widely used by the nation's students. The youth wore clothing indicative of that time such as denim jeans having wide bell bottoms at the ankles. Above the belt line anything that looked cool could be worn. It was usually some article of woven clothing having an aged look that emanated aromatic odors like musk, incense, or weed. Males let their hair grow long, even past their shoulders and women often did not wear bras. While the Mamas and the Papas, sang 'Go Where You Wanna Go and Do What you Wanna Do', activists at campus rallies preached love not hate. For some their preaching was often hypocritical and the love they expressed was mostly in the back of a van. So this new breed of youth rebelled against what seemed like the perpetuity of war for a myriad of unjustified reasons. Certainly to them the defense manufacturers seemed to be one of the perpetrators of what they saw as the abusive and unjust condemnation of America's young males. To the hippies, it was government itself fueled by the huge defense corporate lobbyists that the youth blamed for the killings in a war they did not agree with. Young Americans didn't stop at just their rejection of the war; their issues were varied and well directed. In a nation that preached freedom they felt it was a nation that still hadn't arrived fully within the concept of the word. They were rebelling against the government's reasons for war and the involvement of America. The boys of the Second World War whom had fought in that world conflict were now running the country. Their children were chanting in the streets tired of their history lessons and excuses for war. They were not shy with their chants, such as, "Hell no - We won't go."

Whether you supported their position or defied it, the theory was to nip bad things in the bud. So then should our government adopt a policy of policing the world, sending youth off to fight others' wars? That was the question often under discussion at college campuses. Should home spun culture as it related to war be allowed to perpetrate futuristically against the consensus of the public? Did Washington go too far in assuming that they did not require the support of Americans when choosing to declare war?

In the years to come Americans would find out that most had endured enough with Viet Nam as students across the nation had vehemently protested the war. On the fourth of May, 1970, an event would take place at Kent State College that would make national and world news. Ohio's governor Jim Rhodes called in the National Guard to the Kent State campus to deal with what he had termed, 'Un-American and dangerous student protests.'

The previous weekend, students or revolutionaries as some called them had been in town throwing bottles and anything they could find at passing cars and businesses. It was in reaction to President Nixon's televised address of intent of going into Cambodia even though he had campaigned on promising to end the war. So when on that Monday as students arrived on campus they could not have known what the governor had prepared for them. Some of the most radical students that were throwing rocks and presenting a threatening attitude had set in motion a time bomb. When guards in jeeps tried to deliver messages to students to disperse they were met with thrown rocks. In response, all students who were unarmed whether engaged, just passersby or watching at a distance, were assaulted with military Garand rifles and Colt .45 side arms by national guardsman. Sixty seven shots were fired in thirteen seconds resulting in four dead and many wounded or paralyzed. That event would come to be known as the 'The Kent State Massacre'. The next day four million students across the nation at colleges, universities, and even high schools stayed out of attendance. Most of the students actually thought the guardsman's guns were loaded with blanks, not the live ammo they actually carried. They had no idea that the Governor would go to the length he chose. Of course, intensive investigations followed but with no arrests or prosecutions.

Considering the foregoing discussion of war, Kent State, and a time that utilized the draft to secure fighting soldiers the nation's youth had a right to question the government's decisions. In light of the question one must consider a speech President General Eisenhower, the in the field commander of world war II made at the White House before he left office in 1960. In it he set forth his concern about how when World War II ended the defense manufacturers that sprang up overnight to produce munitions, aircraft, and ships, realized what a profitable boon that manufacturing weapons and defense products could be. Following the war they didn't want to go away and didn't. They had thousands of skilled people in their employ that depended on government jobs for their livelihoods. By lobbying congress and wooing the right government officials they were able to keep lucrative contracts flowing. Eisenhower thought it was immoral but congress failed to heed his wishes. Had they, perhaps Korea, or even the United States involvement with the Viet Nam war would never have happened. The day would come of course that future congressional leaders and Presidents would assume it practical to embrace the concept of preparedness.

The facts were that such huge defense industries created millions of jobs, either directly or indirectly. Many smaller companies sprang up overnight to supply the largest players with the contract assistance they would need. It all trickled down to other businesses and when defense business was good it was a shot in the arm for many other types of businesses. So it was that work trickled down to companies like, 'Supra Consolidated Printing,' where George worked. The work allowed George the job he needed to raise a family, to prosper, and be reasonably happy, that is to live the American dream.

"George is this the print block you were looking for?" asked Blaine Pearson a young apprentice.

"Yep, that's it. Thanks!" replied George.

It was a busy place for the three tradesmen and the one apprentice. Besides George and Blaine, there was Don and Paul. Don was the Linotype machine operator but he was proficient at running anything in the shop. The three were a good team.

"Gosh, sometimes my eyes get to seeing double, Blaine," exclaimed George.

"I think I'll go on break and look over the newspaper. Does that make any sense?"

"If you say so boss," responded Blaine as he walked away from Mr. Miles.

"Hey Sal, How's it going?" asked George, as he entered the break room.

It was due to the printing plants location that the break room could sometimes be a lonely place at lunch time. The shops proximity to a whole host of fine eating establishments along the ocean front was a welcomed benefit.

"Well, its Friday for one thing and that's a good thing," responded Sal.

Salvatore Lennon worked for DYNAMO INK LLC, as the printing ink salesman who sold Consolidated, their ink stock. He sometimes used their break room to quickly scan the newspaper.

"Yeah, I hear ya. Anything planned?"

"Nah, I was going to go watch the midget dirt races, but Claire wants to go to her sisters."

"Sounds like fun."

"Yeah, right, I can't wait," responded Sal.

"How bout yourself," asked Sal as George picked up a magazine.

"I'm going out on Curley's boat, Catalina way tomorrow and do a little fishing, take some food and enjoy."

"Well what's wrong with this picture? I gotta go to the in-laws and you get to go fishing," said Sal.

"Yeah, well I'm sure my days a coming," responded George.

"How's your son Allen doing at dental school," asked George.

"Oh, plugging along. He's passing the classes but now he's not sure if that's what he wants to do. He's considering changing his major."

"Well I'm sure he'll get it figured out," replied George thinking about his son, Jonas.

"And your son, 'Jonas', is he still in school?" asked Sal.

"Ah, some kids. I thought he would pursue professional baseball. It doesn't look like he's going to have much of a future. Helped him get a student loan and he spent half of it on a car. Think he said he wants a degree in the arts or something? What is a degree in the arts, anyway? I don't even know, some future," declared George.

"Maybe he'll be another, 'Brando', George," responded Sal.

"Brando? Oh, that actor? How long would you think I'd have to hold my breath for that to happen," replied George with a serious look.

Sal couldn't hold it in and had to let out a slight laugh.

"Well, you got to admit not many guys I know have been kissed by Marilyn Monroe, George. That'll be one thing he takes to the grave. I sure thought he was all lined up for a career in baseball. He sure was good at baseball in high school. "

"Yeah, I guess. I don't know what good it was?" replied George.

"I remember picking up the paper and seeing Jonas in there a lot," said Sal.

"I tell yah Sal, when he got those baseball scholarship offers from those colleges and ignored them I could have strangled him."

"You know, it could be baseball was just an easy thing for him, you know, like a natural. Maybe his heart wasn't in it," replied Sal.

"Anyhow, you should be proud of your boy Sal, looks like he has a future ahead of him," stated George as he got up to leave the room.

"You know, he may surprise you someday George, you never know about people, even your own kids," said Sal as they both walked out of the room together.

That evening when George got home, Jonas of all people was there. He was coming out of the garage with some boxes in his arms.

"Hello Dad."

"Hi, what have you got there?"

"Oh, clothes and stuff."

"Are you still living with that bunch in Redondo?"

"No, Hank and his girl friend are moving out of their place in Torrance. It's just a little guest house, affordable, so I'm taking it."

"Moving in with Irene?"

"No, Irene and I, well, it didn't work out. Just me moving in," responded Jonas.

"You might as well stay for dinner. Your mother hardly ever even sees you anymore. I'll tell you about a position that's opening up over at our satellite office," said George.

"Where's that Dad?"

"In Corona," replied George.

"Corona del Mar?"

"No, Corona!"

"I can't move to Corona Dad, that's out in the middle of nowhere. Besides, I don't want to work in some factory all my life, like, like...," suddenly Jonas became silent realizing where the thought was going, not meaning to hurt his Father.

"Like me you mean, who worked in a plant to put a family together and gave you a life."

"Sorry Dad, I didn't mean it like that. I don't know what I want yet. I haven't got it figured out," responded Jonas.

"I've set myself down and looked at different college programs in catalogs. I don't want to be a lawyer, or a doctor. I'm hardly a mathematician, so forget engineering. As for business administration, I can't see me sitting behind a desk all day."

"Well this job would be better then where you're working now, wouldn't it? Where are you working now anyway?"

Jonas gave his dad a compassionate look.

"Thanks Dad, but really its Ok. I'll manage. There's something out there for me. I don't know what it is yet. But somehow I'll find it."

George threw his hands up in the air.

"Okay! I can't help you then. Be a bum if that's what you want."

"I gotta go, Dad!"

"Yeah sure!" uttered George.

The two walked away, Jonas toward his aging 56 Chevy, and his father toward the house that Jonas grew up in.

As Jonas drove away his thoughts had not left his father. He thought about how close they were not that many years ago when what seemed like every weekend they were together. The hunting trips, the pro ball games and various other outdoor activities were such that a son never forgets. Now they hardly talked to one another or even saw much of each other.

As George Miles walked back toward his home he thought about a young man he once remembered a long time ago who just out of high school was going nowhere. He recollected how that guy seemed to have so much fun with his friends riding about the range of his father's New Mexico ranch. He remembered a father who wanted something better for that kid than he himself had. And he remembered a kid who rebuked his father preferring instead the joy of rambunctious youth. All that changed when the Japanese bombed Pearl Harbor. Then Uncle Sam pointed his finger at a very young man named George and then he enlisted. That all seemed like a long time ago, and it was.

FOUR

Disperse and Regroup

Years had passed since Jonas lived in Torrance. The purr of Jonas's car could be heard as it made its way down the Los Angeles I-5 freeway. Even though Jonas still had his 56 Chevy, he was now driving a 1970 Plymouth Cuda. His face was no longer the face of an 18 year old, he was now 29. It was 1973 and his body held a maturity. His youthful complexion and wavy brown hair provided him an appealing attractive flair.

Jonas had a wife and two boys. It was the usual love trap thing. Boy meets girl, falls in love, gets married, then come the kids and then you were suppose to grow old together. Jonas wouldn't admit to regretting anything. He loved his kids and his wife. He thought such things to himself as, 'Thank God for Families,' of which without most of us would not be here. Well it wasn't an absolute to have a family to produce kids but it brought some sort of social order. So now he had a wife, Lynn, who was twenty seven, two years younger than he. His two boys, seven year old Calvin, and Charles, five, were the pride of his life.

Jonas had just had a birthday and not yet into the next chapter of life that begins when one turns thirty. Most people looked at the thirties as the last years of their real youth. When one reaches their forties it becomes impossible for most to pass for someone still in their twenties. The Cuda sounded good as it rumbled down the freeway. One of Frank Sinatra's popular hits just came up on Jonas's favorite FM station. The volume was not turned up particularly high as Jonas started to sing along. In fact, some of his comrades at work had remarked how much he sounded like Sinatra, when he sang to himself.

"When you're twenty, forty is old and when you're sixty, forty is pretty damn young," mentioned Gus, a company salesperson. Well Jonas wasn't forty yet.

Jonas was still in fairly good shape. So he had gained a few pounds, but nothing he couldn't get rid of quickly enough if he wanted to, and now he wanted to.

"Things will be different from now on," he thought.

Kind of crazy Jonas singing along with Frank since he had just been let go, terminated, fired for something he didn't even do. How ironic after not so many years after he and his father had a certain conversation about not working in a factory, that such would be the very place he would find himself. Now after seven years employment with AUTO-TECHMORE, a company that designed and built after market car parts, he would be fired, set up by someone in his own department. It was a good bet he knew who it was and his suspicions were true. A co-worker, Jack Shietz, often deliberately pronounced, 'Shits' by others had been stealing parts for resale from the company. When the company realized their in house stock numbers weren't balancing they began a low key investigation. When Jack got wind of the investigation he slyly planted evidence in Jonas's desk. Jonas was an easy target. His independent solitary attitude was at odds with others and since he didn't share the same views on social issues with many of his coworkers, he was often the guy out of favor.

Then there were people like Logan Taylor who couldn't stand to be ignored so he spent a good amount of time talking about other people, just like he did about Jonas.

"I'll tell you one person who is a waste of assets is Jonas Miles. He doesn't do a damn thing. If he only did half the work as the rest of us we wouldn't be so far behind," he would say.

"Have you noticed how long it takes him to finish a project?"

And with Logan, it was non-stop crucifixion.

"Did you notice that Susan Larson came in late again? I don't think anyone even said anything to her, and ...."

Oh yeah, Logan was a hard worker all right. His constant chattering could put any woman's gossip time to shame. Maybe if Logan actually did some work the company wouldn't be behind, as if he really cared.

It wasn't in Jonas's favor that he seldom if ever locked his desk. That was probably because he didn't believe he kept anything in his desk that had any value. He stuck it out there for the same reasons as most everyone else did, it paid the bills. So maybe it was true that Jonas had lacked some enthusiasm, but it didn't seem to be exactly jumping out from others as well.

"I guess every place has its rats and backstabbers. I believe I liked most of the people who worked there, got along with most. You know though one just can't ever tell for sure what's on another's mind. A workplace can be real cutthroat. Everyone knows that," he mused.

"How will I put it to Lynn? At least we have my company stock savings plan and our personal savings until I get another job," were thoughts going through his mind.

As truth would have it justice would catch up with Jack. What went around came around. It was difficult for many to believe that Jonas was the actual guilty one. He just didn't seem the type who would make stealing a pastime. Then there were those who knew who was the real culprit, but it just took them a while to let their conscience catch up with them.

However, as the companies contact with Jonas would follow in a few short weeks expressing sincere apologies, even offering him his job back with lost pay, he would decline the offer. His honest response to them during the questioning were the usual expected statements such as;

"Do you think I am so stupid to keep such things in my desk if I were stealing?" he said at the time of his termination.

They didn't believe him and after being slapped in the face the only way he would keep his honor would be to refuse their apologies and offer of returning to work. But that time had not arrived just yet, and besides, sometimes things happen for a reason.

"Better things would come in life, hopefully," he reasoned. It wasn't that hard of a decision. He didn't like the place, and besides he felt he was capable of doing nobler things.

Jonas and Lynn lived in a nice area of townhomes in Cypress, California. It was gated and had its own park, swimming pools, club house, gym and even a small lake. Such amenities offered some recreation for kids. When Jonas was at work in the first years of their marriage, Lynn had to take some time off from her salon business to spend time with their babies.

Lynn was a hair stylist. Years prior, she garnered some family financial assistance and with the help of a bank loan, financed her own salon. She was very attractive for her age, looking youthful with brunette hair and a slim curvy shape. Because she was good at what she did she had no trouble keeping and attracting clients who tipped well. As Jonas drove up to the guard post of his gated community, Earl the attendant recognized Jonas right away and waved him on through. Jonas was home early, an occurrence that seemed out of the ordinary to Earl but it was Friday. The kids would not be out of school for several hours. As Jonas drove around through the various residential streets he recognized most of the cars. There were a few service vehicles parked around his home, but it wasn't uncommon to have service vehicles parked around the neighborhood. Jonas had to park down the street because there was an unfamiliar car parked across the street from Jonas's residence, a new 1973 Oldsmobile Toronado.

As Jonas reached the front door and tried to turn the knob it was locked. He thought that was unusual because he noticed Lynn's car parked outside.

"Maybe she went for a walk," he wondered.

He quietly unlocked the door and upon entering the hall heard noises like people talking upstairs. He stood there for a moment and then was sure he heard sounds like people laughing and then the laughing stopped. Jonas took a few steps upstairs. Then he heard more noises, those sounds so typical of lovemaking. Conscious of the fact that the steps in his home weren't prone to creaking he decided to walk quietly up the stairs toward his bedroom.

The door was open enough for Jonas to see in, but unlikely that anyone would see him in the dimly lit hall. Jonas had a premonition that he was about to get his finale of a one two punch for the day, first at work and now at home. What he found was his wife in bed with another man. They were now both very vocal with their sounds of pleasures. Jonas considered going back down the hall. At that moment what Jonas really felt like was one of those little black inflated bags that boxers get a rhythm going on with their fists as they practice their jabs. Yeah, he felt like a punching bag considering all that he had gone through that day. What Jonas was hoping for when he got home that day was some encouragement and sensitivity from his wife. What he got instead was another of life's tsunamis. Another may have exploded with rage, but Jonas slowly walked back down the steps to think for a few moments. After all there was a guy in his bed with his wife. But Jonas being somewhat practical considered the options and the repercussions of such a confrontation. What were the facts of their marriage and what was its future.

"Well she's up there right now demonstrating the facts of our future, and the question is how long has this exercise been going on and with how many," Jonas asked himself.

In less then a minute dozens of things passed through his mind. He thought about how his actions would affect his boys whom he loved, but he could no longer live with his wife. He would somehow see that his kids could get through the coming chaos with the least amount of repercussions. He went over to his desk and got his camera. He quietly, but quickly moved back up the stairs and pointed the lens through the opening in the door making sure to get both their faces. The first flash took them by complete surprise giving him enough time for a clear second shot as he pushed through the door. He then stuck the camera in his pocket and stood there looking at them both. The guy looked just as Jonas would figure, suave, good looking, about thirty; perhaps fit, but not anymore then Jonas. The guy got up forcefully but embarrassed as he sought to quickly get dressed.

"So darling this is what I go to work for. How devout you are my dearest."

Lynn looked hurt that she was found out, but kept herself emotionally in control as she pulled the sheets up around her.

"Gosh, I'm sorry if I barged in while you were undressed, Dear! Probably nothing new for your boyfriend I suppose. Or is he married too," exclaimed Jonas.

Lynn was silent, as her face turned red.

"So how long has this been going on or is this just a new guy?" asked Jonas.

The stranger, calmer now with his pants on moved confidently toward Jonas assuming that he was at least a match as he demanded the camera. The stranger, a city council member and a salon customer of Lynn did not want such evidence making it to a review board, or the newspapers. Whoever said city council members were smart anyway.

"Why don't you just give me that camera, old man, and I'll be out of here in a flash," he said in a British accent as he came toward Jonas.

"Old man? Bad choice of words, but none could be any better. Unbeknownst to the intruder he might as well have stuck a cattle prod into Jonas's armpit for choosing his words so poorly, or ignorantly.

Again as some men could be the man of the hour like a sweet talking politician, Jonas never had a problem just being the man of the moment. As the stranger got to within arms length of Jonas it was Jonas's arm that came out and up in a cross cut just catching the stranger under the chin sending him back as quickly as he came, as he fell to the floor out cold with blood trickling out of his mouth.

"Say you wanted to be out in a flash, glad I could help," yelled Jonas.

"You know I thought I had some bad news to report, but I guess maybe it wasn't so bad after all. Anyhow, I'm out of here," said Jonas, looking at Lynn.

"Just so you'll know I was fired today. Since it takes both our incomes to raise a couple of boys I guess they will stay at my parents until things get figured out. At least I won't be paying for everyone else's orgasms anymore. Besides, I can see you obviously don't have enough time for our boys anyway."

"Jonas, we had something once. We can get it back," pleaded Lynn.

"It won't ever happen again," she cried.

"I think it only has to happen once," responded Jonas.

"Well, I have lots to think about now. I'm getting out of here," he added.

By late evening Jonas had most of his important possessions packed to vacate the home. He told Lynn he would be back on Sunday, for the remainder.

FIVE

The Benevolent Rendezvous

As Jonas lay in bed Sunday night a lot was going through his mind. Come morning he had no job to go to. The discovery of his wife's affair certainly caught him by surprise. Though he blamed her he knew it wasn't all her fault. Things had simmered down in their marriage. They had happier days together but now it was like the hands of time had been turned back. For all practical purposes it seemed he was single again at twenty nine. He was a little older and wiser now. Men could be such chumps. A guy could be perfectly happy being single and then comes another one of them dames. One of those gals who just didn't look like a knock out but knew how to act out all those femme fatale personas that drive men crazy. Anyhow, none of that mattered right now. Jonas would not look to rush into anything in the near future, at least if he had anything to say about it.

Jonas had his savings to hold him over for a while. So far Lynn hadn't said anything about the shared assets. This separation between the two would be done amicably. He would just get it over and be done with it when that time came.

Not much had changed with Jonas in some ways. A person becomes whatever the driving force inside of them dictates. If one is confident, ambitious, lacking conscience, calculating, and even criminally inclined, then one might make a good politician. If one is scholarly and compassionate then perhaps a physician, or physicist. If a person is articulate, cognizant, cunning, or even mischievous, perhaps a person would make a good trial lawyer or a detective.

"Well hogwash, I have some of those qualities – so what?"

Just because none of the major professions appealed to him didn't mean he wasn't capable or adept at anything he wanted to do. Nothing had changed over the years. Most of the occupational passions that Jonas found appealing were not necessarily high income professions.

I'll go back to school and enroll in a program that interests me. Surely, learning something is better than doing nothing?

Jonas conducted a self evaluation of himself as objectively possible.

"Ok, am I conceited? Surely, I don't go out of my way toward resurrecting a wall around me, too isolate myself. Do I have trouble relating to people in general? Do I think I'm better than most everyone else?" he wondered.

"How could I be better than everyone else? Look at me and where I am. What's to brag? I need to humble myself and listen to others more. I need to be more personable to others."

"Alright, step one. I need a plan. I got to look at this logically. I'll get a day job somewhere and take some night classes. Yeah, that's what I'll do. I will go back to school and use my savings to tide me over," he thought to himself.

Three weeks later, Jonas was still not working. If they handed out any trophies for first, second, and third place procrastinator he probably would have taken one of them. He had not even been seriously looking for work, but he knew he would have to soon. What was the matter with taking a few weeks off?

When Jonas retrieved Monday's mail it included papers from Lynn for divorce proceedings.

"Well it didn't take her long to get her mind made up either, did it?" thought Jonas.

He wondered how long the shenanigans with the affair had been going on.

"It must have been a short while. If it had been going on for awhile the neighbors must have known? How many times had he talked to Ben, or Sean, when he was washing his car? I guess they didn't know for sure. Probably didn't want to get involved," he mused.

A few days later, Jonas received some more documents from Lynn's attorney. She intended to keep custody of the boys. She wasted no time in securing legal representation. It shouldn't be that hard to accommodate her wishes, Jonas wasn't working. The letter written by her attorney stated she would prove she would have no problem supporting them. The letter also stated that he would have visiting rights, of course.

"Yeah, can't wait for the next surprise. I'm getting very use to them," he thought.

That night at his parent's house Jonas explained to Cal and Chuck, his two boys what was probably going to occur. The boys loved their father, but it became apparent through the ordeal that the boys missed their mother as well.

One might come to the conclusion that Cal was partial to his father, and Charles the youngest, favored his mother. Fortunately the fragmentation of the family occurred in the summer when school was out. Jonas already made arrangements to rent an apartment for himself. His savings that he accumulated over the last decade would last him for awhile. Jonas never really unpacked anything when he left Lynn, except some clothes and a few other needed things. But one thing he would leave at his parent's house would be the signed Marilyn Monroe photo. He never wanted to have to sell that out of desperation.

With the passing of a few days Jonas found himself at an old night club he use to go to with his friends. Now it was called 'Pandora's, but many years ago it was called 'Dominique's'. The club was in Westwood off of Wilshire. It was late Friday afternoon, the place was busy and it had undergone a radical overhaul. The once white plaster walls were now black, as well as the ceiling. The new renovated walls were now heavily decorated with Greek like motifs having flat sided alabaster statues of the gods as well as columns and vases. The wasn't much intensity to the interior lighting. The bar had a full length mirror framed in neon lighting. Chromed panel fixtures were screwed into the ceiling which reflected the modest amount of interior lighting that was used. There were now booths along the walls with fewer tables out in the center of the room. The tables surrounded a sunken dance floor.

It was a popular place. The food was good and the pricing fair. Happy hour was consistent in drawing a faithful crowd. The place was dark, dark enough for people to remain incognito if that was their wish. It wasn't unusual at all to find celebrities passing through the doors of 'Pandora's.'

It had been some time since Jonas seated himself at the end of the bar. It gave him a good view of the whole place. He had been there over an hour. Jonas had always made it a point to know the barkeepers name.

"Another beer, Jeff," said Jonas as he raised his arm to get his attention.

"Sure, coming up Buddy."

Jonas liked looking at pretty women. The truth is marriage never stopped men from looking. Jonas didn't go to Pandora's this evening with the intentions of looking for another serious relationship. He just didn't feel like being alone. So he sat there and listened to the people talk and occasionally conversed with others. The more he drank the more he talked. The normally quiet shy Jonas was changing into the carefree rambunctious character he usually became when he drank.

Meanwhile, across the other side of the room there were lots of other people. Some sat at tables. Some were leaning against the bar or sitting like Jonas, but one man in particular sitting at a table was staring at Jonas. The man's white loosely buttoned up shirt served to expose his well tanned hairy chest. His shirt was tucked into a pair of slim tan Levis that covered the tops of his black suede boots. His dark brown hair was short, neatly combed and fit in well with his handlebar style mustache. He wore a large gold class ring on the index finger of his right hand and a gold wedding band on his left. He was about Jonas's age and his serious dark brown eyes became focused upon Jonas at times as he drank from his mug.

Whenever an attractive woman walked by the strangers eyes took in her whole form. When the couple next to Jonas got up and left, the man finished his beer and walked over and sat next to Jonas. By this time Jonas was well into his other character. There were only two bartenders and they were both busy.

"Lots of nice scenery in here tonight!" interjected the stranger.

"What?" replied Jonas.

"I'm talking about the women."

"Oh, right, yeah sure, nice looking women," replied Jonas.

The stranger looked at Jonas out of the corner of his eye.

"Hey, did you play High School baseball by any chance? You know, I mean at Glendale High back around 62?"

Jonas's easy going grin took on a more quizzical look as his head turned to look at the stranger in a surprised fashion.

"Yeah, as a matter of fact I did, why?" responded Jonas.

"Your last name is Miles, right?"

"Yeah, that's right." responded Jonas.

'Give me a pitcher, Jeff," interjected the stranger. The bartender nodded.

"I don't think we ever actually met in High School, but I remember you. I couldn't play sports though I wanted to. I was to busy helping my dad after school. I did go to some of the Friday night games though. I got to say, you sure hit some homers when it really counted," said the stranger.

"Oh Yeah, thanks, I suppose I hit a few."

"A few, I would say you looked like Ted Williams out there."

"My name is Stanley Guiles. Most just call me Stan. Since my dad died I took over our business, 'Guiles Landscaping.' We've been around for awhile."

"Yeah, I've seen your trucks driving around," responded Jonas.

"Yeah, we do a lot of the celebrities in the hills, Brentwood, all over, besides the commercial stuff."

"Sounds like things are good," responded Jonas.

"What was you first name?" asked Stanley.

"It's like on the tip of my tongue."

"Jonas."

"Yeah, that's it, Jonas Miles. Yeah, you're the guy that was in the paper. You know that Marilyn Monroe incident where she planted a kiss on your cheek or something, at the Golden Globes, right?"

"Yeah, on the forehead, guess I won't forget that evening."

"So what line of work are you in now?" asked the stranger.

"The fact is I'm doing nothing at the moment, going through a divorce, out of work."

"Sorry to hear about that", stated Stanley.

"Oh, no need, stuff happens," responded Jonas.

"Hey, if you're interested, I could put you to work. I've got a foreman who's moving. He'll be gone in a few months. You'll have to start at the bottom for a while, working the yards until you learn the ropes and get the hang of it. Once you get that job, it pays five hundred a week."

"Five bills, that's not bad."

"Here's your pitcher," said Jeff, the barkeeper.

"Thanks!" Stanley gave him a ten.

"Keep the change."

"Hey, thanks pal."

"Sure thing buddy, drink up Jonas, it's on me."

"Yeah, thanks I'll take you up on that. The beer I mean. The job I'd like to think on," responded Jonas.

"You should. Also here's my card in case you're interested. It's not a desk job. Good for people who don't want to stagnate. You'll notice we don't have any fat guys on the crew. You're on the move a lot, pushing, pulling, but its really not strenuous work. It's just active. You know what I mean, easy in a way. Like I said, pays pretty good," said Stan as he noticed the flab around Jonas's stomach.

"Yeah, I'm thinking that," said Jonas.

"Thanks for that offer. I may take you up on that."

"You start at eight in the morning and quit at five. It's as simple as that. I was going to run an ad. I usually don't have any trouble filling openings fairly quick. I'll pay you three hundred to start until you slide into the foreman opening. That's if you decide to stick it out," added Stan.

"Yeah, I'll think it over a few days. I'll let you know this coming week. Thanks for offering me the job."

"Well you don't seem like the indoors type."

"That's right. I don't much like it, I guess?" remarked Jonas.

Minutes went by, and the two finished the pitcher of beer. "Well I got to go. Picking the old lady up at the airport," exclaimed Stan.

"Yeah, Hey glad I met ya. I'll give you a call," said Jonas, as he tried to rise quickly, and shook the man's hand.

"Sure. Who knows? You might like it."

Jonas waved as the man walked away then he sat back down as he watched him leave. He looked at the business card he held in his hand. He put the card in his shirt pocket.

"Another beer buddy?" asked the bartender.

"Ah, no, I never met him before," answered Jonas.

"No, I mean do you want another beer?"

"Oh, no thanks, I'm leaving," said Jonas, as they both laughed and the bartender shook his head.

"Okay pal. See ya next time," as he picked up the empty glasses.

An hour later Jonas was at home sitting on the sofa in his apartment. The TV was on but he wasn't watching it. He was thinking.

"Me, a Landscape Dude? Am I crazy? The more he thought about other professions and tried to transpose himself into them, nothing fit. It must have had something to do with the outdoors. Maybe his dad ruined him. He loved nature and the outdoors. He thought it would be interesting to be a game warden but those people usually held a biology degree. Then he remembered years ago when they were visiting his mother's brother one evening. He was a bank manager in Rancho Bernardo.

'I'll tell you how to become a millionaire.' he said.

'Go get yourself a few trucks, fill them with landscaping equipment and start mowing lawns and......," he had said in so many words. Jonas doesn't know why he remembered that.

Well I guess I'll go to work for this guy and try it out for awhile he thought. At least I won't have to spend anymore of my savings. It was the last thing Jonas remembered thinking before he passed out on the sofa. Hours later he awakened to the crackling gray static of an expired broadcast signal. It was three am.

SIX

Her Name was Gina

On Sunday morning Jonas woke up about his usual time, six-thirty, he felt great. There was an onshore breeze that blew the smog out to sea and the sky was a clear blue. He felt like going for a drive somewhere. He dismissed the idea of driving up into the mountains so he wasn't sure where he would go. An hour later he sat in a booth at one of his favorite places for breakfast, The 'Waffle Strudel Cafe'.

"Hi Jonas," hailed, Gina Thorpe, a waitress.

"Hi, the place is busy," responded Jonas.

"Yeah, never ends, especially on weekends. Where's the family?"

"Oh, things haven't been working out between us lately and we're getting a divorce. The kids are with her for now."

"Oh, I'm sorry to hear that, Jonas," she said with a shocked look.

"Yeah, well stuff happens!" and not wanting to get into any details he changed the subject.

"I'll have my usual. The Ortega Mega with the hot strudel," said Jonas.

"Okay, a number five, with a hot strudel?"

"Yep."

The Ortega Mega was a three egg omelet filled with shredded jack cheese, sweet red peppers, crispy bacon, diced tomatoes, and sautéed mushrooms. The entre was garnished with diced scallions and came with crispy shoestring potatoes and toast. The 'Waffle Strudel Café,' was known to have some of the best waffles and strudel in town.

"So what are your plans for today, Jonas? It's supposed to be really nice out. Almost eighty I hear."

"Yeah, I figured I would go for a ride somewhere. Give the old beast a workout," Jonas responded smiling.

Gina, now 25 had married right out of high school. The marriage lasted five months. She wasn't one who had a hard time being asked out. Not that she had a reputation, it was just that her perfect features held an attraction that sometimes was a curse. There were a few she had worked with that called her a tramp behind her back, but that was because they were jealous of her. She went steady with a few guys since her marriage, but marriage wasn't an obsession with her like it was with some girls. She was still young and she had an appetite for life. Those who knew her well, summarized her as carefree, a person who in most instances threw caution to the wind. Her reddish golden hair was stylishly long and wavy. It was a perfect accouterment to her sky blue eyes and slim curvy figure. Those ingredients with a great sense of humor could bring men to their knees.

"I know some nice places down in Orange County, Jonas. Have you ever been down there?" asked Gina.

"Yeah, sure, sometimes, why?" he asked.

"I'm off at nine this morning and if you don't mind some company I could show you around down there."

Unbeknownst to Jonas there were many women who found him attractive. More than he ever realized even when sober, which really was most of the time.

"Gosh, I don't know Gina. I'm not..."

"Oh forgive me. I shouldn't have brought that up so soon. Well, I didn't mean like it was a date or anything. I just figured I would show you around some places down there. Give you some company to take your mind off things. I know I felt terrible after I split with my husband."

"Your husband?" asked Jonas.

"Yeah, Well I was married once," she replied.

"Hey, let me get your breakfast ticket going so you can eat."

"Sure," responded Jonas, watching her walk away while cognizant of the fact that a girl who looked like that could be more trouble than many men could handle.

So as Jonas sat there waiting for his breakfast he was thinking about Gina's offer, which sounded pretty good. He really never had time to respond before she walked away. He sometimes forgot he wasn't married anymore. It would be a short lived problem. When Gina would return with his breakfast he would tell her he would love it if she came along with him. As Jonas was thinking and looking out through the pane glass window at the busy street traffic, he saw Gina holding her coat walking out into the parking lot. Then he looked at his watch.

"Hey, she said she was leaving at nine. It's already nine. I didn't realize it was so late?"

Like the wind he got up and headed for the door. He reached her just as Gina was closing her car door.

"Sorry Gina, I was kind of thinking about things and didn't realize it was already nine o'clock. Anyway, I would enjoy your company if that offer is still on," said Jonas, with a friendly smile.

While Jonas was talking, Gina was writing something on a piece of paper. He thought his ex, Lynn was beautiful, but Gina was quite a number.

"Here, Jonas. This is my phone number. Go back inside and enjoy your breakfast. When you finish call me. I will tell you how to get to my place and by then I will be ready to go with you, Okay?"

"Yeah, Okay, sure."

"As Gina pulled out of her parking space and then drove forward she said something through the open window at Jonas. It sounded like she said,

"Get ready for the stampede?" and then she laughed.

Jonas wasn't sure he heard her right and it made no sense to him.

"Get ready for the stampede?"

About forty minutes later Gina heard a knock on her door. She opened it to find Jonas standing there with an intrigued look on his face.

"Oh, come on in. Give me another minute. I have to feed my dog," said Gina as her dog looked obviously excited as it sniffed Jonas's pants in an embarrassing place. Jonas quickly took a few more steps into her residence putting the incident behind him.

"Oh, is that a greyhound?" he asked.

"Close, it's a Whippet." The semi small animal was predominantly white with tan and grey spotting.

"Don't eat all this at once Reeba. It's got to last you all day," said Gina.

"Sure is friendly, isn't he?" noted Jonas.

"Oh Gosh, they're wonderful dogs, usually quiet and very mild mannered. They love to go for walks. I get lots of comments from people'" answered Gina as the dog left Jonas to follow Gina into the kitchen.

Jonas heard the food pour into the dog bowl and then the sound of the dog crunching the food. A minute later as Jonas and Gina were leaving through the front door, Reeba reappeared in view. She barked once as if to say good bye and then returned to its feast.

As the two walked toward the street, Jonas's yellow Cuda came into view.

It was a beautiful car, having deep dished polished aluminum Mag's sporting a shaker hood.

"I like your car Jonas. Cuda's have that formidable look."

"Thanks! With gas prices climbing I'm wondering if I should rethink my ride," responded Jonas in a joking fashion.

As Jonas was walking toward the car the thought occurred to him to open the door for Gina, but he dismissed the thought. He wasn't going to open and close the door for her every time they got in or out of the car. In a way he wanted to but he didn't want to give her any false impressions. After they both got into the car Jonas turned the ignition key that started up the high performance V-8 in an instant. The car was as original from the factory, no thumping and popping from aftermarket cams, headers, and blown out gaskets. The engine just roared as the car sped off toward the interstate in a southerly direction.

"Are you working, Jonas?" asked Gina.

"What, oh yeah, I start this new job next week. It addresses local environmental issues," responded Jonas.

"Oh, is that the field your in?"

"Ah, yeah, that's how I would describe it. Sure, it's an up and coming thing this job I'm getting. Yes, the environmental field." answered Jonas thinking if landscape work wasn't environmental then he didn't know what was.

"So we're going to Orange County?" asked Jonas

"Yes, I grew up in Orange County before I moved to LA. It was a wonderful place back in the fifties. It was just a lot of agriculture back then," said Gina.

"Wow, what did you do for excitement," asked Jonas as he turned the cars radio on low and headed for the onramp that indicated, SAN DIEGO - 405.

"Well it wasn't like we were stuck on a desert oasis you know. Corona del Mar is close to Newport and Balboa. Orange County is still a pretty cool place, just a lot more crowded. Nothing seems to stay the same anymore, right?"

"Sure, of course. I wasn't putting it down or nothing," replied Jonas.

"It was really a great place to grow up. And we never ran out of things to do. Sure we didn't have all the museums, parks, and Hollywood stuff. It was different, sort of like out in the country. The closest place I could ride my bike to buy anything was a drive-through Alta Dena Dairy. Every time I could get my hands on a couple of dimes, I would buy me a pint of their chocolate milk," Gina laughed.

Just as Gina was laughing, Sinatra's, 'It Happened in Monterey', came on and Gina was about to find something out about Jonas. Jonas was in a good mood and as Sinatra's lyrics came forth from the radio, she could barely distinguish Sinatra's voice from Jonas's as he sang along.

As Jonas sang he snapped his fingers and Gina just sat there staring at him, listening, smiling and amazed with his voice and act. She noticed that some of the cars that passed them were giving Jonas a good deal of attention as he appeared to sing and snap his fingers. She didn't say a thing until Jonas had finished.

"Well listen to you Mr. Sinatra. I'm impressed. You're really good," concluded Gina.

These days Jonas had few friends. For all practical purposes none really. And no one could know how often he sang along to Sinatra's tunes. No one else could know how similar he sounded like the star, except for occasional occurrences of circumstance when family or friends might have over heard him.

"Oh, I just like the way Frank sounds. Heck, I like Dean Martin too, but I don't sound like Dean. Who could sound like Dean, with that twang in his voice," responded Jonas.

It was a weekday and the freeway was not too congested. While Jonas's car made its way south it also left the worst part of traffic behind. Barely an hour passed before they came to their exit ramp.

"Get off at Fairview," uttered Gina.

Jonas turned off on Fairview Road and headed south. They were in the city of Costa Mesa and were fast approaching a high school, a place that some of Gina's cousins had attended. She pointed off toward the east which was now all homes.

"All this was just a huge field when I was a kid. It was the remains of the old, 'Santa Ana Army Air Base', training station that they built to train aviators for World War II," commented Gina.

The base was a mainstay of the war effort. After the war, they inactivated the base and demolished most of the buildings or relocated them. During Gina's growing years all that was left of the base were a few building foundations, remnants of roads under overgrown prairie grass and weeds. A portion of it was made into the Orange County fair grounds. After much of it was reclaimed by nature it had become a huge playground for kids until it was bought by land developers.

"Yeah, well this ain't Nebraska cornfield land. If it was Nebraska cornfield land, it would still be a corn field. It's southern California. If the bulldozers aren't running, something's wrong," added Jonas.

Gina nodded her head in response.

"If we're lucky we will be able to park by Newport pier. Have you ever been there?" she asked.

"Yes, I've been down there a few times. It's been a while though," responded Jonas.

The two had found a place to park out in front of a bar that had a big black and white sign. It was called, 'Blackie's,' and by twelve thirty in the afternoon they had already walked all around the ocean front area, even on the pier. Some of the business names had changed over the years, but that span of red brick shops that extended along the beach could arouse old memories. It was a place of historical significance, especially for those who called the place home. Adjacent to the foot of the pier on the sandy beach was where the dory fisherman kept their boats. They launched their small wooden boats every morning through the onslaught of the incoming surf, then returned around noon with the day's catch of fresh fish, crabs, and lobsters to sell to their waiting customers.

Gina had something special in mind for lunch. Gina took Jonas to Blackie's, the bar they had parked next to. Seemed like Blackie's had been there nearly as long as anyone could remember. It wasn't a big place but one could always find room for a seat in one of the booths or at the bar. An array of wall decorations such as life size hammerhead sharks and various things of ocean related paraphernalia were adhered to the walls and ceiling. With an ice cold beer in hand Gina was on the phone with her grandfather. Gina's grandfather, Andrew Davies had worked for James Irvine Jr., the largest land baron and ranch owner of the surrounding area. Andrew began work with the ranch in 1913. Five years later while riding the ranch's range land Andy stumbled upon James daughter Kathryn Helena, whose horse had thrown her into an earthen crevice miles from the ranch house.

The rescue of Irvine's daughter resulted in an immense favorable outlook for Andrew. He was soon the ranch foreman, given generous pay, and at a later time was offered an option of one of five special parcels of land originally set aside for family. Not that Andy was a true family member but he was favored by the family and effective at being a great range caretaker. Consequently, the old man obliged when he found out Andy's interest in one of the parcels. The plots were laid out on a short mesa adjacent to the current city of Corona del Mar, offering splendid ocean views. It was the only parcel that James would ever set aside for a non-family member.

"Gina, what a wonderful surprise, I hardly ever see you anymore since you moved to L.A.," stated the senior Davies talking into the heavy black AT&T dial desk phone.

Gina was close to her grandmother Elsie who had passed away three years prior. Now her grandfather was lonely. Gina called her grandfather, 'Grunny', a name given to him by Gina when her grandfather took her grunion hunting one night. They were all running around trying to catch the slippery little fish when they came up on the beach to spawn. That night Andy couldn't seem to keep the Grunion from slipping out of his hand and Gina just kept laughing and calling him Mr. Funny Grunny. Thereafter she always addressed her grandfather as, 'Grunny'.

"Where are you at now?" asked the 84 year old Mr. Davies.

"I'm here with a friend at Blackie's in Newport. We just had a beer and I told him that we have to come and pay you a visit," remarked Gina.

"Well I should say, you better not leave without coming over. And since you're that close why don't you grab an extra- large Pizza for all of us. You know the place, 'Original Pizza,' just around the corner," stated the retired rancher.

"Of course I do, Grunny," responded Gina.

Indeed Gina knew the place. Her grandfather use to bring pizzas home from there all the time back when the old pizzeria king was a younger man. It had been a long time since Gina had a slice of pizza from the ole Italian pizza shop. She was anxious to see if it was still as good. As a youngster she would listen to Italian opera music that blared from some unseen source while the old man sang along and tossed pizza dough. Like any popular pizzeria, when you mingle the aroma of oven fired pizza dough, cheese, toppings, and spices like oregano and basil it only hastens ones appetite.

"Is the old man still there?" asked Gina.

"Yeah, I don't know how much longer. When he's gone I don't know if it will still be the same." responded her grandfather.

"OK. You like the works, no anchovies, right?" asked Gina.

"That's it honey."

"OK, will see you soon," said Gina.

"Sure, and the gate off the highway still opens the same way as always, dear."

"I have never forgotten how to open that gate. Never will unless you change the lock," responded Gina.

After getting the pizza, Gina and Jonas were on their way headed south on Pacific Coast highway. While they were driving, Gina was rambling on about her years spent growing up in the area. She talked about the various landmarks like the Balboa Pavilion, the ferry boats, the old fish cannery and the quaint county airport that had a swing set at the end of the runway for kids to watch planes take off and land. She mentioned some of the more popular restaurants like the Crab Cooker, Hanks Fish&Chips, Bobby McGees , Dillman's, the Villa Nova, and the Reuben E Lee. Newport Beach had always had a sort of colorful history ever since its inception in the late 1800's by its founder and developer, James McFadden. Now it's impressive manmade harbor provided safe mooring for countless pleasure boats and yachts where some movie stars had come to live.

With Gina giving the directions, Jonas made the prescribed turns, left onto MacArthur and right onto San Joaquin Hills Road where Gina had Jonas pull over. There, Gina pointed out all that remained of the old Buffalo Ranch Headquarters, a red stained barn. It was now a real estate and land development office. The old Buffalo Ranch at one time a small amusement park and entertainment site that was located in the grassy foothills of the sprawling Irvine ranch, consisted of a barn like mercantile building called, 'Porters'. There you could buy western wear, some recreational hardware products, and even collectibles. Adjacent to its location was an old grain tank that once served as a burger stand. Besides the various things on their menu they served Bison burgers. The park was run by a private enterprise that leased the land from the Irvine's. At the park one could go horseback riding or even schedule a Hay ride. The most popular ride was to clamber on back of an old fire truck which drove you out to a roaming buffalo herd. Then sadly one year for reasons unknown the Irvine Company declined to renew the operators lease and that was the end of the Buffalo fire truck rides .

"The poor Buffalo, progress always giving them the boot," joked Jonas.

Gina smiled and pointed toward the highway.

She had him turn right on San Joaquin Road. They drove several miles through the green grassy rolling hills of early spring. After telling Jonas to slow down they turned off and came to a locked gate on the right side of road. The property was well posted with no trespassing signs. Gina got out and opened the gate and closed it after Jonas drove through. The car drove slowly along taking in the view as they started a climb up a hill that sat back behind Corona del Mar. Overhead, a cooper's hawk soared and hovered, and then soared and hovered again in the stiff breeze aloft. Small flocks of mourning doves glided along from one thistle patch to the next, searching for fallen seeds. A meadowlark could be heard warbling nearby through the open window as Jonas's Cuda ambled slowly along through green field grass and patches of yellow mustard flowers.

"Wow, this sure is a lot of nature, such beautiful meadows," commented Jonas.

"Yes, for now. The green grass usually turns brown during summer," responded Gina.

"So how long has your grandfather lived out here?" Jonas asked.

"Oh, about Forever it seems."

"By the way, I call him Grunny, but you can call him Andy. He'll be sure to fill your ears with all kinds of stories. You might even like them." said Gina.

"Oh yeah, maybe, sometimes I like to listen to old timers and their tales. And uh, sometimes I don't," Jonas rolled his eyes.

After Jonas had gone a couple of miles from the paved highway they crested the green pastured hill they had been ascending. The first thing Jonas noticed was a fabulous view of the ocean. Anything else that could have been in view for that instant was secondary, even unnoticeable as his eyes searched the distant horizon. In view were the various hues of blue sky and ocean bound together with a myriad of pleasure boats scattered in the distance. Just up ahead there was a fork in the road. The right fork drifted down below and went around the side of a hill. The left meandered down to a missionary style home having a garden type setting. There within the confines of a surrounding wall huge trees sprang skyward and within the court yard the grounds were like a colorful botanical garden. The home was of white Spanish stucco that had archways along the outside corridors. The red tiled roof had two chimneys rising up, one in the middle of the home. The white washed home and red burnt clay hues were in harmony with the lush décor of the paved earthen walkways. As Jonas's car drove closer out buildings sprang into view. There was a separate open ended equestrian building, an equipment building, and a workshop.

"Wow, what a place. Look at that ocean view," remarked Jonas.

"It's one of the oldest homes around, built long before all the homes you see down below," added Gina.

As Jonas drove around front and parked his car, Gina grabbed the pizza and let herself out of the car.

"We better hurry. The pizza's getting cold," said Gina.

It was only about one o'clock in the afternoon. Gina led the way along the brick path and through the wrought iron gate up to the house. She first knocked on the door and then opened it.

"Anybody home?" she shouted.

"Just I, your old hungry grandpa," answered Andy.

"Grunny, this is Jonas Miles, a friend," said Gina.

Jonas, my grandfather, Andy Davies, but only I can call him Grunny. Isn't that right grandpa?" asked Gina.

"Right, been too long and too old of a thing to change now," smiled the senior Andrew.

"Davies was my last name before I got married Jonas," offered Gina.

Within minutes Gina had paper plates out and they were all sitting around the kitchen table eating pizza and drinking beer.

"Oh Honey, it's good. Thank you for bringing yourself and the pizza. I don't get out as much as I use to," remarked Andy.

"Wow, this is good. It may be the best pizza I've ever had," said Jonas.

The extra large pizza was just big enough for the three. Jonas was forced to finish the last piece by his hosts. When Jonas excused himself to use the restroom it was just the opportune time Gina was hoping for.

"Grunny, is 'Brutus' in good shape," asked Gina.

"Yea, funny you should bring it up, Danny and Guillermo dusted it off the other day, washed it and gave it a tune up. They must have known you were coming," said Andy with a sort of troubled look.

"Brutus' was a 1969 CJ-5 Jeep with a Buick V-6 crossfire engine as installed from the factory.

"Mind if I take Jonas out for a ride?" asked Gina.

"Oh dear lass, what are you fixing to do, scare the ba'jeevers out of another one of your friends? What was that last guy's name, Marty?"

Gina held a grin and a mischievous twinkle in her eye. Her tomboyish character may have been what appealed to some men, perhaps Jonas as well. Within her mesmerizing envelope there was an adventurous side that at times seemed to radiate a flamboyant and risky character. In regards to some things she seemed fearless, maybe even careless or just insensitive to danger.

"Are they still out there Grunny?" asked Gina.

"Is what still out there?" asked the old man, hesitantly.

He was afraid he knew what she meant. He had always been concerned about some of the reckless things she seemed to do, but he could only blame himself for her having such a nature.

"You know, the beasts," responded Gina.

"Yea, but I've heard talk not for long. They're looking at Catalina," said her grandfather.

"I envy you sir. What a wonderful place you've got here,"
said Jonas as he returned to the table."

"Yeah, he's spoiled for sure. So glad he and my Grandma Elsie were able to live here all these years," said Gina.

"Oh yes Gina, we've been fortunate to have this place, but spoiled, nah!" responded the elderly man.

With that Gina excused herself and left the table. She entered the kitchen out of view and found a basket. After going through some cupboards and then the refrigerator she found a few things she was looking for and disappeared.

"So Jonas, What line are you in?" asked Andy.

"Well, most recently I was in manufacturing design, but now it looks like I will be breaking into the environmental field," responded Jonas, not wanting to get into the conversation.

"Oh, you must tell me about it," queried Andy.

"Well in regard to a job I've been offered, I really don't know a lot about it yet. I'll probably know more next week."

Honk! Honk! Honk! Someone's horn blasted repetitively.

"Gosh, expecting someone?" asked Jonas.

Andy was quite familiar with that horn. It was that of their Jeep.

"I believe that would be Gina. I'm sure she wants you to go out and meet her," replied Mr. Davies.

The elderly man felt compelled to warn Jonas of possible danger, but held himself back. He wanted to give a hint of what he felt was going to become a probable event.

"Jeep huh, Guess I will go see what this is about," answered Jonas as he got up to go outside.

"Oh, I'm sure you will have a hell of a time out on that range Jonas. A little word of caution, Gina gets a little adventurous sometimes. She's high strung, so hang in there," responded the elder Davies.

Part of the elderly man fought back any compulsion to laugh. He could not forget how Gina described the look on the face of the last guy she took for a jeep ride. Perhaps such thoughts of mischief ran in ones' blood.

"Can you do me a favor and take those unfinished beers off the table and dump them. The trash is right outside the door," interjected the senior Davies.

"Oh yeah, sure thing sir," However, Jonas would take them out to the waiting vehicle.

"Well, nice to have met you sir in case I don't see you again," said Jonas as he shook the lively mans hand.

The elderly man seemed to cringe at the last phrase of the young man's remark. It seemed he had heard others bid him ado before in the same fashion, in similar circumstances.

"And you as well, young man. Take care of yourself. Keep an eye out for Gina, she's precious you know," remarked Mr. Davies.

With that Jonas left and as he closed the front door and approached the gate he saw Gina sitting in an open top Jeep ready to go. The vehicle looked all original with slightly faded red paint. If there was a top for it, it wasn't on the vehicle. It had a period style roll bar, a PTO winch on the front bumper and wide Gates Commando XT off road tires. It was a nice looking Jeep and it looked like it was ready for business. When Jonas got in, Gina told him to put on his seat belt because there were a lot of gopher tunnels under some of the roads.

"Ah, I don't need no seat belt," shot Jonas.

"Okay, suit yourself," she replied as she slightly revved the engine, released the clutch and the vehicle lurched forward.

"Sorry, been a while since I drove it," said Gina.

"Want me to drive?" blurted Jonas.

"Nah, that's all right, I think I'll get the hang of it," responded Gina as she drove back up the road they came in on.

"Where we going?" asked Jonas.

"Oh, didn't you mention something about a nice cool breeze? Well I just wanted to get you back out in it and show you some of the sprawling Irvine Ranch land before we leave to go back to L.A."

When Gina arrived at the fork in the road that they had encountered previously while on their way in, she now turned the Jeep in the other direction which was more like a trail. It meandered down toward the coast for a few minutes until it changed course and then they headed for the higher terrain of the coastal range. The Irvine Ranch as a rule was off limits to 99.9% of all people, period. They had their own range patrol officers and you didn't want to get caught by them. There were a few people around that were granted leniency. People like Andy who had worked for the ranch and retired with them. And there were lots of red Jeeps driving around in the harbor area, but Andy's had two whip poles in the back with yellow flags tied to them. So when trained patrol binoculars found Andy's jeep in its sights they usually didn't make a big deal about it.

There had been prior incidents involving Gina with the ranch people, but such was the understanding that some of those things she chose to do would not be repeated. Those were things that Andrew Davies could not forget, or control. After all, she wasn't a kid anymore just out of High School. The elder Davies gave the ranch people his assurance that those risky and rambunctious things that his granddaughter occasionally did wouldn't happen anymore. And even though he gave his word he was afraid that someday he would have to deal with the problem again.

To him, she was more precious then anything he owned. She was all he had left in his life. He could never forgive himself either if she got hurt or something worse. He would make up excuses to the security patrol again just like he did last time Gina drove the Jeep, and the time before that.

"Did you bring my beer too, or are those two beers yours?" asked Gina.

"Oh, yeah, here yah go," as he handed her the beer she half finished in the house. The two finished their beers and then Jonas put the bottles in the back where he noticed a basket.

"What's in the basket?" asked Jonas.

"Oh, just some refreshments for later in case we get thirsty," she answered.

Gina was now in high gear giving the engine a little throttle as it sped down the dirt road with a trail of dust whipping back in the cool breeze. The short wheel based vehicle was a stiff ride, not much different than a stage coach except riding a stage coach would have been smoother. Gina wore a blue ruffled blouse with a low open bodice. Jonas couldn't help but notice that her trim bra seemed to be fighting a rough assignment at keeping things steady .

Jonas's concentration was doing a sort of tango between the Jeep, Gina, and the changing countryside. Gina seemed quite charismatic with her large brimmed straw hat secured by a red strap under her chin. She looked so delicate, fresh, full of gaiety and yet seemed predisposed to her own thoughts, all the while looking quite beautiful. Jonas wondered if he should pinch himself to make sure things were real. Life had been so mundane lately, now here he was with a young and beautiful woman again. Going out for breakfast that morning turned out to be one of the best bargains in choice he had made in a long time.

Twenty minutes later they were in a canyon that had steep hillsides. The terrain was dotted with few trees, some wild shrubbery and range grass. Jonas had been enjoying the leisure country ride. Then Gina pulled over, stopped, and pulled back a small lever on the floorboard as she was saying something about lofty views. Jonas was watching what she was doing while listening and thinking at the same time. All the close at hand visual comprehensions kind of just floated in and out of his thoughts like a sudden nuance. Gina had something in mind as she put the vehicles transmission in low range. Before she could say 'Hold On', she gunned the engine and let out the clutch. In an instant the vehicle jerked forward in a first gear leap. The forward motion amounted to nothing more then a crawl as the transmission whined. Then she put it in second gear, the gear it would remain in for the next several minutes as she pointed the nose of the Jeep for what seemed like the top of a six hundred foot precipice.

The front windshield was folded and tied down upon the hood. The Jeep was in low second gear with the engine at a high rev and they were bouncing, swaying, and chugging their way forward. The climb seemed extremely steep to Jonas as they went upward, and sometimes nearly sideways. There was no road, no trail, just raw land with trees, bushes, grass, rocks and loose earth under tire. The incline was tremendous as she held onto the steering wheel going around obstacles as fast as they came. Jonas who had occasionally waned in his respects to God now found himself praying to the almighty for his life. He told himself that the first time the Jeep slowed enough he would jump out. He thought maybe if he did just that he might save his life. After all, he was apparently with a crazy woman. So that is why he is here now, to die. I knew it couldn't be something good he thought as the jeep seemed to struggle to maintain momentum. Dirt was being thrown everywhere behind the vehicle like an isolated dust storm, like one would imagine from some desolate and churning twister.

Meanwhile from a distance there were others in the area. There was a glint, a reflection of light on a hillside more then two miles away. It's what happens when the sun meets the ground glass lens of a fine and expensive pair of binoculars. The observer was not happy.

"Dammit, who in the hell is that? Look at that thing tear up the side of that mountain. It looks like Andy's Jeep. I know that ain't Andy driving it. I can't see Danny or Guillermo driving like that. If that's his daughter again then she must be all hell bent on killing herself, or just plain nuts. I'm going to give Andy hell this time. One of these times she is going to roll that thing over and get hurt really bad or worse, I shrug to think."

The man was Ed Ferguson, an Irvine ranch patrolman. The problem with the Irvine Ranch was it just had too much attraction. It was like a three hundred thousand acre park in the middle of civilization, and everybody wanted to see if they could get away with all sorts of things from hunting and fishing, to hiking and four wheeling. Well here officer Ferguson definitely had a four wheeler incident.

"Yup, Yup, there it goes on up to the top of that son of a gun'. Well I'll be damn if I try to drive this Blazer up there. They don't pay me enough. I'll get them when they come down," he thought.

The two were nearing the top of the hill as the Jeep kept purring and chugging. The finely tuned V-6 engine was just about the perfect little match for that hill. Right at that moment Jonas would have gave anything to be back at one of his old jobs selling stupid little car parts, or even pumping gas at the old Chevron station. Finally, when he thought it would never happen, the Jeep, like the little choo choo that could crested the hill and was finally on top. Somehow through the whole ordeal as scared as he had been he could not say a word. He could not let out any sign of fear to be picked up in Gina's eyes. He just occasionally held on to the grab bar bolted to the dash and allowed his hand and arm to hold onto the side body panel for stability. His heart was racing more then he could ever remember. When Gina turned the Jeep around on top to face the ocean Jonas wanted to lay a piece of his mind on her. But by doing so she would take his chastise as fear when in fact it would have been more about what is sane and what is not. Perhaps, if she had given him a clue as to what she intended to do. No, that would have changed nothing except he might have gotten out. Jonas had spent much of his youth four wheeling through all kinds of terrain but never attempted to climb anything as steep on such raw loose earth.

The true amount of fear he had felt would never come to be known. What reality was and what it had become was a long lost emotion thrown to the wind. The experience would never be forgotten. The truth was Gina had done this climb several times before obviously surviving those events, but how much was luck, who could tell. Perhaps this woman sought these kinds of thrills because she had been brought up to believe in not being afraid of anything. Then it could be something entirely different where perhaps somewhere inside herself while engaged in the dangerous melee, she found a form of temporary asylum from the real world. Casual off road four wheeling is one thing, but launching oneself skyward as though in an overland rocket ship was not for the squeamish.

"Well" was all she said as she looked at Jonas with a face as sweet as honey. Her intense blue eye's searching his inner soul.

"Yea, that was fun," he answered. I can't wait until we do it again. You going down the same way?" he asked, pinching the side of his thigh to cause pain. It was an attempt to subdue his desire to let out a ridiculous laugh.

"Oh don't be silly. Going down that way would be dangerous," she answered.

"Look at the view Jonas," as she gazed toward the west.

Indeed it was beautiful. It was like they were on a pedestal overlooking the world and the broad presence of the ocean glittered like diamonds. The offshore breeze stimulated gentle white caps across the cape of its breath. Yachts were sprinkled about the horizon with tiny sails, and Catalina Island stood clear and bold. It's just twenty six miles across the sea, as they say. Jonas was glad that Gina had the front windshield folded down as it instilled an air of openness. Things were sort of surreal as the two sat in silence for a time while they looked around immersed in their own thoughts. Down below they could see cars crawling along coast highway between Laguna and Corona del Mar. Oak trees were sparse in this part of the range, but not more than twenty yards behind the Jeep was a large oak next to a Sumac tree which offered a lot of shade from the sun.

"Like champagne?" asked, Gina.

"Yeah, sure," said Jonas.

"Good ole Granddad. He always has something lying around," laughed Gina as she reached for the basket and jumped out of the Jeep.

"Hmm, Champagne and the perfect spot," responded Jonas.

"Let's go underneath the oak. We got chairs. There's a half dozen tree stumps that my friends and I made. We brought them up here back when I was in High School."

"Oh I see, if only these trees could talk, huh?" laughed Jonas.

Gina smiled.

"So I get it. That wasn't the first time you ram rodded up this hill in a Jeep, is it?"

"No, Butch and Andy drove me up here when I was just a kid. Butch had a Jeep with a Chevy V-8 in it."

"Yeah, a V-8 in one of these is a pretty beefy option," replied Jonas.

Gina was still talking as Jonas was throwing a blanket out on the ground. Gina was removing the champagne and glasses out of the basket. Then Jonas cleaned off the best of the two tree stump seats. The fact that they had the bark removed and been stained seemed to preserve them. Gina kept talking.

"Anyhow, when I turned sixteen most of the girls wanted a sports car or something. Well, when I went on a date with a friend in High School, he had a Jeep. I thought they were fun so then I wanted a Jeep. So Grunny bought me this Jeep. I loved four wheeling when I was a kid, just riding around in the open, sitting up high."

"Sounds like you're sort of a tomboy, Gina?"

"Tomboy?, well maybe in some ways. I guess I do some things a lot of other gals don't usually do," she replied.

"At least I didn't forget the cork screw. Would you mind?" asked Gina holding up the bottle to him.

"Of course," replied Jonas as he opened the bottle filling two glasses before replacing the stopper.

The two sat and talked about old times from the perspective of their young adult lives. Jonas told her where he went to High School, about his sports accomplishments and classes he took in school. It wasn't news to discover that they both were still searching for something that was bigger and better than what they had. Gina was enrolled in an assortment of college night classes. She favored the arts, like theater and music. She wanted to learn how to play the violin which she said was the perfect instrument to set a mood. She also took ballet and singing classes.

The following hour went quickly and the two enjoyed each other's company. They had maneuvered themselves close to each other for ease of conversation and of pouring the champagne. Jonas sat on one stump facing Gina, and Gina sat on the other facing the ocean with her legs outstretched, one crossed over the other. The wine had taken its effect. The two laughed at anything and everything as fleets of isolated floating clouds held their course as passing shadows. Gina removed her hat and her hair played gold and lively in the breeze. Her delicate face and skin took on a radiant glow as her eyes sparkled. It was a face that the observer wanted forever to be with and one that women envied and men wanted to lay claim to. She had some scent, faint but potent. Jonas realized one must live for today and to hell with tomorrow. She held out her glass for more, it dropped and the two lunged for it as they rolled down the blanket, Jonas losing his own glass. The two came to rest facing each other with Jonas half on top of her. The two looked seriously into each others eyes. Jonas gently placed his hand along the side of her face touching her hair and he placed his lips against hers. He kissed her gently at first, and then passionately.

The sound of a climbing jet airliner could be heard overhead. Its accelerating two hundred fifty knot shadow passed through them and then disappeared as the aircraft entered a cloud. Jonas placed a hand alongside her breast. She pushed her hand firmly against his chest to push him up. She smiled and began to remove her shirt, and he his. And quickly, they removed their clothes. Then they pressed themselves against each other. As time went by the midday sun crossed the position of the earth's zenith and dragged its arch across the azure sky. Such a woman as this might breathe life back into a dead man one could think. For the next several hours upon the blanket, in the grass, or within the trees they made love like there was no tomorrow. And then Gina rose, grabbing her clothes was a cue for Jonas. They got dressed and began to gather up their things. When Jonas tipped over the basket while still feeling a little light headed, a holstered gun fell on to the blanket.

"Wow, a gun?" he remarked to Gina.

"Oh, well, there are lots of hungry mountain lions out here," she responded. But that may had not been the only reason she brought it.

Ed Ferguson the ranger left long ago. After waiting an hour he had no idea they would be so long until after he gave it some more thought. Then maybe he had things figured out right.

"A man and a woman up there alone, Hmm, probably not mushroom hunting."

When Gina and Jonas had the Jeep loaded back up again with the picnic items she had other things in mind. She also had no intention of returning the way they came. That was a good thing considering that the other option of leaving was a much more gradual slope down into a distant valley.

"You mean to tell me we could have come up this way instead of the Yosemite Half Dome?" asked Jonas.

"Tell me Jonas. What were you feeling when we went up that hill, were you scared? I'll bet that will be one thing you will never forget, right?" remarked Gina, while looking at him.

Jonas didn't answer. He just gave her a slight grin and looked ahead.

California valley quail could be heard calling across the canyon. Gina found what she was hoping for all along. She pulled out a small pair of binoculars from the glove box. She stood up on the seat and concentrated her attention on a distant herd of animals.

"Hells Bells Jonas, we found them," she exclaimed.

"Found what?" he asked.

"You see way over there, those little scattered dots?" she asked.

"I guess, you mean those cattle," he remarked.

"No, those aren't cattle, they're Bison, you know Buffalo!" she responded.

"Buffalo? Are they leftovers from that Buffalo ranch you were talking about?" he replied.

"Yep, that's exactly what they are, about two hundred of them. That's really why I brought you out here," she answered not thinking of anything else.

"Oh really, glad we found them then. At least your day won't be a total loss," responded Jonas.

She paused a minute and then turned and looked at him.

"What does that mean?" she asked.

"Oh, nothing, just didn't know if you've been completely enjoying your day," he answered, perhaps choosing his words hastily due to a champagne overload.

"Have I not seemed so?" she replied.

"Sorry, forget I said it. I must be blitzed."

"Why, you unhappy about something?" she asked, also feeling light headed.

"No, I'm not unhappy about anything," he added.

Gina sat back down in the Jeep, released the brake and headed for the herd.

"Oh Gina, what are you up to now?" asked Jonas.

"Nothing, I just want to get a little closer so you can see them," she said staring ahead.

"Okay, sounds cool," he responded, and as she drove he was thinking, was this going to be another one of those things that she says I will never forget, he wondered. He remembered back in the parking lot of the 'Waffle Strudel Café,' when Gina pulled away and said something about, 'Stampede'. Now he could only wonder.

Gina drove along toward the herd and as the minutes went by the herd got closer and closer. How could you describe a Buffalo, an American Bison? Buffalo brought other things to mind like all that historic folk lore about cowboys and Indians of the old west. The grand Texas Longhorns with their five foot horns beating a path along the dried dusty Chisholm trail. Then came the more refined beef cattle like the white face Herford's and Black Angus, among others.

One thing for sure, bison weren't domestic cattle. They are a remarkable beast. They are powerfully built, squat and sturdy as a boulder. They would be best described as being shaped like a potato with a shark eye on either side of their shaggy head, to which is added some devilish looking horns all sitting atop a few sets of four by fours for legs.

A truly magnificent beast, they once roamed the Great Plains in herds that numbered in the tens of thousands. When Bison stampeded in such numbers the ground shook beneath the feet of the Indian, settler, or whoever would have been fortunate or unfortunate enough to have witnessed the awesome spectacle. Now, just several hundred yards in front of Jonas was a herd of a few hundred. Though this herd was only a fraction the size of those encountered a few centuries ago, it was still a magnificent sight.

This place, though just a few miles from the Pacific Ocean was amidst grass laden rolling hillsides that was similar to where they once roamed, free and wild by the thousands upon the plains of the mid-west. Gina didn't need the binoculars anymore as she had Jonas put them away. In their place she produced a .357 caliber revolver as the Jeep hurriedly bounded over the raw range land of earth, furrow, and pasture.

Bang! Bang! Two loud shots echoed off the nearby foothills as Gina aimed the gun at the sky and pulled the trigger. She gunned the Jeep straight for the herd. What was once a serene and visual image of behaving beast's, suddenly became transformed into a sudden fury of disturbed animals. Now these beasts were responding to threat no different than the generations of their kind before them. Their reaction was to run. In this day and age to experience a fleeing herd of such animals was practically impossible. The thought of a fleeing galloping herd as exciting as it seemed, was no less stimulating then a close in pack of wolves howling through the alpine woodlands.

Bang! Bang! Echoed the report of Gina's pistol again as two more shots rang out. She sped forward and the needle of the speedometer had reached forty as the vehicle vaulted over the open irregular terrain. They were now beginning to gain on the animals that were just out in front of them. No, this time Jonas would not curse her beneath his breath. Earlier this day, when Gina rocketed her Jeep to the top of her secret mountain, he realized it was a sort of a cold shower experience, an experience that introduced him to her true character. So, whatever it was that drove her, he deduced he liked it. He liked people who went against the grain. So she was a risk taker. People need that something extra in one's ordinary life to make them feel alive. Depending on the challenge and the circumstances in ones quest for success, it can be moments such as these that mean success or failure, life or death, gratification, or dissatisfaction in life.

There was a time when the adrenalin hormone was called upon in humans on a much more common basis than it was today. It was before we covered over the earth's natural environment with tar, before we displaced or eradicated natures wild denizens; those creatures which we feared as much as they us. It was before we reduced nature and a myriad of species either to extinction or to only a fraction of what it once was. One must wonder what role adrenalin might possibly inject into the human animal syndrome, or any animal, a hormone brought on by a sudden need for survival in the face of threat. Perhaps it's something we have not studied well enough.

Surely in our past, humans had to run for their lives, climb trees to escape death, or face that which threatened them. Such was when humanity had to routinely put into practice their learned tactics of flee or fight. These were the rules of survival in a world that only recognized the laws of nature. All creatures crave the same things, shelter, food, comfort, and peace. So this again, was one of those times as they found themselves in the midst of this thundering herd of Bison running at full gallop toward some unknown place. And that unknown place would become the place they would cease to gallop, perhaps their energy spent but prepared to fight if necessary. Suddenly Jonas imagined he was the Indian riding a bareback horse along side of the herd shooting as many arrows as he could so he could feed his family. He found himself staring into the eyes of the beating hoofed beasts, and they his. The herd swerved young and old as Gina drove alongside and within the fringes of their driving fear. From behind, clouds of smoke like dust rose up and then slowly settled to the ground. Jonas stood up on the floor panel of the Jeep as he held onto the roll bar. The vehicle bounced and leapt over mounds and dips.

The day to day life of the 1800's explorer, fur trapper, or gold seeker found on the long trail from Saint Louis to the mountains of the west surely was not the same as it was for those who chose to stay behind in the eastern cities. What today do most experience in their day to day lives that make them feel alive? What to take out of the freezer for dinner? What channel to turn the TV to? Shall I sit on the couch or the recliner? Rarely are there swollen rivers to worry about, or wild animals, Indian attacks, or killer road agents. The early pioneers were dealt death by heat, thirst, starvation, and the freezing cold. Now, several hundred years later after this new nation has seized these lands from the native peoples have those who have displaced them been the best stewards. In one scenario, just to stay alive on a daily basis would probably require a degree of stamina, alertness, and basic survival skills. In regard to the flip side, survival might mean not cutting off a car in traffic or arguing with the boss. The old way of living was an ever changing set of circumstances while the current way is as repetitive and as boring as a cola that has gone flat. Each means of living offers its own version of stimulation, both focused on survival while the challenges are varied and dependent upon one's own choices.

"Hold on," Gina yelled.

Just up ahead was a low berm of earth along an old irrigation canal. The herd jumped over it with the jeep in pursuit as it became momentarily airborne for what seemed like an eternity. Jonas's body lunged forward and only by grabbing the roll bar did he save himself from flying over the hood of the Jeep, or worse, being run over by it. They sped past a small pond partially hidden by cattails. There, an explosion of waterfowl sprang vertically skyward, each bird at first like a slow moving space shuttle until gaining great momentum. Jonas loved this crazy girl, a woman he thought he would like to know better but he thought it only for a blink of an eye.

It wasn't right to feel overshadowed by a female. He was the man. He should be the one providing such a thrill. But it is she who knows of this place, not I, he thought. I know of no place as this. Then he briefly wondered what kind of guy such a woman as this must need and respect. She must have seen something in him. For now, screw all the problems of the world and screw mine. All he felt now was the exciting fear of the proximity of the galloping beasts alongside their bounding Jeep. Forget the prospect of danger, for if that truly was your dominant thought then you shouldn't have even been here.

From across the valley unbeknownst to Gina and Jonas were two vehicles converging on them. They were in communication with each other. One was a white Ford Bronco and the other was a Chevrolet Blazer. The door panels read, 'Security Patrol- Irvine Ranch'.

"Alright, let's move in now," commanded security chief Jerry Kline. Jerry drove the 1972 Bronco towards Ed Ferguson, the patrolman who first spotted them hours before.

The lighter Bronco would be able to give the Jeep a run for its money then the heavy Blazer. But this chase would not be like the last time they came after Gina. That former incident which was promised to be the last obviously wasn't and that one was a long exasperating pursuit. However, this time Gina was caught with far less effort. A half hour later she and Jonas were at the Irvine Headquarters.

Not many knew that the Irvine ranch had their own jail cells. As it turned out they had two separate cells. They were just an interim holding pen until they could have the sheriff over to pick up who ever had been detained. And it wasn't Ed that was really upset, it was Jerry and maybe he was just in a bad mood or having a bad day. It wasn't that Jerry was mean rotten but he could be if he was dealing with mean rotten people. He was only five feet six inches tall but as sturdy as the buffalo their captives were chasing. Ed on the other hand was six foot six, but easy going. The truth be told there was a big difference between a city jail and a small time security office that had an empty cells most of the time. Besides, Jerry probably wanted to give Gina a little something to think about since she had already promised she wouldn't do this stampede thing again. Now Jerry was on the phone to Gina's grandfather.

"Hello Mr. Davies. This is Jerry Kline over at the ranch headquarters."

Soon as the phone rang Mr. Davies had a good idea who it might be.

"I got your granddaughter and her friend in our jail, you know," spoke the slow spoken grizzly character on the phone.

"Oh Jerry, what happened?" asked Andrew, even though he pretty much had a good idea.

"You know what happened Andy, she stampeded our Bison herd again. That's what happened. The charges are, trespassing, leaving the roadway in a motorized vehicle, destruction of private property, using the ranch for a social event without permission, discharging a firearm, harassing wildlife on private property. Do I need to go on Mr. Davies," exclaimed the chief security officer.

"Yes, I gotcha Jerry. What do you intend to do with her? You know how she is. She's always been like a little twister."

"Yah, like granddad, like daughter, I say," responded the officer.

"She's a grown woman. Heck, you know she just came down to visit me. She lives out of town. I think she just wanted to show her friend a little countryside," responded the senior Mr. Davies. The old gentleman didn't really know what to say. He had used up better excuses in times past.

"Well she didn't exactly take him on a leisurely buggy tour.

Andy, the ranch has rules to protect themselves and others, you know that. That's why it's off limits to most everyone," you know that.

"Gee, what can I do, Jerry? I'm eighty four. I know its wrong but that poor guy that's with her. He didn't know what she was up to. Let's not forget we too were kids, once."

There was a momentary silence at Jerry's end.

"Okay Andy. This is the last time I swear that I will ever excuse it. If she ever does it again I'll have to report it to the boss. I'm calling Pete at the Sheriff's office and I'll be delivering them to him, and I'll instruct him to drop them off at your place in your custody. I'm not telling them where they're going. Let them think they are going to the county jail. She's a beautiful granddaughter. She could have gotten killed pulling those stunts," said Officer Kline.

"You can have Danny or Guillermo pick up the Jeep. And if it ever happens again we will just keep that too."

"Okay, Thank You Jerry. I'll make it right for the ranch. I owe ya," responded Andrew.

"No Jerry, Gina owes us. Just like the last two times."

"Yeah, I know," said Mr. Davies.

Hours had passed. The deputy sheriff had dropped the two off as planned, and to their surprise at Gina's grandfathers. In no time they were back in Jonas's car on the way back to L.A. They were both very tired. Jonas's high performance Cuda rumbled down the freeway in the evening darkness. Gina had the seat back and her eyes were closed. Jonas's eyes were only open because he was driving. He didn't know how to describe the day. In the end he was glad he didn't leave the café back in L.A. with out Gina. This would be one of those days in Jonas's life he wouldn't forget, not knowing if he was going to die under a rollover or spend the night in jail. Going to jail would have been worth what he had experienced that day. All Jonas could see was bright headlights coming and going. He looked at Gina. Even after all the wind bashing and rough adventure she still looked beautiful. He wanted to see her again but would she see him? When he arrived at Gina's residence he dropped her off. He asked if he could call her later in the week. She smiled, said sure, and said goodnight. The day would come in the not so distant future that the Irvine ranch people would come across Gina Thorpe again, but not on their ranch and next time she would have a different name.

SEVEN

Changing Lanes

Several days had passed and Jonas could not get Gina off his mind. The very next day after he had dropped her off he called Stanley Guiles the landscape owner who had offered him a job. Stanley wanted Jonas to start right away so it didn't look like Jonas would have much spare time to see Gina. He was to report to Jay Thompson the groundskeeper who did most of the training.

They had a few homes to do off of Laurel Canyon in the morning and later a couple of jobs off of Wilshire. When Monday arrived Jonas showed up at the given address a little apprehensive. He was looking at it as if he were following the advice of his uncle. The one that told him a person could become a millionaire by starting their own landscape business.

"Wow, Dad would be proud," thought Jonas in a humorous fashion. "I guess they'll call me, George's son, 'The Lawnmower Guy'.

When Jay met Jonas his first impression was he would be one of those guys who didn't come back after the first few days. One day on the job and there wouldn't be a second. One thing Jay hated was training new hires the art of the landscape trade and then they never came back. Jay had two other guys with him, Jose and Kim. When a work crew approached a half acre or more of landscape work that needed to get trimmed back in shape in the shortest amount of time they had to be skilled artisans.

"You just don't start hacking at everything," stressed Jay. "It's not the same thing as when most home owners do their own yard work," he explained.

He told Jonas that there had been a number of those they hired that they had to let go just because they couldn't get the hang of it. So he warned him to pay attention.

"All you need is physical effort, a little ambition, show up for work, and you should be okay," said Jay.

At the first residence Jay told Jonas to follow him and watch everything he did. He showed him how to overlap the mower on lawn coverage, how to deliver the right trim perspective on the hedges and the boarders of the lawns. He showed him how to test the irrigation system and how to use all the different tools of the trade. Jonas took on the whole affair as a serious endeavor no matter how elementary it all seemed. It took them a few hours to do the first residence.

When they got to the second residence Jay told Jonas to mow the back lawn while he and the other two would get the front yard whipped into shape. Jonas pulled the mower out and pushed it around the side toward the back of the home. Like many of the homes in the area the grounds had ample privacy with lush landscaping. Besides the rectangular shaped lawn there was also a pool and tennis court. There were the usual lounge chairs and patio tables with umbrellas. There was no one outside using the grounds which was typical when the men were there working.

Unseen to Jonas was a woman drinking coffee and looking out of the kitchen window. She was Lisa Conroy, wife of Anniston Conroy, a well known talent agent that kept local popular night clubs, film studios, and entertainment venues staffed with talented people. He was regarded as one of those people who make it possible for aspiring actors and actresses to become 'discovered,' as they say.

There were not many places in the world where the mid day temperature seemed to hover around seventy degrees all year long, but Southern California was one of them. So the sun was out and there was a comfortable breeze. It was early summer.

"I guess if I can't mow a lousy lawn then I might as well be a door knob." Jonas thought to himself.

He looked over at the lawn.

"Well, it's just another lawn," he thought.

He started up the motor and commenced mowing by overlapping paths, one over the other. He really wasn't too worried about anything. He just looked at this job as something to give him some living expense money and get him back into physical shape. The other guys were out front doing the hedges, trees and lawns. Jonas was alone. He started whistling an old tune. He was a very good whistler. He could almost sound like a flute. The tune was 'Never on a Sunday."

Lisa Conroy had been watching him for a few minutes as she drank her coffee. The window was open and there was a nice breeze coming through the window. She went to the refrigerator to get some milk to prepare a bowl of cereal. As she was pouring cereal into her bowl she then heard a Frank Sinatra song. It was Sinatra's 'Summer Wind'. She always liked that song. After she poured in her cereal she added some artificial sweetener and sliced up a banana for the cereal. She got a spoon and went back over to the window to eat her cereal. She was listening to the song unravel and as she was watching Jonas it took a long surreal moment of comprehension for something to hit her senses. It wasn't a radio she was listening to. It was Jonas singing the song just like it was old blue eyes himself.

Jonas just kept right on singing that song. He could sing just about any song Sinatra sang. He just kept mowing across the lawn as he sang. It wasn't a huge lawn like some estates, but big enough. What was left was good for another ten minutes. As he was pushing and singing the same lyrics over and over he did not notice that Mrs. Conroy was standing yards from him, listening with great interest to his singing.

"Excuse me," she said. He did not hear her as the mower's engine was loud enough to drown out her tone of voice.

"Hey you," she said, this time much louder.

Jonas thought he heard something and turned around to find an extraordinarily beautiful woman looking at him. She was wearing hip hugging tight white denim jeans with a limber sleeveless black twill top. White strap high heal sandals adorned her feet. Her large green eyes, framed in shoulder length auburn hair grabbed your attention. She wore little make up. She looked to be about five foot eight in her heels.

"Was that you I just heard singing or is Frank Sinatra hiding in the bushes?" asked the lady smiling.

"Well I don't know if Mr. Sinatra is in the bushes, but I was singing. I like to sing when I'm busy, it makes me feel good," responded Jonas.

"Well if Frank Sinatra has a beautiful voice then you've one too, because I couldn't tell the difference. You sound just like him."

"Well, thank you Ma'am. There has been some who have said that I reminded them of him when I sing."

"I would say it's a lot closer to just like him. It's amazing. Do you sing his other songs?" asked the woman.

"I sing a lot of his songs. It depends on what mood I'm in."

"Have you worked on our yard before?" asked Mrs. Conroy.

"Ah, no, as a matter of fact, this is my first day on the job with this outfit," responded Jonas.

"My name is Lisa Conroy. What is yours?" she asked.

She realized these landscape people didn't always do the same homes but she wanted to know his name in case he didn't come back. Then she might be able to locate him.

"My name is Jonathan Miles, but I just go by Jonas," he replied, smiling.

"Say that's an easy name to remember. At least I can pronounce it."

"Not too rough' I guess," he responded.

"You know it's my husband's job to find people like you. I'm going to tell him about you."

"Oh, he's like a talent agent? I doubt if I'm that good?"

"Oh, but you are."

"Well thank you."

"You're welcome. You have a great voice. Keep exercising it," added the homeowner.

"Well I'll try."

"Well, take care Jonas, and don't ever stop singing. You sound beautiful."

Lisa Conroy had every intention of telling her husband about her discovery. But Anniston was a busy man and it was unlikely that he would call a groundskeeper up for an audition. His mind was just to busy for that. And though Jonas appreciated the woman's compliments on his singing, obtaining stardom status was something that really never seriously entered his mind. So a mere few minutes later no remnant of her remark remained in his thoughts except for his task of working on her yard. By five o'clock that evening the crew had finished five estate yards, which were sizable. So far Jonas was doing OK, but he was tired and a little sore.

By six o'clock he was at home and in the shower. After showering he got dressed and called Gina's apartment. There was no answer. He decided to drive over to the café where she worked. When he arrived he just ordered coffee because he didn't intend to stay long unless she was there. She wasn't. Jonas asked one of the other waitresses he knew if she had seen Gina. She said Gina worked about half a shift Sunday morning, leaving early after receiving a phone call. She also said that she had called them that morning telling them she wouldn't make it in that day either. Jonas thanked her, finished his coffee and left. He then headed over to Gina's apartment. When he got there he found her car out front so he thought she must be home. There was no parking spot available right in front of her place so he parked a ways down the street. As soon as he shut his car door to walk over he saw her front door open and a guy came out. Jonas got back in his car. He watched the guy take a few steps toward the street and then turn around and walk back toward the door. He began talking to someone in the door that he soon recognized as Gina. Then he saw her come briefly out in a white terry robe and they exchanged a few words and then they kissed each other.

The man was well dressed and got into a late model BMW. After the man drove off Jonas waited about ten minutes. Now a certain anxiety and bad feeling had come over Jonas. He was going to go over and knock on the door, but instead he drove around the corner and called her number from a pay booth. He let the phone ring several times but there was no answer. He didn't understand. It could have been anyone calling her. A relative, her grandfather, or even the guy who just left, but she doesn't answer?

He was peeved. Obviously his recent time spent with Gina must not have meant much to her. He quickly drove to a florist he passed a ways down the road and bought a small bouquet of roses. Then he drove over to her apartment and knocked on the door. When she answered the door she was now wearing a baby blue terry robe and her hair was wet. She must have been in the shower.

"Hi Gina!" said Jonas

She had a very surprised look. It was a look that was familiar to many men's faces that suggested bad timing. Nevertheless, she tried to compose a pleasant reaction to the unexpected visit. It was a forced composure, a look that held an artificial smile that anyone who had a half an ounce of sense could easily translate as,

"Gosh, bad timing dude."

Jonas handed her the flowers.

"Thank You, Jonas! But you shouldn't have bought these, really."

"Oh, it's nothing. I tried calling these last few days but I guess you haven't been home?" said Jonas.

"Yes, I have been out quite a bit. I've been really busy."

"I went to the Café to see you, but they said you had missed some shifts."

"Yeah, I have Jonas. So much has happened in this last week. Actually, I took some work elsewhere making easier money with fewer hours. It goes by quickly and has been giving me the time I need to keep up with classes and such."

"Classes, yes, I remember you said you were going to school? Well that's great. What are you taking?"

"It's like an entertainment curriculum; singing, dancing, acting type classes. I thought I already mentioned it? I'm sorry, but I'm in a hurry right now. I have to be at an audition in a few hours. And I'm afraid I'm not going to have a lot of free time for awhile."

"Oh, alright, I got yuh."

"It's not like that. I really like you Jonas, but I sort of got this opportunity this last week. It's sort of a long shot and I'm going to try to make the best of it," said Gina.

"Oh, I'm sorry if I'm keeping you then, I will get going. Good luck with that thing' then," he said, not forgetting what he had witnessed at her front door between the stranger and her.

As he was walking away from the front door to leave she blurted out a short last sentence that would be the last he would hear her say for a long time.

"Jonas, call me in a few weeks. Sunday's good."

"Sure, okay, no problem, Sunday, okay, Good luck with your audition thing," he said as he walked away.

It's strange how a woman's fervor toward a man can launch him to the top of the world or bring him down like a battleship chased sub, depending on the circumstances. It's what can make a guy whistle or sing when he mows a lawn, or just forgets about life for awhile. The resilient person just lets things go and moves on. It seemed Jonas was getting better at resiliency.

"Oh well, everyone takes a punch now and then and that's life. You just can't take too long to bounce back and dust yourself off for the next punch," he thought to himself, trying to make the best of it. He was not happy but she had every right to pursue her dream, whatever that was.

"There's more fish in the sea," he thought out loud. He was single again and he liked it. Jonas did whatever he wanted, whenever he wanted. In the following months Jonas continued to visit his kids. They always came over when he had something lined up for them to do. They went ocean fishing, and sometimes they would drive up into the mountains and go fishing for trout. He took them to amusement parks and museums or sometimes for a simple walk along the beach. He enjoyed his kids. They were fun to be with because they were kids. Somehow, he still wondered if he himself ever moved beyond that stage of his life. He wondered if he really wanted to.

By eight the next morning he was on the job again. One thing about residential landscape you couldn't start work too early or you would wake up your customers. You get up at a reasonable time to begin work and go home at five. They were working residential that week. The exercise was doing him good. During the day he was always on the move. There was no more between meals snacking. The weekends came quickly.

At first, Jonas didn't go out much anywhere after work. Not to a bar, a restaurant, or even a theater. Being on your feet all day made a person tired. He just wanted to hit the couch, grab a simple bite to eat and watch something on TV. In fact it was getting to be a habit. The extra twenty pounds he had been carrying was coming off quickly. It seemed like almost every night he watched TV, thirty minutes into the movie or program he'd pass out and wake up past his bed time.

Saturday came quickly. He wanted to go see an art exhibit that was being held in an old abandoned brewery building turned art center. He liked looking at the different styles of art and was hoping at least some of the art might be of subjects he could find interest in. However, first he wanted to stop by at a residence and look at an automobile that was up for sale. It was a vehicle he always considered to sluggish for him, but practical in a sense. It was a 1971 Volkswagen Bus. It was a model that had the windows that went all around the edge of the roof. They called them twenty-three window busses and they were very open and kind of cool. Jonas just wanted another transportation option, something cheaper on gas. The owner was a retired United Airlines Pilot who used to drive it to the airport so the vehicle usually did more sitting then driving. It was in immaculate shape. Jonas fell in love with it quickly. The owner wanted twenty eight hundred for it. Jonas offered twenty four and got it for that amount. He told the seller he would pick it up Monday after work, which was fine.

The little one bedroom home that Jonas now rented included a work studio that was converted from a two car garage. The studio faced the ocean but much construction and tree planting came with the passing years, so that there was no ocean view. What Jonas really wanted to do was make use of that studio room and begin oil painting. He had some instruction in painting in previous years but he was mainly self-taught. He wanted to paint people and landscapes. At the art exhibit Jonas suddenly found himself quite excited. There were all sorts of attractive and interesting examples of unique creations from ceramic work, and pottery, to paintings.

Jonas spent the next several hours looking at all the interesting art work. He had picked up an art supply catalog at the exhibit as well as some other printed matter that interested him. When he got home he looked through the literature more thoroughly and decided to order some things from the catalog, like some large sketch boards, paint brushes, charcoal pencils, and a stretched canvas board. He decided to buy other needed things locally, for one, a good strong easel. After he finished filling out the order form he wrote out a check and put a stamp on the envelope. On his way out that evening he would drop the item in the mail.

For dinner Jonas decided to go to a place called, 'The Chopping Block'. He liked it because they offered a multi-ethnic food menu. You didn't have to make up your mind on the way. You could make it up when you got there and it was good food. It wasn't a stagnant production line process with, 'here yah go pal,' food. They had a little of everything. If you wanted a slice of pizza with your pastrami sandwich, or hamburger, you could get it. It was very spacious inside. You could get lost in a corner and read or do your homework with out getting shooed out after finishing your meal. The prices were reasonable, that was one thing that always mattered.

The music was toned down and commercial free. It was a mixture of instrumentals and vocals, both old and new stuff. Jonas ordered a lasagna plate that came with garlic toast and a salad. The meal was delivered to his table by Pete, who was the owner.

"Hi Jonas, here's your order."

"Thanks Pete." smiled Jonas.

"I usually get waited on by someone prettier then you," grinned Jonas.

"Well, I wish you could. Half of them are playing hooky tonight. They're killing me," sighed Pete as he ambled off.

Jonas ate slowly, enjoyed the music and watched the people. How different things were now without family around. He was alone most of the time and he really had no friends. As he ate he thought about his life. It was in a sort of limbo. Less than a year ago he was a family man with an acceptable job. Now he was single with no respectable career to speak of and in his thirties looking at an uncertain future. His memories drifted to a happier time when he was very young. Times spent outdoors with his father and friends. He thought of the disappointing look his father sometimes seemed to cast upon him in regards to himself. Everyone is different. Everyone follows their chosen path in life and not everyone finds the gold at the end of the rainbow.

EIGHT

So We Meet Again

A few weeks later on a cool cloudy weekday morning the landscape crew showed up at Shriner's Children's Hospital. This was the day they serviced charity institutions except for the Westwood cemetery which they would do later in the day.

Of course working the grounds at such places as Shriner's and the Orphans Home could instill a more solemn disposition within oneself, depending upon what one may have seen. There were things to distract a person at such places and usually these places were not the places where everyone was dealt a so called fair hand in life. Without such places there would be countless young people who would possibly have to live with physical defects.

The reasons the kids came were many, some born with deformities, some having vision problems, some needed facial reconstruction, some having unequal pairs of appendages or any number of other conceivable conditions. The surgical specialists volunteered their services for the reward of seeing any degree of optimism in the faces of their patients. Such people could not afford anything more.

Jonas was trimming the hedges and he began to see things that people don't think about much in their daily lives. That was how lucky most people really are. Kim and Jose had become all too familiar to such things as they were used to, that being ailing youth. In the two hours that Jonas was there his working companions took notice of the effect the visual disturbances had on their new companion as patients were transported around the premises. Indeed for all the things that people complain about many never stop to think about how lucky they are.

They finished that establishment by mid morning. The next stop the crew found themselves at was the Los Angeles Orphans Home on North El Centro. It was a much smaller building then Shriner's. It wouldn't take as long to finish up here, thought Jonas. The main door to the building was open and there was a white wrought iron screen door that was doing a good job of allowing in the cool air. As Jonas was happily whistling and trimming hedges he could hear a combination of adults and children talking just beyond the door. It sounded like an adult was saying their farewells to a child and words to the affect that they would be back in a couple of weeks to see them again. The young girl responded with a voice of despair that captured ones sympathetic attention. Again, Jonas realized his good fortune to have had two good and able parents. Jonas watched various kinds of people go in and out of the home. Most of the children that Jonas noticed going in or out of the building he waved and smiled at, or said hello to. He supposed many of them must have been there for a while. They were probably just tolerating a less than ideal situation. Most did not look either happy or particularly sad but just seemed to be carrying on with the business of living. Surely in the fall when school started they would have more to challenge their thinking minds and scholastic abilities.

However, today the drama was not over for Jonas. A car pulled up to the curb. It was an older car, a bluish 1963 Chevrolet Nova with faded paint that showed rust coming through the paint on the hood and trunk. The engine obviously must have had many miles on it and smoky exhaust fumes emanated from the tail pipe. Apparently, previous arrangements had already been made as a young woman got out of the driver's side and opened the passenger door. As she tried to retrieve a young boy of about seven he held firmly onto the steering wheel and didn't let go until she slapped his face. Once she got him out she performed a combination of dragging and lifting to get him to the front door of the orphanage. His leather soled feet sort of bounced over the cement walkway like the rough landing of an airplane. He wasn't going to go willingly. He was crying loudly enough that anyone in the vicinity could hear him. Surely, the boy must have thought that no one heard him that cared, but all of the landscape crew cared. Unknown to the child his pain was everyone's pain that witnessed the scene. Such things as this happened too often.

"Please Aunt Margaret! Please don't take me here. Please don't leave me here. I won't be hungry again. I promise I won't make any more noise, please Aunt Margaret," the boy kept repeating until they reached the door and entered the premises. Jonas could still hear the boy crying inside for a moment than someone shut the front door. It was not a pretty sight and Jonas wasn't whistling anymore. Kim and Jose both looked at Jonas.

"You see what we mean? At first it gets to you but you just learn to go on and do your job. In a few weeks that boy will have made a few friends and might even be happier then where he was. Who knows?" said Jose.

"Yeah, but kids that age ought to have parents or at least one person who cares," responded Jonas.

"Of course," said Jose as he shrugged his shoulders and went back to work.

Jonas was now just as efficient as Jose and Kim with his yard skills. They would trade off; take turns at trimming the hedges, trees, and mowing the lawns. By noon the crew was working the Westwood cemetery. It was like a little rectangular oasis that sat in the middle of a blacktop jungle. There were large shade trees and flowers scattered everywhere about. The cool breeze was refreshing and well appreciated.

The men went to work as they had much to do there. Surprisingly, there were few visitors that day. At noon the men took a lunch break. Jose and Kim asked Jonas if he wanted to go with them for some Café food, but Jonas declined. He had brought his lunch. He watched them drive off as he took his lunch and a cold drink over to a shady bench in a corner of the cemetery. Strange, in all the years he had lived in the region he had never been here before. As he worked that day he recognized the names of many famous people. Now, he noticed that one of the mausoleum marble head stones had a different hue then the rest, a sort of a pinkish hue. There were some visitors lingering around that spot and there they talked amongst themselves before walking to another area of the cemetery. When they left, Jonas out of curiousness walked over to that same place.

He saw that it was Marilyn Monroe's headstone. He knew she was interned at Westwood but he had never given it much thought before. Now he felt a gladness that he had discovered her again, even if it was under an unfortunate set of circumstances. It was an unexpected consequence of his new job.

"Well, so this is it. Just beyond this polished head stone lay the remains of her," he thought.

He was thinking about all the deceased who elected cremation. Jonas thought it was good that the world at least had something tangible here, even if it was old bones and skin. Of course, there were her clothes as well that she wore. It was sort of like religions and their relics. The relics usually being a small section of a saints clothing to put inside of something like an altar which serves to give that thing substance and honor. Not that Marilyn was a saint.

Though to many people she was more than that. Often, when people mentioned Hollywood, Marilyn Monroe was the first thing that could come to mind. Jonas was lucky this day. He seemed to have her alone for a time. He imagined it akin to some kind of prearranged appointment.

"Jonas Miles, she will see you now," spoke the wind through the trees like some invisible voice.

"You have fifteen minutes, sir, well; maybe not quite that much," the spirits echoed.

There were a few others walking around the cemetery, possibly visiting the remains of the many celebrities interned there. Jonas felt a sadness for her untimely death, for her parentless life, and for her many difficulties. Well gosh such circumstances were not hers alone. Then there was all the problems she had with her employer, Fox studios. I mean, who wouldn't show up four hours late to work every day if they were the box office draw and were paid a fraction of what her co-stars got paid. Somehow it sounded so familiar.

Having only eaten half his sandwich and not really feeling hungry, Jonas threw the rest away. He walked closer to Marilyn and placed himself right in front of her. There was no one else around. He saw numerous lipstick marks on her headstone. Over the years there must have been thousands who kissed it.

"So that was what gave the stone a pinkish hue?" he thought.

The stone was so permeated the stuff wouldn't wipe off. One would imagine no other star no matter how talented would have been so missed. Just what was it about this, 'Marilyn Monroe'?

Jonas began to summon his thoughts as he stood there imagining that he could find some spiritual avenue in which to communicate, like some transcendental experience. It was what he wished for but in reality he knew he was just thinking thoughts about Marilyn. He was just simply talking to her in his mind. He said the things he wanted to say and then listened as if he could hear her, but he couldn't. Then he wanted to do for her what she once did for him, he walked over and kissed her headstone.

"Gee, I wonder if I'm the, 'one millionth kisser'? Hmm, is that a word, Kisser? Or, what's that story about a 'frog who would be king'. No, that's in some Neil Diamond song. Not even close. Seems like I remember some story about a frog that kisses a princess, or is that vice versa? Whatever, anyway, Jonas missed her, America missed Marilyn Monroe. She was America's girl and she belonged to the world. It wouldn't be the last time Jonas would come here. The crew came every few weeks.

The rest of that day as Jonas finished out the day working he began to think about things. There are those people who just go to work and sit at their desks, maybe go to meetings to figure out how to make more profit, to squeeze more out of less. It is what society has become, a mechanism based on economics. Then there are those who involve their lives with outcasts and traumatic human situations where they try to make a difference in suffering be it abandoned children, injured soldiers and veterans, the mentally ill or the physically maimed. Such people are the ornaments that sparkle on the tree of humanity. As Jonas worked that day all he could think about was the children at the orphanage and imagined in what way some day he might help.

In the late afternoon after work when Jonas got home he retrieved his mail and then at his door he found a large thin parcel and a box. He opened the box and it contained a whole array of artist supplies that he had ordered, such as paints, brushes, and other items. As he was opening the large thin carton he was sure the contents must be the canvassed boards he had ordered. He found that inside that box was yet another thin carton. So now he was again cutting tape while his mind was thinking, wondering what it was that he was opening because now he could not reason that it was anything he ordered.

After cutting enough binding material to retrieve the item he discovered it was a folded-up life size celebrity figure of Marilyn Monroe. This seemed a little bizarre to say the least. Thinking that he might have received someone else's package he retrieved the packing slip. Strangely, it had his name on the packing slip but made no mention of the contents. Obviously, the catalog center somehow must have sent him something he didn't order. When he called the company to tell them what had happened the customer service agent was initially confused. He told Jonas they didn't sell celebrity cardboard standups so he didn't know how the item got in Jonas's order. So thanking the agent, as Jonas hung-up he considered the extra parcel a very strange and unexplainable phenomenon indeed. There were no packing slips from any other companies enclosed or any other recipient addresses. Jonas placed the folded up Monroe item on the table and decided he was hungry and that he was going to go out for dinner, something he often did. He had a place in mind famous for their chili. When Jonas got there he took a seat inside. The waiter brought a menu but Jonas just wanted a bowl of chili and a drink. When Jonas finished his meal he decided to walk his dinner off on the pier, about ten minutes away. When walking, Jonas almost always kept a fast pace going around people if he had to. He drove his car the same way. If anyone commented about his driving or walking he didn't pay much attention to them. Jonas was easy to get along with.

Once Jonas finally reached the pier he slowed down a bit. Santa Monica pier was one of those piers that allowed motor vehicles onto it to a certain point. He walked to the end of the pier and hung out there for a few minutes. He took some time to watch the fisherman and the few boats that went by before heading back home.

When he got home he sat at his kitchen table and began to look at some of his art supplies. The cardboard figure was dominating the table space so he decided to stick it in the closet for the time being, however, Jonas never made it to the closet. His curiosity did get the better of him as he decided to remove the plastic wrap that held the cardboard Monroe figure.

After removing the protective covering he unfolded the stand up figure. She was wearing what looked like a saloon outfit that resembled a corset. It ascended high enough to cover her cleavage with some fluffy navy colored material. Then there was some white satin skin tight material around the mid section down to the top of her thighs. Her legs were encased in black fish net stockings. Jonas ascertained this outfit was either from the movie 'Bus Stop' or 'River of No Return', he wasn't sure.

He tried to stand it up with the supplied cardboard appendage but it did not seem stable and it took up to much space in his small living room. He decided to remove the rear stabilizer partition and just lightly tack the flattened out figure up against the wall between his kitchen and the living room. He wound up sliding a small section of her figure between the wall and a small hutch where it fit perfectly.

"Hmm, amazing what art and ink can do to cardboard," he thought. In the minutes that followed thinking about what he had done with the Marilyn image seemed a little silly but he would leave it for the time being.

Over the years there had been hundreds of such figures made of all kinds of celebrities that included fast action heroes, movie star icons and even political figures. Jonas had seen a few occasionally in stores and such. Some looked pretty good and some didn't.

"This one didn't look bad," he surmised.

"I guess I won't throw it away," he thought.

Then Jonas thought about the real Marilyn Monroe, the one that he once stood inches away from and felt her kiss when he was a high school kid. He simply showed up at the right place at the right time and got her attention. It didn't seem that long ago. How strange now setting on his bookcase just a few feet away was the clear Plexiglas frame that contained a photo of Marilyn. It was just as pristine as the day she handed it to him. The impression of her lips and her written words were as vivid and clear as his memory of that long ago evening. No one but he knew it was there. He often thought if he had any common sense he would lock it up or at least hide it away. But then he wouldn't be able to see it.

Jonas decided to watch TV. Some nights lately, many nights in fact Jonas didn't make the greatest effort at socializing. Beyond eating out, living extravagantly wasn't something he could afford. Economically, he was being too practical to have any fun. It seemed if he got himself inebriated then he had the excuse needed to blow his money, be crazy and all that. Such times were few. So for the time being in his now too familiar safe and sober world, working the long stretch under summer's sun then passing out in the evening while watching TV was getting to be an undesired habit.

So now, Jonas sat on the sofa and turned on the TV. It could be hard to find something to watch with only seven broadcasting stations. His Zenith 19 inch portable color TV gave a fairly sharp picture as long as the reception was good. Of course most of the old movies were filmed in black and white. He decided to watch an old Laughton and Gable movie. Laughton played Captain Bligh. It wouldn't matter really because Jonas would soon fall asleep while sitting on his plush high back leather chair. He could really sprawl out on it with his feet up on the ottoman. After sleeping for an hour or less he would usually wake up and watch a little more TV until his bedtime. He would feel badly if he missed a program that he really wanted to watch, like a sports game. If it wasn't too late he'd watch a western serial like the Rifleman, Gunsmoke, or the news. On some nights he would stay up late to watch the Steve Allen show. This night when Jonas awoke he saw something he wasn't used to seeing, Marilyn Monroe staring back at him. The clock read eleven-twenty, considerably past his bedtime. Jonas rose and went to bed.

NINE

Uncle Leslie

The end of another work week found Jonas wanting to go on a morning ride with his ten speed Motobecane bike. There was a warm and dry offshore breeze. After retrieving the newspaper and laying it on the dining table Jonas made his breakfast. In minutes he was out the door and pedaling down the street out in front of his residence. He rode south on Washington Street moving along briskly, passing pedestrians as if they were motionless.

Just then a very large shadow of a bird which appeared to be that of a raptor passed along the ground directly in front of Jonas. It seemed highly unusual and becoming intrigued by its presence he looked up only to find a bright sun staring him in the face. It was a distraction he didn't need for it occurred near Washington and Third, a fairly busy residential intersection. He did not know that a young woman was stepping out into the street between two cars. Had he been paying attention he might have seen her but by the time the two met his only recourse was to sharply veer which caused him to lose control of his bike. As the bike went down, so did Jonas. The bike slid across the paved intersection and sent Jonas flying through the air. Fortunately, he landed on a nearby lawn surrounded by foliage. The young auburn haired woman raced over to him to see if he was all right.

"Are you OK?" she blurted.

Jonas slowly rose up as he was a little shaken.

"Yes, I don't think anything is broken," he responded.

"I'm so sorry. I didn't see you coming," said the young lady.

"Oh, it was my fault. I'm afraid I wasn't paying attention," he answered.

As he was brushing himself off the woman ran over to get his bike as it was partly blocking the intersection.

"Your bike seems to be OK too. It doesn't look like anything is broken," she remarked.

"I hope I didn't strike you?" asked Jonas.

"Oh, no, I should have been looking but my mind was too busy thinking about other things, I'm afraid," she said.

"It was my fault, really," Jonas responded.

"Okay, then it was both of our faults," she said her eye's smiling at him.

"I'm sorry, hope I'm not keeping you," he interjected.

"Oh, I was just going to walk down to the store and get a few things," she replied.

"By the way, my name is Jonas."

"Jonas? I don't think I have ever met anyone with that name," she responded.

"Yeah, I don't think I have either," replied Jonas with a smile.

"I'm Kay."

"Good to meet you Kay. Well I'll have to ride my bike more often if it means meeting pretty girls. I mean as long as I don't crash into them," he said grinning.

"Well, it's good that no one got seriously hurt," she responded.

The two spent another couple of minutes chatting until Jonas was beginning to run out of things to say.

"Hey listen, would you like to meet up for dinner sometime?" asked Jonas, thinking he had nothing to lose by asking.

Kay thought Jonas was a nice looking guy and seemed good natured. A little awkward, but she didn't see any harm in going out with him.

"Sure Jonas, I would like that."

"How about tonight?" asked Jonas.

"I'm afraid I will be busy tonight. How about tomorrow evening?" she asked.

Sunday night wouldn't be Jonas's first choice, but if it was the soonest he could see her again it would have to do.

"Sunday night would be fine."

Kay smiled and took a pen and a piece of paper out of her purse. She wrote her number down and told him to call her the following afternoon.

"I'll see you Jonas. Glad you are all right," she said as she walked away.

Jonas watched her walk away for a moment then left.

An hour later Jonas was back at his place. He didn't have a chance to read the morning paper so now he was skimming it for any interesting articles when a news article caught his eye. It simply read,

'ORPHAN CHILDREN NEED YOUR HELP.'

As he read the article he discovered it was about the Los Angeles Orphans Home. It was the place where the woman pulled up in her car and then commenced dragging the young boy to the front door while Jonas was trimming hedges. The article went on to say that there was an open house that day from 10am to 4pm, and that all were welcome. They were going to have all kinds of displays that featured the work and accomplishments of the children that were currently residing there. The home was looking for qualified chaperones to take children to nearby theme parks, museums and such on weekends. It was their annual event that sought qualified people who could donate some of their time during the summer, and on weekends.

When Jonas finished with the paper he was glad he came across the article. Since he had nothing else that he had to do that afternoon he drove over to the orphans home. It was somewhat ironic that he had been hoping he could do something to help out with kids there. Now maybe the opportunity would present itself. He would take advantage of the open house by driving over to the orphanage, going inside and getting a feel of the place.

After arriving he parked out in front along the street. As he walked slowly up toward the door there were a few people standing outside talking. Once inside, there were some tables set up with coffee, refreshments, and donuts. There were other tables that had photos of various children who had lived there years ago, children who had grown up and taken responsible positions in society. There were a few displays set up that provided a history of the orphanage as well as some of the leading figures and employees involved with the institution. The reception chamber was noisy as there were children ambling about and various adults engaged in conversation. A voice caught Jonas's attention from across the chamber that seemed familiar, but as he turned to investigate another voice was directed at him.

"Good morning sir!" came the greeting from one of the attendants as she looked at her watch.

"Yes, It's still morning," she chuckled, as Jonas smiled.

"I'm Susan. Is there anything I can help you with?" she asked.

"Well, maybe there is. Hi, my name is Jonas."

"What brings you to the home today Jonas, are you related to one of our residents?"

"Actually, I saw the article in the paper today and I wanted to learn a little more about your, 'Weekend Sponsor', program that it mentioned."

"Well, that sounds wonderful. Let me direct you to the person who can best give you that information. You see that woman right over there wearing the jeans and green top?" she asked.

"Yes."

"Well let me introduce you to her. She looks busy but I'll let her know what you are here for," as Jonas followed her over to meet her.

"Oh Kay, Kay, pardon me for a second but this is Jonas and he would like to talk to you about the weekend sponsor program."

Before she even finished her sentence, Susan recognized strange and surprised looks on both of the faces of those being introduced.

"Oh wow, this is weird. I had no idea you worked here," asserted Jonas.

It was Kay Lincoln, the girl that he had almost ran over on his bike only a few hours earlier. The odds of the two running into each other so soon wouldn't seem likely. She must have wondered if she had been followed.

"Hi, what brings you here?" she asked rather impersonally.

"Well, it looks like you two might know each other. Glad I could help you young man," remarked Susan before leaving the two alone.

"Will you please excuse me?" remarked the other person Kay had been talking to before she was interrupted by Jonas's arrival.

"I just saw someone I know. I'll be back shortly," said the woman as she began to walk away.

"Sure, just come back when you're ready. I didn't mean to interrupt you," responded Kay.

"Oh, not at all," the woman responded.

"Wow, this is really sort of embarrassing for me. I feel like I have been framed as a stalker. "

While not saying anything Kay offered her silent attention.

"Well, I feel I should provide an explanation here. You see I started this new job a few weeks ago. I was here at the orphanage the other day and I witnessed something that didn't leave a good feeling inside. I saw a boy being dragged to this front door, crying. Well, I thought that kid could have been me. Anyway, after I finished riding my bike this morning I saw this article in the paper about the orphanage. I wanted to see what this, 'Weekend Sponsor,' program was. I thought maybe it was something I might like to do. So, well, here I am, and Susan just brought me over to you. I'm just as surprised as you are. It's very weird, I know," asserted Jonas in an apologetic manner.

With that explanation a very warm smile returned to her face and to her eyes as well.

"Well, you would have to be a pretty good story teller to make up that one. Of course I believe you. Are you sure you are alright from that rough landing thing you did this morning. It looked terrible," she said.

"Oh yes, I'm okay. Just a few bruises," he responded.

The two continued to talk for almost an hour as she explained to Jonas what forms he had to fill out. She also mentioned to Jonas that he might want to take two of the kids if it wasn't any more of a bother. She confided that she herself was currently assigned to two girls. So Jonas filled out the necessary forms while there with Kay. She told him it would take a couple of weeks for the application to be approved.

It was expressed to him that he had no say in which children might be assigned to him, that men were paired with boys and women with girls. However, he would be given a chance to meet them during what they called, 'Ice Break Day,' where the children and the adults spent several hours getting to know one another.

When they had finished with all the formalities Jonas asked her if they were still on for dinner Sunday. Without hesitation she replied that of course they were. The truth was Kay was moved by Jonas's noble effort to help the orphan kids.

"Be here two weeks from today at 10am. Oh, I forgot, I'll see you tomorrow," she laughed as Jonas was leaving and they waved goodbye to each other.

It was 12:45pm, when Jonas got in his Cuda and drove back toward his residence which was about a twenty minute drive away. He stopped at a store for some grocery items and then drove home. He parked his car behind his old Chevy and VW Bus which now took up much of his driveway space. On the way in he picked up his mail. After going inside he put the grocery bag and his mail on the table then he left to go for a walk.

Taking a walk on the pier was practically a daily ritual for Jonas as long as he had the time. Once he was half way out on the pier Jonas stopped alongside the railing and looked down along the beach toward Malibu. There were seagulls soaring about but it seemed they were always there, whether a few or a lot. The cool breeze felt good as it passed over Jonas's face and arms. In the distance there were people walking about in the sand between the pier and a place of historic beach front homes. They were of course owned by the wealthy, and many were the homes of celebrities. He watched groups of kids running through the fringes of the surf with their skimmer boards, screaming and having fun. There were lots of tourists milling about taking pictures and children picking things out of the sand.

After a few minutes Jonas completed his walk to the end of the pier, and then stopped at a sub shop to pick up a sandwich to take home. When Jonas got home he laid the sandwich on the table, popped a beer and ate. As he ate he was thinking about Gina, wondering where she was working now and if she was really taking night classes. He noticed the mail lying on the table which he picked up earlier. He tossed a few junk mail items, kept a couple of bills and all that was left was a large manila envelope from his Dad. As he was opening it he realized he had not been to see them in over a month. It was not unusual to receive things in the mail from his father. In times past George sent his son articles of newspaper clippings about shared things of interest and other such things. So that was kind of what Jonas thought it would be when he opened it. Inside the envelope there was another smaller envelope. It was sent from a law firm. There was a short note taped to the outside of the envelope. The note read:

> *Jonas, did you know your mother's brother, Uncle Leslie, passed on Wednesday. Wonder if this envelope is relative to that. Your mother thought we were being sued when she took it out of the mail box. It was sent here from his lawyer asking us to pass this on to you. I guess it goes with out saying our curiosity is up. We're having a party the first weekend of this coming month, inviting all the usual friends. We will be barbecuing racks of spareribs on the smoker barrel. Hope to at least see you there, since we have not been seeing much of you.*
> *Dad*

Jonas opened the envelope and removed the correspondence which were two sheets stapled together. There was also a document that looked like a deed or something to that effect from a recorders office. On the back of the second page was a heavier board paper with keys taped to it and a few series of

numbers written down. There was also a sealed letter size envelope.
The letter read;

August 11, 1973
DARIN, KLAUS, IVANHO
ATTORNEY'S at LAW
SPECIALISTS in ESTATE PLANNING
REAL ESTATE & BUSINESS LAW
San Francisco- Los Angeles- San Diego

Mr. Jonathan Lyle Miles
468 E Wilson Ave
Glendale, California

Dear Sir,
This is to inform you that Leslie Statler, (uncle), brother of Ariane Statler, (Ariane Miles), your mother, had visited our firm in March of 1955. At that time we executed a 'Living Trust' on his behalf expressing his wishes and transfer of ownership of assets following his death. Now upon his death we are releasing his assets according to his wishes in regards to the benefactors of his trust. As you may know he has since remarried following the death of his wife. His current wife will be taking possession of specified assets. In the trust there are some specific assignments of transfer which we are still in the process of executing. Herein enclosed, this document will finalize his only expressed wish in regards to you. In his trust he has left you a parcel of Real Estate at 902 Kester Avenue, a building structure, and any and all assets located therein and thereon in the city of Van Nuys, California. The parcel is presently developed. Enclosed please find the deed of transfer for the county recorder's office that requires your signature. The parcel is free and clear.
Though we know you regret the loss of you loved one we bid you congratulations on your new acquisition! If we can be any further assistance please do not hesitate to call us at (760) 133-7777. Enclosed are all the accouterments of necessity required for your access to said premises. Also enclosed is a sealed, unread, personal

document from your uncle Leslie.

> *Regards,*
> *Melanie Booth, Assistant A L*

Having finished the letter, Jonas continued to stare at it thinking that there must have been some kind of mistake. He had always been very fond, even close to his uncle Leslie but he never expected to inherit anything from him. His uncle had resided in Riverside where he had started a prosperous plumbing business. He started off by himself until it grew into a modest inland empire. No one ever seemed to have any idea of what he actually owned but everyone was always remembered by him at Christmas time with a nice gift, often a gracious check. When Jonas was a child his uncle Leslie would invite family over for a new year's get together where he lived on his small 29 acre citrus ranch.

Jonas picked up the other sealed envelope that had his name written on it in his uncle's handwriting. He opened it.

Dear Jonas Boy,

Well, I suppose you're not a boy any longer. And I hope I still have at least a few decades left as I write this but one never knows. Anyhow, if you are reading this I suppose I have expired. To begin, I worked hard most of my life, started as a young plumber apprentice and just stuck with it. Can't say I loved every day of it but I never went hungry. In fact I did pretty well. I acquired a few things over time. As you know I had two sisters and no children. I had plans for a son but it did not happen. I loved my wives but they were not my only love. I believe you will come to find this out soon. I know you Jonas and I believe that you have the right stuff in you to appreciate that which I have to give. I'm laughing right now Jonas. I always thought of myself as somewhat eccentric, hell maybe even a little crazy. I never told my wife about some things. Sometimes a guy just doesn't tell the Old Lady about some things. You are about to find some things of mine that I never told anyone about. I remembered when we use to go on picnics how you got excited whenever an old car drove by. Well, I happen to like old cars myself. As a matter of

fact I have a few, or should I say had a few if you are reading this. They're yours now. You're like me, you like things that have real value. These things I worked hard for so I could enjoy them. I hope you will now. I hate to see them all sold off as I worked so hard to get them. I would like to see them stay in the family. You know, some people are too anxious to let go of things that are old and I'm only to anxious to be there when they do. So long for now nephew, and remember life is not the same for everyone. It's what you make it that it is. So go on Jonas, live your life and enjoy life. I did.
Leslie

As Jonas finished the letter he was in a state of stupefaction. Besides feeling a bit stunned he wasn't really sure of what it was that he had taken in transfer of ownership. His curiosity would not allow him any rest until he went to investigate. He just had to go right this minute to see just what it was that was now his. Until he knew what Leslie had given him he had no information for his parents.

Jonas almost immediately drove off toward Van Nuys. As he drove, all he could think about was just what was it his uncle left him. Once he arrived in Van Nuys it wasn't that hard to find Kester Avenue, just east of the 405 freeway. He drove slowly along Kester but couldn't find the address, 902. He turned on a street called Aetna and saw that there were factory buildings behind other buildings and they also were part of Kester Street. He discovered that there was no uniformity in the style or design of the buildings. Some were old with lots of windows, some had very few windows, some had concrete walls, and some were Quonset hut type structures. It was the typical industrial layout that was spurned by the need of products in a hurry spurned by the war effort.

It wasn't until Jonas got to the end of the street that he found 902 Kester and saw the building that was now his. Well, it wasn't any GM assembly plant but it was no slouch either. It was an older looking concrete building. The size was hard to judge from the distance. There was an eight foot tall chain link fence that surrounded the property. The fence was crowned with thick coiled chrome intrusion prevention wire.

There was a twenty foot gate that was heavily chained with a thick hardened steel lock. Jonas opened the gates and drove inside then closed the gates behind him. Just to the west of the building was an undeveloped field which was also part of his new inheritance. When his uncle bought the property back in 1954 he chose to leave the field vacant. The first thing Jonas did was to walk completely around the building. The condition of the walls appeared to be good, basically steel reinforced cement with some small chipping but no fissures or obvious damage. The east side of the building had three large roll up doors and the west side had four.

One of the first things that Jonas thought about was whether the power was still turned on. He tried the light switch by the door and the light went right on. He saw another switch box and tried those switches and the whole inside began to light up from an overhead florescent network. It suddenly became very bright inside. The only windows in the building were some screened rectangular shaped openings that ran along the walls near the ceiling.

The interior was far from empty but everything looked organized. Just surveying from where he stood he could see a few bench tables, chairs, heavy metal cabinets, some tools neatly hung up on wall boards, and other things that weren't discernible yet. But what really dominated the interior of the building was all mostly covered up with dark heavy canvas tarps. The place was dusty. The floor would be the first thing he would clean.

First though Jonas rolled up the doors and let in some fresh air and light which made a big difference in the stuffy atmosphere. The next thing he thought that made sense was to shake off all the dusty tarp's and stack them outside for the time being. Most of the tarp covered objects were congregated either in the front of the building or the rear. Jonas started in the front of the building and pulled off the first tarp cover. He knew what the object was right away because he was so used to seeing them down at the printing shop where his dad worked. It was an old heavy Heidelberg offset printing press. Despite dust everywhere it was quite clean and looked to be in good shape. Then he pulled the tarp off the next large object that stood there. It stood much higher than the printing press, and upon it in heavy embossed letters read the name, 'Merganthaler.' It was a Linotype machine probably manufactured around the 1940's. This was a machine that operators used to make type set. Jonas was sure his dad had the same model of machine in the shop. What he didn't know was that these were the very same machines because his uncle Leslie had bought them at auction.

"Hmm, what was he going to do with these?" wondered Jonas.

Jonas kept removing the tarp covers in that quadrant of the building and threw them out side the roll up doors. He shook them off the best he could and then folded them up and stacked them inside the door.

Next he moved to the other end of the building. Now the tarps found there covered forms of a broader shape and Jonas imagined these items to be cars. You could practically see them through the heavy covers. Jonas just grabbed the covers and started slowly lifting and pulling and as he did what he found was another kind of machinery. The more he pulled on that first tarp the more excited he became and it was a car. It sort of reminded him of those cars the gangsters drove around in. The car had a shiny black paint job and appeared to be in a new like condition. Then Jonas pulled some more on the tarp to reveal another car that had a similar style as the first one but it was a silver blue color. Jonas could not believe the beauty of these two cars and he didn't even know what they were. He could not believe they were his.

After he completely removed the tarps he folded them and laid them near the wall. Then he proceeded to pull off the next tarp to reveal another classy old vintage convertible. As he kept removing the car covers the thrill of his discoveries was more then he could have imagined as one after another of collector car beauties appeared. Beneath the next tarp was a 66 and a 69 Corvette convertible. They looked to be in brand new condition. Under the remaining tarp's Jonas laid his eyes on some of the classiest and most beautiful cars he had ever seen.

"Wow, thank you' Uncle Leslie," thought Jonas.

The more tarps Jonas removed the more excited he became. He could not identify all the cars but what he saw he loved. Jonas fetched his camera and took pictures of every car there.

He shook all the tarps free of dust and neatly stacked them in the corner. He did not recover the cars because he knew after this day it would not be long before he would return. He continued with the cleaning and sweeping until he had the place clean.

Perhaps the most suspense filled object that Jonas found in a room in the building was a large heavy steel gage combination safe. Trying some of the combinations given to him per his uncle's instructions the safe opened. What he found inside were four heavy woven canvas satchels. They all looked identical and had heavy zipper closures. So there sat four bags staring back at Jonas with an envelope leaning against one of the bags. The name on the envelope read, 'JONAS MILES'.

Jonas took out the envelope and walked over to a chair to read its contents.

Dear Jonas boy,

Well, you're probably not a boy anymore if you're reading this. I bet you never thought you'd hear from me again so soon. Well there were just a few more things to say that those lawyer people didn't need to know about. Had I made known all the details of the buildings contents as drawn up by the attorneys, well I, let's just say I wouldn't have felt comfortable with that. Things might be missing. So you found the safe and have opened it up to find this letter.

You know these printing presses were in the shop where your dad worked. When they upgraded, I bought them thinking I might get some kind of news publication or car collector magazine going but I guess time ran out for those projects.

Anyway no doubt you must have found my babies by now, yeah the cars. Aren't they great? I bet your heart was racing like a motor boat. Mine did every time I drove one of them. I think I know you pretty good Jonas. In some ways you are like me, a practical person, meticulous, and a perfectionist. You just need to work on your focus, set some goals and then you will succeed.

I think you know what many of these cars are but I will list them all for you. I have no idea in what order you uncovered them so I will just go down the list. There should be twenty one vehicles in the shop as of this writing. There might be more by the time you read this, but probably not less. I'm afraid my desire for cars is a curse. Yes, I was well off Jonas but I wasn't as they say, filthy rich. You know the guys with the helicopter pad on their front lawn, two yachts in the harbor, a Gulfstream jet, and a car collection to put mine to shame. I'm hardly jealous though, these kept me plenty busy. Anyhow, obviously by now I suppose I'm like that song, 'Dust in the Wind.' You know my ashes scattered to the four corners, or whatever.

Well here goes the list: (1) 1958 Mercedes Benz 190 SL (2)

1934 LaSalle Convertible (3) 1934 Oldsmobile F series (4) 1959 Cadillac El Dorado Biarritz Convertible (5) 1966 Corvette Convertible (6) 1969 Corvette Convertible (7) 1958 Chevy Convertible (8) 1962 Cadillac Convertible (9) 1959 Chevy Convertible (10) 1960 Ford Starliner (11) 1968 23 window VW Bus (12) 1968 RS SS Camaro (13) 1962 Chevy Carryall (14) 1970 Porsche 914-6 (15) 1973 911 Porsche RS Carrera (16) 1963 Porsche 356 C2000 GS Carrera (17) 1969 Jaguar E series convertible (18)1950 Hudson Hornet Convertible (19) 1941 Chevy Special Deluxe Convertible(20) 1969 Boss 302 Mustang (21) 1971 Dino GT Ferrari.

Well Jonas, I know it's kind of a mixed assortment and may not be enough for a car museum but it will get you started. I know you will keep these cars and take care of them. Some of them had at one time been my daily drivers. I just never sold them. The last one I bought was the 73 Porsche. It's brand new. I only got to drive it home before I found out I was ill.

Now let's talk about the four satchels in the safe. I know you must have it open because you got the letter in your hands that I left in the safe. The one bag without a name on it Jonas, is yours. There is a sum of cash to help you keep this place going for a while, pay the taxes, take care of my babies, etc. There is also enough money for you to start a business, go to college if you want. That's your decision. The rest of the bags have names on them. Two of the bags are for my sisters, one your mom, and the other for your aunt Sylvia. The last bag Jonas I would like you to give it to a dear friend. Her name is Esther Margot. She's older now, but in her day she was more beautiful then a peacock's feathers. She just knew me as Lew. She never badgered me with questions. I really admired her for that. I think she knew I was married. We were very compatible Jonas. I don't think she wanted to be married, we never talked about it. I just took care of her, Jonas. She's a good gal. She probably hasn't seen me in some time now and is wondering what happened. Maybe she saw the obituary, I don't know, but make sure she gets her bag. Yes, the one that says Esther. Deliver it to 955 S. Western in Torrance. Make sure when you hand it to her you tell her it's from Lew.

Anyway, at one time I had a lot of other collections of things in this building, but I sold most of it while I could still get around. Remember, I mentioned in the letter there are some things I would never mention to my wife. Well now I think you know why. She would sell everything off. My trust has well taken care of her. So, Jonas, if you would kindly and discreetly give these satchels to those of whose names I have marked on the bags, that should finalize my last wishes.

Well, my boy, wherever it is I'm at now I can only wonder. We all awake to find something else or we just never wake I guess. Good luck to you, keep your wits and hold your head high. Cheers!
Leslie

Jonas went back to the maintenance room and pulled off a large plastic trash bag to put the satchels in. After placing all the satchels in the ample sized bag he closed it up. Jonas locked all the doors and turned off all the lights, grabbed the bag containing the satchels and put it in the trunk of his car. He drove outside the gates, locked them, and then headed for home.

When Jonas arrived home he removed the bag from his car and went inside. He removed the satchels from the bag and set them on the table. He went and got a cold beer out of the fridge, twisted off the cap and sat down and just stared at the bags. He then looked up and there was Marilyn looking right at him from against the wall where he had placed her. He studied her for a long moment. Her face looked quite mortal and attentive even if the rest of the caricature looked like nothing more than colored cardboard. There was something about the face that seemed to have depth and feel. There was an inherent alluring quality within like a magical presence of some kind in a surreal fashion. Call it a spiritual challenge or just some acute perception of Jonas's imagination, but to him for now she was there.

Of course she didn't do any talking but she was a great listener and she listened to everything he had to say. She had no choice in the matter and this pose as she presented herself was a classic Marilyn pose. A pose forever frozen in time as it was originally captured by the famous photographer who snapped it. Like so many of her poses she seemed to be doing it for the benefit of one. It was just you and her in the camera lens, at least that was her usual intent. She was a true artist to the camera. She could be very friendly to it.

"Well Marilyn, how's your day been? Mine has certainly been full of surprises," stated Jonas. Her eye's and lips appearing to smile back.

With that Jonas looked at his satchel given to him by his uncle. He took another drink of his beer. He was still in awe by all that he discovered since he drove to his uncles industrial building. Now all the discoveries served to intensify his excitement when he discovered the cars, the contents of the safe, another letter, and just the building itself. It kind of made Jonas feel like an industrialist.

He reached over and picked up the bag that was for him. He loosened the straps and with a great curiosity opened the bag. When he looked inside all he saw were banded stacks of one hundred dollar bills, some bank receipts and a notarized letter stating for whom the money was withdrawn. Leslie had included a letter and bank receipts in the satchel. Jonas's uncle was a fairly smart man. He had planned wisely. Jonas would not squander any of the wealth bestowed upon him, nor would he cash out items his uncle cherished.

Jonas's mind was already working, calculating, thinking about what to do with all the money and how to manage the factory building and its contents. Jonas had no idea what was in the other bags, but he did not want the responsibility of having them around. He would not leave the apartment until morning upon when he would deliver the remaining bags. "Hmm, now what am I going to do with two 23 window buses?" wondered Jonas.

TEN

Esther's Visitor

That next morning Jonas drove himself and the three satchels over to his parents where he would deliver his mother's bag. However, first he had to tell them all about the package he received in the mail from Leslie. They would wonder why her brother chose Jonas as the mediator of his assets. Nobody knew for sure the answer to that question but Jonas would carry out his uncle's wishes and he could be trusted.

Inside his mother's satchel she found four hundred and fifty thousand dollars in cash. When his mother opened her bag her jaw seemed to drop in disbelief. Leslie had given them cash. The self-serving Washington bureaucrats would not be using any of Uncle Leslie's hard earned money to fund wasteful party agendas or foreign handouts.

Jonas asked his dad if he could help him drop off a car later at a place in Van Nuys which required the senior Miles to follow him. Jonas would then tell his father all about the industrial building and show him the cars when they reached the premises. First, Jonas had a few more deliveries. He called his aunt Sylvia and told her he had something to drop off to her but didn't tell her what it was. So when he arrived at her home he went inside and handed her the satchel and told her it was from her brother. It was something he wanted her to have. Aunt Sylvia was a talker and Jonas knew it would be hard to get away after she started gabbing about anything that came to mind. She talked about everything from the neighbors barking dog to the music classes she had in High School. She talked about some movie she saw three nights ago, than she started talking about the price of groceries.

At first she seemed to take no interest in the bag. She was a widow, living on her deceased husband's social security allotment. Halfway through a story about how to properly make sponge cake she started undoing the straps to the bag. When she seemed to have some trouble with them Jonas opened up the bag but didn't look inside. She kept looking back and forth between the bag and Jonas as she was talking. When she opened up the bag and looked inside Jonas thought it was the first time he ever saw her in complete silence.

"What's the matter Sylvia?" asked Jonas.

"Looks like you just saw a ghost," he added.

"What's in the bag?" he asked, as he walked back toward her but she snapped the satchel shut faster than a shooting star.

"Oh Jonas, there's nothing much really," exclaimed his aunt.

"Where did you say you got this, Jonas? You say it was my brothers?" she queried.

"Well, yeah, you might say I was cleaning out his shop and I stumbled upon this with your name on it," stated Jonas.

"Is it something bad? Here I'll take it away," said Jonas figuring he had a good idea what was inside and having fun with her at the same time.

"Oh no Jonas, looks like it's just a bunch of stacks of papers," she exclaimed.

"I'll see they get some attention when I have the time," she responded.

With that, she shut up and then just stared at Jonas being very quiet.

"Well, I got to run Sylvia, I have lots to do today," he said.

She continued to just look at him as he was headed for the door and then she managed to let out a brief high pitched,

"Bye, Jonas," as he closed the door behind him.

When Jonas got inside his car he rolled down the passenger window and just sat there for a few minutes. Then he heard a woman's voice let out a very audible expletive that would not seem to respectful for a woman of her age. Surely even the neighbors must have heard her.

Jonas had no idea how much money was in the bag. Only Leslie knew. It wasn't anyone else's business what Leslie gave to his sister Sylvia. No matter what amount it was it did not concern Jonas. Jonas started up his car and headed to his last destination, Esther Margot's.

When Jonas finally reached Esther's neighborhood it was definitely not an upscale place. Most of the cars averaged from seven to ten years old. Jonas parked his car curbside out in front of Esther's home as given by address. When he got out of the car he grabbed the canvas bag and headed for her door. There was a white 1966 Ford Galaxie in her driveway. It seemed to be in great condition for a car that was nearly eight years old. Jonas knocked on the door. He could hear the creaking of the wood floor as somebody slowly made their way to it. Jonas turned and looked back behind him at the street, at his car, and then at the neighbor's homes. He didn't notice anyone around. It was an old neighborhood but the yards were kept up.

"Who is it?' called out a voice from the other side of the door. It had one of those tiny observation lenses in the door and Jonas imagined she must have been looking at him through it. Jonas noticed there was yet a sturdy screen door to reckon with before entering the home. The heavy wood door suddenly opened. If she were anywhere around his uncle's age she would have been in her sixties or seventies, give or take.

"Hello Ma'am! My name is Jonas. I'm the nephew of Lew. He passed away over a week ago and I have been instructed by him to bring you this bag."

"Lew, you say?"The door was now opened wide to reveal the face of an aged yet attractively petite woman. The woman suddenly seemed anxious in that she may finally discover what happened to her Lew. She had wondered for a long time. She did not believe he just abandoned her. It was not like him to have just stopped calling without some explanation.

"Won't you come in?"

Jonas just took a few steps inside the door. The roots of the woman's hair were gray but she had shoulder length brown hair with brown eyes. Her facial features were beautiful just as his uncle had mentioned. She seemed to be wearing gardening attire as she had a big straw hat in hand. She was wearing white loose cotton shorts and a big oversized buttoned up cotton shirt.

"Lew, Lew sent this for me?"

"Yes Ma'am."

"Lew died?" she asked with a faint expression and teary eyes.

"Yes, he took ill quite some time ago and never recovered I'm afraid."

At the same time the sadness of his death struck her there was an indelible appreciation to learn that he didn't just desert her. There was a reason he never came back, sad as it was. Jonas handed her the bag.

"Won't you please come in for some ice tea?" she asked.

"Oh, thank you very much but I have to pick up my father," he answered. In a way he wished he could have visited with her, she seemed lonely and he would have liked to talk for a short while with her.

"I think that whatever it is that's in this bag Esther will bring some kind of good feeling for you. Well I wish I could stay and enjoy that offer of tea but I really have to go."

"Okay, well, certainly, and thank you very much for coming. I certainly appreciate you bringing me news of Lew."

Jonas stopped in the doorway then turned and spoke a few more words to her out of concern.

"Miss Margot, I don't know exactly what is in that bag but I have delivered a few similar bags to relatives of Lew. If my assumption is correct about what I think is in that bag it may change your life. I wouldn't hesitate to be practical. I know it's all clean and above board."

Miss Margot nodded and looked at Jonas with a somewhat confused look. With that said, Jonas stepped outside the door still worried that someone may have seen him go inside her home with a suspicious looking bag. He did not want someone breaking into her home just to find out what might have been in that bag.

Jonas turned to look at her one last time as she looked at him. She projected a very surprised expression. Then she simply said,

"Thank you Jonas for coming to tell me about Lew," Then she waved and slowly closed the door and locked it.

When she got inside she sat down and opened the bag. There was another bag inside with a letter on top of the bag. She took the envelope out and removed the letter.

Dear Esther,

My dear girl, did you think I ran off and left you? Never would I do such a thing. (She read on with teary eyes)

I prepared for this day that something not good might happen. If you're reading this, I guess it has. I must have passed on to somewhere but I know not where. The happy thing is that you are still here my love. I have missed you painfully, every time I thought about you not being able to come and see you. I miss going to our quaint little café by the sea, taking our shoes off and walking through the wet sand along the beach. I miss seeing those soul searching eyes of yours, your beautiful face and all the fun we had together. But most of all I miss my best friend and the warm moments we shared. Never has there ever been anyone that I was so glad that I met.

Please Esther remember me if you must but go on with your life. You are still young and beautiful. Live your life to the fullest. Do those things that bring joy to your heart. I kept care of you my

girl while in life as I will do even in death. Well Esther, until we meet again, I love you.

Love,
Lew

While crying, Esther continued to stare at the letter for some time. She read it several times. When she opened the bag in the satchel it was full of cash. More cash than Lew had given to any of the others.

Jonas drove off back to his parents place to pick up his father so his dad could help him get rid of some of the cars in his driveway. He did a lot of thinking about his uncle Leslie. It seemed people didn't know everything about him, maybe very little really. He was a heck of a guy. Soon Jonas and his dad were at the industrial building.

"I figured that old coot was doing well but I had no idea. He mentioned something about a building he bought one time but he didn't say much about it," stated George Miles as they were walking through the entrance door of the building.

"What are you going to do with it?" he asked his son.

"I'm working on it Dad and will definitely be giving it a lot of thought. Always appreciate any ideas," replied his son.

"Maybe you can quit your lawn mowing job and turn this place into a money maker," mentioned his dad sounding a little sarcastic.

"Nah, I like mowing lawns dad!" stated Jonas wondering what took his dad so long to get started as he turned on the lights in the front part of the building.

"So this is where he put those old printing machines?" interjected Mr. Miles as they came upon them first.

"They're still in great shape. Isn't that scent great? It brings back memories. I can imagine myself at 40 again setting up a printing job!" stated the older Miles in a serious reminiscence of memory.

"Yeah Dad, they're built like a fortress. I don't think anything could wear one of these down," said the younger man.

The older Miles lingered there for a few minutes to walk around them and touch some of their parts. Jonas turned on all the lights in the building until the blinders had been lifted from his old mans eyes. Suddenly he noticed all the cars at the far end of the building.

"Oh my God, what is this?" asked the father hurriedly walking in the direction of the cars.

"Well dad, these are the cars of the ages. Probably some cars you remember as a boy. Aren't they gorgeous?" responded Jonas.

"They are beauties. How many?" asked George as he proceeded to count them all.

"Looks like twenty one cars," he stated.

"Yeah, twenty one I guess," sighed Jonas.

Jonas let his dad take his time looking at the cars even though he did have to get ready for a date with Kay later on. At that hour there was a kind of long lost reunion between Jonas and his father over such things as old cars. Of course, George knew a lot more about the older cars then Jonas did. They spent time looking under the hoods, sitting in them and walking around them. Then they completely toured both the inside and outside of the building. They walked around in the adjacent undeveloped lot. Jonas parked his old 56 Chevy inside that he had since high school. Then he locked up the building and they drove away.

Several hours later Jonas was home getting ready for his Sunday night date with Kay.

"Let see. Casual I told her. I'll wear my brown Dockers with matching top sider shoes, a white collared button shirt and a brown corduroy sport coat."

While he was dressing he was thinking about what to do on a Sunday evening. He had to be at work early the next day. He would just plan on dinner, then a movie. They would go see, 'The Sting', it had excellent reviews. They would eat at, 'Marco's,' Italian restaurant.

When Jonas located Kay's address he parked on the curb across the street from her place. It was a charming small one bedroom apartment. The grounds were neatly landscaped with colorful foliage and shady trees. As he walked toward the front door he could hear familiar music. It was Roberta Flack, 'The First Time I Ever Saw Your Face.' Jonas paused a moment before knocking.

Jonas knocked on the door lightly and waited but there was no response. He knocked on the door again, louder this time and someone turned the music off. Kay opened the door and looked so stunning he wasn't at first sure if it was her. Her presence was breathtaking as she stood before him wearing a white and red polka dot knee length dress, and white high heel pumps.

Accentuating her petite waist was a wide red patent belt with a white clutch purse in her hand. Draped over her shoulders was a white alpaca sweater for the cool evening. Long wavy lush auburn hair framed her radiantly stunning face. Jonas felt himself falling deep into the abyss of her spell binding blue eyes. Her presence left Jonas nearly speechless.

"You look gorgeous," said Jonas.

"Thank You. And you look very nice as well. Shall we go?" she asked.

"Sure, I guess we shall," he answered.

As they walked toward Jonas's vehicle it wasn't until then that it struck Jonas that taking someone out who looked as hot as Kay in a VW Bus wasn't the smartest thing he ever planned.

"Gee, I just bought this bus a few months ago. I have been so busy today I didn't even stop to think. I could have brought my other car," said Jonas.

Her thoughts were of that old worn out cliché she often heard,

'Oh, but you should see my other car.'

"Oh Jonas, I don't mind. I think it's a very nice looking bus," answered Kay.

Then Jonas remembered, he didn't just have another car or two, he had lots of mind blowing cars. He didn't have any intentions of telling anyone about such things at the moment. Jonas wasn't as materialistic as most, but he appreciated fine things, old things that could not be got anymore and had a respect for such. Jonas opened the door for her to get in and couldn't help but notice her flawless shapely legs as he shut the door. He then got in, started the engine and drove away.

"So I guess we will go to Marco's for dinner, than a movie? If we plan it right we should get there in time to catch that new release that's out, The Sting."

"Yes, I wanted to see that. I heard its really good," responded Kay.

"Which theater did you plan on going to?" she asked.

"It's at the Egyptian," he responded.

"Sure, I like the Egyptian," she remarked.

Jonas reached over to turn the radio on. The volume was turned way up and Howard Cosell's voice flooded the cab announcing a sports game. Not what Jonas wanted to hear at the moment. He quickly turned the station to some softer music.

"Well lots of traffic, as usual," mentioned Jonas.

"Oh yes, I doubt if that will ever change," responded Kay.

The usual dialogue went back and forth all the way to Marco's where they found a place to park. It was a popular place because it was semi casual and had very good food. Jonas and Kay went inside and the hostess took their names. They were seated in less than ten minutes at a corner booth. The waitress handed them their menus and asked if they wanted any wine. They ordered imported beer, then Kay ordered a veal dish and Jonas ordered Lasagna. During the meal there was much discussion about different things. They were the kinds of questions most ask when getting to know each other. After dinner they each ordered a slice of cake. It was then that Jonas casually mentioned that a talent agent's wife heard him singing while he was working and that she had said that she wanted her husband to listen to him sing.

"Oh really," exclaimed Kay with some sense of excitement.

"What is the agent's name?' asked Kay.

"Ah, Conroy I think."

"Not, Anniston Conroy?" she asked.

"Yeah, Anniston Conroy," he responded.

"He's one of the biggest talent agents in Hollywood. He helps with fund raisers for the orphanage. I've talked to him. He is really nice," she added.

"And what type of song were you singing when his wife heard you?" she asked expecting it to be a rock ballad, or something.

"I was singing Sinatra's 'Summer Wind', he responded.

"You sing Sinatra?" her face filled with excited energy.

"Oh, I'm probably not that good really," said Jonas, holding to his modest character, down playing himself.

"Who could really sound as good as the real Frank," he added.

"I don't know why this Conroy would be interested in me anyway, Sinatra is still performing in Vegas, right?" he asked.

"Well, you know Sinatra's style is a very popular one and he can't be everywhere, especially when so many like to hear his songs. I'm sure there would be plenty of demand at night clubs and stand in's at concerts. Oh, I'm sure he would have work for a good Sinatra voice," she interjected.

When the two finished their desert, Jonas asked for the check and paid for their meals. The drive to the theater didn't take long. The ticket line was about average as movie ticket lines go and from the time they arrived in the parking lot until they were seated was about fifteen minutes. The picture had a good line up of actors starring Paul Newman, Robert Redford, and Robert Shaw as well. The movie started at 6:45 which meant they would get out about 9:15 pm. The theater was full with few empty seats.

When the movie was over people began dribbling out of the theater. Everyone seemed to enjoy the film. The movie utilized the old tried and true plot of the perfect con job and capitalized on the good natured villains who got away with the heist.

"Would you like to go for a walk? It's not too late," asked Jonas.

"Sure, I think that would be nice," responded Kay.

Even though it was Sunday evening there were still a lot of people out walking about. Hollywood Boulevard was always busy as it was a world wide tourist attraction. So Kay and Jonas enthusiastically proceeded to walk down Hollywood Boulevard. It was fun observing all of the different people. It was early November but the weather was comfortable and the fall atmosphere added a tone to the air. Jonas noticed all the eye catching attention Kay got as she walked with him close by his side. She truly looked like a movie star. There was some phenomenal thing about her as if she possessed some mysterious unexplained extravagance. It was something in her eyes, her smile, and her bodily ambiance that could be so strangely attractive to both sexes.

After walking a spell Jonas and Kay were passing a well known night club and they decided to go in so Kay could rest her feet and have a drink. They didn't intend to stay long, just one drink but of course they had two before leaving. A short way down the boulevard there was a small four man orchestra playing for donations. Their instruments comprised a clarinet, a saxophone, a small drum set, and a horn. Jonas and Kay stopped for a minute to listen as did others. Both Kay and Jonas were by no means staggering from the two drinks but they both felt good. That was when a devilish idea came to Kay's mind.

"Jonas, please sing me a Sinatra song?" she asked Jonas'

"Oh no, I couldn't. I'm really not prepared," he stated.

When she looked at him with those baby blue eyes, together with his mediocre high, he caved in.

"Okay, what do you want me to sing?" he asked.

"Right now I would like to hear, 'Nothing but the Best', can you do that one?" she queried.

"Yeah sure, I think so!" he replied.

So when the current number was finished Kay asked the band leader if they knew how to play Sinatra's, 'Nothing but the Best'. The band players gave a quick look at each other, said a few words to the affirmative and said they could.

"Why do you ask?" asked the leader.

"Because my friend is going to sing it for us but I got to warn you he might be drunk," she laughed, herself feeling a bit high.

"Well, I think this sidewalk drunk can sing that song," asserted Jonas.

"Yeah okay, sure miss, we'll play that for you. Here's the mic, buddy," said one of the band players.

So as the band began playing the tune for, 'Nothing but the Best,' Jonas took the microphone and started singing. The reaction from the people whether just standing around or walking by was nothing short of fascination. Some of the more distant people across the street began to look thinking it was just a recording of Sinatra, or wondering if he was really there. They weren't really sure. As Jonas got into the song the consensus was pure joy as the lyrics and melody sprang forth to fill the gathering crowd with a good feeling.

When the music wound down and Jonas had finished he took a bow and the crowd clapped fiercely. He handed the mike back to the band member and the crowd shouted for more, but Jonas didn't want to turn it into a concert and it was getting late. He needed to take Kay home and he had to get up very early to go to work. Kay was the last one to stop clapping.

"Oh, Jonas, you amazed me. I had no idea you were that good. You sounded just like him. You know, I could feel you stirring peoples desires," stated Kay.

"Oh really?" remarked Jonas.

"Oh yes. If you were shorter and was wearing one of those fedora hats...," she exclaimed.

"That song was the best part of my whole evening and I truly enjoyed everything tonight, Jonas," said Kay in a sincere way.

After that, Jonas and Kay walked back to his VW and they headed back for home. The vehicle traffic had lightened up which was fairly typical for a Sunday night at that late hour.

"Don't forgot this Tuesday evening Jonas, you're supposed to be at the orphanage to meet the kids," said Kay.

"Wow, its Tuesday? Gosh I'm glad you reminded me. I thought it was next weekend," he responded.

"No, next weekend is when you come by to pick them up," she replied.

"The kids?" mentioned Jonas.

"What," queried Kay?

"Oh, I was just thinking. I hope everything works out with the kids," said Jonas with a mellow high from the two stiff drinks.

"Whatever it is you just have to try to do your best, right?" she responded.

"Right," he answered.

When Jonas got back into Kay's neighborhood he stopped by the curb in front of Kay's house.

"Don't worry about walking me to the door Jonas. It's late and I'm sure you have to rise early. I'll see you Tuesday at the orphanage, OK Frankie!" smiled Kay.

"Yeah, Frankie, oh, you mean as in Sinatra, ha, I doubt that, but thanks," responded Jonas. They both smiled and then Jonas drove off.

ELEVEN

A Standup Roommate

Considering all that occurred over the weekend some of the Miles family members might have had too much to think about for sleep. That wasn't the case for Jonas he slept like a baby. The evening spent with Kay turned out memorable. The weeks whirled by and a month later Jonas found himself back at the Conroy residence for their monthly yard work. By this time both Jose and Kim were not just working pals with Jonas, but friends. They worked great together. They were a good team. Stanley Guiles was pleased with Jonas's work and Jonas no doubt might find himself with that foreman job soon. However, once Jonas was promoted he would be moved to another crew and location which wasn't what Jonas really wanted.

The morning sun had slowly risen over the mountains and Jonas's energy was at a peek with perhaps some added boost from his morning coffee. This time instead of mowing he was trimming hedges up close to the Conroy house and all seemed quiet. In fact, it appeared no one was home but luck or good fortune, whatever you wanted to call it seemed to follow Jonas lately. Anniston Conroy had usually already left his home by now, to be found at his Beverly Hills office or having breakfast at one of his favorite spots. But this morning he hadn't left the house yet.

Jonas began the morning in quiet thought. He was thinking about the past weekend as he trimmed the hedges. There was lot's to think about because a lot happened. He felt happy and his thoughts turned to Kay and how radiant she looked the previous night. Jonas wouldn't stay quiet for long when he sizzled with energy or felt happy. A song came to mind so he started singing Sinatra's, 'Fly Me to the Moon'. Jonas sang the song confidently and formed his words distinctly. The morning air was cool, fresh, and pungent of the scent of flowers. There was a slight breeze from the west. Jonas's singing probably couldn't be heard by either of his comrades for they were on the far side of the residence. But the window was open in the study room on the west side of the home. Jonas was just outside Anniston's open office window as he sat at his desk in deep thought. He was working on an entertainment lineup for the following month. There was a noise, a distraction of some sort outside his window.

"Grounds keepers playing their radios again," he thought. When he looked through his open window all he could see was a man's back. He like many people loved Sinatra's songs, but it was a distraction for him at the moment. Jonas was still singing when Mr. Conroy spoke up.

"Hey buddy," shouted Anniston.

Jonas turned and looked at him.

"Could you please turn that thing down or use ear phones or something, I'm trying to concentrate on work in here," stated the home owner.

"Yes sir, I don't have a radio but I'll keep quiet sir," replied Jonas, thinking the man could just close the window.

"Thank you very much," responded Anniston as he sat back down.

Forty Seven year old Anniston Conroy was not a tall man by any means. Though his thin, five foot six inch frame was not a generous height, his robust energy and vocal dominance seemed to provide an impressive platform for him. Aeton was always's well dressed out in public and his dark hair and thin mustache could have reminded one of an actor. Particularly the one who placed, "Frankly my Dear", on the Hollywood list of famous phrases. In reality, Anniston favored comfortable clothes, like the loose cotton shirt and slacks he was now wearing.

As Anniston sat back down he was enticing himself to think about his projected entertainment line up again. Then something was bothering him as he got back up out of his chair.

"Excuse me again," he said to Jonas.

"Yes sir?" Jonas responded.

"I just distinctly heard Frank Sinatra singing but you said that you don't have a radio?" asked Anniston.

"That's right sir," responded Jonas.

"Then where was that song coming from," asked the man.

"From me sir," stated Jonas.

"From you, do you mean you were singing that song?" asked Anniston.

"Yes Sir," replied Jonas.

"Do you sing any other Sinatra songs," asked Mr. Conroy.

"Yeah, lots of them. I mean most of his popular stuff," answered Jonas.

"Really?" responded Anniston, while scratching his chin with his eyes distantly focused on some unknown object across the yard.

"I'm coming outside," said the anxious talent seeking mogul.

Before he went outside he stopped by his desk and opened a drawer and took something out of it. Once outside he had a few more things to say.

"How would you like to be an onstage performer? Have you ever given any thought to that?" asked Mr. Conroy.

"Well, I have wondered about it at times, but never anything as to be so serious about. You know, I mean Sinatra is alive and well, still performing, right?" stated Miles.

"My name is Anniston Conroy. Most people call me Aeton."

"Sure Mr. Conroy," responded Jonas.

"That's Aeton, call me Aeton," the talent agent repeating himself.

"And what's yours, name that is?" asked Aeton.

"Jonathan Miles, but, I go by Jonas," said the young man.

"Hmm, Jonas," responded Aeton, changing his expression.

"Jonas, well, we'll work on that later. Here's what I would like you to do. Take this and record me some of your Sinatra stuff. It can be anywhere quiet. Maybe an empty school auditorium, I really don't care. I just want to hear your voice singing Sinatra songs and then bring the tape to my office. Just give it to my secretary. I will tell her to expect you. Here's my card. Got all the information you need right there, my direct number. I want to listen to what you got and if I like it, well, we'll set you up for a formal audition with a band and just go from there. Sing your best, okay," offered the busy entertainment professional.

"Well, okay, sure. I'll do that," responded Jonas in a sort of state of shock.

"Hey, don't look so surprised kid, you just might be on your way up," answered Conroy.

"Yes sir," answered the young man as Mr. Conroy walked off back to his home.

After work when Jonas got home he put the tape recorder on the kitchen table and sat down.

"Wow, Marilyn, it sure has not been a boring week for me," he said looking up into her attentive captivating face. Again this unusual cardboard facsimile of the actress seemed to take on a surreal presence, like she was actually there if nothing else but to be some sort of artificial roommate.

"Me, a performer, I don't know. I don't know if I am the right person for this. I guess it's about fear isn't it? Its fear we have to over come. Hell, what am I getting anxious about? I don't know if he will even like my recordings. I'm totally jumping the gun here. Right, Marilyn?" he said looking up to the icon.

He thought he saw her lips move as to say something. Of course they couldn't have really.

"I suppose I'm being a little pretentious. Nothing set in stone. At least not yet. I think I can do this though. I just got to want it bad enough," thought Jonas.

There was no denying that this had been a week filled with serendipitous karma for Jonas. He might have to make some decisions and know what to do when the time came, if it came.

On the Kitchen table there was a thin magazine pamphlet that arrived in the mail. It was about Los Angeles Historic places. On the cover was a color photo of Union Station. Jonas picked it up and went over to his canvas and started replicating its features in charcoal pencil. It was a court yard view that included tresses, colorful plants, trees, and vines. When he finished drawing in the subject matter he put his sketching charcoal down.

"There now, it's drawn in just got to paint it sometime, right Marilyn?" Then he turned to walk out of the room. He didn't realize it then, but that would be the last time he would touch his art equipment for quite some time.

The evening was getting on as Jonas sat down on the sofa and turned on the TV. The Alfred Hitchcock show was on. Thumbing through the TV Guide he noticed that following the Hitchcock show was the movie, 'Stagecoach', and yet on another channel was, 'Gunsmoke'. The Western series TV shows were currently popular. The networks were filled with them.

Jonas got comfortable on the sofa with his feet up on the coffee table and finished off the Hitchcock show. Ten minutes into Stagecoach he fell off into a deep sleep. It was his typical thing. He usually slept sitting up with his head back, or worse slumped forward on his chest. Not an ideal position to sleep in. Then of lately there were the strange dreams, some he remembered vividly when he awoke while others were vague. Some of his dreams were of fantastical situations which manifested themselves in fantasy. One of the dreams was of him and Marilyn living in an apartment. In one dream they had an argument over burnt TV dinners of which they threw away. Then they decided to take a walk. Marilyn put a scarf around her head and wore her dark sunglasses. They headed toward the pier. When they got down near the ocean front they were walking by a fish and chips place. It was called the 'Sand Dabber', and out emanated the familiar scents of freshly fried battered seafood. They knew when they were hooked and submitted to a table within. The two were now in a much better mood. Jonas would say something funny and Marilyn would let out her familiar sexy audible laugh that was so familiar to all who knew her. In so doing, people began to stare. Hank the owner came over and said to Marilyn that she looked familiar. He said if he hadn't known Jonas he would think that the girl he was with was a famous person. Marilyn was still wearing her shades and scarf. With a very surprised look Marilyn told him she had great fun wearing the scarf and sunglasses because people often thought she might be some famous person. Hank asked her what famous person that would be? Marilyn asked Hank what person he thought she was?

"Ah! I got to get back to work," said Hank, shrugging his shoulders and walking away.

Then a man at a table next to them who overheard the conversation leaned over,

"Sister, I can't tell for sure with the scarf and shades, but seems like you could double for Marilyn Monroe."

Marilyn, giggling, leaned over and asked,

"Do you really think so?"

Things were heating up and Jonas just wanted to get out of there, so they quickly ate and left. The dream went on.

After dinner, a good walk was needed so they walked toward the pier. When they approached the end of the crowded pier, Marilyn's scarf came undone and blew off exposing her vibrant blonde hair and as she tried to grab it her glasses came off as well in the wind. A woman grabbed her scarf while Marilyn reached to pick up her glasses. Then things got hectic as the woman was returning Marilyn's scarf.

"Why, you're Marilyn Monroe," she practically shouted. Then people began to take notice. Suddenly crowds of people came closing in. It was a frightening sight and in that instant Jonas realized the fear she some times felt when crowds came at her. There were times when people really wanted a piece of her, whether it was a shred of clothing, or even a strand of hair. In that moment Jonas felt like jumping off the pier was an option, but then he woke up.

There were several other occasions he dreamed of Marilyn in the house while he was sleeping on the couch and then waking, but he really wasn't awake. It just seemed he was awake with his eyes half shut seeing Marilyn sitting on the couch watching television wearing only a white robe. She would just look at him in silence with that vulnerable looking face before he eventually awakened, disappointed to just an empty couch. Then, he would get up and go off to bed.

However, this evening there were no dreams and after about ninety minutes passed, Jonas awoke and watched the last twenty minutes of his movie, 'Stagecoach,' disappointed that he fell asleep. After the movie he watched a few minutes of the late news and then went to bed. In the morning he was supposed to meet Kay at the orphanage to become acquainted with his pair of orphan children. He imagined himself looking forward to the weekends with the orphans, seeing the excitement on their faces. In a sense, it was to make them feel they were part of a family and if possible feel like someone cared about them. Isn't that what all humans wanted? The challenge of the endeavor was to one day look back on his efforts as something to feel good about.

TWELVE

Cram and Jam

Upon late afternoon, Jonas was on his way to the orphanage. When Jonas arrived Kay had already been there for a time. His expectations for that day were positive. He came prepared, ready for the challenge of being a surrogate brother, a friend, or father figure if that was what was required. He didn't know what would land in his lap as children go. He reasoned he was here because he wanted to try to fill a void to that which these children had been denied. He was in it for the duration, whatever that was.

"Hi, Jonas!' greeted Kay.

"Hello, Kay."

"Jonas, this is Wanda," placing her hand gently on top of a girl's head who had black hair and green eyes.

"Hi, Wanda, glad to meet you," responded Jonas.

"Hello," she replied.

"Connie here just turned eight last month," said Kay, touching the other girl on the shoulder. Connie had blond hair and gray eyes.

"Nice to meet you both," responded Jonas.

"I guess you're both going to Vine Street School?" asked Jonas.

"Yes," said Wanda, with Connie nodding her head.

Depending on their own personal histories some orphan children had been stood up and knocked down much of their lives. That was especially true for those who didn't have much luck getting picked up by a foster family or adopted. Of course, what all children really needed was to be raised normally by their real parents. After all, how would anyone feel after being brought into the world only to find that your parents ditched you. Typically many had little faith in the words spoken to them of promises and predictions. What they needed and what they got were often two different things.

"Jonas?" a voice seemed to echo from behind him.

Turning, he saw Martha. She was in charge of the weekend field chaperon program.

"Hi Martha."

There were two young boys standing on each side of her.

"I want to introduce you to two boys that would love to get outside these walls, at least on weekends," said the woman.

"Hi!" responded Jonas.

"The lad on my left is Fred, and this other guy right here is Matt," stated Martha.

"Hi guys," said Jonas with a smile.

They both acknowledged Jonas with a similar greeting.

"Well boys, you know Kay and the girls. I think it would be nice if you went with them and Jonas right now. It looks like you'll all be spending some weekends together," stated Martha.

"Let's go outside and catch some fresh air and walk around a little bit and talk. How does that sound everyone?" said Kay as they all agreed.

So they headed outdoors. Matthew was entertaining himself with a small rubber football, tossing it up in shallow spins above his head before catching it. They decided to just walk around for a while, maybe head to a park or get something to eat. Jonas began asking the boys and girls questions as they began to express some interest in talking. Also, as they walked along the business districts they window shopped and bought a few things to eat. When they came to a park Jonas asked Matt to throw him the ball. Then Jonas threw it to Fred. They had a little passing game going while the girls watched. Before long, Kay suggested they head back to the orphanage which they did.

As they walked they continued to talk amongst themselves. Jonas was careful of what questions he asked while also attempting to get some kind of perception of the children. He knew he wasn't going to have a grasp of their complete personalities in this one visit. The kids were fairly talkative as kids go but the girls seemed the quietest. By the time they got back to the orphanage there was no reason to believe that anyone would not get along with each other.

Jonas asked everyone if they liked barbecued spare ribs. Matt and Connie said they never had any kind of barbecued ribs. The only things they ever had off a barbecue were hot dogs and hamburgers. When Jonas mentioned that in the coming weekend he could take them to a fun outdoor barbecue they seemed interested.

When they got back inside the lobby Jonas went into more detail with Kay about the big annual barbecue that his parents had thrown every year.

Since lots of other children would be there Kay also thought it would be alright to attend. With that they bid each other farewell.

When Jonas left it was almost dark. No doubt the kids at the orphanage would be served dinner soon. Jonas turned on the radio in his VW Bus. The long hollow interior of the vehicle seemed to amplify the stereo speakers that were attached to the roof. He tuned into the middle of, 'Born in the USA.'

Jonas did not feel like cooking and then cleaning up the mess that followed. There certainly was no shortage of eating places in L A. Whatever you wanted they had it. Jonas stopped at 'Shanghai Dragon,' a local food place popular with the locals. Tomorrow was a work day. A simple evening at home with TV and a takeout dinner seemed easy.

Once Jonas got his dinner home he grabbed a cold drink and headed for the living room. While passing Marilyn he stopped and turned to at least say something.

"Hi Marilyn, wanna watch some TV? I can't guarantee we'll agree on the programming, but I'll do my best," he remarked with a grin.

It seemed like her lips moved but that was probably the human mind again playing its tricks. The facsimile of the famous star was in an advantageous position to both the kitchen and the living room. The practical placement of Marilyn on Jonas's part was really the only possible place where there was room. She could watch TV or listen to his conversations at the breakfast table. Of course, in a logical sense if she were real, a thought that Jonas might imagine and she were cognizant of her surroundings, why would she choose to confine herself to a thin sheet of cardboard, really?

"Well, It shouldn't take long to browse the entire seven channels," he was thinking, but he didn't get that far. There was no mistaking Howard Cosell's voice. It probably would not be what Marilyn wanted to watch.

"There you have it, there you have it ladies and gentleman here in Los Angeles, with Ali apparently holding back on his Bee Sting punches until later, but no shortage of Rope a Dopes. Ali, Mohammed Ali barely taking the fourth round as these two very intense fighters go back to their respective corners," drawled out Cosell in his unique style of event hosting.

"Oh crap, I forgot there was a fight tonight," Jonas said out loud to himself.

It was already into the fourth round between Mohammed Ali and Ken Norton and it was right there in L.A. Actually, it was in Englewood. The two just fought last March and that fight wound up being a split decision going to Norton. Ali had his axioms, his techniques of style down such as the 'Rope a Dope', and the 'Butterfly, and the Bee Sting,' to name some. There was probably no man with more conceit, confidence, or talent, whichever it was than Cassius Clay or Mohammed Ali, as he now called himself. He would come walking down the isle to the boxing ring throwing a few shallow jabs claiming to be the most beautiful boxer that ever lived.

"Look at this face. Have you ever seen a boxers face so beautiful, so pretty," he would say. Another one of his favorite claims was shouting into the networks microphones, "I am the greatest. I am the greatest." In the end, the fight went the full fifteen rounds and was another split decision, this time going to Ali.

During the fight strange things would happen with the TV. The channel would change and Jonas would have to turn it back to the fight. In fact, it happened five times. Although he never thought much of it before, now he did. This wasn't the first time this strange phenomenon had happened. It had been going on for almost two weeks. It had been going on long enough that Jonas began to see a pattern. It didn't seem to happen when he was watching certain genres of movies. The channel changing seemed to occur only when he was watching a sports program or various western movies. The only logical explanation was; well there wasn't a logical explanation except that someone or something other than he was causing the channels to change. It was like someone didn't like what he was watching.

After the fight the local news followed and not surprisingly Jonas didn't make it through the segment before he fell asleep. One second his mind was processing input, his eye sight transmitting bits of information to the brain from the TV set and then suddenly he was out like someone yanked his cord.

The fight was over by nine o'clock and for far better than an hour Jonas was out cold as if Ali himself gave him a solid left jab. The sports channel was just going to a commercial when the station mysteriously changed to a local network that had just gotten into a movie. The movie was, '99 River Street,' filmed in fifty- three, with John Payne, and Evelyn Keyes. By the time Jonas would wake the movie would be over. That KTTV channel stayed true to its air wave frequency the rest of the evening. A little after eleven Jonas woke up, looked at his watch, got up, and turned off the television before going to bed.

"Good night, Marilyn!" bided Jonas on his way to the bedroom. In Jonas eyes she seemed to understand and respond with a certain look.

Nearly two days had passed since the Ali fight. Jonas had made arrangement with his work crew that he wouldn't be going in on Friday. There was something he wanted to do. He wanted to use his time that day and record his Sinatra songs for Mr. Conroy. He had given it some thought and decided that if he just sang the songs without any background music the effect might be terrible. He had found a band that could play his background music for a reasonable fee.

In truth, Jonas was not sure yet he had what it took to go up in front of people on stage. He wanted to do the recordings for the challenge, to see what Mr. Conroy's reaction would be. Would Conroy even call Jonas back? He was to meet the band at an offbeat night club called, 'Sam's Place'. It wasn't a big joint as clubs go but big enough. It was clean and had live music in the evenings. The kind of stuff where one guy would play a piano or a Spanish guitar, and a woman with a sexy baritone like voice would sing songs, sometimes in French. Jonas loved to listen to women sing certain songs in French even if he didn't know what they were saying. The place also enjoyed a degree of notoriety for its food and reasonable prices.

At 10am that Friday morning Jonas met the group of five musicians at the club bringing only his voice and Mr. Conroy's tape recorder. The manager, Jake Sims showed up early to open the place as a favor to the band. The extra twenty bucks he would make off of Jonas for the use of the premises was just easy pocket money. When Jonas entered the club, he began to get quite nervous. He asked himself why he was even bothering with all this preliminary fantasy façade crap, but it was too late to call it off without looking ridiculous. Who did he think he was anyway? Then he remembered all the people who had complemented him before when he sang. The club had a long bar on the right and lots of tables along the far wall. As they headed toward the back stage things got roomier. There was a piano over in the corner. Jake walked over and reminded everyone not to touch the piano.

"Keep your paws off of Daryl's piano. He's real sensitive about that," remarked Jake.

Then, Jonas handed Jake twenty bucks and thanked him for the use of the place.

"No problem," said the lean tough looking man.

Jake figured coming in a little early for some easy money was no big deal anyhow. Twenty bucks was twenty bucks. Jake went behind the bar and started sweeping. About the time Jonas was about to start to sing Jake finished his sweeping, grabbed a newspaper and then disappeared into a back room. Jonas had already provided the band with the music list to the ten songs that he wanted to sing.

Jonas set up the long playing tape recorder and told the guys he wanted to do a few minutes pause between songs so he could turn the recorder off and get ready for the next song. Once Jonas tested the recording system with the plug in mike he was ready to go.

"Okay, ready, Jonas?" asked Tom, the bands saxophone guy.

"Yeah, I'm ready," he answered.

So the band let their stuff out and they were good, surprisingly good for the fifty bucks that Jonas got them for. Musicians were a family and they all needed each other. They weren't there to laugh at anyone. They were there because they loved to make music. They probably would have done it for ten bucks or even for free if the guy was down on his luck. They had no idea as to the talent they were about to hear, so when their instruments came alive and Jonas began to sing, 'That's Life,' it sounded just like Sinatra. It was so good that when he finished they forgot about the recorder that was still playing and started clapping. Concerned, Jonas reminded them that the recorder was still running.

"Are you kidding? That clapping will only add to your agents haste in sealing a deal with you," they told him.

"And what happens if I sing a song that you don't like?" asked Jonas.

"Well, we'll clap anyway," he replied and they all laughed.

So Jonas knocked off all the remaining songs like a pro. There was, 'Fly Me to the Moon,' 'Nothing but the Best,' the same song he sang for Kay on Hollywood Boulevard. And then there was, 'Come Fly with Me,' 'The Lady is a Tramp,' 'Summer Wind,' 'It Was a Very Good Year,' 'Autumn in New York,' 'My Funny Valentine,' 'and finally, 'The Good Life.'

Jonas hadn't noticed that the club manager came out of his office after the second song and was sitting back behind the band clapping as well. When Jonas went to turn off the recorder Jake told everyone to come on over for a few drinks on the house.

"Say, I've heard a couple of guys try to do Sinatra but you are really something else fella. I think whoever it is that you are recording these for is going to fall off their chair. Who are you recording these for anyway?" asked Jake.

"Well, I met this guy on a job named Anniston Conroy and he..," Jonas was interrupted. Seemed everyone had heard of Conroy, but Jonas.

"Conroy! You struck gold if it's Conroy who likes you. He was in here once. I served him a couple of drinks. He seemed to enjoy the place. Funny, I thought he might have come back but that was the only time I ever saw him. Something tells me that we haven't heard the last of you. Heck, what is your name anyway?" surprised he hadn't thought to ask before.

"Jonathan Miles, but everyone calls me Jonas," he responded.

One drink led to another and after the first few on the house everyone bought a round. Jake soon had to open the place up for the noon lunch crowd. Later in the day some of the club's performers started dribbling in. One who came through the door was Trish Langley, an attractive buxom honey blonde. She prided herself as an adept singer, stage performer, and indeed she was quite capable of arousing the audience with her coquettish style of songs. Following close behind was her piano playing partner, Daryl Dungren. Trish was not use to having patrons arriving at the place before she showed up. Then she recognized the band players but not the unfamiliar face. She didn't give it much thought as she seated herself next to Jonas while Daryl took some things into the back room.

"Hi guys," greeted the young lady. They returned her hello.

"Are you ready to knock them dead tonight, Trish," asked a band member.

"Oh yeah, sure, I'll knock them dead all right if I can ever wake up," was her reaction.

"I've had my share of those days," said Jonas looking at her.

"You certainly don't look tired though," he added.

"Well, I can't afford to at work, but I'll just let myself unravel when I get home and get some sleep," she replied.

"Trish, this is Jonas alias Frank Sinatra," interjected Jake with a chuckle.

"Frank Sinatra?" queried Trish with a sort of surprised look.

"Yeah, you ought to hear him sing. Close your eyes and you'd think it was old blue eyes himself."

"Really?" she responded looking at Jonas with an interested look.

"Well I would love to hear you sing a number sometime," she stated.

"Come on Jonas, sing a song for her," said Jake with a gentle jab on his shoulder. Jonas was a bit modest and did not seem anxious to jump up.

"Sing a song? I'm not sure I can even stand up," he said with a grin.

"Hell, Sinatra was probably half bombed every time he sang," interjected Jake.

"Oh, come on Jonas. Sing me a song," said Trish looking at him with her large girly eyes. Her perfumed scent was faint but potent and had the effect of arousing the senses in men. It was what ladies often sought in a fragrance. He felt powerless to refuse her especially in his present state of intoxication. In that place, she probably was used to getting her way with the men succumbing to her whims of fancy. Like most women she was an actress, but better then that she was a well learned one. At that moment, Daryl took a seat on the other side of Trish.

"Well, what song is your choice?" he asked, being conscious of the fact that Sinatra sang a lot of songs over the years.

"Hmm, let me see," she said with a moment of contemplation.

"How about, 'Tell Her You Love Her,' do you know that one?"

"Well Guys?" asked Jonas looking at the band.

"Yeah, sure we can play it," they responded.

"Well, I think I can do that one," Jonas acknowledged to the woman.

"Yeah, we played that one for a wedding last year. Remember, guys," remarked Tom, the drummer.

So it wouldn't be a problem. They had a sheet for it. Jonas was glad she picked it. After the band had a few minutes warm up practice Jonas sang the song. The lyrics and tempo were romantically upbeat.

Considering Jonas had his share of drinks he sang the song quite well. He noticed how absorbed Trish was with his singing, but he also sensed it was something more for her. Shortly after he started singing she turned away facing the bar with her eyes closed. The song must have hit a sentimental chord with her. When Jonas finished the song everyone clapped right away but Trish. She seemed to have placed herself in another world while Jonas sang. Then as if to suddenly stir from her hibernation, she began to clap. Her eyes looked teary.

"You are so good. That was incredible. I'm not sure if you sound just like him or better," she remarked.

Jonas again thanked the band for playing so well.

When Jonas sat down he told Trish he didn't know exactly how he sounded to others, he just sang the best he could.

"Oh Jonas, you were perfect. You sound wonderful," she reiterated.

"Does that song have some special meaning for you?" he asked.

"Oh, perhaps," she said, silently looking away momentarily."

"Anyway, my name is Trish Langley. It was a pleasure to hear you sing Jonas," she added.

"Well, it is a pleasure to meet you Trish," he responded.

"If you're not in a rush you must hang around and listen to me sing, at least one song," remarked Trish.

"Yeah, you should Jonas. Gotta warn you though she has been known to put a spell on guys," interjected Jake.

Daryl didn't say much since he got there. He mumbled something. The dark haired piano playing musician was of average height with a slight build. Although he was not romantically involved with Trish, he had the desire for it. He was very jealous of the men she paid attention to. So when he had uttered some indiscernible remark, something which Trish was use to when she was paying attention to men she barely noticed.

As the evening wore on the guys in the band talked amongst themselves as Jonas and Trish got to know each other better. The two found out they had many things in common and found themselves in lively conversations. It seemed appropriate when they exchanged phone numbers which was initiated when Jonas asked Trish if she would care to go out some time. That was when Daryl once again could be heard mumbling something to himself.

Not just the evening but the whole day seemed to fly by to Jonas. In his drunken state he had taken the perfect antidote; 'liquor,' which served to disguise his calmer character and sensitive side. He had lots to say and he laughed long and hard. He was aggressive yet considerate. Jonas was having an effect on Trish Langley. Jonas became a little obnoxious that evening, even acted as an outspoken guru of the way things were, the way life was and he joked and laughed with anyone around him into the late evening. He stuck around to hear Trish sing. Jonas's musicians had already left and the clubs band for the night had already set up. The club was a pretty popular place for its regulars. The place catered to the kind of people who liked to drink, eat, have a good time and listen to people like Trish sing the night away.

"Good evening ladies and gentlemen. For those of you who are newcomers tonight you are a very lucky audience, said the announcer.

"Tonight we have Dale Creighton doing his comedian acts, and Johnny Canton will be playing his Spanish guitar. Also, Jackie Clairer with his blues band and others will be here. Tonight we will start you off with the very adorable vocal seductress, Trish Langley. Her first two songs for the night are, 'Its Magic,' and then, 'The Man I Love,'" came, the announcer.

So now Trish was up on stage after changing into a blue shimmering tight fitting dress that served to offer the best of her female assets. The bottom hem was amply above the knee to show off her fabulous legs and matching blue sequined high heels. Her voice was saucy, sexy, and very entertaining as she moved along the stage using the piano, the vertical columns that supported the ceiling, and a few props to glide around and through as she sang. The song selections and the lyrics seemed perfect as they reminded you of new found friends, people who might fall in love. Jonas imagined this was just another night for Trish, another evening on the job. He was just another bloke passing through the doors. Only time would tell anything different. He hung around until the end of her first set of songs and when she came back out of the dressing room she came over to Jonas and suggested they sit at a table. They talked more. They laughed and told stories until it was time for her to go on again. He was tired. He had been there since mid morning. He told her he had to go. They kissed each other.

"Call me," Jonas thought he heard her say as he walked away.

THIRTEEN

The Last Barbecue

On a breezy cool afternoon Jonas drove his bus over to the orphanage where he would meet Kay and the children. They were going to his parents for the barbecue. The plan was if they had time afterwards to head over to Queens Park. Queens Park was the new name they had given the old Long Beach Pike.

Historically the famous amusement park began construction in 1902 and featured quite a stimulating roller coaster ride built on pier pilings that jutted out over the ocean. Through time, since its inception there arose many arcade games and concession businesses along the boardwalk of the Pike.

When Jonas drove up to the orphanage he was surprised to find Kay and the four children waiting alongside the curb. He double parked long enough for them to get in and then they were off. Kay had Frederick sit up front with Jonas and she and the rest sat on the seats in the rear.

"I thought I would show up a little early. I was sort of surprised to see you all there waiting," remarked Jonas.

"Well life's full of surprises, isn't it," smiled Kay.

"Hmm, I guess so," he responded.

Jonas had told his mother about the orphan kids and she was expecting them. She was surprised, but thought it admirable that Jonas had gotten himself involved with orphans since he had a couple of boys of his own. The truth was that Jonas didn't discuss the facts of his personal problems much with anyone, including his parents. Lynn, his ex, was currently involved with a wealthy businessman and she had begun exerting a great influence over the daily itinerary of his two boys. Lynn's new boyfriend had been giving the boys costly material things which must have been well appreciated. Today though was a day that Lynn could hardly avoid or deny so soon after separation. It was participation in an event that in the past they had all attended annually. Lynn was going to drop the boys off at the outdoor feast and then pick them up at five sharp.

Jonas pulled out some 8 track tapes from a considerable stack near his driver's seat. He was trying to drive and look at them at the same time.

"Now don't let us take a bite out of that truck up ahead," mentioned Kay.

"Yeah, ditto that," added Wanda.

"Ditto that? Yeah okay, I got yuh," replied Jonas with a serious look.

"Okay, what will it be Tommy James, Hollies, or Bobby Darrin?" asked Jonas.

No one said anything as they looked at Jonas.

"Okay then, I'll put them all back and just reach in and pull one out. That's what we'll play then, whatever it is."

Jonas reached in his bag of tapes while watching his driving and pulled out a tape that had the hits of different artists.

"Well, this is interesting," he said while inserting a tape into his 8 track player.

Jonas looked into his rear view mirror and noticed everyone was looking at him.

"What? You don't even know what it is yet," said Jonas as the VW Bus puttered its way through the congested Saturday morning LA traffic, headed toward Glendale.

The first song up on the hit list was, 'Walk Away Renee,' by the 'The Left Banke'.

As Jonas drove his mind became occupied with, of all things, that day he spent with Gina when they were riding around the coastal hills in her Jeep. What made people put their lives in danger? Take rock climbers, those people armed with only a rope, a small hand pick and a few other things only to scale sheer rock cliffs. What about people who swim with sharks. Certainly, thousands jump out of airplanes, would he do that?

There were times when Jonas had done crazy things, wild things and stupid things. He loved that buffalo stampede, it was exhilarating, thought Jonas. What is life without risk? Living in fear is no way to live. Jonas wondered how things might be different now if he was seeing more of Gina. He might not be here in this bus right now. Maybe he wouldn't have made the decision to help out at the orphanage. Yes, Jonas had strong feelings for Kay but Gina and Kay had two different personalities. He imagined Kay being stable, practical, and sensible, and he loved being with her. Gina seemed to be more wild and adventurous. She was of that percentage willing to put herself at risk for something better even if only for a thrill. She liked the wind in her face.

Gina seemed to want the world and wouldn't settle for anything less.

Suddenly, Jonas began snapping his fingers, slapping his trousers, and bouncing his hand off the steering wheel to the beat of the music. Jonas noticed Kay looking at him with a grin in the rear view mirror. However, Fred was giving him one of those sanity check looks.

"Oh, come on, Fred. That's a great song. Doesn't it make you want to rock? Today you guys are going to have a good time. We're going to go get some of those famous barbecued ribs and beans at the Miles place and then head for the beach. How can you beat that?" queried Jonas.

After the VW bus pulled into the long driveway of his old childhood home it only took him a second to jump out of the front seat. In a flash he was opening the passenger side sliding door to let everyone out. Kay, exiting first was poised holding a canvas bag that had some side dishes she made.

"What's that?' asked Jonas.

"Well I couldn't see coming without bringing something," she replied.

"Oh, you didn't have to you know? He replied.

"Nonsense, it's just potato salad and deviled eggs," she answered.

"Okay, than I'm sure it will be appreciated."

Even though it was still early guests were already parked out on the street and the driveway. It would only be a few hours later those cars would be parked everywhere up and down the street. People who weren't even invited showed up, friends of friends, sons and daughters of friends, and even people who lived in the neighborhood that the Miles didn't even know. Yep, everyone knew that scene. So called party crashers. That may be alright at some BYOB parties, but George only bought enough ribs for those who were invited and he knew who was invited. Last year, George ran out of ribs before many of those invited could even put some on their plate.

The Miles had a very large back yard , ample room for people to play a game of Croquet, throw horseshoes, or play a fast game of ping pong. The kids also had plenty of room to toss a ball. Jonas had introduced the kids from the orphanage to some of the other youth after they arrived. He was hoping that they would hookup with other children. Things were slow at first but people just kept arriving. Wanda wound up playing Croquet with a girl name Julie. Connie was having some fun at the ping pong table, and Fred and Matt were throwing Horseshoes. Kay was helping Jonas's mother while Jonas was talking to his own two kids, Cal and Charlie near where his father was cooking.

Jonas's boys were nearly a year older now since Jonas and their mother separated. Cal was pushing twelve and Charlie nine. They seemed to act a bit tight lipped about their new arrangements and surrogate father figure. They did say that Thomas, their mom's new boyfriend was very strict about things and that he was already having discussions about their future.

Soon after helping Jonas's mother Kay had come over to be with Jonas and meet his kids while she walked into an ongoing conversation. Jonas had not said anything to anyone yet about his inheritance other than to his parents. The last thing Jonas wanted was for Lynn to get her hands on any of Uncle Leslie's money. He wanted a divorce done and done quickly. After all she started the divorce process in more ways than one. So now she's got a new guy with money, the kids, and she's got her own business. She didn't need the shirt off Jonas's back as well.

"So Jonas, are these your two handsome boys?" asked Kay.

"Yes Kay, this big guy here is Cal and this other fella is Charlie," responded Jonas.

"Well, glad to meet you two guys. Your Dad has spoken of you often and I'm sure you make him proud," replied Kay.

While Kay was there, Jonas thought it would be a good time to explain to his kids what his intentions were with the children from the orphanage. He held a desire to give some of his time to children who had been left behind, to those who were far more unfortunate then others. It would turn out though through time that Jonas would give far more than he could have imagined. And it was good that his boys appeared to understand him. When possible he wanted all the children to be together including his own kids as well. The concept had Kay's approval as well. It would be like having a large family. All of a sudden the isolation and loneliness that Jonas occasionally felt on weekends would vanish. He did not know yet how everyone would get along although he hoped for the best.

Jonas had fruitful conversations with his father that day. They reminisced about all the outdoor adventures that decades earlier they had shared together. How they hunted and fished extensively the lakes, valleys, deserts, and meadows of the region. It was all back in a time when it seemed they had the world to themselves.

Jonas also had a very pleasant visit with his mother. He talked some more with her about Mr. Conroy and his Sinatra renditions that he made for him.

She seemed delighted with the news and encouraged him. They made fun of old times and places and laughed while she prepared food for the guests. Jonas saw some of the same people he already knew from previous parties and met many new ones as well.

As the afternoon unfolded Jonas's boys met the children from the orphanage as they wandered, mingled, and joined in the fun and games. Jonas and Kay became like kids themselves as they played each other at ping pong. And when the ribs were done and all the food was laid out on the tables everyone was served. There was enough ribs and food for everyone. As time would have it nothing could have moved the day along quicker then the ingredients of good people, tasty table fare, and good conversation. So as it was the plans of going to the beach at the end of the day would not materialize as it was getting late.

It was a completely uneventful and sober ride back to the orphanage. When the VW bus pulled up around four thirty in the afternoon one would have thought the children would be tired but their energy levels never seemed to wane. They were all quite talkative during the drive home. When Jonas pulled up to the curb he helped with the unloading and then Jonas was off, solo once again. Although the day was enjoyable being with the group, sometimes a person had a place they liked to go to if not to just be alone, but to think.

When Jonas got home he didn't want to be inside. He parked his VW, fetched a light windbreaker jacket and headed for the pier. Yes, that place he seemed all too often to find himself if only to allow the cool salty air to bathe his spirit and work its magic. When out upon that sturdy platform of wood and concrete that held itself fast to the earth he like many others looked out over the sea. That place seemed to remind you with each breaking wave that your days were numbered and that your life was measured and it reminded you that you wanted to make sure every single minute counted. It was a place to let out ones thoughts that seemed to leave you feeling relaxed and free, like a mirage of wandering gypsies in the wind.

Perhaps it was just as well that the children had not come down to the beach this evening as the air was getting cold. The sun was down low on the horizon as the golden glimmer of its radiance sprinkled its luminescence upon the rhythms of the ocean. One could imagine that all the people who were now roving about here at the seas edge were rewarded with wondrous things to see. The wildness of nature could never be boring for it was conceivable that many others across the continents had their own horizons of beauty. However, here and now, there was something about groups of soaring seagulls extravagant in their own right living the life of the free spirited. They seemed to be as much a part of the sea as the very salt in it. Their low toned squealing squawks instilled kindred imaginings as they glided along effortlessly upon outstretched wings.

In the distance a small school of porpoises skipped along upon the seas surface like perfectly thrown pebbles. More than once Jonas had sat at the piers end on moon lit nights to witness the giant hulks of migrating whales. To see their huge tails smack at the surface or silently slip through the seas salty blackened glow.

Jonas thought about Trish Langley, the singer he had met at 'Sam's Place'. As beautiful as she was there seemed to be a hollow loneliness in her eyes. Jonas wanted to see her again. Surely she was working tonight? He had thoughts of going to Sam's Place. He liked her voice. It would be nice to hear her sing again.

Two hours later Jonas was at the night club sitting at a table with a pitcher of beer listening to Trish sing as her partner Daryl Dungren played the piano. When the song ended Daryl's eyes wasted no time finding Jonas, giving him the eye in the crowded smoke filled room.

FOURTEEN

Yesterday is Not Forever

There was enough of a crack in the heavy curtains to allow a bright ray of sunlight to strike Jonas's face. It was enough to awaken him so that he could take notice of the unfamiliar surroundings. Slowly looking around the room he began to recall the evening. Next to him lay Trish Langley. Jonas had much to drink at the bar. Completely recalling what had happened was a struggle. He remembered when leaving with Trish there was a slight confrontation with her pianist partner, Daryl. Besides being naturally protective of her he could also become quite jealous of her occasional romps with men. He would be concerned about Trish leaving with guys who had trouble walking a straight line. Once she went out the door he always worried about her.

Now, while the room was still dark and Trish still asleep, Jonas rose, gathered his clothes and left the room. Near the kitchen he completed his dressing and noticed a tablet and a pen on the table. He would take a minute to write Trish a note.

> *Trish,*
> *Very much enjoyed being with you.*
> *Enjoyed your company. Loved your songs.*
> *Will see you soon.*
>
> *Love*
> *Jonas*

About an hour later Jonas was at home. After showering and dressing he thought it nice to have a day off from work. He thought now would be a good time to drop off his voice recordings for Conroy. Jonas wondered how many submissions Conroy garnered on a weekly basis. It didn't matter, either Conroy would be interested or he wouldn't. Jonas did his best, it was all he could do. Just as he was finishing up the package the phone rang.

"Hello," said Jonas.

It was his sister Liz. Her voice seemed tormented. Her usual glee like mood was challenged as her voice came out scolding Jonas in an urgent tone.

"Where have you been," demanded Elizabeth.

"What?" he replied in a confused tone.

"Dad had a heart attack about an hour after you left yesterday. We have been trying to reach you for hours," was her immediate statement.

"Oh no, is he okay?"

"He's alive, he's in the hospital of course."

"Glendale Memorial?" he asked.

"Yes, mom and I are here now."

"I'm leaving right now. I'll see you when I get there."

"Okay, don't get in an accident. We don't need someone else in the hospital. They have him stabilized. He will be in surgery soon."

"Okay Liz, I'm gone," was all Jonas said before he was out the door.

Ten minutes later Jonas arrived in the lobby of the hospital where his sister was waiting for his arrival.

"Hurry, they are going to take him into the operating room any minute," Liz blurted.

They both were practically at a trot they were walking so fast. When they got to his room there was a nurse and some aids prepping him for surgery. When George saw his son he tried his best to minimize the seriousness of his condition and to diffuse as much distress as possible his family might have. After all he was about to go into open heart surgery. However, in his father's own eyes few could miss the truth that read like a story book. All expressed a degree of worry. Everyone was worried for George. And though they were there to comfort him it was George who tried to deliver to his family a good measure of hope and confidence. After all the medical staff at the Hospital were competent professionals. At least no one had heard otherwise. After the nurse had finished with her prep work she left for a few minutes to give the family time to be together. It was then that Jonas said things to his father that he never had said before.

"I love you Dad," said Jonas.

"I love you too, Jonas," replied the elder Miles.

The surgery would take about four hours. After they wheeled George into surgery Jonas tried waiting, but he told his mother he was going home and that he would be back. Jonas just wanted to be alone. He wanted to go home to pray and think. Everyone liked George. He went out of his way to make friends. Others came to the hospital to provide comfort for the family.

When Jonas got home he sat at the kitchen table. Jonas looked at Marilyn. Sometimes Jonas talked to himself so it didn't really bother him to direct his conversation at the famous star. If none of the rest of the printed facsimile of Marilyn Monroe looked real against the wall her face did. Sometimes it seemed her face was nothing more then what it was, that printed cardboard likeness of a celebrity who had a blank stare. At other times her face took on a surreal, attentive, living appearance. She could project a lifelike presence in the room even if it might have seemed illusionary. People could make claims about all sorts of things, some false and some true. In most instances it was something one experienced when alone like a special moment to peer into another's world, or light plane, or whatever it was. The perception of what he saw and what he believed is what gave Jonas cause to believe in a spiritual world after a mortal existence.

She seemed to listen, offered a perception of eye contact, and presented herself in an attentive manner. Jonas worried that at times she might do something that was considered taboo in her spirit world. That is, crossing the line and exposing her illuminated spiritual self out of a moment of compassion. Of course granting any mortal such patronage would be forbidden and even harmful to the mortal recipient. There would be a price for one to pay. He sensed at times she may have wanted to temporarily cross but he would never wish it, and surely it was just poor interpretation on his part. That concept was just part of Jonas's imagination. Jonas would often say things to her like, "Now don't you get in trouble over me," then walk away.

There were times when he got fed up so chastising himself for being crazy enough to talk to a piece of cardboard. Whenever he said such things a look of sadness came over her face. So he became reluctant in those times to criticize himself for fear of hurting her which made him feel even crazier. Jonas did not believe that the cardboard cutout was Marilyn Monroe, but he simply philosophized that she could be allowing the image to serve as a communicative medium. In time he would come to believe this even more so as stranger things would happen.

The whole thing Jonas realized was probably just some fantasy creation in his mind. Whatever it was he decided he would not discuss it with anyone. At any rate, Jonas was beginning to accept something that he kept trying to dismiss. His own self paradigm of what was rational and sensible. He had become what people call eccentric or even worse. Perhaps he had become influenced by some of the books he had read of esoteric knowledge.

So, within Jonas's conscious mind existed an apprehension of the spiritual existence of the famous star Marilyn Monroe. So he talked to her and she had plenty of time to listen. After all, he talked to her in real life once though brief it was. That long ago evening when she had been so close in the flesh he felt a strange feeling. When he finally was able to look into her eyes he only saw a lost and sad soul within a body of beauty. And her face held you spellbound as the iconic star's magnetism drew all your energy to her. During that long ago incident his conscious mind was blind to everyone else present that night and all the hoopla around went deaf to his ears, except Marilyn's footsteps, her aura, and her own voice. That must have been how it was with any fan fortunate enough to get so close to her. Now years after her passing who is to say that there couldn't be some kind of esoteric relationship between the mortal and immortal in the realm of the spiritual? As Jonas sat at his kitchen table and talked to her this day tears welled up in his eyes as his grave concern for his father dominated his thoughts. He had her attention but he learned not to stare at her. She did not seem to like it when he occasionally did so. Her eyes became un-attentive and she slowly reverted to a lifeless look.

Jonas mentioned to Marilyn about his father's serious situation and he told her about the wonderful times they had together. Jonas was passionate, telling all about his father. He mentioned how he was sad that she grew up without any real parents of her own. Of course Jonas did all the talking and she listened.

Without realizing it, several hours had passed since Jonas left the hospital. He was cognizant of the need to get back to his mother's side as he rushed to pick up his keys. Near the door he bid his famous cardboard roommate farewell hoping that she somehow might have some effect on a favorable outcome. Just what was it that a warehouse shipping error had sent, if it was a warehouse? Just where did the folding caricature come from. Perhaps somewhere beyond comprehension, but she seemed a supernatural friend. One that he got along with very well but one who really never had much to say.

FIFTEEN

Stairway in the Forest

Barely a week had passed since Jonas had returned to the hospital. He would never forget the news that came too soon, the worst news of his life. Jonas's father, George Miles passed away on the operating table. All they were told was that, 'they', the doctors were very sorry. That's when a family starts asking themselves questions like would it have been a different outcome had they had another doctor or been at a different hospital? Who the hell could know?" Everything in life is like a spin on the roulette wheel. They are questions that most will never know the answers to.

There was much grieving those first few days and the sorrow would take time for healing. Not having George around in the Miles family was like California not having Catalina. He was their rock. At the funeral Jonas had seen his father out in style. It was held at the country club where his dad played golf. He made sure his father had a memorable ceremony, one the attendees would not likely forget. There was a huge send off party that followed. Of course, all the Miles family members were there as well as the usual friends and relatives. Jonas hired a band to play Jazz, George's preferred music. Following the catered meals Jonas gave the opening speech about his father and then a couple of Georges friends spoke. There were display photos of George that captured him at some of the highlights of his life, many of his happiest times. The event took up the whole afternoon. For the burial ceremonies Jonas brought in some of his uncles old classic cars to deliver attendees and add an element of nostalgia to the event.

Jonas drove his uncles 58 Chevy Impala convertible to the ceremony. It sported a gorgeous gloss black paint exterior and a red and white leatherette interior. The 348 engine could throw you back in your seat with a slight tap of the throttle. Jonas had invited Kay to the ceremony even though she had only met his father that one time at the barbecue. She readily accepted. Jonas had no other friends really except Jose and Kim, his work comrades. Trish was not there. He did not invite her. Even though he considered her a friend she didn't know his family. The alliance that brought them together was by circumstance a mixture of booze and loneliness.

Several weeks had passed since the funeral. Jonas had gotten home from work and he was about to barbecue some hamburgers when the phone rang. It was Anniston Conroy. He had been so busy he had just now found the time to listen to Jonas's recordings. He sounded like he had been quite excited about Jonas's talent.

"Jonathan, I have never heard anyone sound so much like Sinatra. Can you be here tomorrow morning about nine?" asked Conroy.

"Yeah, sure," responded Jonas.

"Think about a first name. Your last name is OK. We just have to come up with a better first name. I'll do a little thinking this evening. It shouldn't be that big of a deal. Just don't pick Frankie, OK," kidded Conroy.

"Frankie? No, it won't be Frank."

"Hey, by the way it would be a good idea to have a few suits and ties if you don't already. Maybe buy yourself a fedora hat. I will have you get together with one of our guys, Sam Preston. He will get you set up with a band to do a little practicing with your numbers," stated Conroy.

"Yeah sure, but Fedora Hats?" responded Jonas thinking things are starting to sound a bit rich.

"So I'll be wearing those, really?"

"Oh Maybe, don't worry about that right now," responded Aeton.

"Maybe I should just do Don Ho? All I need to do him is a straw hat and a Hawaiian shirt," added Jonas.

"Hey, good idea, do you do Don Ho, too? A few evening beach performances might be a good idea," replied Conroy.

Jonas Laughed, but Aeton wasn't kidding.

"No, I'm not a Don Ho."

"Hey, I appreciate what you are doing for me but what is Sinatra going to do about some guy singing his songs who lives right in his back yard?" asked Jonas.

"Don't worry about Sinatra. I know him. As a matter of fact I will probably see him at a big event I'm going to this Friday night. I'm going to mention you to him. At least he can't say I never said anything about you. I'm just going to tell him I got a guy who is pretty good at impersonating him. I don't think he will mind. The world of entertainment is full of impersonators," said Conroy.

"Yes, but we all know what kind of friends he has that live in places like Jersey and Chicago, if you know what I mean," added Jonas.

"Forget about it lad. There are not going to be any headlines like, 'Sinatra Impersonator Found wearing Cement Shoes'," laughed Conroy.

"Yeah, that's because those people never get found," Jonas replied jokingly.

"Hey I got it, 'Glenn', how about Glenn Miles, interjected Conroy.

"How about, 'Rex'?" responded Jonas.

"Let's see, "Rex Miles'? Well I don't know about Rex. Keep thinking. We'll work something out. See you tomorrow morning. I think you're going to be glad we met up. Yeah, think about Glenn, that fits you," ended Conroy.

"Okay Aeton, I'll see you in the morning," said Jonas.

"Glad you remembered kid, that's my name, Aeton," said Conroy hanging up before Jonas could even say bye.

When Jonas hung up and sat down that was when the news really hit him.

"Glenn Miles? Maybe Glenn does sounds better then Rex," he mused as he once again looked at the strikingly realistic form of Marilyn, only feet away.

"Wow! What is happening here Marilyn? Did I actually plan for all this to happen? I wonder what I'm getting myself into. I guess I never really thought I sounded that good," thought Jonas.

"I just need to chill, it's not like I'm a star or something. I'm just an impersonator. Why do I get this feeling I'll be seeing one of Sinatra's lawyers after my first performance? Worse yet, maybe he'll set a wrath of the underworld upon me. Oh, like I'm sure there's going to be a couple of overfed Mafioso's named Tony and Al sitting with frank watching me perform. Nah, I'm sure Sinatra has better things to do then watch a green impersonator sing his songs," thought Jonas.

Jonas grinned as he humored himself. He would later mention the humorous thought to Aeton.

"Well Marilyn, it looks like I might have the chance to gain a little local notoriety. Oh, my new name will be Rex, Rex Miles. How does that sound?" asked Jonas, speaking to the figure on the wall. He thought he saw her frown.

"Hmm, maybe she doesn't like Rex?"

Her look seemed aloof this evening, like she was either just not interested or maybe she wasn't even around. That was what Jonas believed. That her free spirit was a busy force involved with many souls. Her sole existence did not evolve around him. In fact, surely, she must have been in many other places. However, at the moment there was no reason to try any attempt to appeal to her cognitive senses. He could see she wasn't around.

Jonas had no idea how soon Aeton would be booking him or where. He decided while the evening was still young to go looking at suits to see what he could find. Maybe take a look at some hats as well. He only got about two blocks before he decided he had to tell Kay the good news. He wasn't sure she was home. When she answered the door a feeling of relief came over him. When he told her about the good news she seemed more excited than he.

"I'm really not surprised Jonas. You sound so much like Sinatra. Even your speech sounds like him," she exclaimed.

"It looks like my new name is Rex Miles," he said.

"Rex?" she queried.

"Yes, Conroy suggested 'Glenn', but I mentioned Rex for a first name," he replied.

"Well, Rex' sounds a little prehistoric, don't you think? Maybe Glenn does sound better," she said.

"Well, whatever it becomes will be final tomorrow morning. I'm supposed to get a few suits and a fedora hat. I do not like the hat idea that much."

"I was just on my way to see what I could find when I stopped by to tell you the news," Jonas added.

"I'm finished with my school work. I'll go with you if you would like me to give you some ideas," she offered.

"Wow! That would be great. I'm not much of a suit specialist. I guess it just boils down to fit and color," he responded.

"Well let's go see what looks best on you," she remarked.

As the two left the house Kay was looking about for the bus when he led her to the fifty-eight Chevy and opened the door for her. The car was just over fifteen years old, but it was clean and sweet.

"Did you get another car?" she asked as he closed the door.

"Yeah, I got me another car. What do you think?" he asked.

"I love it." she added.

"Oh, I better put the top up," he responded.

"On a day like this, don't bother. I have something in my purse for my hair. I love convertibles."

Hours had passed and Jonas had his suits, one brown and one black. After the shopping they had cruised Ocean Avenue and drove down PCH, better known as Pacific Coast Highway. They headed toward Malibu talking, laughing, and enjoying the fresh salty open air ride. When they got to Malibu they stopped at a place to eat. It was off of the Highway. The place was called the 'Sea Lion'. There was a salt water pool out front with real seals. They often greeted the patrons with their friendly barks and clapping appendages. The owner would often greet customers when they walked through the door.

The place offered a great view of the ocean. While the two enjoyed their meals they talked of the orphanage, the kids, and of Jonas's new shot at show biz. When they finished their meal the two headed back to Santa Monica and spoke of such things as dates, times, and appointments for their busy schedules. When they finished discussing these things the two grew silent as the engine spoke up as it rumbled down the coastal highway, cutting a path through the on rushing air. Funny sometimes how silence seems louder then words as each strained to hear the others thoughts, or became lost in their own. Kay's normal long reddish brunette hair now glowed like fire in front of the setting sun.

"Well I guess you might as well take me home Glenn," she said with a smile.

"I knew you liked that name, 'Glenn'. It doesn't sound bad really. Maybe Rex is to sharp," responded Jonas.

"It's going to be your name so you better pick what you like," she answered.

"You know, I have been thinking about changing a little something myself," she said.

"Really, what would that be, not your name?" asked Jonas.

"Oh no, nothing like that, at least I wasn't planning on it," she stated.

"Hey, before I take you home we can stop by my place real quick? I will show you where I live. I can offer you a beer, wine, whatever?" He suggested.

"Ok, maybe a soda, but I can't stay long. I have some things I have to do," she replied.

"Sure, you know though everyone always has things they have to do, right?"

"I know, I didn't mean it to sound like that. I think we both have busy lives. And Saturday, we have to be at the orphanage again, remember?" she said.

"Oh yeah, I know, we are taking them to Griffith Park, It will be fun," he responded as he quickly pulled into his driveway.

"Well here it is. Now you know where I live," he stated.

"You have a long driveway," she remarked.

"Yeah, it works out for me," he replied.

As Jonas was walking toward the front door he suddenly remembered something that he forgot about that would be somewhat embarrassing for him to explain. It was the Marilyn cardboard figure. No one else ever saw it before. Well, there was no escaping it now, besides considering his current relationship to it, to her, he didn't know if he could ever bring himself to even take it down. Somehow, it seemed like there was a person inside the stirring image. He would not humiliate her by shoving her into a closet. If a friend could not accept the harmless article then perhaps it was they who had a problem.

The first thing that caught Kay's eye was his painting easel and art equipment.

"Oh, you are an artist?" she asked.

"Well, I try. I'm just an amateur I suppose, but in time I hope to improve. I haven't done much with it lately. I have been distracted with a lot, I'm afraid," he answered.

"What are you drinking?" asked Jonas.

"I'll just have a cola, thanks."

Jonas removed two ice cold bottles from the refrigerator. He opened them and handed her a beverage.

"Well show me more," she said as her eyes caught the Monroe figure. She said nothing of it as Jonas began to show her some of his prized collectibles. Afterwards, Jonas took a seat at his kitchen table where they finished their colas. After the two had seemed to run out of idle talk, Jonas got up to take her home.

"I see you like Norma Jeanne?" mentioned Kay. Jonas was caught off guard, surprised she would use Marilyn's childhood name.

"Oh, of course you saw her. I was surprised you took so long to offer a mention of her? Well, she's just been kind of hanging around the place of late," he answered as he looked at Marilyn hoping his response would be taken in jest. Marilyn's eyes looked aloof and distant and Jonas felt Marilyn was absent.

"I'm glad you like her or do you love her?" asked Kay, studying his face.

"Hmm, well you know, she's an American icon, a sort of self-made institution I imagine," he responded as he looked into Kay's observant eyes.

Then Kay looked on the shelf and saw the photo of Marilyn with her kiss and the note she wrote. She took it all in quite quickly, but said nothing.

"Do you think she was lonely, Jonas?" she asked.

"Everyone has gotten lonely at sometime," he responded. Then he looked at the cardboard facsimile again.

"You know what's weird? I never bought this. It was left at my door, included in a shipment of art supplies. I don't know. It was some mistake," remarked Jonas.

"Maybe you didn't receive it by mistake Jonas."

As the two left the house Jonas thought about the last thing Kay had said as he followed her out the door. There were other things he thought about. He was trying to be as rational as possible, but to Jonas, Kay looked much like Norma Jeanne. How eerily strange the tide had turned for Jonas since he had taken in his new cardboard roommate. He had gotten picked up by this huge talent agent like magic.

"Is that how it happens for most celebrities, some fairy comes floating down waving their wand and taps them on the shoulder and says your next," wondered Jonas.

"No, it wasn't really that way for Jonas. Sure, he might have been at the right place at the right time. Really though, it took a serious and coordinated effort of work and commitment. Why, certainly such had been required of everyone who ever made a name for themselves.

SIXTEEN

Metamorphosis

When Jonas arrived at Conroy's office on Friday morning his secretary beeped Aeton letting him know that Jonas had arrived. Aeton came out the door with his brief case briskly sweeping Jonas up in his path hurrying him out the door. He was taking Jonas to breakfast at a little place called JON'JON's. Mr. Conroy put the top down on his new Jaguar. Soon they were buzzing down Beverly Boulevard with the radio blaring while Aeton talked. Aeton was in a cheerful mood as he talked about his two dogs, which were Great Danes. He had expected them to take the grand prize in an upcoming dog show. He talked about a new sailing yacht he had on order as well as his mountain cabin retreat next to his favorite fishing spot. He talked about how everyone was overcharging him from engagement halls and performance centers to attorneys and taxes. It was kind of humorous that the song that was coming out of the radio was 'Hominy Grits' by Dean Martin, since they were on their way to breakfast.

JON JON's was typically a busy place, very popular with the local crowd which included the rich and famous. They only served breakfast and lunch. They closed by 3pm every day except Sunday. They were closed on Sundays.

Once they were seated at the restaurant Aeton ordered 'The Works,' commonly referred to as a number seven. The entrée consisted of two slices of toasted wheat sourdough topped with poached eggs and on the side was bacon, sausage, shoestring potatoes, ham cubes in gravy and silver dollar pancakes. Aeton preferred the house blueberry syrup. Perhaps a strange coincidence, 'The Works' was the same entre that an over weight celebrity was feasting on the previous year when she keeled over dead from a heart attack. After Aeton ordered, he excused himself to go see someone across the room. Jonas noticed Aeton had the newspaper on top of his brief case so he decided to take a glance at it. On the fold of the back cover was a photo of a woman and an article. The caption read,

'Pavlo Picks Unknown for Lead Role.'

The short one paragraph article mentioned the woman's name as Eleanor

Marore, but Jonas recognized her right off. It was Gina.

"Gosh," thought Jonas in shock. Well, she sure doesn't waste any time. Jonas knew she was the kind that if she wanted something bad enough she could get it. In a few minutes Aeton returned to the table.

"Well, Glenn, did you find anything that looks good? Anything you want, it's on me," said the famous agent sitting down.

"Yes, I believe I did. Just about everything on the menu looks good, doesn't it?" remarked Jonas.

"Oh, I decided to choose the name that you suggested, I'm gonna go with Glenn," said Jonas.

"Oh you are, fine, fine, it's a good name, a smooth name."

"I just scanned the cover of your paper and saw an old friend on the back cover," mentioned Jonas.

"Oh, Hope it isn't bad news?" responded Aeton while picking up the paper.

"No, she apparently just got picked by Pavlo to do a movie. Looks like it will be her big break in the movie business," responded Jonas.

"Really, oh is this the article?" asked Aeton, pointing at it.

"Yes."

"Eleanor Marore, huh, I suppose she already has an agent. What's her real name?" Aeton asked. He knew that rarely anyone used their real name.

"Well I knew her as Gina," answered Jonas, deciding not to give any more information..

"Hmm, OK, Looks like both of you have a debut coming up then? Let's talk about you now Glenn. You should get use to that name as well as your friends. It might be your new name for a long time," stated Aeton. Well, not that many will have to get use to it," stated Jonas. I really don't know a lot of people.

"Well, I would rather have one good friend then a bunch I couldn't trust. I have plenty of those," responded Aeton.

In the following hour the two discussed business, ate their breakfasts and consummated what they could. Jonas still had to take some papers that Conroy had already notarized to an attorney for review. That is whenever he found one. He hadn't even done a gig yet and already needed a lawyer.

Aeton mentioned that he wanted to have Glenn's first performance at the Hollywood Bowl. A lot of famous people had performed there as it was a really popular place. Aeton told Jonas he was booked in with a very popular group and that he would be like a side performance.

"I want you to find all the flicks you can find on Sinatra singing. Study him, how he moves when he sings, how he talks and what he says in between songs. You will never be perfect but it's always the illusion that is important when you are impersonating someone," he told the kid.

After finishing breakfast Conroy drove Jonas back to his office. As they were about to walk their separate ways Aeton had a few more things he wanted to tell Jonas.

"Plan to be singing by next Friday. Probably Saturday too," remarked Conroy.

"Glad to see you need a haircut. Leave it that way. We will take care of that. A quick butcher job somewhere could finish you. You'll be hearing from me," he said as he turned and walked away.

Life was getting busier now by the day for Jonas, alias Glenn Miles, copycat Sinatra singer. While driving down the road a lot was going through Jonas's mind. For one thing in the morning Jonas had to pick up Kay on the way to the Orphans Home. He was also somewhat in a bit of a surprise about Gina. He knew she was taking some acting classes and such, but wow, scheduled for a movie now and all this happened so quickly. He would love to know that story.

The next morning when Jonas got to Kay's house he was able to park right out front curbside. He really had made few walks up to her front door and he made them each time a little nervously. He found her almost too beautiful to be around and he always noticed whenever they were in public, the guys took notice.

"How long could this last, not having serious competition?" he wondered.

As far as he knew there was no one else. Something seemed strange here. It simply couldn't last. Eventually someone else would come along and Jonas would have to roll up his sleeves. It was what life was all about; competing and fighting for what you wanted most.

He pushed the button for the door bell, but he never really thought it worked because he never heard it chime. He knocked on the door. Just as times before when she opened the door he was taken aback by her beauty, but he wasn't prepared for what he would find this day. The person who opened the door resembled Kay but the first thought that would go through anyone's mind standing there was that they were looking straight at Marilyn Monroe. She was wearing a yellow combo pants and top suit of a body hugging style that served to define her curves. Her long luxurious shoulder length auburn hair was gone and she now had a short bright blonde upswept full head of hair. It served to give her an impeccable Monroe look, but she was a woman named Kay Lincoln.

"Is that you Kay?" he asked. You are the same Gal I had dinner with the other night, right?" he asked.

"Well, remember you mentioned you had to change your name and I mentioned I was thinking about a change as well? I always wondered how I would look blonde. What do you think?" she asked.

"Did I mess up?" she queried with an almost childish voice.

"Have you not imagined who you look like?" responded Jonas.

"Not really, who do I look like," the question presented again. Jonas fantasized the blonde actress stood in the doorway.

"Oh, by the way you should try to remember to call me Glenn from now on. I don't know how long that this will last but I better not quit my day job yet," he said kidding.

"Okay, Glenn, let me grab my purse and we can get going."

A half later they had picked up the four youngsters, Connie, Matt, Wanda, and Fred. The reactions on the faces of the four when they first saw Kay was amusing. Matt and Wanda didn't seem to know who she was. Fred just sort of stared at her and Connie simply told her that she looked way different, but that she looked really good. Connie also said that she liked her old look just as much. After the initial shock and comments they were soon headed for the Ferndale area of Griffith Park. Once they arrived and found a spot they liked they unloaded the ice boxes, food, and chairs.

As they were setting things up for their picnic Jonas asked the kids about school. He seemed concerned about their progress and how they were doing. Kay told the children about Jonas's up and coming singing debut.

"You guys are supposed to call Jonas, Glenn. That's his new name."

"I don't care what anyone calls me. Jonas, Glenn, Mack, Buddy, it all pretty much gets my attention," he said with his hands on his hips looking at the adjacent picnic table with the food preparations on it.

Kay thoughtfully had prepared much of the food the previous evening. There was deviled eggs, baked chicken and tuna sandwiches and for sides, potato and macaroni salad, chips, dip, fruit, and apple pie.

"Wow Kay! You don't mess around. You brought some yummy looking stuff," remarked Jonas.

"Well thank you, I guess I did, didn't I?"

In no time it seemed they were all seated enjoying the food. It was a busy day at the park. The seventy six degree weather was just about perfect. Jonas noticed that once again all ages of men were giving Kay the eye. A few of them looked like they were just about to invite themselves to the show of exorbitant food selections.

As Glenn was eating his sandwich the youngest resident Connie had some questions for him. She liked to ask questions with words such as why, where, what and how?

"Glenn, are you going to be a movie star," she asked Jonas, with her piercing jewels of eyes.

Jonas grinned; she was already calling him Glenn.

"No Sweetie, I'm a singer, not an actor."

"But I bet you could be a star. I bet you could be anything in the world you wanted to be," remarked Jonas.

"You think so."

"I know so. You just have to try. If you don't try to get what you want in life then you will never get anything, will you?"

"I'll give you a little secret Connie. The earlier you know what you want to be in life the sooner success will arrive."

"When I was young, I knew what I was good at but I gave up what was important choosing the easy life of fun and games with my friends. I don't even know where they are today or what they became in life. I would be embarrassed to let them in on my life. Maybe I could have been a pro ball player, and now you know what I do for living? I mow lawns and cut hedges but I whistle and sing while I do it. I couldn't do that when the bosses were around when I worked in a factory designing car parts."

Jonas went on.

"Of course, when you know what you want to do it should be something that you would love doing."

The group spent the remainder of the afternoon enjoying the food and taking walks around the park. The kids threw the Frisbee and played hide and seek until the mid morning sun was no longer overhead. The days light now cast long reaching shadows that spread their dark fingers across the landscape. It was time to leave so they packed up their gear and left for the return drive home.

The bond between Jonas, Kay, and the children of the Orphans home was an evolving one. Some might call these children the unfortunate ones, but they had a roof over their heads, were fed and cared for, kept warm, and given proper schooling. They had Jonas and Kay for chaperones as well as for friends. In time, perhaps they would think of them as much more.

When they arrived back at the orphanage the kids fetched their belongings and Kay told them she would let them know when and if anything would be planned the coming weekend. Jonas continued to be stunned at Kay's new image. A man could feel a real ego boost, take up a sense of appreciation when in the company of such a female attraction.

As Jonas had been waiting in the lobby for what seemed like too long of a time for Kay, he heard some laughing which he recognized as Kay's voice. When he looked down the Hall he saw a neatly dressed man standing in the doorway of the hall engrossed in conversation with Kay. His name was Grover Samuelson and he smiled as he seemed to take a step back and give Kay a serious look over, as if examining her. He was a wealthy business investor and was one of the orphanages most faithful donors. He seemed quite immersed in her presence and was so soft spoken that Jonas could not really hear what either of them was saying. Periodically, they would both laugh out loud in perfect synchronization which was really stroking the jealous chords of Jonas's conscience. After more then fifteen minutes of this man's invasive interlude Jonas's patience was rapidly becoming exhausted. It was clear he was becoming quite angry at being ignored. Just about when he was going to walk in and interject himself upon the two, the man went back into the room and Kay came walking toward Jonas.

"Jonas, I mean Glenn," she said with a smile.

"I have a ride home with Grover. He is one of our donors and he has invited me to see some special paintings at a museum and we might go to dinner. It sounds like fun so I'm going to go. That way you won't have to take me home."

"Well taking you home has never been a bother but if that's what you want," he answered with a tone in his face.

"Some art things he wants to show you, like what?" queried Jonas making a face.

"Like, whatever, I'm not sure. I don't know," she replied.

"Okay, fine," he answered smartly.

"Jonas, you seem upset about something?" she queried with searching eyes.

"No me, upset? Nah, you and Grover there have a good time," he murmured as he walked toward his vehicle.

She stood there for a few seconds watching him walk away and then turned to walk back toward the home. She didn't think it was anything to get upset over. She quickly forgot about it, at least a lot faster than Jonas did.

SEVENTEEN

Take Me - I'm Yours

It was Thursday afternoon, five days had passed since Jonas had last seen or heard from Kay. He was removing a coat of wax from his 58 Chevy after thoroughly washing it. It bothered him that he walked away from the home the other day the way he did. He could have hidden his emotions better but he was upset. He couldn't fathom himself keeping someone waiting on him and he didn't think Kay would do such to him. Suddenly it occurred to him that he really didn't know all that much about her, like where she was employed, that is if she did work. The Orphanage was volunteer work. He had never brought up such personal matters with her. As a matter of fact he really didn't even know anything about her family, where she was from or how old she was, none of that?

Using steady hand pressure Jonas carefully removed the wax that covered the cars smooth black glossy paint. When he had finished the car took on a sheen like a black pearl. Then he retracted the black top which exposed the contrast of its vibrant red interior. After putting away all his cleaning and waxing equipment he locked up the house, jumped in the car and headed for the freeway which would take him to his mother's house. When he arrived, Ariane was sitting at the kitchen table looking at pictures and photo albums of the family and such. A couple of boxes were placed about on the floor and she was sorting items that had accumulated over the years in each of the boxes. Each box had the name of one of her children, Elizabeth on one and Jonas the other. There was a whole host of things there that was their father's belongings. The amount of articles were astronomical and she asked Jonas if he could help her with the sorting of his father's stuff. Of course, he replied but it could take days to go through. His plan was to come back another day with his bus.

He offered to take his mother to lunch. At first she wouldn't go but he talked her into going to a local soup and salad place. Once they took a seat in the restaurant he brought up the latest information concerning his life and that his new name was Glenn. The news seemed to perk her up and her mouth formed the slightest smile. The most he had seen since the day his father died. He told her about his debut Friday night at the Hollywood Bowl and that he was already nervous, wished he never heard of Anniston Conroy. His mother looked at him right in the eyes with the tears of a proud mother and said what a good mother would say.

"Nonsense, you go to that Bowl and you sing your heart out and you'll find everyone loves your singing, Jonas. You do it for your father. You do it that first time like a pro and then all the other times will be easy. The audience will love your singing Jonas. I've always known you have a good voice. Do something with it," said Ariane as she raised a spoonful of soup to her slowly aging face.

She rarely wore much makeup, certainly no mascara or eye liner, just some powder foundation, brow pencil and pale lipstick. She wasn't much for ear rings nor painted nails either. She had always been an attractive lady. She never really became so absorbed in the cornucopia of feminine entitlements that goes with the gender.

Jonas told his mother about the trips planned with the orphan kids and that he rarely even saw his own kids anymore. He went on to tell her that with his ex-wife Lynn being engaged she made it difficult to even see them. Most of his contact with them had been on the phone. They were always busy. Everyone was always too busy. That's the way society was now too busy for family but plenty of time for things and gadgets he told her.

"Yes, I know. Some things never whither and disappear like people do," she answered.

They finished their meal and Jonas took his mother home. He would be checking in on her more often now since his father was gone. Elizabeth had moved out, had a full time job and was now engaged. She worked as a salesperson in pharmaceuticals and was well paid. Now that Ariane was alone her world had dissipated from a family household of four to just herself in what seemed like a few years.

A few minutes after Jonas got home Aeton called. He told him he had been trying to get a hold of him for the last several hours. He told Jonas what hotel he was to check into and even knew his room number. He told Jonas he would be picked up by a limo to be taken to the event. He would have a PR person there, a hair stylist, and a rather small entourage of others to make sure things went smoothly for him. He told him to relax and that if he sang half as good as his live audition he would be fine. Jonas didn't tell anyone about his singing engagement except Kay and his mother. His mother wasn't the type to fight the traffic to see a show at the Hollywood bowl. He thought Kay might go, at least he told her about it.

That evening Jonas laid out everything he would need for his gig. A suitcase with all the suits and any other clothes he would need. And there were several other small bags with all imagined essentials from a compact medicine bag to men's toiletries and extra shoes. When he finished he went into the kitchen and took an ice cold mug out of the freezer and poured himself a beer out of a fresh quart bottle. He looked out the kitchen window. The sun was quickly setting over the few rows of roof tops that stood between himself and the surf of Santa Monica.

Jonas gazed in Marilyn's direction. He walked towards her to be close enough to see her face distinctly in the fading light. Her eyes were on him and her face was alive. Her face was the only thing that ever either looked alive or defunct. Nothing else of the caricatures form ever gave any slight hint of the living. "Well, Gal, this is it. I'm on tomorrow," he said.

"I hope those people like Sinatra because I intend to give him to them. How far can this go? I don't know, we'll see!"

"Hey, there is this acquaintance of mine that got her picture in the paper. Seems she is going to be in a movie. That should prove interesting. I might just want to go see that flick. If she should make it to the top I doubt if she would give me a second look," Jonas remarked, as he looked at the stars smooth face with her attentive lively eyes affixed on him.

"You must have been nervous at times under the film camera? A little different than live stage work though, isn't it? What makes people do it, you know, go through with it?" he asked.

Her lips seemed like they moved to answer him. This perception was rare and far more occasional then the norm. There was nothing vocal, no sound of course. Sometimes, it was like you were pretty sure you noticed her lips moving in some sort of fashion. With large captivating eyes and an alluring face of innocence came a comforting answer.

"Because no one else can do it better," was the understood response. Well, her lips seemed to flutter so fast or move so slow he couldn't be sure they moved at all. So it was just easier to not spend much time trying to rationalize the phenomenon.

Nothing about Jonas's relationship with the cardboard recreation of Marilyn Monroe was sexual, as if it could be. That said, the fact that it would be difficult or even impossible now for Jonas to remove her from the wall as if to throw her away had much to say about his feelings for it.

It, her, she, thing, how should one sanely refer to the strange phenomenon of things that occurred even if only in his imagination.

'It', was her, she was her, Marilyn Monroe in his home, at least some of the time. The usual things one would call it like one of those, 'stand up celebrity cardboard things', or a 'life sized gag prop,' or whatever you called them no longer seemed an appropriate reference to that which adorned his wall. In fact, to refer to her as such could be disrespectful or even hurtful, considering the place that she held in the conscious mind of her fateful friend. What about values? There seemed to be an exchange between the two of such attributes like trust, appreciation, consideration, and support.

If the thin cardboard rendition was indeed a phenomenon of sorts to Jonas then what if anything could the public conceive of it by witness to its presence. There would be those who simply would not bother to investigate it. There would be some who would want to investigate it or even make a scientific study of it. The scholars might label the topic something like, 'The Quantum Theories of Spiritual Displacement,' so how deep would they delve into the equation? If they chose to consider the truest sense of the physics of it then which laws of physics are utilized? Scientific notation could take months or years to work out but most probably would be a waste of time with such a questionable topic. Surely, it wouldn't be anything anyone would even bother with. The whole idea itself might be ridiculous which brings us back to the reason why that first group mentioned would not bother with it at all. To Jonas, it wasn't physics or about things that seemed impossible in the universe, but were things possible that could never be explained in the realm of science.

Finishing his beer Jonas stepped outside to take a short walk. He decided to walk over to Ocean Boulevard and back just to get out of the house for a few minutes. Once he got there he eventually made his way to the end of the pier and came back via Wilshire. When he got back home he made sure his cars were locked and then went inside. When he opened the door he heard voices and saw flickers of light upon the wall. His TV set was on. After a quick memory search he ascertained he did not turn on the TV. Again, conscious of the fact that it was a remote control TV the chances of someone else's control unit affecting his TV were possible, but not likely.

The Carol Burnet show was on. It was an extremely popular comedy show. Jonas thought things over. It was not unlike when such strange happenings occurred before, he didn't think it wise to challenge that which reeked with mystical connotations assuming her, Marilyn, was responsible. He wasn't going to make things difficult if they didn't have to be. He was not going to question little things that thus far seemed harmless if the TV set going on by itself was harmless.

"Well I like the Carol Burnett show. Chances are I was going to watch it anyway," Jonas said to himself.

He left the tuned in CBS station alone. Tim Conway had a special knack for being funny as did all the stars of the show. About three quarters of the way through the show Jonas got up to get a frozen dessert out of his freezer. The show was winding down and so was Jonas, the sugary desert spiked his blood glucose and made him drowsy. When the show was over Jonas used the remote to flip through the few available channels, not counting the UHF frequencies which he seldom used. The Big Valley western series had been terminated but they were showing reruns. It wasn't one of his favorite westerns but he favored it to the alternative programming so he tuned in to the ABC network show. It didn't really matter much though because he had a destiny and it didn't have anything to do with Sinatra. It did have everything to do with sleep as he passed out in just a short time after eating his snack.

Upon such a time later after the wall clocks hands had spun around Jonas awoke. Some of the open windows in the house had allowed in the faint scent of Jasmine that emanated from a bush on the side of his house. The back of Jonas's neck felt stiff and uncomfortable, probably due to the nearly vertical angle of the back of the big cushiony leather arm chair. He looked at the wall clock. It was after eleven. Johnny Carson was on TV which was fine but only his show is on NBC. Jonas remembered he had the station on ABC. At least he thought he did but he wasn't sure.

Jonas walked around a bit and then closed the windows. Then he noticed that some things were out of place, a couple issues of his LIFE magazine collection were out on his writing table. One was the August 7th, 1964 issue, and the other was the August 3rd, 1962 issue. On the cover of one was a picture of Marilyn and it was the two year anniversary after her death issue. The cover article title was, 'What Really Killed Marilyn?' Jonas was familiar with the author's words. It was a well written article. He liked the article in the 1962 issue better, titled, 'Marilyn Monroe Pours Her Heart Out'. That article of course was published just before she died. So why were the magazines out and who left the article open? Was there supposed to be something there for him to see? He had already read it before several times. Perhaps he would read it again someday soon but he wasn't going to think about anything at the moment but to go to bed.

"Tomorrow is another day," said Jonas as he turned off the TV and house lights saying 'Good Night Marilyn,' as he walked by her headed for his bedroom.

"I guess I will soon know everything she likes to watch," he said to himself as he headed to bed.

Jonas was up by six, finished breakfast and stretched his legs out with a morning bicycle ride. He then showered and was done by nine. Anniston Conroy wanted his new star Glenn Miles at the hotel by 11am, so Jonas began loading up his car with the needed bags and cases. He had dressed himself with casual light slacks and a dark sports shirt.

Jonas was nervous, he wondered about those virtuous few, whomever; that had that ego that seemed to be in some celebrities. They made it look so easy. Some seemed to be so infatuated with themselves they gave you the impression they lived on cloud nine. They couldn't wait to get on stage to perform because they were doing the world a favor. It must have made it so easy for them. But in front of such large crowds as found at the Hollywood bowl, that surely wasn't Jonas. Instead he was the sort that was too self-conscious and unpretentious. He realized how wise Conroy was to book him with the others. If he didn't show no one would even miss him. He could call in sick right now and that would be the end of the whole thing. It could only be the people who had guts that could make it in show biz. Of course they had to have the talent, too. Every time Jonas thought about the easy way out he remembered what Marilyn had seemed to say, "Because no one else can do it better!"

That was it, he was going. There is nothing that can be said about failure that is too bad if you at least try. Isn't that what he told little Connie? He needed to follow his own advice. Enough of this damned stage fright. When he goes on stage he will do the job he was hired to do, that's it. He will reach down inside himself and find his way to mimic the giant singing star, Sinatra.

At times, Jonas's way might have been fueled by desperation but only for the purpose of achieving a desired outcome. Jonas sat down at the kitchen table. He dialed Kay's phone number. He let it ring seven times but there was no answer. He hung up. He dialed Lynn's number. Perhaps one of his children would answer but no one picked up. He felt like he had to talk to someone. It never became so apparent as now that he really had no friends. Not like he did in high school. People you go out and do things with. He hadn't seen Trish Langley in several weeks or heard from her. He wanted to tell her about his singing engagement. He was looking for a little moral support from someone or anybody really. He dialed her number.

"People are never home when you really need to talk," he mused. No answer there either. He spent the next twenty minutes pacing around the house and then the phone rang. It was Elizabeth, his sister. She called to give him words of encouragement. She also had a short message to give to Jonas from his mother. The message was derived from a true story that she read in one of her husband's letters to her brother, Jonas's Uncle Leslie. The one that had passed away.

"Oh yeah, what's the message?" Jonas asked.

"Well it doesn't make any sense to me, it's just a name," she remarked.

"What Name is that?" he asked.

"Dume LaCross, if that means anything?" she said.

It had been many years since Jonas heard that name. Dume was that baseball pitcher he had hit a home run against the last game of the season in high school and won fifty bucks for his dad. Now that he thought about it, Dume must not have made it to the majors. He never heard his name mentioned again. Whatever, it didn't matter. There were countless High School sports heroes whose future was never meant to feel the grass or dirt of a professional stadium.

"Tell mom thanks, Liz. I better get going, its time," he said.

"Sure Jonas. I mean Mr. Glen Miles. Forget about the audience. They are just there to clap," she said.

Jonas thanked her as he hung up and tried to call Kay one more time, still no answer. This was no time to reason or imagine where she might be. It was time to leave. He had to get going.

Jonas decided to put the top down on his 58 Chevy. He didn't care if his hair got all messed up, he wanted some air. He wanted to be under the sun and feel that comfortable perfect weather that southern California was known for. He opened his car door, got in and shut it. He started the engine. He noticed in his side door rear view mirror that the post man was walking down the other side of the street. As Jonas was momentarily distracted he felt the car slightly move as the sound of the front passenger side door closed shut. He didn't even see it open but there was the sound and feel of the passenger side car door being shut. It sure seemed so, but for there was not anyone there, at least not that he could see.

Now Jonas was really beginning to wonder about his sanity. Maybe he wasn't getting enough sleep. He thinks his TV comes on by itself, changes channels at its own discretion and his car door apparently opens and shuts by itself. There's something else, Glenn Miles is going to sing Sinatra numbers at the Bowl for free because he just realized he never even discussed money with Conroy. What then does that say about Jonas's lawyer, the one recommended by Aeton, himself?

Jonas had heard about this one film star who had this attorney named Lou Castle, of 'Castle, Bench, and Rowden,' so Jonas chose them. Maybe not a good reason but he didn't know anything about all the hundreds of others in the yellow pages. He also remembered that Mr. Castle had mentioned he had eaten lunch several times with Anniston Conroy. Why should that be a bad thing, there was no evidence of anything wrong with Mr. Castle.

"Oh well, I'll deal with that later," he thought.

Screwed into the bottom of the dash was an 8 track stereo system similar to the one in his Bus. But he wasn't going to play a tape. He'd just turn on the AM radio. Jonas backed out of his driveway and then pointed his car toward Wilshire and then throttled forward. Jonas turned on the radio as he entered the heavy traffic of Wilshire. 'It's Only Make Believe,' by Conway Twitty bellowed out of the speakers. There was a layer of brown haze on the horizon.

So the car sped forward toward the Beverly Wilshire Hotel where Aeton's agency had him booked. Actually, it was better than he expected. I guess they weren't going to put an unknown first timer up in the Beverly Hills Hotel. Jonas made his way through the surface streets of the busy Los Angeles basin. At stop lights there seemed to be unusual compliments from drivers, especially truckers. One guy whistled and said,

"Hey, ain't she sweet," and from another,

"Mighty fine looker," and yet again at another intersection,

"Absolutely gorgeous."

Then one block from the Hotel another couple of guys in a furniture delivery truck came along side of Jonas and unbeknownst to him kept staring at his car. Their eyes were affixed to some aspect of Jonas's car that seemed to greatly interest them. Then the driver hollered out a ridiculous remark.

"Hey, is it true Blondes have more fun?"

Jonas couldn't imagine they were talking to him, but that seemed how it had been since he left the house. He wasn't even sure that he heard what he thought he heard.

"Who you talking to?" shouted Jonas.

"Well now, do you have blond hair," asked the Driver.

Jonas looked at the guy like whatever he had for his last meal must not have been food.

"What blond hair? What are you talking about?"

Jonas concluded the man's remark was not applicable to anything that made sense. Jonas was further evaluating the situation when the light turned green. The driver of the truck hit the throttle but was short on clutch as the gear ground in and made a loud annoying crunching sound.

"Moron!" mumbled Jonas as he passed the truck looking at the driver. His car certainly had its share of attention that day. To be sure it was a nice looking 58, but it was fifteen years old. Jonas thought most of the remarks on that short drive to the hotel came from a different class of guys then the kind he was use to with auto aficionados. Was there a blonde in his car? Someone he couldn't see but maybe others could? Jonas was really beginning to wonder. When Jonas arrived at the Hotel the valet parking service people took his car and delivered his luggage to his room. But before he got to the room he encountered a couple of people in the lobby holding cards with his name on it, 'Glenn Miles".

"I'm Glenn," said Jonas looking at two people who were standing close together.

The two who were assigned to assist Jonas looked at each other and then one spoke.

"Hello, Glenn, I'm Bert Callahan. I'm the guy who is going to help you be a smash with the audience this evening. Lorraine Schwartz here is the gal who is going to help you look almost as gorgeous as her," remarked Bert.

"Well, Flattery will get you everywhere," she said laughing.

Lorraine Schwartz was of average height for a woman at five feet six inches. At age forty-five her current weight of 128 pounds was a challenge to keep under control and her straight semi long dark brown hair perfectly framed her heart shaped face. She was dressed in a mid-length casual denim skirt and a green open necked ruffled blouse. White high heeled sandals adorned her feet. Jonas didn't have a clue what the provocative scent was that emanated from her. Other than having a full bridged nose she might have been a nine when she was younger, not that she looked bad now.

"Glenn, I'm going to give you some ideas and suggestions about how to cope with all this stuff you're probably not used to. You ever go to a big wedding or any event where you got to wear a tux and do this and do that and maybe there is a little nervousness?

"Yeah, I suppose I have," answered Jonas.

"Well, we're going to help you learn how to overcome the fear of audiences. Well, let's get out of here and up to your room," suggested Bert as the three headed out.

When they got to Jonas's room Bert wasted no time.

"OK, show me the clothes you brought for the event," asked Bert.

Jonas opened his suit case and showed him the really nice suits that Kay helped him pick out.

"Hey, these are really nice Glenn, but you know what?" asked Bert.

With an apprehensive and not too sophisticated reply came Jonas's quick response.

"What?" asked Jonas.

You know Dean Martin and Frank Sinatra can get away with wearing these suits all day long because they are already big shots. And even they wear tuxes a lot. I think we need to get you a tux. And there is a tux shop less than the distance of a Leon Wagner home run from here. Lorraine will take you there and she is going to be with you for the next several hours while I take care of other stuff. That is, unless you would rather have me take you to the Tux shop," asked Bert.

"Nah, I think Lorraine will be fine," laughed Jonas.

"Yeah, that's what I thought," responded Bert.

Bert Callahan was better than six feet tall with the usual trademarks of young southern California male residents; slim, tan, and muscle toned. His eyes were hazel and his thick sandy blonde hair was neatly trimmed, short on the sides with medium cropped full bodied wavy hair at the crown. In a way Bert reminded Jonas of John Kennedy without the accent.

Hours had passed. Jonas had been fitted with a tux and given a haircut by none other than his escort, Lorraine. Her superb hair cutting talents and polishing skills rendered Jonas a very handsome and suave image. Bert informed Jonas about the orchestra that would be playing for him. They were the same people who had backed up Sinatra, Como, Martin, and others at the Hollywood Bowl. All he had to do was sing. He told Jonas about the special blackout lights he could request to have turned on if he didn't want to see the audience while he sang. He tried to reinforce the need for Jonas to stay calm and relaxed. He gave Jonas a card with little one liner jokes on them. He told Jonas to treat the audience like they were guests in his living room and that everything would be fine. He told him if he blew something it was better to make a joke of it then standing there in a panic.

"Laugh it off and take up where you left off. But you are not going to have a problem. Everything will be fine," Bert reminded him.

The day went by fast, like a hot air balloon in a stiff breeze and it was already time for the short Limo ride to the Bowl. Bert wanted Jonas there by seven.

"It's time for the world to meet Glenn Miles," Bert said to Jonas.

Normally, agencies like to get their copy of the program schedule weeks in advance but Bert had only just received his copy a day prior, so he didn't have much time to review it with Jonas. The only thing Jonas knew was that he was supposed to sing seven numbers. He didn't even know which ones he was supposed to sing yet. That night, the Box Office draw was 'The Carpenters'.

EIGHTEEN

Let's Go Kid

Upon arriving at the Bowl Jonas met Conroy. Aeton often attended the performances of his new clients. It was just good sense business practice. If his clients grew out of favor with the public he had no choice but to drop them. He had an image that he had to maintain. Tonight, especially since it was Jonas's first gig he wanted to help him get relaxed. He also wanted to apologize for not getting the night's song line up to him quicker.

"This is not the usual way I run my agency Glenn, but it happens sometimes that I'm at the mercy of the event organizers. OK, you got about two hours to get comfortable with this song line up."

"Two hours? Wow, Yeah okay," responded Jonas.

"That's the spirit. I knew I was going to like you my boy!" exclaimed Aeton putting his hand on Jonas's shoulder.

"You know, if you get into trouble remembering things your mind just needs a few seconds to catch up. A little improvising will get you through that, a joke, a comment, whatever. You know what I mean," remarked Aeton as he handed Jonas the song list while padding him on the back again.

Then Aeton walked off in another direction, he wanted to talk to Mike Larson who was the moderator at the bowl.

Jonas looked at the list of songs, 'The Way You Look Tonight,', 'My Funny Valentine,' 'Fly Me to the Moon,' 'The Good Life,' 'Moonlight Serenade,' 'Put Your Dreams Away,' and Young at Heart.' Most people didn't know that Sinatra had recorded more than eight hundred songs by that time. Here were seven of his best. So Jonas spent the next couple of hours going over the songs and then he thought it a good idea to memorize at least a few of the jokes that Bert gave him. In the meantime other side show performers preceded the Carpenters. The Carpenters would of course be the main draw, the finale. Depending on how much of the crowd remained after their show would determine how many people Glen Miles would have the pleasure of to hear his singing.

The Carpenters were always a huge draw. That night they "would resonate with the audience with songs like, 'We've Only Just Begun,' 'Close to You,' 'Ticket to Ride,' and others. After the Carpenters had finished their performance, Jonas was up. The moderator introduced him as an upcoming talented and gifted singer whom he promised they would hear a lot more of in the near future.

"Ladies and Gentlemen, I give you Glenn Miles," he said with a sweeping arm pointing off in the direction that Jonas would approach from. When Jonas walked out on the stage he simply psyched himself into believing that he was Frank Sinatra. That was the only way he could go through it, believing he was the real deal, the guy everyone paid their money to come and see. Jonas thought it best to take Bert's advice and talk to them like they were guests in his living room. It would make things easier. He simply bid them a good evening, introduced himself and told them that he was a regional native, born and raised locally and that he had some special songs to sing for them.

"Well I have some popular songs to sing for you tonight. I only hope I can sing half as well as the guy who usually sings them. Ah, so let me begin with my first song, 'The Way You Look Tonight.' I won't bother telling you what the rest of the song titles are, I'll just sing them. If you can't figure out what the other song titles are as I sing them, then I better not quit my day job." The remark was followed by a few laughs.

After that, there were a few seconds of silence and then the orchestra began the music for, 'The Way You Look Tonight.'

Sinatra songs usually consisted of a slow tempo. Lucky for Jonas, he didn't have to do a lot of fancy footwork or body movements. All he had to do was hold the mike with one hand and the cord with the other. Perhaps sway a bit, a few snaps with his fingers as he walked loosely around while singing. Jonas sang the song superbly and one could tell the audience loved it. He and the orchestra were in perfect synch. His voice was so close to Sinatra's that surely many imagined it was him.

While singing, Jonas noticed a very familiar face in the audience having blonde collar length hair. It sure looked like Kay on the far left as his eyes roved past the audience just behind the box seats. His mind was so occupied in its state of concentration he simply could not think about it as much as he wanted to. He had just started the song 'Moonlight Serenade,' and effortlessly sang it all the way through. When he sang, 'Fly Me to The Moon,' and 'The

Good Life,' they didn't stop clapping for what seemed like forever. The audience had responded to Glenn Miles with a very loud and noisy applause which put Jonas more at ease.

"Hmm, seems they really like me," he thought to himself.

He had learned to relax, walk around and move his arms like the authentic singer himself. And after that song the next song 'Put Your Dreams Away,' went just as great. Then he mentioned he had one more number to sing.

"My last song will be 'Young at Heart.' People should pay close attention to that song. It's because you're never too old to do anything you feel like doing. You're never too old to do anything that's possible, right?"

"Okay folks, so here it goes."

As in all theater's and various entertainment establishments there will always be people who want to beat the crowd out to the parking lot, so some were already leaving. Jonas was into this last number when his roving eyes caught the face of that beautiful blonde again. She looked like Marilyn Monroe, but it had to be Kay. Her new image seemed a near perfect reflection of the star. So Kay had come to watch Jonas after all he reasoned. It had to be Kay as this time his eyes locked onto her face and her face seemed to be filled with admiration for his performance.

Then, Glenn looked down closer into a seating territory that he hadn't before, apparently gaining the courage to really take in the faces in the crowd now. He was looking down into the box seats section where he saw mostly pleasing faces until he thought he saw something that bumped his blood pressure up about fifty points. He would have to look one more time so there wouldn't be any mistake. While looking again during the song he saw something that nearly caused him to miss his vocal range. For there, right in front of him was Frank Sinatra and an overly large man on one side of him, and an older thinner guy on the other. Both were wearing shallow brimmed felt hats and gangster like coats. It was just like Jonas had jokingly described to Marilyn in his kitchen just days earlier, and to Aeton as well. He had humorously mentioned to Aeton about Sinatra and two Mafioso's coming for him. It was all a joke, at least it was supposed to be.

So there was Frank shaking his head from side to side in slow shallow movements just staring at Jonas with that straight mouth and thin lips. Glenn Miles managed to finish that last song still managing to hold onto some degree of composure.

"Of course, I should have expected this," thought Jonas, as the audience clapped and Jonas thanked them through the mike.

When the moderator came out Jonas handed him the mike, took a bow and walked briskly off the stage. He didn't have the nerve to look at the real Frank after that look he gave him. Also, Jonas never noticed that Frank and company had left a few minutes before Jonas finished his last song. Jonas was a good sized man normally not intimidated by much of anything but he was no match for heavyweight celebrities like Frank Sinatra with possible heat packing cronies. He would find Bert and Aeton and just get back to the hotel. But Bert and Aeton did not seem to be around anywhere. Did he really think Aeton would still be there?

"Where in the hell is Aeton?"

"What is with these guys, anyway? Two hours heads up on the song list and nothing to be found of Aeton's staff. How am I supposed to get back to the hotel?"

About all that was left hanging around was the stage crew. Now, quickly from behind Jonas came heavy and deliberate footstep's made by two serious looking men.

"Hey sonny, that was pretty good singing. I would like to shake your hand," came a somewhat stoical remark from a man bearing a reserved menacing look. Jonas recognized both as the two who had sat next to Sinatra. The gangster type character spoke up again.

"Wow, for a minute there, I mean, wow! You know who I thought you were for a minute. I thought you were Frank Sinatra, but then I shake my head. Wait a minute. This can't be Frank. I'm sitting right next to Frank. Yeah, that was very good Sonny."

As the man brought one of his hands out of his coat pocket to shake Jonas's hand he clumsily brought out a handkerchief that got caught up with a pair of brass knuckles. They hit the ground with a solid clang.

"Oh, those damn things are always falling out. I swear, I swear, I'm gonna throw them away. Besides who needs brass knuckles anyway when you got hands like mine," said the man with a grin. As Jonas and the large man firmly shook hands Sinatra's guy had hands like bear paws and slightly crushed Jonas's hand.

"Hey, it looks like you don't have a ride. What do yuh know? Everybody leave or something? It don't matta really cause Frankie would like to take you for a little ride," said the other man with a hint of sarcastic politeness and a devilish grin.

Jonas wasn't going anywhere with these two if he had anything to do about it.

"Oh, for a little ride, huh? So Frank Sinatra wants to take me for a ride in his car? Why would he want to do that?" asked Jonas.

"I don't know kid. Why don't you ask him? His car is right around the corner," said the hefty man whose name was Alfonse Bertelli. He pointed in a general direction looking more irritated and losing patience. He threw his used up cigarette on the ground and rubbed it out with his shoe.

Now following his move the other more aged persona wearing the appropriate hat and coat for sadistic film noir spoke up. His name was Doc Flaminio. It was said that he earned the name from back in the forties when he worked the east coast rackets. He was one of those guys who got his reputation performing gross malpractice surgery on losers outside the approval of the medical board. He favored his custom made folding ivory handled doctors knife that did quite a nifty throat job. They called him Doc because he was frequently seen carrying what looked like a doctors medical bag but no one ever seemed to know exactly what was inside. So it was unfortunate for that sad and sorry lot of victims that the doc had left his calling card back in years past. However, as of lately his most recent visits hadn't been as fatal to some of his assignees since moving to the west coast. The Doc never had much of a conscience, he just did a lot of gross dirty work for thick stacks of greenbacks.

"Don't keep him waiting kid," said Doc as something resembling a gun barrel was suddenly sticking out against the inside of the man's coat pocket pointing toward Jonas.

"Oh, so what's that poking out of your coat pocket now, a gun?" responded Jonas in a manner that concealed any fear he had.

"Oh, you think this is a gun? Nah, actually it's my dick kid. You see, I was born with all kinds of deformities with everything out of place. Truth is, you're giving me a hard on. I'm afraid if you don't get in the car real quick I'm just gonna do yuh right where you stand if you know what I mean. Yeah, in this little dark corner of the Hollywood bowl," the thug replied. Alfonse grinned.

"Geez, Doc. Don't waste him right here."

Jonas turned and looked around. There was no one close by on the stage, just people still leaving the event in the distance. Jonas surmised the situation. Running would be stupid. This whole thing must be some sort of misunderstanding. He would reason with the heavy weight star. They marched Jonas off into the darkness to the waiting limo of the huge mega star. Upon reaching the automobile Alfonse opened a rear door and there sat Frank with those blue eyes looking at Jonas, not smiling or even grinning, just burning a hole out the back of Jonas's head with a pair of indifferent blue eyes. Frank was wearing a felt Fedora hat. Jonas felt naked.

"Get in," said Frank's bodyguard Alfonse nudging Jonas inside. Jonas got in and then the cigarette smoking hippo got in next to him trapping Jonas like a boulder on a slug. The Doc got in the driver's seat of the black late model Cadillac and the car slowly rolled forward at first, and then sped up. The vehicle drove down through the darkened streets and neighborhoods of Hollywood in a southwesterly direction in complete silence except for the sound of the quiet engine and rolling tires.

"How many times have I seen this scene before?" thought Jonas.

It was the same scene he had seen in a hundred old B&W movies. Now it was Take 20, cameras roll, but this time for real, two hulks squeezing some gumshoe in the middle of a back seat. Only Sinatra wasn't a hulk and Jonas would seem to be the person of interest. It was then that a lot of things were rushing through his mind. Would he just disappear off the face of the earth? And what about his mother, or Kay and his landscape comrades, whomever, wouldn't they wonder what the hell happened to him. What about Marilyn? No, Marilyn would know what happened, she wasn't limited by mortal boundaries.

"Shit, am I really thinking about a section of cardboard when I'm on my way to get my brains blown out? That Aeton tells me all's cool with his dear friend, Frank."

Another breakfast at JON JON's would have most likely been good news for Jonas. He just had to have another breakfast with Aeton, contemplated Jonas.

What Jonas didn't know was that Aeton did know Sinatra and he had met up with him at the engagement that he attended. The same event as mentioned to Jonas by Aeton a few days previous. Just like many events that serve liquor as the night wears on, one thing leads to another. Things could transpire even if not necessarily as desired. So after several drinks Aeton was talking to Sinatra about his new guy Jonas. Jokingly, he told Frank about Jonas's vision of Sinatra putting the rub on him. They both got a laugh and Frank thought it was hilarious. He suddenly quit laughing when a sinister thought of sorts came to fruition in his mind. A thought that Frank could not pass up for Frank was a guy who was a practical joker. He told Aeton that he had a plan and that if he would go along with it he didn't care about Glenn Miles copycat performances.

"This kid has got to be good, though. If he ain't good you got no use for him. You can't book him and he wouldn't be good for me either if he is less than stellar," stated Frank.

Aeton at first wanted no part of it. He just didn't do that type of thing to his stars. Frank could be very persuasive though and Aeton gave in on the condition that his participation was simply no participation and that nobody got hurt. Sinatra agreed and a caper was planned, but it turned out it wouldn't quite go down the way as planned.

After several minutes of silence Jonas was about to say something when Frank broke the silence.

"So you trying to push me out kid," said Sinatra to Jonas.

Jonas was profusely perspiring. He turned slightly to look at the face that he had seen in so many movies, the face that sang on so many shows, and whose image now and then adorned the pages of newspapers.

"Hardly, Mister Sinatra, if people are trying to emulate you with their voices isn't that a compliment? Besides, there is no originality in what I'm doing," said the copycat hostage while conscious of the fact that many of the songs Sinatra sang were previously copyrighted material as well.

"Originality," blurted Sinatra.

"What does originality have to do with it," asked the older star.

"Well," said Jonas with a long pause.

"Well, what? What if you sing my songs better than me?" asked Frank.

"Maybe you got Vegas Billboard lights in your dreams. Glenn Miles in, Frank Sinatra out, is that it?" challenged the Icon.

"No sir, I'm just trying to make a living. Trying to see where things go, that's all I'm doing, Mr. Sinatra," said Jonas.

Frank didn't really like the idea of someone sounding like him using his material but he figured the whole thing with Jonas would just fizz out and go away on its own. He really felt the kid had earned himself some repercussions from the master even though Sinatra was somewhat impressed with his performance. The truth was after watching Jonas sing Frank had taken some interest in the kid.

"Well let me tell you something buster. You were pretty damn good, maybe too good. I was really impressed. Someone told me there was going to be this guy singing my stuff and I had to check it out. You know what I mean?" queried Sinatra.

"Yeah, I know what you mean, but the truth is I just like your style, and I like singing your songs," responded Jonas.

"Yeah, I know you like singing my songs. That's why you're in my car, sonny?" queried Frank.

"Where are we going?" asked Jonas.

"Well, where would you might imagine we are going?" asked Frank.

Suddenly, the car came out onto a busy street. There were lots of cars, street lights, and stop lights.

"Is anyone hungry?" asked Frank.

Normally, Jonas would have been very hungry as he hadn't eaten for hours but the intensity of his emotions must have obliterated his hunger sensations. However, the more Jonas thought about the question he concluded that, 'yes,' was the right answer.

"Well, I could eat something, boss," responded Alfonse.

"Really, no kidding, you got an appetite?" replied Frank sarcastically.

"I'm kinda hungry," blurted Jonas.

Frank gave Jonas a blank stare.

"Really? You're kinda hungry? Well, so happens I always fatten up my copycat impersonators before I deliver them to their destination?" grinned Frank.

"Well, let's get ourselves something to eat before we deliver the kid here to his destination," said Frank, as the two Mafioso characters let out husky laughs which only confused Jonas more. So were they trying to insinuate it was going to be his last meal?

Jonas never thought he would be sitting in the back seat of a car with Frank Sinatra, especially considering he impersonated the star. His life as of lately had been like a nonstop roller coaster ride.

"Where do you want to eat, Boss?" asked Doc.

"It's kind of late. Anyone ever hit that big prime rib place?" asked Frank.

"You mean the place called ANJUSHAUS," boss?" asked the Doc.

"Yeah, that's it," said Frank.

Frank was thinking to himself. He would be expecting the usual treatment. We'll all go in and they will probably want to take my picture and put it on the wall. They'll ask for autographs, I'll be nice and they'll probably give us a big break on the meals. It had happened many times before.

"Sure Boss, it probably ain't half bad anyway. It's in a nice area, so? Well you know," remarked the Driver.

"I could eat anything right now, Boss," said Alfonse again, his mass still squeezing in on Jonas.

In no time they found a parking spot right on Sunset Drive. The 'ANJUSHAUS,' dinning establishment specialized in prime rib, but also served most other cuts of meats as well as some seafood items. They all went in with a juicy prime rib on their minds. They offered three cuts, The Rancher, The Captain, and The Empire. When they were looking at the menu Frank offered to take care of the tab. Alfonse ordered the Empire cut. When he did, Frank gave him a quick sharp look. Everyone else ordered 'The Captain', not wanting to be a rich with Frank's money. Frank also ordered a lobster tail to go with his.

"Anyone want to order a tail?" asked Frank. Everyone declined even though they probably would've liked one. When the dinners were ready a male waiter brought everything over on a cart with sides like baked potatoes, salad, beans, and rolls. Everyone was sure to get their fill and the food was good. It was Frank's luck that there were a couple of sports news reporters there eating after a local ball game. He was hoping to escape the reporters this night. They were trained to have roving eyes and they always carried their press cameras with them everywhere they went.

Jonas's concern about being put through the ringer or even getting roughed up a bit was beginning to look a lot less likely, he mused. Surely such a famous person as Frank Sinatra wasn't going to fatten someone up and then throw them down a well shaft, or something. Everything pretty much went as Frank said it would. The establishment and customers asked for autographs and took pictures. Frank couldn't do a very good job of evading the patrons even in the dim light. Frank's silhouette and voice were a giveaway. They said they were going to put his picture up next to the other stars they had on the wall.

Anyway, Frank did everything he could for all the people who asked him for an autograph. He was very nice to the waiters and even managed to accommodate all the patrons who wanted an autograph. He finally had to tell the waiters to keep the people away so he could eat his dinner. When they were done eating Frank let the waiter know. Soon the waiter returned somewhat nervously with check in hand.

"Mr. Sinatra sir, this is the first time you have come here, yes?" asked the waiter.

"Yes, it is my first time," replied the star.

"Well I just wanted you to know if this was my place this check would be a little different," stated the waiter as he put the check in a folder and laid it on the table in front of Alfonse before walking away.

The remark left Frank with a quizzical expression as he looked at Jonas.

"Okay, I guess the waiter pretty much spelled it out," remarked Frank as he looked at the Doc. Frank asked Alfonse to take a look at the check.

"What's the bottom line?" asked Frank. It was not really a big deal but Frank really went the whole ten yards tonight.

"It looks like $80.99, Boss, with the drinks," answered the big man.

The usual charge for a good dinner at a nice restaurant with a couple of drinks for one person should average about twelve bucks for the meal.

"Hey Boss, I intended to pay for mine, you don't..," the heavy weight gangster was cut off in mid sentence by Frank.

"Don't be ridiculous, I'm paying for this," as he took the ticket from Alfonse and looked at it. It was the same look he had when Jonas first got in Franks car but there was no mistaking his expression. There were enough times that Frank's popularity didn't earn him a free ride but he had never went so far out to please people as he did this night. He looked so mad that Jonas thought maybe he should start worrying again because he looked like he wanted to kill someone at the moment.

"Everything okay, Boss? I never figured you to pay for ours," asserted Doc.

"Don't be ridiculous," changing his expression to that cool look he was known for.

"Let's get the hell outta here," he said, while getting up. He left a fair tip for the waiter. When he was at the register he pulled out an American Express credit card. Some stars didn't like to write checks because some businesses wouldn't cash them electing to keep the signature on the check as an autograph. The result was that celebrities could have hell keeping their books properly balanced. The up side was that they always had more money in the bank than they thought.

"Wow, What a place. Are you the owner?" Frank asked the person completing the transaction. He was a man with graying hair who appeared to be in his early fifties.

"I guess you could say that. At least I'm one of them. It's a family owned business," said the man.

While the man was writing on the charge slip Frank looked at what was supposed to be the establishment's celebrity photo board. "Wow, is this your celebrity photo board?" asked Frank.

"Yeah, it sure is," replied the owner.

It only had three photos on the board. One was of Jack Benny, another was Milton Supman, and then there was a photo of John F Kennedy sitting at a table back when the establishment first opened. Frank did not any longer have any great love for Kennedy.

"I thought you guys have been here for quite awhile?" said Frank.

"Since 1959," said the man.

"In fourteen years you only have had three celebrity photos taken," he queried.

Oh no, the big one we had was stolen when our place was broken into last year. We had quite a few, ah, about ninety three photos of celebrities.

"How could you have a Kennedy then? He's been gone for over ten years!"

"The wife had some extra Kennedy autographed photos," the man replied, smiling as he pushed the slip over to Frank for him to sign.

"Oh I see, Hey mind if I see those Polaroid's again you took of us. I had a little bet with the guys here about something," stated Frank.

Other customers were now backing up behind Frank wanting to pay and possibly also hoping for an autograph.

"Does it really help when celebrities eat at your place? I mean does it really help that much, the publicity and all that?" Frank asked, practically whispering.

"Oh yes, I think it helps a lot, especially now that you have dined here it sure can't hurt," answered the man smiling as he handed Frank the three snapshots.

"You know these are really horrible photos. Look at the Doc. Do you like this photo of you, Doc?" he asked the Killer.

"As a matter of fact I don't approve of the photo," responded the mobster. Following that statement Frank started tearing up the photos in little pieces and then put them in his pocket.

"Anyhow, hope everyone got all the autographs they wanted.

"Excuse us folks. I just wanted to tell my friend here something in private. He will be right back," said Sinatra as he walked the graying owner over by the front door.

"I think I went all out for you guys. Lots of autographs, photos, I was generous to your waiter, friendly to your patrons, employees. Now what kind of generosity did I get from you for all that good will? Just a big tall glass of ice water, right?" said the big star softly speaking while looking around.

The man just looked at Frank with a confused expression.

"I'll tell you what I got in return," said Frank smiling as he turned around to make sure no one could over hear his words. "Okay, what was I saying? Oh yeah, and I wanted to tell you what I got from you for all my opulent generosity. Not a God Damned thing! Not even a drink on the house, you cheap..., ah forget it," the star spoke in a low tone in the man's ear so the reporters wouldn't hear him. Then he and his entourage were quickly gone. It wasn't his kind of place, anyway.

Once they were all in the car, Doc spoke up.

"Where to, boss?"

Though the whole kidnap thing was an act regarding Jonas as far as Frank was concerned, Frank considered the arranged gag long over. The two coats were actually Mob members loaned for the night to Frank by an old but not so favorite associate he once had an arrangement with.

"Okay, look, don't call me Boss anymore," said Frank.

"This game was over when we went in to eat dinner. Now we are just going to take Glenn home. That's your name, right? 'Glenn'," asked Frank.

"My real name is Jonathan Miles. Jonas is what everyone calls me."

"Jonas?" said Frank with an apathetic expression.

"Yeah, Glenn Miles is my stage name."

"Okay, Glenn. If I were you I would shuck Jonas. At least if you intend to be somebody around this town. Stick with your new name kid. Now, where do you want us to drop you off?" asked Frank.

"The Beverly Wilshire would be great."

"Okay, you got it, kid. Did you hear that? The Beverly Wilshire," Frank said to the driver.

"I heard it Boss, I mean Mr. Sinatra," he responded.

As the car headed for Wilshire Boulevard Jonas reached into his shirt pocket and brought out the only thing he had that could be written on. Realizing now his life was never in danger and that Frank wasn't really upset with him, he wanted to get the stars autograph. After all, it seemed like everyone got an autograph in the restaurant but Jonas and he was riding around in the stars car.

"Mr. Sinatra, could I get your autograph?" he asked.

"I'm afraid this is all I have for you to write on," he said as he handed it to him.

Frank looked at it and saw it had a bunch of type written words on it.

"Doc, can you get me one of those stock photo pictures out of my glove box?" he said to the driver. Then Frank looked at Alfonse sitting next to Jonas.

"I guess you can get back in the front seat at the Hotel," he said, looking at Alfonse.

"Yeah, I was thinking that, Boss, I mean Mr. Sinatra," the large man said looking straight ahead. As Doc was reaching for a photo Frank was reading the card which had the jokes that Bert had given to Jonas. There were four really good short jokes on the card and after Frank read the first one he started laughing.

"Hey, listen to this, guys. What do you think of this one," he said as he read the first joke and everyone laughed. Then he read all the rest of them and everyone was laughing all the way to the hotel. Frank said he never heard those jokes before and asked Jonas where he got them. Then he asked Jonas if he ever used them. Jonas told him he hadn't. Frank asked if he minded if he kept them. Jonas told him that wasn't a problem with him but he had no idea where Bert got them.

When the car pulled up to the Wilshire Frank took out one of his photos. Then he took out his fine point Sharpie and wrote something in the corner of it. When he finished he put it back in the envelope and handed it to Jonas. The valet service opened the door and let Alfonse and Jonas out.

"Well you don't have a problem with it then Mr. Sinatra," asked Jonas as he got out of the car.

"A problem, no, I don't have a problem. Just don't sing my new stuff. Leave my new releases alone. And Glenn, call me Frank! You can call me Frank anytime. Stick to that new name kid, 'Glenn Miles'," said the star.

As the valet was shutting the door Jonas yelled out one last thing before the big black caddie drove off with Frank Sinatra and two guys who didn't really seem half bad.

"Thanks for that dinner," yelled Jonas as the door closed and the tires slightly screeched as he watched the fading taillights disappear down the practically deserted boulevard.

It was after one in the morning. When Jonas entered his hotel room he was exhausted. He just wanted to go to bed. The only thing he wanted to do before he turned out the light was to read what Mr. Sinatra wrote. He took the card out of the envelope. It read,

"Hey, Jonas my Pal, if it's alright for me to call you Glenn, then you can call me Frank. Hope all the Stars will come out for you my man," signed, Frank Sinatra.

Jonas would place that autographed photo in a Plexiglas protective case on the same shelf where his signed Marilyn photo was. The next morning in a local highlights section of the Los Angeles Times there was a photo of Frank at ANJUSHAUS Restaurant, with Jonas sitting right next to him. Those two sports news guys probably got a pat on their backs for the photo. Frank might have a little explaining to do sitting next to a known ex Mob hit man named Doc Flaminio. As for Jonas, that photo was a shot in the arm for him as a singer however long or short it would be. Three months later Jonas watched Frank perform on TV and in between songs he had some very funny jokes to tell.

NINETEEN

Alone Again Naturally

The day following Jonas's Hollywood Bowl debut and the surprise kidnapping caper Jonas's sister called. She wanted to let Jonas know that she drove their mom to watch the concert. They sat in the back because they didn't want him to know they were there.

"You were great! Jonas. We took some home movies and we also taped your songs," his sister stated.

"You made mom so happy that whole night. It was good to see her that way. She hasn't laughed or looked happy since dad died, you know," she said.

"I'm glad she liked it and thanks for shooting it on film," responded Jonas.

"Well I thought it would be something good to look back upon in your old age."

"Maybe it will at that," he replied.

"Well, I just wanted to let you know we were there. I have to run. So, you did great and mom wants you to come over more often," said Elizabeth.

"Yeah, I should try. I get pretty busy with things I suppose."

"Well, I'm glad you took mom to the event Liz. I mean, since it turned out okay."

"Stick with it brother. Who knows? Maybe you'll wind up a big star."

"Hmm, I'm not holding my breath."

"Okay, Bye Jonas, talk to you soon."

"Yes, thanks Liz, Appreciate the call," said Jonas as she hung up.

The phone call from his sister was about all that happened on Saturday except that Aeton also called. He wanted to let Jonas know he performed great and that Frank called him.

"Yeah, the kid is okay," were Franks words.

Aeton informed Jonas to expect more bookings at various events. During that day Jonas only went out once to take a walk. The rest of the day he just hung around the house, watched TV and slept. On Sunday morning he took his time about everything. He made a big breakfast and read the newspaper while listening to some classical music. When he had finished he decided he was not going to do what he had done the previous day which was to vegetate all day doing nothing. He looked over across the room where the kitchen and dining area overlapped. There were a lot of things keeping his mind busy. Marilyn seemed to be looking his way. Her face looked delicate, fresh, like a meadows carpet of dew laden droplets. Thereon, she had big eyes that wooed him. It was a new look, one he hadn't seen before. It was the look of one who felt comfortable with another, of one who considered you an equal but he hardly thought that. However, he had at least stood in the lime light of that thing regarded as a theater, a place of performing artists and got through it without any major embarrassment.

Gazing further around he noticed the neglected painter's canvases which he had the inclination and desire for, but lacked the time.

"Someday I will paint again but when, hmm, I just don't know."

Then there was the matter of the factory building with the show cars, the printing press machinery and the cash he inherited from his uncle. The cash had just been sitting in the bank collecting interest in a diversified portfolio of certificates.

Looking again across the slight distance of the small room where Marilyn stood against the wall, Jonas found that her lively spirited eyes were affixed on him and she was obviously paying attention. So Jonas felt she was open to conversation. At least if one did not mind doing all the talking. In that world of Marilyn's present existence, to go to whatever effort that it took for her to assimilate herself within a cardboard caricature would seem to suggest that she had some interest in Jonas. That idea was a thought that often perplexed him.

Of course there must be other Marilyn Monroe cardboard stand ups in at least some people's homes around the world. They've been selling them for years. What was their perception of that item that they acquired? Was it anything beyond just a fun thing for show or a conversational topic? Did their imprinted cardboard panels have anything to do with their TV sets changing channels, car doors opening and closing? Did their cardboard standups have an attentive look? Did theirs have a smile, a frown, look happy, sad, aloof, or bored?

All possessors of celebrity cardboard cutouts by any measure of sane thinking, would, should, just see some plain and fancy cold lifeless look into oblivion; that look that sees right past you and not at you. But now, the face upon the wall was offering her personal attention and it seemed she had been around a lot lately for whatever reason and Jonas was glad. She wasn't always there with him. He knew that. He wouldn't expect it nor want it so. He knew she had to be at other places for whatever reasons. It was like she had a part time day job somewhere, but in the evenings she seemed to be around, perhaps to watch TV, he wasn't sure. He didn't really know her personally, how could he? He could only guess, but she knew him. Did they have some sort of agreeable interests? Maybe she liked to watch movies?

"Nah, it couldn't be that, could it? That's not what life after death is about, right. To come back to watch television? I would hardly think so."

Jonas went out of his way to watch some movies that he might not had been crazy about just for her benefit. After all, he just couldn't watch everything he liked. It wasn't easy with only a few network channels to search through. In the back of his mind something had to change. How long could he go on thinking, practicing such madness?

"For God's sake it's just a piece of cardboard", he had said a few times before but never would repeat it again. One time he said it out loud. That time he did he could see the mood change in her face from one of friendly happiness to one of being hurt. In fact, Jonas learned not to speak of anything that was other than complimentary about Marilyn or else risked being shunned and ignored for days. She could be anywhere. He couldn't write anything to others or even speak of her in a low tone without risk of being overheard. He never knew where she was, exactly.

Jonas went over and sat on the armchair of his small sofa facing Marilyn. When he talked to her he would look at her closely and then look away, and then look at her and then look away while continuing to talk. He realized that if he just kept staring at her she realized that you were just pressing her, hoping for some memorable interaction that you were never going to get. She was not about to allow a mortal to formulate definitive conclusions about the reality of her presence at any particular time and place. That is to say, she would never provide clear evidence of her undeniable presence for any mortal's recall. Those recognizable gestures that are given gratuitously by her, that occur within fractions of a second are only meant to hold her bond's fascination and such things are most aptly and easily dismissed as a figment of one's imagination.

As Jonas sat he looked at her face. He began talking to her about things and then was reminiscing about his teen years. He spoke of his high school days and was telling her about how he thought he could have done great things in sports, especially baseball.

"You know Marilyn, I can be really stupid sometimes. Why didn't I listen to my dad? You knew what the secret to success was, didn't you? Its passion, isn't it? If only I had one ounce of passion when I needed it back in High School, it would have been different. If I was playing ball today it would be a whole new, well, it would be a lot different. At least I would have found out if I had what it took. Now I will never find out. I'm already in my thirties," he said searching her face for a sign that she was listening.

There were things that went on that were probably allowed in Marilyn's existence of the higher worlds that gave her the freedom to wink, blink an eye, move her lips or at least let one think such occurred, even if they couldn't be sure. So whatever it was she did it was enough to let Jonas know she understood.

"I am going to go over to Kay Lincoln's home and see her about things. I haven't talked to her in a while. I haven't heard anything from her about the coming weekend schedules for the orphan kids. I hope she isn't upset with me. I'm sure I saw her at the concert."

"I'll see you later," he said to Marilyn while getting up to leave.

"That is, unless you want to come along? I don't go anywhere really where you wouldn't be welcome," He paused, catching himself.

"Second thought, you might want to sit this one out. I'm not sure what's going to happen," he said looking at Marilyn before leaving.

Marilyn Monroe was not someone nailed against a wall as if some immovable object. The fact was even though she spent a considerable amount of time with Jonas she continued to circulate herself around the world. All those of the higher worlds were busy people. So if Marilyn knew what was going on to a broad extent in that higher world that she was of, then she certainly knew what was going on in this lower mortal world that she came from. She was coming along to make sure Jonas would be okay.

As Jonas's car pulled out of the drive way it was then he got the thought that he should have just called Kay before he left but now he was already like some part of a hunk of metal in motion. It was too much effort to turn back. "It wasn't far to the lass's place," he thought. He was excited. He had news to tell her.

When Jonas arrived at Kay's he knocked on her door. He heard some music playing. It was 'American Pie,' by Don McLean. It was one of the longest songs that ever played. If you didn't slumber you could begin an oil change on your car when the song started and it would still be playing when you were finishing.

Kay opened the door with an initial look of excitement that quickly turned to a surprised look.

"Oh, hi Jonas, how's it going?" she said as she stood there partly blocking the opening in the doorway.

"Well it's going pretty good actually."

"That's nice," was all she said.

"Well are you going to leave me standing out here?" he remarked with a noticeable expression.

"Well, okay, come in, but just for a minute. I'm kind of expecting someone," she replied, leading him in just a short ways past the small entrance hall.

Kay looked like a million dollars. What a change she made to herself with that blond coiffure. She was wearing some fancy dress, heels and emanating some delightful scent. Jonas knew that she was a pretty solid specimen of a kind of man magnet.

"What's new?" asked Kay.

"Well, I guess I can't tell you anything about my Bowl performance, I saw you there," remarked Jonas.

"Saw me where?" she asked with a surprised look.

"At the bowl, Friday night, I'm sure I saw you there toward the front, behind the box seats?" stated Jonas.

"No Jonas, I wasn't there. Not at the Bowl."

"Are you sure? It sure looked like you," he responded.

"No, I was out with someone Friday night."

That statement hit Jonas like a quick tossed drink in the face. He knew the two hadn't been in the sack yet, but he had barely met her only weeks ago. He figured it was just a matter of time. He had his plate full with so many things, there was Aeton, the inheritance, his landscaping job, his dads death, not to mention other things. They really hadn't been out that much yet. So what did she expect. Why all the bother, and the orphans? he wondered.

Just then, there was a knock on the door. Somebody must have practically been at his footsteps or running behind him. Kay was thinking it was the worst time to have Jonas there. Jonas had his suspicions and bets already laid out on the table. He figured he had a good guess whose presence would soon fill the hallway.

"Oh, hi Grover, won't you come in? Jonas is here. Jonas was the person I was telling you about that I went to Griffith Park with that day you and I went to the art museum. He just stopped over to tell me about the singing engagement he had, ah, was it Friday night, Jonas?" she asked, while turning her head looking at him with a casual indifferent look.

Now the quick tossed drink in the face had been replaced with a sharp stab. Just when you think you have some kind of solid relationship taking shape with someone you really care about, you discover that apparently you couldn't have been more wrong. You discover that once again that the person that you met that you thought was going to be the one, wasn't. Perhaps she was testing him. It didn't matter. He really didn't care anymore. Besides if it was a game, he didn't play those kinds of games.

"Jonas was just leaving. So glad that things are going great Jonas," was all that she said as she opened the door for him to leave. Grover extended his arm for a handshake. Jonas reciprocated.

Some women may at times humorously refer to themselves as felines, and as upon the savanna there may be many lionesses in a pride, but who knows how few may be kind or gentle, even to their own. In this case the lioness was human and her words may as well have been claws or fangs. It took little effort on her part but after she had finished Jonas's wounds ran deep and he did his best to bind them. Jonas was bigger and stronger then times before but once again he had allowed himself to be overtaken, to be devoured by one he trusted. So now he best scurry off, lest she finish him.

"Yes, it was this last Friday," Jonas said, looking at Kay. "Have a nice evening."

"Mr. Samuelson, Kay has made mention of your generous acts of contributions to the Orphans home. How wonderful of you. Nice to meet you. Maybe I'll see you around," said Jonas, as he walked off leaving the two looking a bit bewildered.

Kay then momentarily closed the door before reopening it. Apparently they both decided that they were leaving as well. Jonas got into his old 58 Chevy, started it up and did a few low revs as the healthy engine seemed to make the ground resonate. Almost as quickly, Grover was leading Kay toward his new Bentley. Grover was looking in the direction of Jonas's car than he watched in amazement as Jonas's passenger side front door mysteriously opened and then slammed shut, but no one was there. Kay had been looking in her purse and didn't see what happened.

"Did you see that?" Grover exclaimed.

"See what?" she asked.

He, realizing she hadn't witnessed the incident decided he better not repeat what he saw.

"Oh, never mind. It wasn't anything," he said, still looking at Jonas's car with an incredulous gaze.

Jonas appeared to see it happen but by this time he just resigned himself to accept as much as he could handle in his own world of surprises. He was not yet completely use to that world, the bizarre one that Marilyn lived in. As the passenger door closed Jonas put the car in 'D' for drive and hit the throttle.

"Hmm, Okay, this time I'm pretty sure I saw the passenger door open and close. She must have come," he thought, not feeling too surprised as he seemed to be getting use to some degree of the bizarre.

As Jonas sped away a stunned Grover Samuelson was staring in Jonas's direction as he opened the door to his car for Kay.

"OK, I'll head over to 'Sam's and surprise Trish. Might even get a charge out of the look on her partner's face, what's his name? Oh yeah, Daryl, when he sees me walk in," Jonas thought, thinking to himself as the car rumbled down one of the streets of Santa Monica a few blocks from the ocean.

Still thinking, his thoughts were now elsewhere. He lifted his arm and moved it back and forth through the void of space next to him, but his arm encountered no resistance.

"Doesn't appear anyone is here," soliloquized Jonas.

Then Jonas got the idea maybe Marilyn was in the back seat so he leaned backwards to run his arms through that area of airspace. He felt ridiculous. While doing so he nearly lost control of the car.

"Watch where you are going!" uttered a woman's voice.

"What? What did you say?" he asked.

There was no response.

"Please, say something. I know I heard you. I know what you said. I'm not going crazy. I can't be going crazy," repeated Jonas as he looked at the empty space in the seat next to him and behind him, but there was nothing to be seen.

"If you are not going to say anything how can I talk to you?" queried Jonas.

There was no reply to his statements. He just kept driving through the busy traffic of downtown L.A., making his way toward Sam's Place. Only now it wasn't night and though Marilyn had allowed herself to be seen by the public on other days she had no intention of such today. Such rare and generous sightings would be extremely scarce to the public. That recent time Marilyn did so vividly allow herself to be seen by others as that shiny black Chevrolet convertible floated down the boulevard, was just merely a gist of a whim in her, an accolade for her friend.

"Maybe there were some pedestrians I didn't see? Was that who yelled out to watch where I was going? Maybe that's what happened," mused Jonas.

"Ah, just forget about it dude," said Jonas out loud.

"Yes, forget about it," echoed that woman's voice again, followed by a short quip of laughter.

This time it scared Jonas. He was sure he heard that voice. So, was he losing his mind or was he just one of those people who heard voices which was the same thing. On the other hand could the person he thinks is in his car actually be in his car? He went through the same rigmarole all over again.

"What did you say?"

"I know what you said."

"Why did you say that? Say something!" He kept repeating such, but nothing answered.

"Okay then, just forget it," he said to the one with the silent voice.

"Yes, forget it. That was what I said the first time," came the woman's voice again as Jonas pulled into the parking lot of, 'Sam's Place'.

After parking his car, Jonas just sat there saying nothing. He was not going to waste his breath. He was just going to roll with the punches and float down that creek of uncertainty with an open mind.

"Okay, so I hear voices. Lots of people hear voices. So what? So my car door opens and closes by itself, so what? So my TV changes channels by itself, so what? What of those other things I noticed like the smell of perfume, blond hair on my couch pillows, noises in the house, so what, so what, so what," iterated Jonas out loud.

This time a woman's high pitched abrupt laugh...., then silence.

Okay, I'm going into this joint. I don't know how long I will be," so Jonas let himself out and closed the door.

"I do open the door for ladies but obviously no one is here but me," he said as he walked away.

Once Jonas was inside 'Sam's', Jake saw him and extended a friendly greeting while Jonas pulled out a bar stool and sat down.

"Hey Jonas, how are you?" he asked.

"Well Jake, I thought I was doing okay."

"What's wrong?"

"Oh nothing I guess, just crazy stuff."

"Oh, you want to know about crazy stuff. Forget it. It's a crazy world," responded Jake.

"Somebody was in here and was talking about this guy he saw singing Sinatra stuff last Friday at the Bowl, was that you?" asked Jake.

"Probably," responded Jonas.

"Well he said he thought this guy's name was Glenn Miller or something. I told him that Glenn Miller was pretty much dead," laughed Jake. Jonas also laughed in response.

"Yeah, I guess my name is pretty close to Millers."

"Hey, see', you're feeling better already fella," remarked Jake.

"Yeah, this guy said he went to a 'Carpenters', concert, but was glad he watched your gig. He said that from where he sat he pretty much thought he was watching Frank Sinatra. Anyhow, thought I would pass that along," said Jake.

"Well thank you, Jake. I need all the encouragement I can get. I actually met Sinatra that night but that's another story," said Jonas.

"No kidding? So you met him, really!"

"Hey, is Trish coming in tonight?" asked Jonas.

"Ah no, she quit almost a couple of weeks ago."

With that statement Jonas's plans were on par for the whole evening. He was batting a big fat Zero.

"You know, her partner the pianist pretty much loved her. I think she saw one too many guys for him. Poor guy, he couldn't take it anymore. They had a fight and he split. She went to New York with this other guy. I don't know if she is even coming back to town," said Jake.

"Wow, really," said Jonas as he stared into the mirror on the back wall looking at his face sticking above dozens of liquor bottles.

Jonas was really hoping to see her. There were two sides of the coin for Jonas. On one side everything was going great with the new line of work and on the other side his romantic life was going down the drain. He just wanted somebody to talk to, to cruise around with and hit the night spots. He wanted to feel alive. He wanted to talk to someone about his future, the bookings, and his love gone bad. He needed someone's shoulder to lean on. He wanted to hear someone say, 'Atta boy, you can do it,' and 'Keep plugging,' the next gal has got to be the right one.

After about an hour and a few beers Jonas left and got back in his car. He sat there for a couple of minutes. There was no passenger car doors opening and closing. It was about three in the afternoon when he left. He headed for the freeway. He drove to Long Beach and even though the freeway was noisy, it was like a slow motion silent film to Jonas. The only thing he heard were thoughts in his mind. He drove to the harbor, stopped at a pizzeria and bought a large slice of Cheese pizza and a beer. He was pretty sloshed, not even walking that good. He made it over to the ticket booth for the harbor cruises. He got on a boat and went up to the top deck. The breeze felt good, kind of a misty cool and he could smell the salty air. He was feeling a little better now. More people boarded. A whistle blew and the ship shoved off.

TWENTY

Christopher Sailing

It had been over a week since Kay had shown Jonas the door and he hadn't made any effort to contact her. Surprisingly, she phoned him on a Friday afternoon. She seemed to be in a mood of some gaiety when she spoke. She said she wanted to apologize to him about things. She also told Jonas that Grover persisted in asking her to marry him. She said that sadly she wouldn't be at the orphanage any longer because she feared it would be too difficult. It was Grover's suggestion that she work in one of his art galleries. She told Jonas that she never planned on getting serious with Grover, it just happened. She said she kept saying no to him and explaining why. She let Grover know that she wanted to finish college, not rush into something as serious as marriage at this time of her life. She told Jonas that she had somewhat of a problem with his age being nearly thirty years older. The determined Grover wouldn't take no for an answer, offered to pay her way through college, buy her new cars, clothes, the whole bit. It was when he promised her that she could leave anytime she wanted, that he'd agree to a divorce if such were the circumstances. That was when she made up her mind.

"I'm sorry Jonas. I do really think you are a super person. No doubt we could have been heading for something serious, but I just never expected this. I hope you and I will still be friends."

Jonas was thinking about when he was over at the orphanage. When he first saw Kay with this guy and also when he was last in her home. It kind of seemed obvious who was on the top of her list. Still upset as Jonas was over her recent behavior and her decisions he did not hate her, nor could he remain angry with her. Besides being beautiful there was something different about Kay that made men want to be around her. What would it accomplish by telling her off? One person cannot force another to love them or commit to them if it's not their choice. Love has to be by one's own choice.

"Friends, Kay? Yeah, if you still want to be my friend, I mean I guess we could be friends. Of course you will be married soon so it doesn't look like we will be spending any time together." Thinking, she didn't have time to answer before he spoke again.

"So, when's the big day?" he asked.

"We haven't set it in stone yet, but should be soon."

"I trust you have given all this at least some practical thought. If he seems like a nice guy, then, well? I hope you have made some effort to peer a little into his past. Nah, forget it, I'm sure he's fine," stated Jonas.

"Oh, there is one thing I would like to ask of you," thought Jonas.

"Yes, what's that?" she responded.

"I intend to keep seeing these kids out at the orphanage. I don't want them to feel like they have been abandoned again. It would be nice to keep the group together. I'm sure I can handle it. Can you see what you can do out there. You might have a word with somebody about it?"

His statement hit a chord with her and made her realize she was abandoning them. It was the last thing she wanted to do.

"Yes, of course."

"Don't worry Kay. I'm sure they will understand that you're getting married and that it changes things beyond your control. Maybe, my being there has something to do with it. I understand."

Kay's thoughts turned to Grover's concerns about Jonas. Grover wanted to eliminate Jonas from any participation at the orphanage, but Kay wouldn't allow it.

"I intend to talk to them about that. It's not like I won't ever be there again," responded Kay.

"So, Kay, can you let those people know my intentions over there, that I would like to keep all four of them together," remarked Jonas.

"Sure, I'll tell them Jonas. One chaperone having four children is a little unusual but I'm sure I can arrange it. I'll make sure Grover sees to it, if there should be a problem," she answered.

"Good, but I don't think it will be a bad thing. I think four is actually better than one. They'll have each other and me. I want it to be their family."

"I would also like to know more about each of their backgrounds. What were the circumstances that brought them there?"

"That sounds logical, Jonas. Yes of course. I will get that information for you. I have to say that I had no idea how important they were to you. It's wonderful of you. I always thought I would be there for a time to come, but life throws you a loop sometimes."

"I felt the same about you with the kids. Not sure I picture you sitting in a gallery," said Jonas.

"Yes, but I like art, and you know what I'm hoping is that I will be able to get a lot of school work done while I'm putting in my time there," she remarked.

"Yes, I suppose you might."

Jonas wouldn't believe that money was the big part of the equation with her, but then it usually always was with most people. In that case, many got over the age difference. He thought Grover would be like an anchor tied around her neck.

"Well, I got to go Jonas. I hope that whatever it is you want in life, well, I hope you find it," said Kay.

"You know, sometimes you think you found it but then you find out you haven't, then you just keep on or give up," he responded.

"I know you Jonas. I'm sure I will be seeing you around. Stay with Conroy as he'll take you places, I'm sure," remarked Kay.

"Goodbye Kay."

"Not goodbye Jonas, until next time. I will get those history details that you want sent off this week," stated Kay.

With that, they both hung up. A week later Jonas received all the historic details about the children, at least as much as was possible. Kay had sent him a wedding invitation but as she suspected he did not show up. His heart was slow in letting her go but she was right, she did see more of Jonas as 'Glenn Miles' in the months following her wedding. There were write ups in both newspaper and magazine articles and even occasional TV film clips on the local evening news. His singing engagements were meeting with much success. Entertainment critics were throwing heaps of outstanding publicity in Anniston Conroy's favor. Conroy's, 'Glenn Miles,' had become so popular that he hired a song writer to come up with original music so Glenn could have his own hits. As it turned out, in less than six months after his first performance at the Hollywood Bowl Jonas had cut his first single hit titled, 'Only You.' It was a remake of an older song titled, 'You're the One,' with a rearranged score. Aeton had already made plans for Jonas to do more recordings. Frank Sinatra wished the stars to come out for Jonas and it looked like that they were.

With all the things going on in Jonas's life he had of course quit the

Landscaping job. He had gained a friendship of sorts with Jose and Kim, but they certainly understood his decision to quit the crew. They said that he would be crazy not to quit. Stanley Guiles, the owner, the one that had offered Jonas the job nearly a year prior when they met at 'Pandoras', decided to throw a party at that same establishment. It would just be for the four guys. After a couple of hours Jonas had drunk more beer than he ordinarily drank in a week. That afternoon, Jonas shook the hands of three people that he called friends for what would probably be the last time. It was then that Jose and Kim had something else in mind. It seemed nearly an oddity that they never even brought it up before, but they were both involved in county league baseball teams. Kim played for the Glendale Tigers, and Jose played for the Culver City Pirates. As they were leaving the club Jose handed Jonas a card with contact information about enrolling in L.A. county baseball leagues. Jonas never discussed any sports with the two including his High School playing days so they may had never considered him interested.

"What's this," asked Jonas.

"Well, we didn't know if you would be interested. Kim and I play the county baseball leagues. We just thought we would tell you about the opportunity to have a little after work fun," grinned Jose.

"Wow, are you guys telling me I could have been playing ball with you all this time?" asked Jonas.

"Well, I guess none of us ever brought anything up about sports. Does that mean you would like to play?" asked Kim.

"Yes I would, it sounds like a lot of fun but I have Aeton making out my concert schedules so I can't say at the moment if I can make the meeting times. I'm also spending a lot of weekends with these orphan kids," said Jonas.

"Oh man! That's great, Jonas. You'll look back and be glad you did this. They will probably never forget you, you know. That is really more important than anything," responded Kim.

"Yeah, a year ago I would have never thought I would have found myself with the career I have now and helping orphan children. Something has sure changed my life. For now I'll just keep my fingers crossed that things will work out," replied Jonas.

When Jonas drove away he was thinking about what Kim had said about he and the orphans. He rarely saw his own kids anymore. They never called. Whenever he called Lynn, his ex wife, she would just say they weren't home.

Truly, they rarely were. They were out with their friends doing what kids liked to do. He too, seemed tied up with things. Now he had cut his own single and Aeton was sure it would be a hit.

Jonas would get one thing straight with Conroy. He would have certain regular days off each week so that he could have some kind of private life. Jonas was hardly the only person Conroy had under contract. He signed on a lot of people but not everyone would make the big time.

On Friday morning Jonas had driven over to his industrial building in Van Nuys. It was autumn, and the seasons change with the bite of cooler air could have an effect on people. Along the southern California coast the October sky filled with a westerly flow as the offshore breeze blew in from the Northern deserts. The skies became a clear blue as the abnormal wind direction would often blow the valley air pollution out to sea. Walking amongst his cars Jonas dreamed at the moment he would really like to take one of the sportier cars out for a spin, but that would have to come later. He had other things in mind. He was planning on taking the orphan kids sailing Saturday morning and he didn't want to leave a rare car sitting out alone in some public parking lot.

Jonas decided that if he was going to get anywhere with these kids he wanted them to like him, and kids like adults seek out fun things to do. Jonas saw an ad in the paper offering up a sloop for daily rentals. It was a Catalina 30, which meant it was plenty big enough for the whole group. The boat was down in Newport, about an hour drive south where he and Gina had driven to. He wanted to teach them sailing basics and planned on just sailing around the harbor or maybe even taking a trip outside the harbor toward Dana point.

The owners of the sailing craft were the Carlson's. The Carlson's home interiors business was having a bad year and rather than sell the craft they wanted to try renting it. When Jonas picked the kids up to take them sailing they were thrilled. They left at eight in the morning which was the soonest the orphanage would let them leave. When they arrived at where the boat was located they were greeted by Mr. Carlson. He got them acquainted with the sloop and they checked the gas tanks to make sure they were full. Then while Jonas and the kids loaded up the boat, the owner hung around to make sure they were acquainted with everything, like life vests, emergency items, and control functions.

Jonas wanted to give the kids a quick introduction to sailing basics before they shoved off. The 1970 vessel was only a few years old. The craft could be operated by one person. The entire length of its thirty feet was in practically like new condition. Jonas instructed the children to put on their life vests. He called them over for a quick training lesson. He explained some basic sailing terminology and taught them how the components of mast, boom, jib, and mainsail functioned. He taught them about safety protocol and how to use the radio for emergencies. He explained what port, starboard, bow, and stern was. Once they understood some of the basic nomenclature Jonas started the engine and guided the vessel out into the harbor. For the time being he was just going to cruise around the bay as there were lots of interesting things to see.

They cruised by the old fish cannery, now a restaurant. He pointed out the prominent Balboa Pavilion built in 1905. It was the first building built on the peninsula. The entire whole Newport Harbor area below the bluffs was at one time nothing more than a broad dangerous sand bar with various pockets of treacherous waters. It was during a period at the dawn of the twentieth century that a number of people lost their lives trying to enter the harbor. Prior to the harbor being dredged for deep water navigation the entrance met at a conjunction of jagged rocky cliffs and strong ocean currents. It was the place where many lives were put in peril, or lost to the strong ocean currents that could batter a vessel against the rocky cliffs. A safe passage couldn't be assured until following the dredging, elongated jetties constructed of cement and boulders were extended out to sea from the inlets. Jonas pointed off toward the far eastern end of the inlet where the Back Bay estuary lay. It was a place of salt water marshes where wildlife and fisheries flourished. They cruised by the ferry boats that made the short trip between Balboa Island and the Newport peninsula. The children saw John Wayne's house. Permanently moored in the bay along Coast Highway was also a popular restaurant known as the 'Reuben E Lee,' which was a mock up of a Mississippi river boat.

The sailing vessel was now fast approaching the old Gillette Brother's house near the harbor entrance. It was noticeable that the house had a dividing wall that made two residences out of one. One side was brick colored and the other cream. The story goes that the brothers had a significant disagreement of sorts so a dividing wall was installed in the middle of the home. Eventually, the Gillette's sold and a myriad of subsequent owners bought the home.

After Jonas's vessel left the harbor he had to let the sails out or 'ease' them as they called it. The craft would be under port tack. The ocean had a moderate rolling swell. The craft would be heading down toward the south. Their destination was Dana Point harbor, another man made harbor that was smaller than Newport. It too was created solely with the use of earthen materials, rock and cement. Dana Point harbor had a considerable number of slips for boats where shops and restaurants were close at hand. Jonas thought he would take the kids there for lunch and then come back home before the late afternoon.

"OK Fred, come over here. We are still under motor power. You see that ship off that point in the distance?" asked Jonas.

"Yes sir," answered Fred.

"Well, I want you to steer this vessel right at it. It's going away from us so we are not going to run into it. I have to let the sail out so we can switch to wind power. Take the wheel," said Jonas.

So Jonas was now beginning to see himself as a factor that could have some affect on the formative years of the lives of these children. They had already been out together several times at his parents big barbecue bash and the picnic with Kay at Griffith Park. While Jonas was tending to sailing nomenclature he was also thinking about the children's backgrounds as given to him by Kay.

First was Frederick Kester. He was the oldest at fifteen. He had been at the orphanage for five years. His tall medium build, sandy colored hair and green eyes bestowed an attraction that others were jealous of. He possessed a motivated cheerful personality with a touch of that typical youthful arrogance and didn't seem to be afraid to try anything new. About a decade earlier things seemed to be OK, he and his mother were doing fine while his dad Paul was overseas fighting in Viet Nam. Then one day the Kester's received the bad news of Paul's death. Eventually his mother met another man and started dating him. In the mean time she had delivered Fred to an uncle to stay with until she got on her feet with a new job and hopefully a permanent relationship. After nearly a year she discovered her boyfriend could be very physically abusive. He had told her she had better never try to leave him. He was an alcoholic to the worst degree. Unfortunately, she didn't get away from the guy in time. The relationship came to a conclusion one day when neighbors concerned about not seeing any activity around their home called the police. They found the body of Fred's lifeless mother in her apartment, beaten to death. In less than two weeks the police finally found her murderous boyfriend in a cheap motel several miles outside of Beaumont, Ca. He surrendered without any resistance and was sentenced to life in prison which went to appeal.

Then there was Wanda Daniels, age thirteen. She came to the home as an illegitimate child of an unknown father and mother. She was left on a park bench as an infant becoming a ward of the state. The man who found her was a jogger named Jeffrey Daniels. The first on scene officer was a woman named Wanda Simmons. So the story was that whoever filled out the official forms not knowing the baby's real name, wrote Wanda Daniels, the first and last names of the two that rescued her. That was how she got her name. After a number of years she went up for adoption but she didn't get picked up so she was accepted at the Los Angeles Orphans home. Wanda has dark brown hair, brown eyes, with features that suggested that her parents were possibly of a mixed race. Wanda seemed to always be smiling and she brought home some of the best grades for her class at Vine Street School.

Connie Morely was considerably behind the rest in age and brought to the home at age five. She was a cute young girl having honey blonde hair and large gray eyes. Connie is either very quiet or would talk your ears off depending on the circumstances. It often seemed when everyone else was quiet, Connie became the life of the party. That would be a part of her character for the rest of her life. She either had all kinds of questions or she would tell you about this and that, or anything that came to mind. She liked to carry her little transistor radio around and listen to music. When you set the four in a group for a picture it seemed that the cute little Connie was the one that stood out.

Connie's dad managed a bowling alley until his drinking and drug abuse robbed him of all his practical decision making senses and he just quit going to work. Connie's mother was separated from her husband. She had at one time or another just about worked every kind of job one could fathom on the late night strip. Occasionally, for extra money she often did those birthday stints where a stripper comes out of a cake at parties. So, she was not really first choice material for a mother.

The wellbeing of young Connie had been completely ignored. She had no love and no friends except a rag doll named Donna. One day, when no one was home but Connie as was often the case and there was no food in the fridge as usual, she took a walk down to the corner neighborhood market. She carried her friend Donna with her. When she got there all she knew was that she was hungry so she tried to hide some chocolate milk, cookies, and a jar of peanut butter in Donna's blanket. When she walked out of the store she got caught of course. A seven year old is not the best candidate for a perfect heist. That is when they called the police, discovered her situation and delivered her to the Orphans home.

Finally, there is Mat Shaver. Mat's mother left his father Doug for another man when he was four. Doug Shaver was a pilot for L.A. Airways helicopter service. On one early June morning departure in foggy weather, the helicopter that Doug's father was flying collided with a student pilot's light aircraft. The aftermath of the incident resulted in complete loss of life for both aircraft. Unfortunately for Mat, the only reason his father was flying that day was to cover for another pilot who was sick. Doug's sister took the boy in until she lost her job, then she could no longer afford to take care of him. Mat came to the orphanage at six.

That first day when Jonas was driving over to the orphanage to meet Kay and the kids he told himself he would not draw any conclusions about any of the children based on appearance. Even young kids have developed some form of personality. Jonas would be interested in what they had to say about things. He was simply there to help out. Jonas didn't know if any of the kids would be difficult. He decided he would just be friendly and try to get to know them.

"Just keep the bow pointed at that boat Fred," said Jonas again as Fred was drifting slightly off course.

Jonas finished letting the sails out and warned the kids he was going to swing the boom across to port side.

"Okay, boom coming across."

Upon executing the command the wind filled sails put the vessel in a modest roll position as it sprang forward. The surge caught some of the children off guard as they momentarily grabbed something to hold onto. The boat was now moving much faster than it had been under motor power. Brilliant feathery white clouds lay streaked across the blue sky as a forceful breeze filled the sails and propelled the craft through the march of the oncoming swells. Occasionally, frothy spray came up over the bow or sides of the vessel and on up into the air, where its salty bitterness sprinkled its refreshing zeal alongside the faces of the fledgling shipmates.

"Ready to jibe," said Jonas as he turned the boat using the rudder toward the other downwind quadrant. The children were all entranced and excited by the whole experience.

"Here Fred, hold the wheel. Steer it just like a car. Keep the bow pointed toward that big yacht in the distance," said Jonas, as the distant yacht popped in and out of view from the pitching of the sloop's bow as it rolled through the swells. Now Jonas told everyone to yell 'boom coming across'.

"Boom coming across," they all shouted as he moved the boom to the starboard side of the vessel.

All the lads seemed to be having a unforgettable time with the adventure, while Connie seemed to be making an extra effort holding onto things to keep from losing her balance from the pitching vessel. Jonas showed them how to use the jib and boom in relation to the wind direction to drive the craft. So they sailed the relatively short distance to Dana Harbor where they furled the sheets and motored into the harbor. After docking, they walked around a bit, ate lunch and then launched the vessel for the return trip back to Newport. On the return trip the craft was heading in a generally windward direction so the craft was close reaching as it was tacking through the wind. After the boat pulled back into its slip in Newport Harbor the kids had been fed a lot of information, too much to remember everything. Sailing was an art where there was a lot to learn before one could call themselves a master seaman. Certainly, Jonas never considered himself a master.

Fred and Wanda seemed to show the most interest in their sailing adventure with Fred asking the most questions. When they got back to the slip they all helped to clean up the boat as much as possible so the Carlson's might let them rent the craft for future excursions. They soon were back in the bus and on their way home.

"Well did you all have fun?" asked Jonas.

"Yes!" was the general response from all.

"Don't you think we were all lucky to go?" asked Jonas again.

"Yes," they all replied.

"Now let me ask you this. Would it be wrong or right to tell all your friends at the home how much fun you had?" asked Jonas.

This time there was no quick response. The question seemed to force a little more thinking.

"I don't think it would be good," answered Wanda.

"Okay, what about the rest of you. What do you think?" asked Jonas.

"Wouldn't that be like bragging?" responded Connie.

"Yes, exactly, don't you all think that would be like bragging?" asked Jonas.

"Uh huh, yeah," said Matt.

"I think it might make your other friends jealous and envious, don't you agree?" asked Jonas.

"Yeah, I see your point," remarked Fred.

"It's okay to tell people about fun you've had. Just think a little about the other person before you do it. If they have the same opportunity then it's okay, see my point?" stated Jonas. However, it would come to be that the discussion would not serve its purpose in regards to a future excursion they would all partake in.

The trip home seemed to take a little longer. Jonas parked the car curbside and helped the kids with their stuff and then escorted them back inside. It was 3:45 pm when he looked at his watch. Gale, one of the gals on duty offered Jonas a cupcake and coffee which Jonas accepted. The two boys and Wanda thanked Jonas for the great time they had and took their things to put away while he, Connie, and Gale sat at a table with their cupcakes.

Gale started talking about all kinds of things while Jonas listened. Connie just sat on the edge of her chair with her hands folded underneath her chin staring at Jonas with those big eyes, while Gale talked. There was a newspaper on the table and something caught Jonas's eye just like it had before when he had breakfast with Aeton at Jon Jon's, months prior. It was a front page headline, 'Marore Earns Rave Reviews'.

It was Gina again, but of course still using her new name, Eleanor Marore. It mentioned her outstanding performance in her first movie which would be coming to the theaters in the coming weeks. She had already signed for her next film, 'REDEMPTION.' Now, the critics were forecasting her as an actress to be taken seriously. Jonas would look forward to seeing the movie. When Gale paused long enough for someone to say something, Connie stepped right in.

"Are you going to take us anywhere else?" she asked.

"Not today, sweetie, but yes, I hope we can go to lots more places," responded Jonas.

"I saw you on TV," said Connie.

"You did! When was that?" asked Jonas.

"It was on the news a few nights ago. They showed you singing," she replied.

"Oh yes, a lot of us saw that on the five o'clock news. They had some clips of you," stated Gale.

"Well, I hope I didn't sound too bad," said Jonas.

"Not at all; you sounded great," she replied.

"Well I try. I better get going. Thanks for the snack."

"My pleasure," said Gale.

"Bye Connie. You were a real sailor today," said Jonas.

"Thank you. I'm still going to think of a new name for you," she responded.

"You mean, other than Glenn," he answered.

"Yes! I don't know what it is yet. I have to think," she stated.

"Well take your time Sweetie, bye- bye you all," said Jonas, as he left.

As Jonas was walking out toward the car he was thinking, "Perfect," that's all I need is three names. I wonder what she will come up with. So far, Aeton had booked Jonas for shows each week of the coming month.

When Jonas got home he had stuff to put away from the sailing trip. Of course, he brought all the equipment and things such as food and drinks. For the time being he just put most of the stuff on the kitchen floor. Finishing that, he drove the VW back over to his industrial building to deposit his Bus and pick up something a little more exciting to drive. The problem was, many if not most of these were show cars. He didn't want to use most of them as a daily driver. He really wanted to drive the 68 RS SS Camaro, at least for a while. It was only about six years old. The odometer read 12,007 miles. It carried the original factory paint, a golden bronze metallic with a black vinyl roof. The spokes of the thick American mag wheels also had a golden frosty glitter to match the paint. At night, the boulevard lights would lite up the car like a king's crown.

Jonas assumed his uncle bought the car to have fun because he had made a few modifications. The engine now sported some aftermarket Edelbrock and Isky components like a new heavier cam, and high rise manifold, headers, and a Holley carburetor. Jonas had no idea when the car was last started. The building had much of the tools and equipment necessary to maintain a vehicle and work on them. There was an engine removal hoist often referred to as a cherry picker. There was a hydraulic jack, a battery charger, and rollaway with lots of hand tools and various other auto related tools. So Jonas wasn't too worried if the car didn't start up right away. He had the resources there to get the job done if necessary.

Jonas released the parking brake, put the car in neutral and pushed it away from the other cars. Then he opened the hood, checked the oil and tire pressure and then got inside the car.

"Bet this guy hasn't been started in ages," thought Jonas. He inserted the key in the Camaro's starter switch and turned it to the first click. The fuel needle jumped to indicate that the tank was three quarters full.

"Okay, looks like the battery might still have some juice," thought Jonas.

Jonas was thinking it all through in his mind what would be occurring inside the engine block once he turned the key over. It was sort of strange the way his mind worked, but that was the way Jonas was at times.

So Jonas turned the key all the way over as the electronic fuel pump began a rapid ticking vibrating noise as the device began pumping fuel through the fuel lines into the Holley 650 dual feed carburetor. The carburetor then introduced a measured amount of fuel down through the manifold tunnels as it found its way into the cylinders that were now stroking in rapid up and down rhythms drawing in oil which had been alien to the cylinder walls for some time. Now the cranking cylinders were sucking fuel and air in their respectful chambers directly below the engine block heads driven by the cranked start motor. Meanwhile the battery was delivering the needed energy to the spark plugs that was introducing a charge to the combustion chambers.

As the start motor was cranking, the engine finally started and there was a lot of hissing, popping and coughing noise until it achieved a healthy degree of idle. The engine sounded rough with black carbon build up coming out the tail pipes, then finally there was a loud awesome rumble of power with Jonas holding the RPM at 1500. He revved the engine up and down searching for a smooth roar. Once he was satisfied the engine would idle under its own he let off the gas and got out of the car. He loved the sound of this car at idle, the tempo of the slow thump, thump, thump, thump of a properly mated cam, crank, and engine, as each small explosion of the cylinders threw the remnants of its force down through the pipes of the headers where each bang sounded like a blast at one end and a bellow at the other.

Jonas left the factory building and soon found himself cruising down the

405. He was now not alone in that familiar car arena of fast vehicles. There were other Camaros, emblazoned with different emblems like the Z28 with their high compression engines, and other models having various engines. Even the second generation of Chevy Camaros was on the scene. Also roaring down that southbound gateway was GM's competition with Mopar products with the likes of the Challenger, Cuda, and Duster. The Cuda was one of the models Jonas himself owned, the one he used to drive down to Newport with Gina. Ford had their own offerings with some of the Mustang models like the BOSS 302 and Mach I. Carroll Shelby took the Mustang model to new heights with his renamed, 'Shelby's', giving them bigger engines and post engineering alterations. All that said many of the well to do would not give any of these cars a second look as they drove their preferred Jaguars, Maserrattis, Ferraris, Porsches, or other expensive imports of which some housed twelve cylinder engines.

All that really didn't matter at the moment to Jonas as he was enjoying the ride as his Camaro roared along under the sun down the asphalt path of the freeway. The front flat black grill with the hidden headlights and false valve covers on the hood served to lend a sporty package to the designation of the RS SS model package. So were the 'SS' emblems a stigma of some GM design engineers sinister vision of feared forces out of man's past. Of course what the two SS letters really represented was that the model was a 'Super Sport.' GM branded many of their products with the familiar emblems.

Jonas was lucky. Thanks to his uncle he had many cars to choose from. At the moment he was enjoying his ride as many other awesome powerhouses went by in the opposite direction or passed him as he listened to a loudly tuned in Janis Joplin number, ' A Piece of my Heart.' However, even she couldn't drown out the cool sounding bellows of that WWII radial piston fighter aircraft that was being fantasized in Jonas's mind as the car was hurling down along the three lane blacktop corridor.

Jonas was thinking about how everything in life can change so fast. It wasn't that long ago he was having a good time with Gina Thorpe and he was hoping that he could see her again. Then there was Kay, everything was going great and then it wasn't, at least not his relationships. It looked like Gina was on her way to stardom, and Kay got snatched up by a multi- millionaire debonair. While Trish, perhaps not meeting with the same amount of notoriety as the fateful other two, was now history, gone to the east coast for reasons unknown.

When Jonas pulled into his driveway his neighbor an elderly woman was watering her lawn. She paid a lot of attention to Jonas's car as he was parking it. When Jonas got out of his car she gave him an eye of curiosity. They had never spoken.

"My, How many cars do you have?" she asked.

He could understand her reasoning. He had parked quite a few in the driveway including his Cuda, the VW, the 58 Chevy, and now the Camaro. Jonas was hoping to introduce her to his poor man's Ferrari soon, the Dino.

"Well, I get so attached to my cars I just never sell them. I park them in this old factory building. When I get bored I just grab something different," he responded, grinning.

"My name is Glenn," stated Jonas.

"Oh, I thought your name was Jonas Miles," she responded.

"What made you think that?" he asked.

"Well I got some mail in my mail box the other day that wasn't mine, had your address and it said Jonas, so I just thought..?"

"Well yes, my name is Jonas and it's also Glenn," momentarily drawing a strange look that faded rapidly.

"To make a long story short my agent had me change my name but I hope we can keep it between us," he added.

"Oh, you're in the entertainment business, huh? Yeah, sure why should I care how many cars and names you have? It's none of my business. My name is Carla Masters," she answered.

The conversation continued a while longer ending with Jonas thanking her for the piece of mail delivered in error to her box. She mentioned to Jonas that the mailman had already came today and that he should grab his mail on the way in.

There were five pieces of mail that Jonas threw on the table. One was from the Anniston Conroy Agency that was sent monthly by Aeton's secretary. One was from the Los Angeles County Department of Recreation. The other three were bills. First, Jonas opened the envelope from the county which had all the information for playing baseball in the coming season. He looked the pamphlets over, read the information and wrote on the back of one of them. Then it was getting on toward evening. Jonas decided to go to the store to buy the necessary ingredients to make one of his favorite dishes, spaghetti.

TWENTY ONE

In Dreams

The spaghetti was perfect. He cooked it pretty much the way his mother always had adding only a few ingredients of his own. Like so many other people who grew up with their mothers cooking some recipes just seem to get passed down through the generations, and fortunately for Jonas he cooked a few dishes well.

It had been a long day out on the boat. The event had left him a little drained. He just wanted to hit the sofa and watch TV like he so often did. Before television came to the world people listened to the radio or read books. Now color televisions were for sale in all the big chain department stores. Jonas was planning on buying a new TV since he had finally gotten his contract finalized with Aeton. Now he knew how much he would actually get paid since it had a lot to do with each of the events' total take based on percentages. He would also get a modest monthly salary. The fact was that it looked like he was going to be doing much better than he had been doing at any other job he had. It was time to buy one of those new 25 inch big screen color console TVs. The 19 and 23 inch round color tubes with their splotchy undefined images had gone away. Now they were being replaced with square tubes that had improved picture quality. Some of the most common brands of the day were Zenith, RCA, Sylvania, Admiral and Magnavox.

Jonas walked up to the Marilyn cardboard image and looked at her. Feeling her presence he felt confident his words would be heard.

"Well, Marilyn, I don't know if you were with us on our sailing adventure today but everyone seemed to have a great time."

Though Jonas usually addressed her as Marilyn, sometimes he called her Norma, or Norma Jeanne. It wasn't easy to carry on any kind of conversation with someone who did not respond with spoken words but with perceived expressions, or who could know, telepathic responses. They were expressions that only he saw and they could run the full gamut of emotions. Usually he would just sit and talk about all kinds of things as she just listened. He saw in her a valid sincerity and faithfulness and perhaps unfortunately so, more then he come to know in his own personal world of people.

"Well Marilyn, I feel that I had a good day, like I accomplished something. Any day you can bring joy to others is a good day," said Jonas as he grabbed a 45 record out of a pile and placed it on the player. Often, Jonas would pick up a record at random leaving the selection to fate. Now I'm going to put a little ice in the bottom of a glass, pour in a little Liqueur and watch some TV," said Jonas while looking at Marilyn, catching a glimpse of her lively look.

Then Jonas got out his TV guide that had Peter Falk on the cover. He flipped through it trying to find something that they both might like to watch. Often, he felt he was not fair enough with her when he would watch a sports game or a western. So tonight he hoped to find something they both would like to see. For all he knew maybe she didn't mind baseball or westerns, but he was pretty sure she did not like the fights. He found something on that was kind of old but was a pretty good movie.

"How about the Bond movie 'Gold Finger'," asked Jonas as he strained his neck to look at her, then he turned on the set to the proper channel.

Jonas extinguished all the lights except a small desk lamp. He took off his shoes and sat back on the sofa placing his drink on a side table, while resting his feet on an ottoman. He could lean his head back and be very comfortable that way. The James Bond series of movies was very popular. So Jonas made himself quite comfortable, his head resting on the built in cushions of the plush leather arm chair as the thick cushiony arm rests served to keep him comfortably afloat. His drink was only inches away. This type of movie had the typical theme of many adventure flicks, especially the Bond movies.

"You do like the Bond movies, don't you Marilyn?" asked Jonas, turning and straining his neck again. She was about at a forty five degree angle behind him upon the common wall not too far away. Jonas enjoyed the taste of his drink. It had a sweet taste as most liqueurs. Jonas felt good as the ice chilled drink sent a warm chill through his body. Later on, the movie advanced into a race scene where Sean Connery was racing his heavily armed sports car from pursuers. Then there was a strange mild sound. It was the sound of something so typical. Again, a fast action movie failed its intent upon Jonas as he was fast asleep.

There has been much said about the paranormal, things that happen around the world or in certain people's lives that are unexplainable. This has nothing to do with the usual stuff like being the sole survivor of an incredible airline crash, or of a revelation found in a dream, or an unexplainable ghost sighting, or even those who have claimed to have seen a UFO.

We're talking about certain things that few of us experience that the rest of us were never meant too, leaving the majority of us feeling very skeptical of any claiming witness or exposure to a paranormal event. This is understandable as most would be blind to what others believe is real. It's far easier for us to just say they are the crazy ones. It's about the things that happen that we cannot explain that gives us pause to wonder. To witness the supernatural is beyond the powers of most of us. Most mortals cannot see such because they simply are not in harmony with their being and their own self cosmic energy resists any alignment to the spiritual world that surrounds us. So it wouldn't likely be individuals who claim they have seen the supernatural that people should believe for on the contrary, it is likely the ones who say nothing. They could be anyone; one of your co-workers, a foot soldier, a homeless person, or the lone tenant across the street. One most aptly would not find the gift in those whom are of an aggressive or vex character, nor vain or boisterous, but more probable in one whom is modest, quiet, considerate, or contemplative. What about those who won't budge from their claims of having witnessed a paranormal event or supernatural occurrence, or however it be referred. If someone makes claims to have witnessed a most bizarre paranormal experience we find comfort in being great doubters and possibly rightfully so. Such people will keep things to themselves, or decline to tell their friends because they know everyone will make a good laugh of it. If humor cannot be got from it then many resort to caustic or cynical remarks. Could it be that paranormal things do happen and supernatural life is there. Most just cannot see it, or them, or the things that are there. Also one need not be in a conscious state to become a participant, or find oneself in the midst of acts or things paranormal of the spiritual world.

So, as it was in various evenings within the walls of Jonas Miles home, the dim light of the lamp gave off a faint glow to the room as the variance of light from the TV reflected its shadows on the room's walls. Then suddenly there was another light that cast its luminance there about. It was familiar and commanding, eerily human in form, subtly aglow like the moons lustrous throw of brilliance upon cascading waters. The phenomenon for the moment stood poised and motionless. The form presented itself as perfect in posture yet slight compared to the height of Jonas who had a generous mans height. There was an array of hues and imposing definitive definitions on the forms brilliant mass where most humans might easily identify the image. Then the body of the form began to move around the room just like she had done so many times before while Jonas was fast asleep. She was his unconscious secret hidden within the dark shadowy walls of the night behind drawn curtains and closed doors. The form glided over to the record player. The sound of the TV suddenly went mute and in the invisible stillness of the quiet room the record player began to play. It was the record that Jonas placed on the player and forgot to play. It was Roy Orbison's 'In Dreams.'

Jonas was a collector of many things so therefore had many things that others might find interesting. His book cases were filled with many contemporary books and many of the classics. He collected tiny carved figures from around the world, coins, old postcards, magazines, press photos, western belt buckles, and money clips amongst other various things.

The beautiful glowing figure suggested a harmonic cadence in movement as the female form seemed to dance around the room studying things as they were picked up and set down, not by any form of human appendages but by an apparent science of levitation. Books came off the shelf and rose up into the air and pages were flipped and set back down. She had studied with interest many of the things that Jonas had lying about on tables, in his curio cabinet, upon his desk. She didn't seem to venture beyond any room but where her cardboard form was attached therein, within the area of the kitchen and living room.

Based on what we may or may not know about the supernatural and the belief by some that paranormal occurrence's may entail evil, common sense would argue where evil lives evil follows, but nothing evil dwelled or existed herein. If spirits be the remnants of a prior mortal's existence then let their actions speak their words and let their nature reveal themselves. In mortality we accept as good that which has never been proven otherwise.

So the glow of light that emanated from the beautiful apparition as she appeared was nonthreatening yet commanding. There was no reason to fear that which was there but on the contrary her purpose was akin to pure and wholesome causes, and her attraction had once been a gift to the world. She was as special as was everything that is unique in the universe as we all are. Her talent became something magical which forever embossed her essence into the impressions of time, within pages of books, upon people's minds, on words spoken and an unlimited plethora of photos, movies, and memories.

From where then does such a being come one knows not, but perhaps driven upon by desire or a lofty fellow's whim. She's having tarried upon this place for a time and who knows of the time to come. She is akin to an Angelic Aphrodite storybook having arrived as if a mystic sojourn that was delivered in an instant upon the beat of wings. So it has been at this place for reasons not known that she has placed herself in time, where time has progressed from hours to days, from days to weeks, and weeks to months, and not a thing could a mortal friend prove of her spiritual existence. Nor, would any true friend mortal or otherwise pursue such redemption as impossible as it could be of a supernatural being which can lie hidden in the wind, ensconced in space or even flutter like a hummingbird upon a field of flowers. What mortal could capture such a spirit whom dances on the treetops of mighty forests, sleeps on the cushions of wispy clouds or embodies herself within a colorful sheet of cardboard if she so chooses to do. Certainly, mortals will live their lives never knowing the slightest secrets to the universe, not seeing beyond the planes of light that defines the entrapped environments they were born in. Perhaps, one only has to call her name twice, or thrice, to summon her from the cosmos, from that place where only few might go.

She may communicate with one but not with spoken words. So, if one such as Jonas can see a smile in her eye or feel the gladness of the inimitable flow of her being as she conveys her thoughts, then how could one not reason that the luminescent figure described is indeed the embodiment in manifestation of the one called Marilyn Monroe.

No other spirit or mortal could convincingly impersonate the very unique idiosyncratic mannerisms of her unique persona, that glowing bodily form that now glides around the room as gracefully as a ballerina. One only had to look at the spirit of her to see her face as proof which none could deny.

The intense piece of music by Roy Orbison continued to play as she moved and danced around the room, stopping here and there in breathtaking form, picking things up and putting them down, such things as books and magazines, old and new. Then she seemed to practice specific controlled physical movements that were suggestive of disciplined dance form. There she was in this physical stature, twirling, and executing free style movements like slow motion across the floor.

Then a solemn stillness came about her as the song came toward its end.

She slowly walked around the room within a poise of folded arms, appearing to be looking at something. In a fashion of levitation from across the room she raised the photo she had signed for Jonas as it came near her glowing luminescence, she gazed upon it. Then in the same fashion noticed the photo Frank gave Jonas. She glided over to briefly look at the sailing gear that Jonas temporarily set on the kitchen floor. She continued to walk around Jonas a few times looking at him. Then she turned her attention to the TV as she gently sat next to Jonas with her arms in her lap as she gazed at the TV.

Who could say that she wasn't what she once was, a lover of the cinema. Who could say that she didn't still love what she once did. She was an actress, a lover of the art. She turned and looked at Jonas and whether it was natural or simply discretionary she carried her familiar face and form with her all about that place she shared with him at such times. So now this face that looked so closely upon Jonas was a familiar and beautiful one. She leaned over and kissed his forehead just like she had done that long ago night, then she rose up and as the TV volume returned, she vanished. She possibly went back into the cardboard wall figure or could have transported herself across the sea, or even a galaxy away for all anyone knew. However, she must have sensed that Jonas would be awakening within the moment.

TWENTY TWO

Strange Days

As the months went by Jonas showed up where and when his agent had scheduled him to perform. Aeton was careful that he would not place his guy anywhere near where Sinatra was performing which was usually in Vegas. However, for a time Jonas did perform in and around Reno. Aeton made a wise choice booking his Glenn Miles at the Cal Neva on the shores of Lake Tahoe. It was a place Frank had once shared as owner in partnership but wanted nothing to do with anymore. People flocked to see Glenn perform at the Cal Neva because many of them use to frequent that place when Frank sang there along with his Rat Pack friends. With a few drinks down the hatch and dimmed lights in the Sinatra room one didn't even have to close their eyes to think it was Frank himself that was singing. Aeton also booked Jonas on extended international shows with stays that lasted several weeks in such places as the Hawaiian Islands, Great Brittan, Canada, West Germany, France, Spain, Brazil, and Argentina. Besides all the international traveling Jonas even hit many of the big cities in his own countries major hubs. Aeton never promoted Jonas with any reference to Sinatra's name. He just presented his star Glenn Miles, had him sing the songs Frank sang and that was all that was needed.

The public knew who he sounded like and enjoyed his shows even if it wasn't the real deal. The facts were Frank didn't perform in every city of America, not even most of them. If you wanted to see Frank you had to go to him, so Glenn Miles was only too happy to take his concerts to them as long as he was paid as well as he was.

'Glenn Miles,' had reached a hefty degree of notoriety around the world. He had cut two more of his own songs, 'Midnight Ride,' and 'Gone Again.' Jonas was good enough that even Frank couldn't help being exposed to his progress. In fact, Frank called Aeton up to get Jonas's phone number so he could congratulate him on a new singles hit, 'Gone Again,' which Frank liked.

"Hey Kid, kind of reminds me of one of my own. Sure you didn't just do a little surgery on one of my old songs?"

"Yeah, that's what makes my version better," shot Glenn.

Frank laughs.

"Okay kid, keep it up and I'll sue you for my cut."

"Yeah, sure, not so fast," responded Jonas.

"I'm just joking kid. It's good. I like it," remarked Frank.

One day when Jonas went out to the mail box he saw the usual bills, especially the one for the monthly rent. Aeton had suggested several times that Jonas should look for a nicer home up in the foothills. Jonas himself had given thought to the idea but he hadn't seen any need to live in a big home. When Jonas opened his rent bill he also saw a letter from the owner informing him that he had decided to sell the property. Jonas had sixty days to vacate. Jonas liked the home because it was in a good location and close to the things and places he liked. Being interested in the home Jonas secured an appraisal of the property and upon his second offer to the owner, the home became his. As it would turn out Jonas would live in that house for the rest of his life.

As Jonas went about his daily life he soliloquized about many things as one does from time to time. He thought it strange how often he would be in a crowded place like a store and find himself confronting individuals whom intensely radiated a familiarity to the movie star Marilyn Monroe. It might be someone who looked like Norma Jeanne, the pre-Marilyn Monroe version of the star or it could be the later version, the blonde version. He didn't go looking, intending, or insisting for such things to happen. He didn't go into places prepared to transfix a label on an unknowing candidate. These random incidents where Jonas had interactions with women that seemed to project a strong resemblance to the star were considered noteworthy occasions to him. Depending on the incident, he might even have written down notes on a particular experience, especially if a conversation had ensued from it. Jonas was ardent in keeping records of such things, writing things down for later reference even if it were just a few words. As it were, the women just presented themselves suddenly at times and places. Just like the blonde woman who had been at his very first performance that night at the Hollywood Bowl. He thought it was Kay watching him with her new shade of hair but she swore she wasn't there. Then who was it? In fact Jonas experienced three similar incidents just all in the past week. Monday he had been waiting in a busy doctor's office and an elderly woman came in, probably in her sixties with a bleached tone of silvery blond hair. She had a face very similar to Marilyn's.

There was just something different about her. She sat just over and across from Jonas and there just seemed to be this pleasant magnetic energy that emanated from her. Jonas studied the rest of those in the waiting room but for some reason she seemed like a silver dollar in a pile of dimes even if she was older. She had this presence about her and though quite older than Jonas, he couldn't help but taking occasional looks at her. He noticed her frequently looking in his direction but for some reason he never allowed their eyes to meet. In retrospect, he wished he had. It seemed sometimes people went out of their way to prevent their eyes from meeting.

A few days later in the grocery store another incident. A woman with dark reddish hair came over to him while he was looking at some cold cuts. She started talking about things as Jonas was deciding which product to buy. Her voice stood out alive and explosive and when Jonas first turned to look at her there was an immediate strange sensation that went to his core. He became a touch nervous and excited at the same time for in that instant he believed she was Marilyn. As the woman spoke all he could do was consciously absorb what the woman was saying as he placed his presence near her. Why in all the years of his life void of any conscientious spiritual or psychological provocations did his life one day suddenly become immersed into that of an icon, one that possibly inhabited his home within the facsimile of her cardboard self? When he looked into the woman's face he hadn't planned this interlude of fantasy. All one can do in any event that lends itself to mystery is face that thing whatever it is that challenges your beliefs and then commit to a rational evaluation. One can only strive to come to a conclusion by a process, preferably a sensible one even if it isn't scientific.

Her face and voice were certainly familiar if not indistinguishable from the persona of whom Marilyn Monroe was while living on earth. In the passing seconds it took for him to recognize her as whom he believed she was he knew he had to try to engage her in conversation. Jonas would control the topic of the conversation and try to force her thoughts to adapt to his remarks and questions. The strategy didn't work as the woman just continued to speak about the topic she seemed to be stuck on. If this woman was the one and the same that he imagined her to be then how could one rationally conceive to outwit a spirit? This deed was possibly excessively arrogant in of itself. Perhaps a sly degree of forbearance in thought would be enough to mask any craftily perceived notion of trickery on his part. After all he was a very calculative individual, a formidably worthy mortal thinking opponent. On the other hand Jonas could be just pressing along on the outer fringes of that so called fine line. Jonas had read a book recently in which the author stated something Jonas thought true in some regards.

"That society now justifies as sane nearly anything previously considered insane as long as it accommodates economic function for profit, or psychological liberation," the author also stated that,

"Modern civilized society as a whole can now only exist by practicing insanity and the effects of the species orchestrations for survival will in time cause mankind to self-destruct, along with the normalcy of the environment he came from. So if left unchecked, humanity will revert and nature will then reclaim the planet taking any surviving species that can coexist in the earths radically changed environment. All this happens because according to the author, humans never took any steps to control their population numbers driven by monetary profit," recalled Jonas.

So when was all this supposed to happen, thirty years, a hundred?

At any rate, in regards to the strange liaisons with the satirical women of Jonas's life whether imaginary or otherwise it seemed something unexplainable was responsible for the past events.

"Isn't it possible that we mortals are confronted with spiritual rendezvous in our lives that we can't recognize at the cost of something worthwhile?" thought Jonas.

On the other hand Jonas could just accept any future surrealistic exchanges with persons, spirits, phenomenon, whatever they were with a closed mind and develop his spiritual prowess no further than the tip of his nose. That would be what psychoanalysts call normal and that is the zone we are all suppose to assume. These women are just people who in some cases just happen to look like her and sound like her. Perhaps there are people who look just alike. In his heart however he would believe otherwise.

Whatever the reality was this woman had these gray bluish eyes. Jonas found it a great pleasure to look at her while she talked. She talked about mostly grocery things, farmers markets, sea food places, how she cooked halibut. Jonas occasionally picked up a food item and looked at it while she talked or added some conversation of his own. Jonas lingered there unusually longer then it normally takes to make up one's mind about which item to choose, as did she. Then Jonas, exhausting all conventional grocery conversation reluctantly wandered away. As he pushed his cart slowly in one direction he had an uncontrollable desire to go back. He suddenly realized he had to see her again, he wanted to ask her if she would like to meet sometime but when he turned around she was nowhere to be seen.

That very afternoon there was another person, a young woman in a hardware store. We are all told from the earliest days of our schooling that no two leaves are alike, no two human faces, voices, hairs, or even grains of sand. Every living and possibly physical thing that exists in this world is unique biologically and or physically. At least that is what we are taught. It's just a fact of life and what we experience and what we come to know as we live our lives.

Sometimes though, these beliefs seem to become challenged by daily events. After all, there are babies born twins who look like each other but are different enough so that a mother can tell. So again, such a thought touched Jonas momentarily as he was standing in line at a checkout station in a hardware store. He espied this face that leapt out at him as she was talking to the customer in front of him. She had the face of a young woman who was very friendly and talkative as she was paying for her items. She looked exactly like Norma Jeane. Jonas wasn't making a movie. He wasn't looking for actors and actresses to play roles. He didn't need to see people as anything other than who they really were, but it wasn't his fault that he saw something more than the common person sees. In these few individuals that Jonas had met most people didn't have the knowledge or even the concern to see what Jonas saw. Surely, if one could rewind time and retrieve Norma Jeanne Dougherty out of the past and place her behind a cash register no one would likely recognize her, just another pretty girl. They would not know who she was. Here however was a young Marilyn and Jonas couldn't help himself when his keen eye removed her luxurious golden brown hair and replaced it with a blonde upswept replacement. He knew what he saw and what others could never know. Whatever relevance this may have had, sane or otherwise in Jonas's life, he continued to have these confrontations for the remainder of his life.

TWENTY THREE

The Baja

Two years had passed since Jonas had taken the orphan kids on that first weekend sailing adventure. Jonas managed to take them out on other sailing trips since that time not counting all the other things they did together. One time they left the harbor very early and made it all the way to Carlsbad before they turned around. It was Americas bicentennial year, 1976 and Jonas was now 32 . He had been seeing so much of the fast aging children they were like family now. In fact, Jonas had been giving that concept much thought.

Jonas rarely saw his own kids anymore. He felt his ex wife had completely alienated them from him to where he only occasionally saw them such as at little league ball games or their grade school graduation ceremonies. Their new stepdad had done well by them, buying nice things, fun things, like a Honda Trail 90 dirt bike. He also had bought them all kinds of outdoor camping and fishing tackle, ten speed bikes, not to mention the sea going power boat he bought to take Charles and Calvin out on weekend cruises. Their step dad hadn't bought them anything that Jonas couldn't have bought them, but those toy things and unwarranted extravagant gifts helped to keep Jonas out of sight and out of mind from Cal and Chuck. Jonas didn't believe it was their wish to not see their father but he knew Lynn exerted a great influence on them. It wasn't to say Jonas hadn't had some good times with them following the divorce, but to be fair his Sinatra gigs had claimed much of his time as Aeton booked him across the country and around the world. Jonas was becoming tedious impersonating the master who had his own legacy to be proud of. Jonas had been more excited by his own original recordings. To date he had a total of eight. Like many vocalists, one day you just arrive on scene and you find you have many competitors who are really good, and then one day perhaps you find there's just no stage for you to get on anymore. Jonas didn't know when that day would arrive but it hadn't yet.

Jonas often thought about the orphan children. He imagined that in life each human being was a victim of something, each person has their own psychological set of circumstances. He knew he had his as well and as time went by he learned more about each child. He came to an understanding of what he thought each child needed.

Jonas was a bachelor. He enjoyed his independence and individuality. He was a responsible person who sometimes found it difficult to understand the plain stupidity of people even though no one could escape doing stupid things. Sometimes, he thought maybe it was his fault that he may have not been the best candidate for marriage. His potential partner might aptly have had a rarer type of personality to match his own, whatever that was. Not that he was so special in the ordinary sense. It was just that he saw himself as considerably different from most people. He thought he found the kind of partner that would keep him from getting bored in Gina Thorpe and in Kay Lincoln as well, whom he had such hope for in his plans. She was so full of energy and he was falling in love with her until she was so abruptly taken away. Well that's life as they say, love is a battle field. Jonas had a formidable competitor within Grover Samuelson's bag of tricks, and by the time he realized the threat it was too late.

With Gina, all made sense when he thought about her and who she seemed to be as a person. Whatever it was that drove her in life to achieve her goals must have come from some deep resolve for now she was a movie star. As for Jonas he was alone. Was he perhaps subconsciously a loner by choice? His plans in his personal life were unpredictable for much was dependent upon where Aeton sent him. He never knew where he would be from one month to the next.

Jonas was driving his Camaro trying to think of where to take the kids, not his true kids but the ones he thought about adopting, Matthew, Wanda, Fred and Connie. It was July, so a desert camping trip was out. They had done a lot of things together in the last several years, some more than once. The car radio was turned on and Jonas had been listening to an annoying long string of commercials when James Taylor came on with his hit, 'Mexico'. As Jonas was listening to the song it hit him. He would take the kids down into Mexico.

The following week Jonas and the four quickly growing kids were in his VW Bus headed south on the San Diego Freeway. They were pulling a pop up tent trailer as well as all the gear and bodies that were in the vehicle. He also brought a carton of a popular brand of cigarettes even though he didn't smoke. It was amazing what a pack of cigarettes could do for a gringo down in Mexico.

Anything, other than the Mexican 'Horse Shit', brand was worth their weight in gold. The fifty horsepower engine could be heard noticeably straining on the uphill grades and then it felt like it was floating on the downhill runs. Cars were passing his bus like a sprinter passes a pedestrian. It didn't matter as they weren't in a hurry.

"Joni, where are we going to spend the night?" asked Connie.

Connie had mentioned a considerable time prior that she was going to think of a name to call Jonas, well, 'Joni', was her idea of an improved version of Jonas. No one argued the choice, his old high school friends use to call him Joni.

"I'm planning on making it to Rosarito Beach the first night. But first we will walk around TJ for a while," answered Jonas.

"TJ, means Tijuana, doesn't it?" asked Connie.

"Correct," he answered.

They did not get an early start. They hadn't even left Los Angeles until two in the afternoon. Jonas wanted to make it to camp before nightfall but it would all depend on how much time they wanted to spend in Tijuana.

In years past when Jonas was younger and went down to Mexico, he and his old high school buddies would just park under a remote freeway overpass. There they slept off their beer highs in their cars before crossing into Tijuana. As teenagers working for minimum wage they didn't have the money for motels. Jonas didn't have the option of parking underneath a bridge on this trip, not with the girls along. He decided to just drive on to Tijuana and walk along the popular shopping streets that were frequented by all the American tourists. He planned on giving them each a purchasing allowance for a short shopping spree. Hopefully with enough daylight left they would drive on to Rosarito Beach for the first night's camp spot. It wasn't that far past the border.

Soon they found themselves in the hectic traffic flow of the Tijuana boulevards. When they parked their car and got out they were immediately deluged with kids selling gum, watches, and even others promising to watch their car for a small fee. The merchants that did business there in that so called tourist zone belonged to a coalition of sorts that kept the streets and sidewalks clean. The area was largely void of much of the riffraff that existed in other locations in Mexico. They tolerated children trying to make a few cents but that was about all.

Soon, they entered a shop full of tourists.

"Jonas can I have a pair of these?" asked Wanda.

"Yeah, I want a pair to," said Matt.

They were called Huaraches and they were a type of crude sandal. They had become a popular fad in the states. Their construction was rather crude, the soles being essentially a couple of die-cut stamped out car tire treads for soles with leather surface overlays, and upon that was affixed heavy natural leather straps for securing to the feet. Of course those soles never wore out, but the poorly cured leather tops did.

"Me, too," said Connie.

"Me, too, my old ones are shot," said Jonas. Jonas bought everyone huaraches.

They walked on down the shopping avenues, in and out of the back alleys and across the busy streets where weekend shoppers caused cars to slow and stop. There were many interesting things for sale that were made out of the most common resources available like leather, marble, Mexican jade, wood, and textiles. Consequently, things like chess boards, purses, blankets, baskets, ponchos, sombreros, clay pots, belts, and buckles dominated the shelves and racks.

"Jonas can I have one of these?" asked Fred as he pointed at what looked like a pearl handled switch blade knife.

"Well Fred, tell me what I'm going to tell the Orphanage when they ask you where you got it?"

"I'll tell them I found it," replied Fred.

"Yeah, that's just great unless somebody gets hurt with it. Then they will find out where you really got it," said Jonas.

"Fred, someday soon you will be down here on your own no doubt and you can buy yourself one then,", responded Jonas.

As the afternoon shopping excursion continued they were soon all carrying some kind of bag. Nothing too large was bought. The huaraches would come in handy on the trip. Jonas wanted to make sure they only bought stuff that might be used on the trip. Extra ornamental stuff would be dead weight. These types of things might be considered on the return trip.

"Jonas, can we buy some of these?" asked Matthew pointing at some cherry bombs, M-80's and various other packs of common firecrackers.

It was against Jonas's better judgment but he remembered when he had been down to Mexico as a kid with his friend and his friends father. What young boy didn't want something that went boom and blew things up?

"Okay," he said giving in to their pleas. The switch blade probably would have been safer.

The day's shopping list was filled for the boys with the addition of some belts and western buckles. The girls got a few more things they wanted. The sun was going down. It was time to get out of Dodge as they say.

The sun seemed to go down fast and in no time the moonless night insured that the pitch blackness of the road up ahead could only be lit up by their vehicles headlights. Jonas decided to put the crowd up at a beach called Del Mar, only a short ways from Rosarito Beach. As he pulled into the parking area there under the limited lighting of the buses headlights could be seen a plethora of sleeping bags spread out across the sand.

Even though the hippie era was heading toward it's end, probably brought on by the demise of the Viet Nam war, there were many who never thought it had anything to do with the war. Some who had been part of the movement moved on with their lives as they grew older while others found that carefree lifestyle hard to let go of. So when Jonas's party got out of their car it didn't take most of them long to realize that the whole beach reeked with the smell of burning cannabis. There was a couple in a sleeping bag only yards in front of the bus having sex. They were quite obvious with their expletive moans and they didn't seem bothered by headlights, nor seemed to care. Jonas looked at the boys and they looked at him. They had it figured out as they turned and headed toward the rear of the vehicle. They would all sleep under the stars that night just like the rest of those scattered about. Here the waves that approached the beach gently folded themselves upon the compacted sand and were faintly heard as the bunch quickly drifted off to sleep.

When morning arrived Jonas extracted the gas stove and cooked up some eggs, bacon, and toast before they hit the road again. When they got to Rosarito Beach they stopped there for a short time and walked around. Jonas had planned for this to be a three day trip. He had promised to have the kids back by Sunday evening. His intent was to drive on to La Fonda where there was a nice hotel, a restaurant, and a KOA campground across the highway that had ample hygiene amenities. They would spend some time there and eat lunch at the restaurant of a popular hotel at La Fonda. before moving on down the Baja peninsula.

They were back on the road early, rested and fed and the kids seemed to be excited by the whole idea of the foreign adventure. Of course in Mexico there was a huge absence of development of the kind that the kids were use to in California. The surrounding countryside was barren and undisturbed. The regions flora was mostly grasses with seascape scenes intermittently coming into view. When they reached Ensenada the strong scent of fish filled the air as that locale was largely a fishing village. They continued on south until they came to a place called 'Bulfadora.' The translation was somewhat akin to the meaning of, 'blowhole'. Here, the ocean current came in upon a rocky precipice that had subsurface caverns. After every so many series of tidal repetitions a column of water would shoot straight up in the air to a great height. It became a local attraction. Here again, they all got out and watched the phenomenon for a time before continuing their journey. Soon, the highway veered away from the coast as they were headed toward Santo Tomas. Here they found themselves surrounded by low lying hills as they drove across a vast flat valley. The valley was mostly planted in crops. They espied a woman dressed in black in a field next to the road that seemed to be cooking something. They stopped and watched as she was stirring ears of corn in a big black cast iron vat. Jonas didn't know if it was like an appetizer to them or it was all they had to eat. Jonas bought everyone an ear of corn and the woman gave them some red chili sauce to put on it. The corn was quite good but a homemade tamale would have had more substance. Jonas tipped her a few dollars which would have been an ample amount in any stateside restaurant. In Santo Tomas there were just a few small buildings, one was a gas station. The pumps were the very old kind that had large clear glass vessel tops of which you could see the liquid fuel inside. Jonas wondered about its purity but never the less they needed gas, so they filled up.

The next stop was San Vicente where there was a small store. The man in the store spoke fairly good English and he told them about a dirt road that went to some ruins that they passed back up the road. He also said if you followed the road it would take them to the ocean. In San Vicente they bought a few grocery items and then turned the bus around to visit the ruins. From there they continued west on the road which seemed to be nothing more than a faint trail through a cow pasture. Eventually they could see the ocean as the ground became sandy and the road was like a trail which the bus was handling well.

Then a very strange and startling mirage appeared only it wasn't a mirage. There standing out in the middle of nowhere all by himself was a Federale with a rifle slung over his shoulder. He was standing next to a poor excuse of what would be described as an entrance gate. The road ran between two wood posts that had barbed wire strung from each one that ran off into opposite directions. There was a shabby old sign that read, 'Los Positos,' nailed to one of the posts. Beyond were countless undulating sandy moguls that lay before a vast and beautiful shoreline. It stretched as far as the eye could see in either direction. Here the deep blue of the pacific lapped at the endless sandy beaches under an azure blue sky where no other souls were in sight.

So it seemed that all there was that lay between paradise and the bus of adventurers was a Mexican soldier. In Jonas's mind there was only one thing they could do and that was to see if the guard would let them through. So Jonas knowing little Spanish would try to contend with the situation. He would try to see if he could communicate with the man enough to get permission to camp on the beach. If successful, they might have the whole place to themselves.

"Hola Senor!" said Jonas.

The man said nothing as Jonas drove right up to him with his window right next to his face.

"Espanol, English," said Jonas. The only Spanish Jonas ever learned was in high school. He already forgot a lot which wasn't much to begin with.

This time the man grinned showing some missing front teeth.

"No Engliss," the Federale responded.

"Esta es Playa?" said Jonas pointing toward the beach. Then Jonas pointed at himself and the kids.

"Mis ninos el campo el playa por dos diaz," said Jonas pointing again at the beach smiling.

The Federale looked up and scratched his head.

"Huh."

"No muy bien por Americano el campo playa," said the Federale.

Now, Jonas was scratching his head. He points his finger up toward the roof.

"Un momento, senor amigo, Ustedes es cigaretta?" asked Jonas, not sure he said what he meant correctly.

"Mi cuanto dos packs," said Jonas holding out two packs of cigarettes for the soldier. Jonas's Spanish barely making much sense.

"Ah, Si," said the man looking interested.

"Dos mas," responded the official.

Jonas understood he must have wanted two more plus his offer of two. Four packs would be a bargain for camping on this beach.

'Ah, un-momento," said the soldier knowing Jonas did not know much Spanish.

Si, senor," replied Jonas smiling. He just wanted to get this episode over with. Connie looked a little frightened.

"Diaz dollas, diaz dollas," said the soldier.

Jonas now understood the guy wanted money too. Ten bucks plus four packs of cigarettes was still a pretty fair deal considering. Jonas imagined theoretically once he passed through the gate and was finished with the soldier he could stay five years or more, now that would be a real bargain compared to the states. In California it might be five bucks a night but that would also be sharing a beach with thousands of other campers. So, four packs of smokes and ten bucks was a cinch for Jonas. Jonas gave the man what he wanted.

"Entre?" said the Federale, as he pointed toward the beach. Jonas began to drive forward.

"Wonder if he intends to charge me again when we drive out of here?" was a thought that entered Jonas's mind. Then suddenly the soldier wasn't through with Jonas.

"Alto! Alto!," shouted the Federale, grabbing the bus's window frame scaring Connie as if Jonas had made a big mistake by moving forward. Then the Mexican soldier opened one of the packs of cigarettes and put a smoke between his lips and made a gesture for a light. Jonas struck a match and lit the cigarette as the soldier took a drag on it. The soldier had a long face and his leathery skin was pock marked on one side. His several day's growth of beard stubble was minimized by his heavy black mustache. The soldiers green eyes stared sternly right into Jonas's olive eyes with a brazen look while he puffed on the cigarette. Then he smiled showing off an array of yellow and tan teeth. There was an upper and lower tooth missing. He seemed to have stuck the cigarette within the notch of a missing tooth. Jonas gave him a couple of books of matches.

"Entre, Senor, entre," said the man again sweeping his arm in the direction of the beach as he stood aside. Jonas drove ahead waving as he proceeded to negotiate the shallow beach moguls toward the ocean as he followed the seldom used remnants of ancient tire tracks.

Just then the soldier got a call on his radio. It was from his captain.

"Como esta?" asked the voice at the other end.

"Ah, a VW Bus full of gringos, a man and kids just went through," the sentry responded in good English.

"Okay, well?" responded the Captain.

"Four packs of cigarettes and ten bucks."

"Tomas, Tomas, you are to kind. Enrique just got six packs and twenty bucks. I tell you most of them will pay more. Next time six packs and twenty bucks, okay," his superior responded in English as well.

"Si, I got it cap'i'tan."

"Okay, hang in there, we will be out there and pick you up this afternoon, before dark," remarked the soldiers superior in Spanish.

"Si, maybe you better come sooner if you want or I might smoke up all the cigarettes standing around here," answered the soldier.

Once the group got past the sandy moguls Jonas could see what looked like rocky cliffs several miles to the south. From where they were currently parked the ocean breakers were a hundred yards away. Jonas asked the group if they wanted to check out the cliffs in the distance. It was a unanimous, yes! When they arrived there they were able to drive right up on top. There were signs of previous campers and looking down over the cliffs edge the water was crystal clear, sort of a bluish mint color. Very large abalone shells were scattered about the shallow sea floor at the base of the cliffs. Jonas and the girls were looking down over the side of the cliff as the ocean swells came up and smacked the rocks with tremendous force sending water spraying in all directions. The aftermath left only sea foam within the receding momentum. Suddenly, the three had their attention stolen by something small and bright going over the edge followed by a very loud cracking boom. Matt and Fred had taken out the fireworks and were already having fun. Jonas looked around and there was no one in sight so this place was a good as any to light a few.

"Be careful when you light those. They will blow your fingers off," said Jonas.

Jonas hadn't realized they also bought some packs of what looked like firecrackers but they were as thick around as ones little finger. Before long they were tossing M-80's, cherry bombs, and setting off strings of firecrackers. A formation of Pelican's, came soaring down upon them moving quickly along the cliffs edge with wings spread wide and heads held high. They occasionally flapped their wings to maintain their altitude and forward momentum. Swoosh, was the only sound they made as they went by. All that was really missing thought Jonas was the rumble of Harley engines as they passed.

Even Jonas took a few liberties with the fireworks tossing an occasional cherry bomb or M-80 over the cliff. In the distance could be seen the colorful sails of a whole slew of sailing boats as there must have been a race in progress. Within the hour the boys had made short work of the fireworks and the girls were getting bored.

"Let's head back to the beach and find a good camp site," said Jonas.

They found a great campsite in a small compression like valley within some moguls and set up the tent trailer, extra tents, a canvas privacy room and a large umbrella canopy. Strewn about were inner tubes, an inflatable raft, tables, chairs and a large bag of charcoal. There was also a surf board, skim boards, and fishing poles besides the cooking stuff and ice box.

"No wonder this bus was so slow on the freeway," said Fred, causing everyone to laugh, even Wanda who often only seem to grin at humor.

They would spend the next two nights there enjoying that beach and having it all to themselves. They had the fun equipment to do just about anything. In regards to meals they would want for nothing having brought steaks, hamburger, hotdogs, and on the last night they had fresh lobster and abalone which Jonas dived for with his snorkeling equipment. In those two days Jonas felt satisfied that the kids had a wonderful time, as had he. The nights were just as wonderful with the roaring campfires they roasted marshmallows while Jonas would tell some pretty tall tales. He could get that way after drinking some of his favorite spirits. Once in the sleeping bags away from the contamination of city lights in that far off place, how stupendous was the heavy saturation of stars of faraway galaxies that could only make you wonder. Such sights had been there since the beginning of time but were now mostly obliterated by light pollution in big cities. Here, it seemed shooting stars were nonstop with pin points of lights streaking everywhere. Civilization with all its convenience's does not come without paying a price. The troop spent their three days having the time of their lives and when morning arrived they packed up and left. They never saw the Mexican sentry again.

When the kids got back to the orphanage they were tired as was Jonas. It had been a long day and a lot of driving. They slept sound and fast that evening they got home. With the arrival of the following morning the excitement of the trip and the tales of their adventures was hard to keep to oneself or even a group for that matter. By noon the next day every child in the orphanage knew all the details about their comrades' long weekend. Nobody seemed to really know who told who, and what they told. Every time either one of the four heard what they had done coming around for the second, third, or even fourth time, the reality of their actual experiences seemed to have changed.

TWENTY FOUR

Celebrity Gala & Tommy Roscoe

The difference between people who get what they want in life and those who don't is the fact that some people are just determined to make things happen. On the other hand, maybe it's nothing like that at all and it is about being at the right place at the right time, or some of both. Whatever it was, now Eleanor Marore the movie actress who was previously Gina Thorpe a waitress in a strudel bakery café had plans for the evening.

Eleanor had spent the whole day soaking in a hot bath, having her hair done, conditioning her skin, and getting fitted with a new dress for a charity ball. Afterward, she was going to a party hosted by Larry Casolva, the producer of an upcoming movie, 'Madrid 3917,' a suspense picture.

There were a lot of celebrities scheduled to be there for a fund raiser for CCR, the local Community Childhood Resources Center, and COSA, the 'Competitive Olympics Society of America.' Both were organizations dedicated to helping either underprivileged or handicapped children. Guests contributing twenty thousand dollars or more got their choice of special dinner entrees while seated with the celebrities that were in attendance.

Another person who would be there was the singer, 'Glenn Miles.' Even though he was somewhat excited about going he didn't think he was in the same league as some of the big names that were scheduled to be there. However, Aeton put him on the roster and he knew it was for a great cause. He had been asked to sing a few of his own original hits. He rarely sang Sinatra's stuff anymore, mostly under special arrangement. Besides, Frank would be there to sing some of his own hits. Jonas thought it would look unbecoming to attend the ball alone, so out of convenience he asked a woman he recently met if she would like to accompany him to the event. Her name was Margo DaSilva, a very attractive brunette and he had developed a friendly rapport with her over the last year. Nobody needed to know anything about her except that she was with him. Besides, the reason she really wanted to come was to meet the stars. It didn't really matter to Jonas why she wanted to go, ultimately he knew everyone would wind up smashed anyway.

In times past these charity events like many events hosted in Hollywood were occasionally held at the Palladium, the Ambassador Hotel, the Hollywood Roosevelt, and one time even at the Forum in Englewood. This year, the Beverly Hilton was the site selected. Glenn had never performed at the Beverly Hilton before. When he and his friend were dropped off by the chauffeur driven limousine camera bulbs were flashing everywhere. Not because Glenn Miles was there but because just about everyone who was anybody was there. So, as the reporters were busy interviewing various stars and celebrities Jonas walked slowly alongside Margo toward the entrance doors. He really wasn't expecting many people who showed up along the red carpet runway to really be that interested in him as he occasionally waved as he walked. He could not help but think how strange fate is as never in a million years did he expect to be walking at the same place, inside the same ropes that many years prior a very famous movie actress walked as he called out to her at the Golden Globes. Now, it wasn't the reporter's who were stopping him, it was faces in the crowd who recognized him and called out to him.

"Glenn, will you sign my record?" and, "Glenn, can I have your autograph?" came the calls of fans of various ages. Jonas fought back the tears that wanted to form in his eyes. Very few of the big stars seemed to be giving autographs to the general public. Some were caught up with the broadcast network interviewers. Jonas wasn't a huge star, at least not in his mind. Even if he had been he just couldn't walk away without giving a piece of his time to people, especially if they bought his records. Jonas spent the next twenty minutes talking and signing autographs, much to the delight of his greatly excited and impressed escort.

Jonas decided he would just take the evening in stride and plan on enjoying himself. He would sing his numbers as best he could, enjoy the food and conversation and tomorrow was another day. Once inside there were lots of people. It was a very busy place with the celebrities and charity donors combined. Now, all the big stars that had been reluctant to sign anything while outside were now busy with their pens and markers signing autograph books and making general conversation with the donors. Even Jonas had brought a simple small cardboard note pad not much bigger than the palm of his hand. Pursuing autographs was also a wonderful way of breaking into conversation with stars where one might ordinarily be too nervous to approach.

Not even a half hour had passed and Jonas already had nearly a dozen signatures from some of the biggest stars. Margo had been so excited by the whole affair she had drifted away from Jonas, seeking her own desired celebrities. Glenn Miles the singer had been asked to sign autographs by many of the guests. Just after Jonas managed to get Yul Brenner's autograph someone tapped him on the shoulder. When he turned around to see who it was his composure took a hit as he was staring straight into the face of Gina, or Eleanor Marore as she now called herself. She had been trying to tear herself away from people long enough to see someone that she hadn't talked to in a long time.

"Hello, Jonas," she said, with a smile and a sparkle in her eyes.

"Hi, Gina, I thought you might be here. I saw your name on the list. It's good to see you again," he responded noticing her tight form fitting dress. Suddenly she seemed to be taking something out of her purse. It was a 45 record of his hit, 'Marquette'.

"Good to see you too, Jonas. I remember when you were singing in your car on the way down to Newport how beautiful your voice was. I'm so glad you got caught up in the limelight and that your songs are so popular," she commented.

"Oh, how nice of you to say so, and it seems I'm not the only one who has been busy. Your wish seems to have come true, you're making movies," replied Jonas.

"I saw your first movie. You did an amazing job. It hit me like a Buffalo stampede." The two laughed.

"I'm sure you will have many more proud movies to follow," remarked Jonas.

"Well, I guess time will tell, but I hope so."

"I brought this record for you to sign. Gosh, this record is so amazing. I love 'Yesterdays Smile,' on the flip too. I love them both," she added handing him the record.

As Jonas was signing the record he continued to talk.

"Should I call you Eleanor or Gina?" asked Jonas.

Gina laughed. "I guess Gina Thorpe doesn't sound that great for a movie actress. I'm trying to get used to my new name," she replied.

"Well, I'll call you Eleanor then. But you seem more like a 'Roxy' to me," he said, remembering her gutsy though reckless moves while four wheeling the Irvine Ranch foothills.

"Hey, I like that name," she said with a smile.

Jonas was thinking about her new name, Eleanor. He was wondering how her name came about.

"Okay, I got to ask how you got your new name."

"Well I really didn't have a lot to do with it except they asked me if Eleanor would be okay. They wanted something unusual. They said the name Eleanor was timeless and stately. The producer said it took them a whole day to come up with that name. Then she laughed.

"One of the stage hands said I got named Eleanor because that was the song that was up on the KRQ radio station when they went into the cafeteria. You know the one, by the 'Turtles?'"

"Hey, I like that song," responded Jonas.

In that busy place guests were eyeing Eleanor and some were now practically pulling at her sleeves for autographs. Her presence near Jonas now spurred more people to ask him for autographs as well. As Margo was heading back over to Jonas, Gina reached into her purse and pulled out a pen. She quickly wrote something on a piece of paper and gave it to Jonas. That was about all she could do before she was overtaken by wealthy fans that paid their dollars to mingle with the stars. Jonas put the item in his coat pocket.

"Bye Jonas, call me when you can," was about the only thing she had time to say before she was enveloped by people.

"Gosh, you sure seemed to get Eleanor Marore's attention?" remarked Margo.

"Did you get her autograph?" she asked.

"No, I somehow forgot," he replied feeling stupid. He would blame it on the short rush of time.

The evening went off without a hitch. Jonas sang his songs, met a lot of famous people and was even given some contact information to a few parties and events.

When Jonas woke up the following morning he had no reason to believe that it wouldn't just be another normal day in his life. He had been quite intoxicated by the time he had left the charity ball. He remembered talking to many of the stars throughout the evening. He remembered running into Frank Sinatra at the bar. Jonas told Frank that Eleanor Marore wanted him to sign his record, which seemed to make Frank a little jealous that she didn't ask him to sign a record.

"Which song was it?" asked Frank.

"Summer Wind", responded Jonas.

"Summer Wind? Since when did you start recording my stuff?" asked Frank. Then, Frank started accusing Jonas of stealing his material. Jonas couldn't help but keep the gag going as it was fun to see Frank getting excited. Of course, Jonas never recorded any actual Sinatra songs. Frank had been drinking steady, like a lot of people who were there. Surely, by morning Frank would have forgotten the whole thing. Anyway, all that was now history and today was a new day. Jonas remembered the note that Gina had given him. He went to get his coat and retracted the note. There was very little to read, but enough. There was her phone number and below a jotted suggestion that they do dinner sometime. Jonas tacked the information up on his note board so he wouldn't lose it.

Jonas ate breakfast then he went jogging around his neighborhood. Afterwards, he bought a paper, went home, showered and dressed. He talked on the phone with Aeton about his next singing engagement and then drove over to his mother's home to help her with some projects that required lifting.

By the time Jonas got home it was lunch time. He was planning on eating out but decided to write out some checks for bills before he left. After about ten minutes there was a knock at his door. He couldn't imagine who it might be. When he opened the door it was two county sheriff deputies.

"Are you Mr. Jonathan Miles, also known as Glenn Miles?" asked one of the deputies.

"Yes I am," answered Jonas.

"Sir, we are placing you under arrest. Then they read him his Miranda Rights:

"You have the right to remain silent. Anything you say, can, and will be used against you...."

When the big six foot five deputy finished, he led Jonas outside.

"What is this, a joke? What is this all about?" asked Jonas as they handcuffed him and led him to their squad car. Jonas's next door neighbor, Carla Masters was out watering her lawn again as she often did at this time of day at the expense of much embarrassment to Jonas. She watched the whole thing as they drove Jonas off in their squad car. She couldn't have imagined what Jonas could have done to deserve such treatment, 'He seemed like such a nice man'. They took Jonas down to the county jail, finger printed him, and told him he had the right to be appointed a counselor or he could get his own. Presently, Jonas only had a contract lawyer. He had never needed nor foresaw the need for services of what apparently would require a criminal lawyer.

"You get one phone call," said the guard.

Jonas thought about calling Aeton, but what if he wasn't home? He only got one call. He decided to call his mother. She would be relentless toward following Jonas's instructions. As of yet not even Jonas knew what was going on. Jonas's mother got a hold of Aeton and told him what her son had said happened. Currently, nobody within Jonas's circle of people even knew what the charge was until he went before a judge. Aeton sent his own personal attorney, Sid C. Byron to help Jonas. Sid quickly made his way to the county jail in time to talk to Jonas before the inquest. Sid was not just any lawyer he was one of the top five in Los Angeles. He didn't need a pass to get into the judge's chambers. Before talking to Jonas in his cell Sid found out that the charges against him were child molestation. It seemed one of the children in the orphanage whom Jonas didn't even know, had spread around a story about Connie and Jonas. Word spread quickly through the orphanage and the little story soon reached Grover Samuelson, who pressed to force trial hearings. If the accusation was true then Grover wanted Jonas punished to the maximum allowed by law, so he had put his own personal attorney, Jack Parsons on the case.

When Jonas was brought before the judge he was informed of the charges against him and asked how he pleaded. Of course, he pleaded 'Not Guilty'. Before being released on a $20,000 bond, he was informed that during the trial he was not allowed to try to make any contact with any of the orphan children, especially Connie, Wanda, Matt, and Fred. He was not even allowed to be within one half mile of the Orphanage.

Upon his release, Sid Byron brought Jonas to his office to ask questions of Jonas. He wanted to establish in his mind that Jonas was innocent so he would have confidence in defending Jonas. Then he completely went over everything that would be involved in the case, how he would approach the facts and how he would select the jury. For now, all Jonas could do was go home and live each day as best he could until it was all over. It didn't take Jonas long to realize that after the local and national news got a hold of his predicament his career could be in real jeopardy. It would take a miracle to rid one of the stigmas of such a charge even when innocent. Jonas wanted nothing more than to talk to Matt or Fred, and find out who this kid was that spread such lies, lies that would make it all the way to Grover Samuelson's ears.

The next day, Aeton called and even he didn't sound like the jolly old Aeton that Jonas was accustomed to. Jonas imagined that even he must have been skeptical of his innocence. Aeton called to apologize to Jonas about what the incident had forced him to do. He had to cancel a number of Jonas's upcoming engagements until the trial was over.

"Obviously this is best for everyone, my man. You don't want to go on stage with the public not knowing the facts and that won't come out until the trial is over," advised Aeton.

"Believe me, I've been in this business a long time. This isn't the first time I've had a client get hammered by all sorts of accusations and bad news coverage," he added.

Aeton went on to say that for the time being because he had faith in Jonas's innocence he would continue paying him the $300.00 weekly salary which was nothing compared to the gross receipts percentages, but at least it was something. Neither one of the men terminated the conversation feeling upbeat but both sensed the painful possibility of one's career being snuffed out as quickly as a sheet being drawn over a corpse. It was Jonas's darkest thought of the day.

The courts system in Los Angeles due to its extensive backlog could put some criminal proceedings as far back as months. It was only because Sid knew the right people who were also his golfing and bowling buddies that he was able to get the hearing moved up. Sid had talked to the four children, especially Connie and had felt perfectly fine that the accusing words never came out of their mouths. The children told him how they had told a lot of the kids about their trip to Mexico. They told Sid that they think jealousy had something to do with the perpetuated lies. They did exactly what Jonas warned them about. They blurted out everything just like they always did. After all, they were just kids.

The trial went on day after day with occasional news bits in the media while Jonas's records sales dropped to practically nothing. On the sixth day of the hearing the truth finally came out that a nine year old named Tommy Roscoe made up the story. He did it because he became angry, jealous, and disenchanted with life feeling he had been deserted by everyone. Sid articulated the whole investigation simply as a process of elimination, from where the story terminated to where the rumor began, and it all led to Tommy Roscoe.

The story of Tommy was a sad one. He didn't exactly know who his biological parents were let alone their names. He had been the child of a nineteen sixties era free love couple from Frisco. The mother's boyfriend forced her to give up the baby as the story goes. Tommy was taken in by a devout and loving couple who had adopted him. Unfortunately, and unbeknownst to the two new adoptive parents they would in time suffer one of the worst fates not just to themselves, but to the son they had adopted. Ivan Roscoe, Tommy's new father was a foreign news correspondent and his wife Janet was a grade school teacher. She was to pick up her husband coming in on a flight from West Berlin. Whilst she got closer to the airport to pick up her husband she had no idea that the captain of the DC-10 aircraft her husband was on had lost some of the major functions of the aircraft's flight controls. It was a miracle that he even got the bird down on the ground in any kind of horizontal attitude. The landing was basically a belly crash, sparks and skid to stop landing. In the end, when the aircraft finally came to rest there was major structural damage that resulted in the jet breaking up, but some sections remained intact with about a fifty percent loss of life, Ivan included. The strange thing was that his wife would never be there to learn of the news of the ill-fated flight, let alone pick up her husband. She was killed that same hour when her car flipped over on the freeway. Another driver cut in front of her from the far lane to make an off ramp causing her to swerve, resulting in her car flipping over. The jet crash was on the news one night and then the horrible story of Tommy's parents the next.

Then Tommy was once again alone at age four. He wound up with a family in Compton who temporarily took in foster kids. He spent nearly a year there before he was delivered to another home in Pasadena. More than a year later he wound up in a home in Baldwin Park. Then a couple expressed an interest in adopting the boy. They had invested several months taking him out on weekend excursions such as theme parks and such just like Jonas had been doing with his group of orphans. Suddenly, the woman's husband became seriously ill, and they gave up the idea of taking in Tommy. Finally, he was accepted by the Los Angeles Orphans Home. He had been there since the age of seven years and three months.

Tommy had no outside friends and the only places he got to go outside the orphanage was school, as well as the few trips the orphanage organized. He was one of the few kids who had no weekend chaperones like the others. There were some summer weekends when just he and a few other kids were the only ones left at the orphanage.

Tommy admitted that he made up the story because he felt abandoned, betrayed by everyone and left behind. Of course he envied the others who were having fun outside the orphanage while he seemed to be confined within the homes walls. So he became jealous. Tommy chose to make Jonas a victim, like he, of the person who didn't include him in the weekend fun. While Tommy spoke tears flowed from his eyes as well as from many in the courtroom. Then, as the Judge moved to excuse Jonas, Tommy the boy, wept on the witness stand for several minutes but it seemed much longer. The jury couldn't stand to listen to it anymore as they wiped tears from their own eyes.

It was Aeton's attorney whose counter questions revealed the unfortunate history of the boy prior to coming to the orphanage. Everyone present felt sorry for him and when he cried almost everyone cried with him. So here, perhaps Grover planned to have Jonas convicted and it all turned out to be a neglected boy fabricated story. They couldn't try the boy as an adult. He was simply called to the witness stand to tell the truth.

Being a boy didn't justify what he had done. The counselors convened into the judge's chambers to discuss some appropriate penalty for the lad who was just an eleven year old boy. Sid would also be conveying the wishes of Jonas, the person most affected by the whole ordeal. When it was time for the judge to sentence the boy the Judge told Jonas he was free to go.

The bailiff asked Tommy to stand up. Since Tommy was just a child there would of course be no incarceration, not in the real sense of the word. After Tommy Roscoe rose looking frightened, not knowing exactly what was going to happen at the plaintiffs table the judge spoke.

"Tommy Roscoe, are you truly sorry for the aggravation you have brought upon Mr. Miles," asked the Judge.

"Yes sir," he answered.

"Do you realize the scope and severity of damage that lying, bearing false witness can cause to one's good character?" asked the judge.

Tommy, not fully understanding the question looked at his attorney who whispered something to him.

"Yes, your honor, I do," responded Tommy.

Then considering Tommy that you are sorry for all of this, I sentence you to report with an appropriate escort for eight hours each Friday and Saturday morning to the custody of Jonas Miles for eight weeks. You will do whatever yard work he asks or any other similar and appropriate job an eleven year old young man like yourself might do, such as washing cars, cleaning windows, etc. Upon your return from each Saturday's penance you will write out a full written report of everything that you did for Mr. Miles on those days. Do you understand the instructions of this sentence?" asked the Judge.

"Yes sir," answered Tommy appearing emotionally affected by all that had occurred that day.

"Good, then this court hearing is concluded and all parties are dismissed," added the judge.

The results of the hearings hit the evening TV news, the newspapers, and even the gossip tabloids. Even though it was made very clear to those present in court that Jonas was completely innocent, just as Jonas imagined there would always be the doubters that weren't present in the court to hear the real facts of the case. Those doubters would even include some of his former fans. Jonas Miles, alias Glenn Miles the singer wasn't sure yet what his future would hold. Aeton booked him for a month's lineups of shows hoping that his fans would stand strong, but even the media's vindication of any wrong doing came out like some badly written abstract. Consequently, it didn't help and for whatever reason the concert attendance was a washout and very embarrassing for Jonas. His record sales never really picked up again. He received cards and letters from other stars and fans, some praising his resolve and talent and others from the public refusing to believe he was innocent and calling him sick names. Three months later, Aeton sent Jonas a letter of release from his contract saying that he would no longer be receiving any pay from his firm. He wanted to give him the news in person but he couldn't face Jonas.

In spite of all that happened, young Tommy Roscoe just as ordered by the courts and requested by Jonas came over on the first scheduled Friday and Saturday weekend to fulfill his penance by the judge. So, Tommy mowed Jonas's lawns and whatever work he was asked to do. When Tommy was done he asked Jonas if there was anything else that needed to be done.

"Is there anything else? Mr. Miles," asked the boy seeming very self-conscious about how he had been reminded by the orphanage that he had ruined Mr. Miles life.

"Is there anything else? Is there anything else?

"Yes! I believe there are some more things to do," said Jonas putting away all the yard tools.

"Let's go for a walk. Let's just walk around and see what we can find," said Jonas. So they just went walking over toward the Palisades. They walked over to the pier, bought a slice of Pizza and a drink and found some men painting one of the buildings.

"Let's sit down here on this bench and watch these men work," said Jonas. So they sat there and ate their pizza and drank their coke and watched those men work for more than an hour.

"You want to go somewhere else?" asked Jonas.

"Yes sir, I do," said Tommy.

"Then let's leave. Let's go somewhere else," said Jonas.

Soon they were over by another spot along the Palisades where they found some men laying a block wall near the public restrooms.

"Let's sit here awhile at this bench and watch these men work," said Jonas.

So they sat there for well over an hour and watched the men hard at work laying a block wall and sweat was rolling off their brows. By now the post noon sun was at its peak.

"Do you want to leave yet?" asked Jonas.

"Yes sir," answered Tommy.

"Want to go somewhere else?" asked Jonas.

"I guess so, I mean yes sir," answered Tommy a little hesitantly.

Jonas walked around and soon he found some workers at a construction site where there were framers putting up walls. He rearranged a lumber scrap pile to make a suitable place for them to sit.

"Let's sit here on this lumber pile and watch these guys work," said Jonas. So they did. They sat there and watched the framers frame, and some plumbers digging and threading pipe. After about an hour Jonas could see that Tommy was not too much interested.

They went back to Jonas's house and he let Tommy get in the front seat of his Camaro where the rest of the day they drove around to places watching people work. They went to a factory where Jonas knew a guy who let them watch the workers cut metal on huge lathes and mills. In the process red hot chips of metal spun off and occasional strays burned the operator's skin.

The following Saturday Jonas took Tommy to a poultry farm and egg ranch and they watched workers shoveling poultry excrement, feeding the hens, and collecting eggs. Then Jonas took Tommy to a police station where they drove around in a squad car for a while. The officer gave out a ticket, and Tommy watched the driver of the car yelling rude remarks at the officer. Then as time was running out for the day he took Tommy to a short order café to buy him dinner before they went back home. They watched the cooks cook, the waitresses wait tables and the helpers wash dishes. Then that was all the time left for that eight hour day as Jonas put Tommy back in his car and took him home where he was picked up by a person from the orphanage.

For the time being Jonas spent his Saturdays with Tommy while picking up the other kids on Sundays where they would go out and do things like before. He never again had to tell the kids not to tell anyone about their weekend trips after what had happened. They knew Jonas's career as a singer seemed to be over.

The next Saturday Jonas had Tommy vacuum the carpets and clean the kitchen sink before they took off again in search of watching people working. Jonas took his car to an auto shop for new brake pads and they watched mechanics work on engines, and tire busters change tires. They watched cement workers put in foundations and road workers shovel tar. They watched line workers replace telephone poles and ship mates swab decks. They watched skyscraper window cleaners and roofers put on roofs. The third week they did more of the same as they did in the fourth week. It was toward the end of the fourth Saturday that something really unexpected happened. They were at the Kaiser Steel Mills where they made steel and aluminum. They were down in the underground tunnels and it was noisy, hot, and there were huge furnaces everywhere. They were watching the men that operated the machines that pounded red hot metal into rolls and cubes. When Jonas looked at Tommy this time he could see that something was coming over the boy. They left and went back to Jonas's car.

"Please Mr. Miles I don't want to watch anymore people working," said Tommy with tears in his eyes, crying.

"I'm so sorry I hurt you, Mr. Miles. I'm so sorry I ruined your life," said Tommy.

Even though Tommy certainly had some significant involvement with Jonas's demise, Jonas knew who was really responsible, and it wasn't Tommy.

"Ruined my life, Tommy? I don't know if you ruined my life. You certainly changed it, that's for sure. Sometimes change happens for the better in people's lives. I just took you to all these places so that you might see what people have to do to earn a living. Did you see anything you think you might like to do?" asked Jonas.

"No sir, I didn't see anything I think I would like to do," responded Tommy.

"Then what do you think you would like to do?" asked Jonas.

"I want go to college," answered Tommy.

"College?" blurted Jonas, followed by a pause.

"Wait a minute. You mean I have been wasting my time showing you all the different kinds of jobs that you could do when you get older and you planned on going to college all along. Well I guess all of this watching people work was sure a waste of time, wasn't it?"

Tommy said just what Jonas wanted to hear. He wanted Tommy to succeed more than any of the other kids because he knew after the life that Tommy had been dealt it would be hardest for him. Yes, Jonas heard just what he was hoping from the boy.

"So what do you think you would like to be a dozen years from now?" asked Jonas.

"I never thought about it much until just a few days ago. I want to be either a fighter pilot or be a doctor," responded Tommy.

"Wow, that's two very different things. I had a surgeon who once operated on me who was a national guard fighter pilot so I guess you could do both?" said Jonas.

"Maybe," but I'm sure glad we have all those kinds of workers that we watched though or we wouldn't have much of a world to live in," responded Tommy.

Jonas thought the remark to be a very intelligent comment for a nine year old.

"Well now, just maybe you are smart enough to be both a doctor and a pilot. Where would we be if we didn't have people who had those job skills? It wouldn't be a very pretty picture would it? It takes the job skills of each and every one of us to prosper and sustain a quality of life, doesn't it?

"Yes, Mr. Miles."

"Tommy, you don't have to call me Mr. Miles. My name is Jonas. Call me Jonas from now on. You will be coming with the rest of the gang on our weekend trips, okay. I will be your chaperone. It wasn't easy to arrange but I had some help. From now on you will be with me and the other four of your brothers and sisters. It might not be every weekend but we will get out often enough. We are family, all of us, myself, you, Wanda, Connie, Matt and Fred, okay Tommy?" remarked Jonas.

"Okay Mr. Miles, I mean Jonas," said Tommy with tears forming. From then on Jonas always included Tommy with the rest of the kids and they always did everything together.

After dropping Tommy off at the orphanage Jonas went home and put a TV dinner in the oven. He looked at the Bulletin Board and then over at Marilyn. She seemed to be looking right back at him.

"Hi Marilyn, whats new?" he asked. No answer as usual.

Jonas walked over to the bulletin board and saw that many weeks had passed since Eleanor Marore had given him her phone number. He picked up his phone and called her number. An unfamiliar woman's voice answered the phone. It was Eleanor's house keeper. She said Eleanor was out and took down Jonas's number. She said that she would pass the information along.

TWENTY FIVE

A New Path and Theo Scott

One morning a few weeks after Jonas promised Tommy a permanent seat in his VW bus he was listening to some 45 records while reading the paper. He had put aside some recordings from a substantial accumulation of hits. His Motorola stereo unit could stack up to eight records for long play enjoyment. At that moment a song titled, 'O-o-h Child,' by The 5 Stairsteps was half way through its play time. As Jonas read the paper the celebrity in attendance possessed eye catching realism as she watched Jonas read his paper. She may have been listening to him talk. Jonas was feeling depressed. He was concerned about his future. Considering the stature he held in life only a few months ago he hardly wanted to go back to mowing lawns for a living.

"Hey, look, the county baseball leagues are starting up again in a couple of weeks," remarked Jonas, giving Marilyn a quick glance.

Of course, he never expected her to respond, he just wanted to see if it looked like she was paying attention. With Jonas deeply missing his father's presence he thought about times of long ago when his father had urged him to play. Now he felt more than any other time in his life a real confidence and passion to play the game. He believed that with hard work he could do well. He knew it was not likely he could break into the majors but maybe he could get noticed enough to make it to the minors. He might be a little old at 32, but he wasn't too old. Jonas called up the county parks department to enroll for the spring sessions so he could get assigned to a team. He had no idea what team he would be assigned to or where he would play. At any rate, nobody had to report anywhere for several weeks.

In the meantime, Jonas knew he had a lot of physical catching up to do. He was about twenty pounds overweight and he needed to get his full muscle strength back. In high school, try as he did with his six foot two height he could eat all he wanted and could not get his weight over 165. Now he was at 215, a little too heavy. No more fried foods or sodas for awhile. All of his food would be prepared at home. He would stick to nutritional basics like meat, eggs, low carb produce, vegetables, and plenty of water.

In the first few days Jonas started off by running two miles. He realized he was out of shape as those two miles did not come easy. He rode his bike to the gym where he did aerobics. He lifted weights and swam laps in the pool. Some days he ran down along the beach at surfs edge. He also radically changed his appearance. He grew a short neat Go-Tee and got a flat-top haircut. In less than a week he really didn't look like Glen Miles the singer anymore. Not that he had anything to be ashamed of as Glenn Miles. He was proud of all that he had accomplished in the last several years. In regards to what really destroyed his singing career, Jonas would try to forget about him. Jonas thought he was just going to take his girl, but he just about took everything else along with her. So now Jonas had to start over. It must have been so disheartening to Grover, that the boy who started the rumors confessed that he made the story up. Of course there would be those who would not give complete vindication because to those people there was always an underlying evil in people. Besides, celebrities made easy targets.

At any rate, now Jonas had been incubating this aspiration for baseball born of long ago memories and the desires of his father. He wanted to believe that his father could still be proud, because Jonas believed spiritual life outlived our mortal existence.

After about a week the county baseball application showed up in the mail for Jonas to fill out and mail in, which he did. He just put his name down as Jon Miles. It was amazing how many names you could get out of Jonathan. He wasn't particularly trying to escape from anything, he just felt he wanted some anonymity while in pursuit of his new goals in life.

Jonas also went down to a place called, 'Pro-Pitchn'Hit'. It was one of those baseball pitching parks where machines threw fast balls and people could get their batting practice in. Sometimes it was so busy that you had to wait for people to leave before you could get a spot. Each pitching machine was lined up in a row or column, about 75 feet long and about 20 feet wide. There was netting that incased the column so hit balls would stay within a confined area. Jonas went to the batting park three nights a week. He got in his warm up practice before the first meet day.

A few days later on a Saturday, Jonas and his bunch from the orphanage were driving up toward the hillside country just north of the city. Tommy was along as well as a woman from the orphanage named Sandra Steinman. Jonas didn't give up on the kids. He had put time and effort into their lives and he didn't want to throw it all away. He also didn't want to have to ever be put under the spotlight again like he recently went through in court. Everyone agreed it would be wise to have another escort like they originally had, before Kay left. Steinman was that person.

Sandra Steinman just turned forty so she was about eight years older than Jonas. She worked out of her home as a sales agent for a plastic materials company. She got all the perks, a new car every two years, a pension plan, a base salary plus commissions. The job allowed her evenings and weekends off which was perfect for spending some time at the orphanage. She had a soft side for kids, especially disadvantaged kids. She had only been onboard a few weeks and was a very outdoors oriented type of woman. She played tennis, occasionally shot trap and skeet, loved horses, and belonged to a bowling league. It had been her idea to go horseback riding and the kids all seemed excited about it.

It turned out to be a busy day for riding because by the time they reached the stables eighty percent of the horses were already out on the trails. That didn't necessarily mean the best horses were gone. The stable keeper came out with some good rides; there was an Appaloosa, a Roan, a couple of Buckskins, a Palomino and two Arabians. The stable keeper claimed all the horses had good dispositions.

"We have no choice but to get rid of any horses that act too wild or flighty. They might be okay for riders who know how to handle horses, but not for kids," exclaimed the middle aged man with hairy blond sun burnt forearms, wearing frayed blue denim pants and a weathered straw hat.

Connie and Wanda were saddled on the most easygoing horses and the group trotted off toward the ridge tops up behind the stables. The weather was cool and breezy under the feathery cirrus like collage of clouds. They saw numerous coveys of quail, coyotes, a road runner, lizards, and soaring hawks. The air was dry and the hooves of the horses constantly kicked up dust. Occasionally they galloped, but mostly they trotted in single file behind one another as they ascended or dropped down over the rolling hills.

The minutes quickly became hours and before the adventure seekers knew it their two hour trail ride came to an end. The sun was making its way to the western horizon where in a few more hours it would be lost behind the peaks of Catalina Island. By then, Jonas's party was tired, thirsty, and hungry. Before Jonas drove them all back to the orphanage he stopped at a mom and pop burger place and bought everyone a meal.

The following week Jonas received a postcard in the mail saying that he had been assigned to play for the Inglewood, 'Ravens'. He was to report to coach Theodore Scott, at Centinela Park. When Jonas called up to find out why he couldn't play in his own city of residence they told him that people have to go where there are still openings on their roster. Santa Monica had been booked out weeks earlier. When Saturday arrived Jonas found himself at Centinela Park in Inglewood, and it was just a matter of finding the right group. There were two large baseball diamonds with groups of people at each diamond.

Over a decade had passed since John F Kennedy stood up for the rights of African Americans in their quest to secure the same rights that other Americans enjoyed. Consequently, most of those now milling about on the ground near Jonas would have most likely not have been at this location during the pre-Kennedy years, at least not in this section of the county. In many locales realtors didn't show homes to people of color unless you were a celebrity, or someone of importance. Now most of the people who were here this day were Black, or Hispanic. In fact, Jonas was wondering if he should even finish his walk up to the congregations of people that he saw. Not that it bothered Jonas what color people were, but he felt on the contrary it might bother them what color he was.

"Well, I didn't come here to quit so we'll just see how it goes," he thought.

It could be dangerous for a white person to get caught up in the middle of certain neighborhoods in Los Angeles County at the wrong time and place. The same went for people of color. Since Kennedy died, LBJ had signed into law the Equal Rights Act of 1964. Of course, one couldn't just pass laws to force instant change in regards to how one feels about or treats another person, but it was a start.

Just the same, you must assume that all people are inherently good unless they prove otherwise. This was supposed to be about team sports, a community recreational offering for the fun of people playing a game. As Jonas got closer he could hear what appeared to be the coach calling names off a roster. There were about fifty people present ranging in age from about 19 to 50. By far, the bulk of those who were there looked to be in their twenties and thirties.

The six foot three black man now speaking had a very strong clear and deep voice. He was a stocky man with hefty shoulders and a thick torso. He had a larger then average head that sat on a stout neck. His skin was very dark, and you could barely see his eyes because he wore aviator type sunglasses that had very dark round lenses. Besides his hulk of a size, the glasses seemed to enhance his presence. Jonas didn't know exactly how many players were there but counting himself there were no more white people then the fingers on one hand. Jonas just stood in the back as the names were read off.

"Devan Childs, Rocky Folmer, Jose Luz, Ramon Noriega, Ernest Sampour, Angel Smith, Brutus Livingston, Franko Llamas, and the names kept coming off the roster one after the other, followed by all kinds of acknowledgments from a faint, 'Here', to a sharp and loud, 'Yeah'. Many of them had wives or girlfriends that came along or other family members.

"Jon Miles," shouted out the coach.

It was just another name off the roster like everyone else's name. No one had seemed to stare at people when their names were read. Of course, there were others who had to look at you so they could confirm who you were, or looked to size you up. However, when Jonas responded with, 'Here,' a multitude of faces turned around to look and stare at the face from which emanated the reply.

"Is there such a thing as a white person's voice? I guess so. What were all those pairs of eyes thinking? Were they all mumbling words beneath their breath or was that just his imagination," wondered Jonas.

The coach gave Jonas a longer than expected observation. Then, after reading off all the names the coach spoke of other things.

"Well it's 1976 and I will be your coach for our nation's centennial year of Americas Freedom, or should I say the 'Freedom of Many'."

At that statement many let out a slight laugh or made some kind of muffed response or short expletive like,

"Yeah, right!, or Uh huh."

He went on to say,

"Or most peoples freedom that is," the coach enjoyed his jest than pausing gave a few fair skinned people that were there the eye of his attention. However, they could not see his eye's, they were hidden in the shadows of those round dark lenses.

Some in the crowd found the remark humorous while others seemed to take the statement in a more serious impartial note. At any rate, the coach liked to pour on a minute of sentiment that favored his soul brothers on that first day of practice. It was all about humor to him. He always threw in a few one liners to see what kind of reaction he got. He always found it amusing if he could arouse any degree of embarrassment or concern in the faces of any of the lighter skinned athletes.

"Of course, we're all about baseball here."

"My name is Theo, Theo Scott," he yelled out with a crisp clear deep resonation while looking around slowly, left to right. "Anyone that decides my name is Theodore means that they want to be either a bat boy, a water boy, or someone's boy," he exclaimed, drawing laughter.

"This is my fourth year with the Los Angeles county leagues. Many of you know me already. You may also know that I am a former pro player out of Chicago. I was also an assistant coach for Arizona State, and prior to coming here a batting coach for the University of California. I take winning seriously," he remarked.

"Do we have any ex-pro players here?" asked the coach.

No one answered.

"Do we have any ex college players?" A few raised their hands.

"Is there anyone here who doesn't know how to play baseball?"

No response.

Then Theo handed out various pieces of literature such as the season game schedules, places to buy their uniforms, various items of equipment, their cost, as well as some background questionnaires.

"On the questionnaires I don't need your life history. Just tell me something about yourself, such as if you're going to school and where. Where you're from? List any hobbies if you want, where you work, that's up to you. For instance, I'm from Illinois and one of my hobbies is popping coconuts in the palms of my hands. Does anyone want to see me put a squeeze on a coconut?" said the coach with a gruff voice looking slowly around.

One of the players a half foot shorter then Theo started laughing. Theo walked up to him and put the palm of his hand on top of his head. With his long thick fingers on one side of the man's skull and thumb on the other, he applied a little pressure. The man stopped laughing.

"Is something funny?"

"Does anyone else think my hobby is funny?" asked Theo looking around.

The man who looked to be the oldest spoke up. He was a white guy, over six feet, thin, noticeably aging, but sinewy looking.

"Do you think I'm too old to play for you, I mean with these guys?" asked the man.

Theo looked at the man for a few seconds before he spoke.

"Are you saying that you feel intimidated by these physically younger and superior black athletes?" asked Theo, followed by a second of silence and then reinforced with scattered grins.

"Well, I don't personally judge a person by their appearance, or by the way they look or how old or young they are like some people."

There were a few low key vocal jabs at that remark.

"I judge a person by the way they act, by the way they carry themselves. How I arrive at my conclusions about them as an athlete is based on what they can show me. So sir, don't look around here upon your teammates and make premature decisions you might be sorry for. When it's your turn to bat, step up to the plate and get a hit. When it's your turn to get someone out, make the catch. Not until then should you look around and answer that question for yourself," responded Theo.

Then there was a short pause.

"No matter what though everyone who chooses to stay will be playing ball. If your good you'll be playing in the championship games and we will be making it to the championships. But everyone gets to play in the league games," responded Theo.

"I'm glad to see that a lot of you brought mitts and those that didn't, that's okay. I want the people with mitts to pair up about five yards apart and practice throwing the ball back and forth. After every ten throws take ten more steps backward and throw ten more at each other. Keep doing that until I say stop. The rest of you will practice batting," stated Theo.

Jonas brought the old mitt he had in High School. Bringing it along was an afterthought as he had been so busy with other things. It really didn't fit as good as it once did but he planned on buying a new one anyway. What's more, not one person here seemed to recognize who he was nor would he expect any would. No one ever even raised an eyebrow while throwing the ball back and forth. He did truly look like a totally different person.

That Saturday morning introduction to his team lasted four hours, from 10am to 2pm. As Jonas practiced throwing the ball with the others it appeared that some of the players were not very friendly even though he tried his best to be friendly, even humorous. Jonas could be very patient, he would give things time. Time could work for or against one. He was betting it would work for him.

Here, Jonas was a minority. He didn't really think that things could get so bad. However, part of what prejudice is, is failing to fully recognize the person standing next to you. Regardless of color, the empowered who practices prejudice may deny one or many the opportunity to that which they seek in life. In America, every true and patriotic citizen should have a right to seek and attain any respectable or worthy place in its society. Jonas had hoped he would not be denied his opportunity. It was possible that he could be ostracized but he did not think it would be committed to him by this group and he would not quit.

County sports leagues as established by local governments of their respective cities were never meant to be taken so seriously as pro sports teams, or even High School teams. They were organized for fun and recreation. That was where the bureaucratic control in these leagues ended. Unless a coach was so abusive to cause bodily harm or use excessive psychological tactics, coaches were never removed from their positions. Theo Scott took anything he coached seriously as many coaches would. He only cared about winning. Nothing else mattered to him when it came to the game and he was not alone. There were others who were in these leagues for more than just the fun of the sport. It didn't matter if you were a player or a coach, most wanted to get something more out of the game. They wanted recognition. They wanted a way to climb higher. In reality it was what Jonas wanted too.

Though Theo could have drove a brand new Cadillac if he wanted, he drove a gloss maroon 1962 Thunderbird convertible, or T-Bird as they called them. There were other T-Birds on the road in the vicinity as well, but if you saw a black man driving a maroon T-Bird convertible, especially with a cigar in his mouth it was a good bet it was going to be Theo Scott. Theo couldn't be described as anything other than conservative when it came to politics. He thought of life like a defensive fortress where he doled out sparingly what was needed to achieve his goals all the while scrimping and saving any amassed exuberance of what he held in esteem, be it people or assets. Then, if really needed he would call on his extensive resources to confront or finish the job, any job.

As a radio and TV antenna manufacturing entrepreneur, Theo Scott had been enjoying a boom in sales as CB radios were all the rage. Freight line truckers and the public had been spending big dollars on wattage boosters, sidebands, and state of the art antennas which increased the effective range of the radios. Sometimes on a good day people in California could talk to people in Hawaii, or other faraway places when the atmospheric skip was right. Theo being resourceful as he was had secured all the technology know how he needed to form his company from his local library. He simply used his imagination and known prior technology to make his product stand out from the rest. His company, 'Sky-Skipper Antenna,' employed forty five full time employees.

He liked to smoke expensive cigars and play golf on Sundays. His wife and he enjoyed their four bedroom upper middle class house in a better than average neighborhood in the city of South Gate. His two children had grown and were attending out of state universities. Theo had a taste for nice things, but wasn't foolish. In regards to baseball he was extremely zealous.

That evening Jonas went out to a sporting goods store and bought some equipment like a mitt, cleated shoes, some bats, and a uniform.
He took the equipment home with the intention of putting his own bats to use that evening at the batting park. First he had some work to do to the handles of his newly purchased bats. It was a known fact that weather and competitive tension could play havoc with a players grip on a bat. For decades there had always been some pros who exercised a little wood working finesse at that grip area of the bat to give them a little edge. Jonas had read that Ted Williams used the sharp edges of bottle caps to scuff up the handle area for a good non slip grip on the bat.

Upon arriving at home Jonas proceeded to change into his baseball shoes to get a start on giving his new sports equipment a workout down at the pitching park. The machine threw most of the balls straight and fast, which Jonas didn't find to difficult to connect with. He hit some fouls of course but most were good solid hits. A pitching machine threw balls fairly consistently as they could not duplicate a seasoned pitchers slider, breaking, or curve ball as they were referred to.

Late Monday afternoon Jonas found himself at Centinela Park ready for practice. The coach wasn't there yet and some of the players were taking turns at batting while others were throwing a baseball back and forth. The way the pitcher and catcher played together suggested they had been a paired team for some time. The pitcher had a great fast ball and a pretty slick slider pitch. Suddenly, you could hear the rumble of an engine as Theo came rushing in with his T-Bird and a cigar stuck between his lips.

"Good, Good, I like that," said Theo giving a thumb's up signal.

"Talking about self-discipline are you guys motivated or what?"

"Okay, now we need to do some warm ups every day to get limber and strengthen some of those flabby muscles that some of you have," remarked Theo.

"Okay, let's do some 'jump'n-jacks.' Line up here guys. Give me five rows right here," the coach ordered.

After doing the exercise they followed with sit-ups, pushups, and running around the field several laps.

To many the exercises were expected but some of the candidates were obviously far out of shape, overweight, and too old. Some would not return for any further practice and that was just part of the weeding out process. The leagues were under the auspices of the Parks and Recreation department. They were meant to be an activity for fun and entertainment, but as mentioned by Theo any such sports would always be about competition, first and foremost. There were others like he who aged past the heyday of their prime, who had nowhere else to go for the thrill of their game, but to coach.

"Okay, everyone who didn't get to bat last time line up along here. The rest of you guys start throwing baseballs like I had you last time. In a little while I will show you how to practice picking up grounders," stated Theo.

It soon became clear that Theo knew a lot about baseball and that he had a lot to show to anyone who wanted to learn. He would talk about a particular aspect of baseball and then he would do a few demonstrations, and have everyone practice that application of the game. They practiced bunting, catching high flies in the sun, and picking up hopping grounders. Theo was relentless in regards to the importance of practice.

"Baseball is a fun sport gentleman, but it's always a lot more fun when you win," he remarked.

There may have not been anything new about that statement but one could not argue as to the validity of it being factual. Theo was sort of like one of those warriors who collected things from the conquered to prove the act occurred. Those things to him were the trophies that lined the shelves of his study, his fireplace mantle, and his office wall. There were trophies from his

High School days, from college, his pro years, and college coaching terms. Now he had collected trophies from the county parks to add to his collection. It was not uncommon for pro baseball scouts to stop by occasionally and take a quick look at county players, but to see if there was anyone they might be interested in.

TWENTY SIX

Angels, Hoodlums, and Trout

Considering all the cars Jonas now owned he preferred the 58 Chevy to drive around town. Sometimes he drove his Cuda, which he still liked immensely. When driving around with the orphan group he usually drove the VW bus. On occasion Jonas also had a soft spot for the 60 Ford convertible and the Starliner. Like his 58, the Ford Starliner had a bench seat which he really liked. The Starliner also supplied plenty of punch with the ample 390 V8, and the automatic trans provided comfortable care free driving. Unfortunately, in the latter part of the sixties bench seats either fell out of favor with the public or the manufacturers would just not install them anymore. However, Jonas never lost his fondness for those old car couches. Marilyn's spirit was frequently with Jonas much of the time when he drove his cars around from place to place. He never knew when she was there of course, at least not so as he could see her. It had always been that Jonas only knew her however spiritually it was through the cognizance of his own minds desire. Always so observant of that colorful and vividly reproduced figure at his home he believed there was something more there than others had any chance of seeing. If only Jonas had a notion of how close her spiritual presence was to him at times while driving his car, or at home, not to mention various other places. As before, at times the public might see her but not so as to understand who she actually was, and Jonas was blinded to the vision of her apparition by necessity.

Naturally, no one else who saw her really thought it was Marilyn, she was deceased. After all, there were plenty of Marilyn impersonators to go around in the world especially in Hollywood. It wasn't unusual for guys at traffic slow down's or stop lights to say bold things to her. Depending on what they said, some she ignored and others she might have thrown one of her familiar poses that radiated that sex she was so adept at portraying. It happened often enough and Jonas just thought some guys were throwing smart ass remarks at him. He just imagined they were weird or it was just part of the usual Los Angeles craziness that could be found in people. He was wondering why suddenly he was becoming such an attraction and he wasn't comfortable with it. Sometimes when driving around town on a nice warm day, Jonas anticipating crass remarks towards him chose to drive with the top up. He just wasn't in the mood to waste his thinking on what it was that made people say stupid things. There were other not so favorable events that occurred. These incidents were significant enough that it became necessary for Marilyn to intervene on Jonas's behalf. One evening long past midnight Jonas affected with insomnia decided to take a walk along the Palisades. Heading for an overlook above Coast Highway he surprised four thugs who seemed to be not only acting strange, but saying crazy things. Upon seeing Jonas alone with no one else around they quickly approached him. They weren't like the normal street people looking for spare change.

"Hey Man, Do you got money?" one asked brazenly.

Jonas didn't have any money on him because he had left his wallet on his dresser. That was where he always placed his personal things after emptying out his pockets before retiring for the evening. He simply didn't think about these items when he left the house.

"No, I don't. I'm just taking a walk. I couldn't sleep," responded Jonas.

"Hey, you know, we got the same problem. We can't sleep either," said another, when the four let out a half hearted laugh that only themselves could find amusing. It was almost instantly apparent that there could be trouble with these guys. Jonas started surveying his options. He could run and possibly out run them but what if they had a gun? He could stay and fight them but there were too many. He wasn't Bruce Lee.

"I know your lying though. You got money," said the one who seemed to be the leader as he pulled out a switch blade and with the push of a button a four and a half inch polished steel blade flashed in the moonlight, as it sprang open.

Jonas put his hands up as a gesture then reached inside his front pockets and pulled them inside out. Then half turning around he lifted his shirt and showed them his empty back pockets.

"Pretty obvious I got nothing," shot Jonas.

"Hey, don't show us your ass man. We didn't ask to see your ass," said the thug followed by more laughter.

"Well, if I had a few bucks I might make a donation to your favorite charity?" Jonas replied sharply. The hoods let out an abrupt but hardly amused laugh.

"A donation to our favorite charity, he says. Oh shit, is that funny or what?" but no humor to be found in any of the faces.

Better take off your clothes, socks, everything and throw them over here," said the knife wielder, grinning, revealing a dental nightmare.

"Maybe he's got some gold in his jaw," said one who hadn't spoke yet, causing two to laugh some more.

Thinking again Jonas thought about their last request. He needed his shoes and pants. His shirt he could do without. Taking off his T-shirt he approached the man with the knife as if to hand it to him and at the last minute swirled the shirt around his fist. The man lunged at it like a bull lunges at a bullfighters cape. With Jonas's other hand he grabbed the man's wrist and managed to knock the knife loose from his hand. The four men were obviously high, either on drugs, alcohol, or both. It was when the other three men had moved in on Jonas that Marilyn decided she had to help.

Some people call them dust devils or dirt devils and others call them miniature tornados, but the effect is the same. However, the spin wizard that Marilyn created had much more force. She brought it up over the Palisades from the sandy beach and it was saturated with sand as it engulfed the five people, Jonas included. A torrential whirlwind of air suddenly had the five men spinning around fast enough to set those within off their feet. Quickly, Marilyn extracted Jonas out from the twirling phenomenon. Jonas wasn't sure at first who or what was responsible for the adrenalin inducing spectacle than he thought maybe he had an idea who might. Now as an observer he watched as the four hoodlums were caught up in the air current spinning around, falling down, getting up, frantically trying to maintain their balance as they stood, fell, and stood and fell. Intermittently, they became aware of Jonas standing there watching them in his own awestruck fashion. Jonas was now a good 10 yards from them throughout the entire melee. After a few minutes, Marilyn caused everything to slow down until everything came to a complete stop. The facial expressions of the men as they stood there enshrined in seaweed and crabs projected a swift and just gratification for Jonas. Then the hoods looked at each other in complete shock and fear as they ran off looking like alien creatures.

Jonas walked over to where the incident happened, saw the knife laying on the ground, picked it up and dropped it in the nearest trash can before he walked home. Through the whole ordeal Jonas never saw Marilyn, and he was just as astonished as the thugs but he suspected that perhaps she had something to do with his rescue.

Another late evening a lonely Jonas after watching TV until all the stations had signed off didn't feel like going to bed. He left his home to go for a drive in a 63 VW Bug that had been his uncles. He was driving around in the early morning hours listening to radio talk shows. He had no clue that he wasn't alone. Marilyn happened to be with him as she often was, again unbeknownst to Jonas. Marilyn once an insomniac herself and lonely many an evening as people sometimes were understood exactly the guy behind the wheel.

From out of nowhere came alongside Jonas's car an old large black 63 Lincoln Continental cruiser. All the windows were open in the car as a boisterous and rowdy bunch within the car's interior shouted obscenities at Jonas, for no reason. On one side of the boulevard was the huge expanse of the fenced 20th Century Fox lot of which no one could turn. The only turns Jonas could possibly make were left turns, the same side the Lincoln cruiser was on, so Jonas was boxed in, being herded like an animal. He couldn't turn at all. The unruly bunch in the car would match Jonas's speed as he sped up, and slowed whenever he did. They laughed at him and threw empty wine or beer bottles at his car, or on the street. They were so close Jonas smelled the tobacco from their cigarettes, the unmistakable scent of weed, even the breeze was steady enough to usher in the scent of the alcohol they were drinking. Who knew what else they were high on. If only Jonas had one of his race horse cars, but his little 40 Horsepower VW engine was no match for the big Lincoln's power plant. There are times in people's lives when they really wished they would see a cop, but there was nothing in sight. Not even another pair of headlights. Occasionally Jonas would sail through the few stop lights that were always green, and the black demon car would not go away.

Marilyn had apparently had enough as well as she was waiting at the next intersection for the big heavy Lincoln cruiser. At the last second she placed herself entirely visible in the crosswalk to the driver of the Lincoln. In a flash she was directly in his path wearing something very similar to her 'Seven Year Itch,' outfit', complete with wind flounced skirt. Not believing his eyes the driver sharply swerved to avoid hitting her before entering the crosswalk. The car went out of control, crashed through a U.S. Postal mailbox, a street sign, and came to a sudden stop when it hit a large diameter steel light pole. Jonas stopped and looked at the car with steam coming out from underneath the hood. In a wink, Marilyn was back next to Jonas. Jonas did not realize that Marilyn was responsible for his rescue or why the driver swerved headed for certain intercourse with city infrastructure.

Marilyn took a look at the wrecked car and then looked at Jonas as she rested her arm along the top of the seat at Jonas's back. They then both turned their heads back to the street and Jonas drove on. Jonas would never know why the car veered and went out of control. About a mile up the road Jonas found a pay phone and reported the crash. He felt confident with any luck the occupants of the other car might have outstanding warrants.

Why would Marilyn Monroe be spending any time with Jonas Miles, people might ask? The answer may not be so simple. Maybe it was because Jonas had picked himself up just as she had done so many times when life had a way of knocking you down. Maybe it was because Jonas had his share of lonely nights, as she too often had, even when at her greatest level of fame and popularity. Maybe there was something more to his character then she had ever known before in others or maybe it was because he had taken it upon himself to help children. Whatever it was, she was there and no one could know the day that might be otherwise.

After losing his employment with Conroy, Jonas had little income from his recordings. His assets were everything his uncle left him, the cash, the cars inside the industrial building, and those cars were what kept him from renting out the industrial building. There were so many of them he would just have to keep them elsewhere if he leased the building. He also hadn't forgotten about the old but useable printing presses that were there, that use to be in his father's shop. He had ideas about all these things going on in his head that he would have to think on. Regarding the cash his uncle had left him, Jonas not being stupid had invested most of it. Being a bit frugal he also had a good portion of the money left over that he had made while singing under contract with Anniston. He would have to come up with something else though to avoid cutting into his investments.

Jonas wasn't a predictable person, at least not in the sense that you could guess his next move. He had a spontaneous nature and only planned things in advance if it were out of necessity. The only thing Jonas probably did about the same time each day was to get up in the morning. He might have lunch at one, and a light dinner at five, but he never let up on his workouts for baseball. Coach Scott would probably be making some decisions soon as who he thought would make a good starting lineup. Jonas continued to walk, run, and ride his bike. The weight lifting was rapidly making noticeable changes to his body. In fact, within the next few months with Jonas's short hair and improved physique it would take a trained eye to recognize the character that was once Glenn Miles.

Weekends were about the only time Jonas could pick up the kids so when Sunday morning arrived, Jonas picked up Sandra Steinman and the kids from the orphanage in his 59 Cadillac El Dorado. They headed for a weekend drive into the mountains. First they drove to Wrightwood where they all got something to eat, then crossed over through Cajon Pass than headed up through Crestline toward Lake Arrowhead. While Jonas and the kids went fishing from shore, Sandra took out her art easel and drawing board. She began to sketch the tree lined lake scene with Jonas and the kids in the foreground. She was nearly finished when a breeze came up and suddenly the calm surface of the lake changed to small rolling white caps. The wind caused the air to become cooler as everyone put on a sweater, or jacket, until Sandra finished her sketch. Meanwhile, Jonas and the young anglers caught a grand total of four trout of which Jonas removed the entrails and wrapped them in old newspaper. They put everything in the ice chest. Then they left the lake to do some more local exploring before driving home. Everyone had a great time and the kids especially enjoyed the fresh mountain air and the blue gem scenery of the lake that was woven into the tall whispering pines.

TWENTY SEVEN

Watch and Weep

Though certainly noticeable to the pitcher it could be obvious to anyone all the different stances and styles batters adopted at the plate. Some batters squatted down and let their bats hang loose draped over their backs. Others seemed to have their legs turned in the direction they wanted to hit the ball. A few waved their bats around like they were stirring a pot. Some kept practicing a follow through right up until the pitchers wind up. Some seem to stand far away from the plate or even a little close. Like one's signature or personality trait most batters seemed to never stray from the way they stood at the plate. Others were not so flamboyant, like Jonas. He just walked up to the plate, reached his bat out to the far edge of the plate to set his position and took a few practice swings. He stood semi erect and held the bat high up behind his head, and he held the bat steady until he swung.

Jonas was at batting practice and Theo was taking a look at who could bat. Theo had his best pitcher throwing all kinds of balls. Theo was comfortable with his team as many of the players were carry overs from the previous season. His favorite pitcher was Angel Smith, and there weren't that many batters who could consistently hit off of him.

"Okay, next! What's your name?" asked Theo.

"Jon Miles."

"Okay, show me your stuff," remarked Theo, feeling pretty sure he was talking to someone mediocre at best.

Jonas walked up to the plate and set his position. Took a couple of slow follow through swings and then leaned in at the ready.

In many ways there was just things extraordinary about Jonas. All of this was kept perfectly concealed inside a very modest and humble shell. He would never say it to anyone but he knew he was different in ways, but then everyone was different from each other in one way or another. He knew he had a gift. Whether it was his reflexes, his coordination, his eye sight, god's grace, or a conglomeration of it all, he had known since he was young how lightning fast his reflexes were. It didn't matter if there were things falling off of shelves at home or people tossing things quickly at him, his reflexes were about as fast as anyone ever saw.

Of course that didn't mean he could hit any old pitch. If the ball came in way outside of the plate it was no good. If the ball came to far inside it was no good. Of course, if the ball was too high or too low it was no good. However, if the ball came in anywhere else over that plate, most good batters should get a hit. The truth was Jonas was a very good batter, he always was. It was like he had some kind of computerized robotics that did all the math calculations where speed, trajectory, and distance were concerned. It didn't make any difference if it was a curve ball, a slider, or a fast ball, most of the time he would get a good solid hit when the odds were stacked against it. He didn't need pills, steroids, or a priests blessing. He just tried to be as good as he had diligently prepared himself. Angel decided to give Jonas a fast ball right over the center. He did his wind up and let the ball fly. With a loud solid smack the bat and ball met, sending it over the center field fence. Next Angel threw an inside pitch for a ball. Then he threw an outside high pitch for a ball. Jonas wasn't going to have any of those sucker pitches. Next a slider came in high but dropped low headed for a strike. Jonas's bat met it with a powerful upward swing sending the ball over the left field fence. Theo took notice, but so far it was just a couple of lucky hits. Some of the guys much bigger then Jonas watched in amazement as he continued to hit speedy grounders, long distance fly balls and numerous home runs. Angel Smith, a slim tall man of remarkable talent as a pitcher became quite frustrated with Jonas's success. Finally, he had to wonder if the team now had quite a hitter on their side, as did Theo.

"Damn!" Theo whispered to himself while Jonas was at bat.

"Okay next," Theo kept saying repetitiously to each batter as he watched every one try their hand with Angel Smith.

When everyone was through taking their turn at bat, Theo told the guys to take their mitts off and to practice throwing and catching balls with only their hands, on the hop, and throwing to first base. In the meantime Theo took Jonas aside. He had some questions he wanted to ask him.

"When I asked if anyone ever played college or pro ball, did you hear me?" asked Theo.

"Yeah, I played High School ball," responded Jonas.

"How did you do then?' Theo asked.

"I was pretty good."

"How old are you?"

"Thirty two."

"Where do you live?"

"Santa Monica."

"You couldn't get on a local team, that's why they stuck you over here?"

"That's right."

"Well, are you having a good day or do you always hit like that?"

"I don't know, maybe I'm just having a good day."

Jonas looked at Theo's dark lenses, as the coach took a long silent look at him.

"You sure you want to play for us," said Theo, as he looked at Jonas for a few seconds. Jonas looked off toward the ball players.

"Why wouldn't I?"

"Well I guess it's up to you to make things click," said Theo.

"Click?" responded Jonas.

"Well you know, getting along. Playing sport's is all about team work. It's about everyone playing as a team. I've got no problem with you. It's hard telling with some of these guys. Depends on what life has dealt them. If you didn't hit or play the field well I would not give you any encouragement. I know in some of these leagues around here a white guy trying to get into a black club is like a Black guy applying for a bank manager position. He probably isn't going to get the job. The way you hit, some of these young guys want to play pro. Not sure they will cheer you on. I'm just saying you will have to take care of yourself here."

"I always take care of myself."

"Okay then, why don't you get over there and get some throwing practice in?"

Later on after Jonas left, Theo had a talk with some of the other guys. He asked them to be cool with everybody. .

"Take that man Jonas, if he be cool then you be cool, okay."

Jonas continued with the days practice and then he went home. He was tired and it had been a long day. But he loved the game more than ever. He wished that he had the same passion when he was a kid. It was the only thing he really had to look forward to now that he was no longer performing as the once popular Glenn Miles. He liked it better then singing. When you sing the same songs over and over things could get too familiar and a little boring. In baseball you never knew what was going to happen.

Jonas decided to call Gina, alias Eleanor Marore one more time. No doubt all the high profile negative publicity he had gone through in the last several months had scared her off as well. He was surprised she still had the same number when she herself answered the phone. After a short conversation they had arranged to meet near the pier. They were going to drive down Coast Highway toward Malibu. Jonas was planning on picking her up in his Ferrari, than he thought it wasn't a good idea. So he picked her up in his daily driver, the 58 Chevy. Wisely he left the top up. The car was eighteen years old now. Other then looking like a new, old car, it was really just a nice car. It was nothing real special in the public's eye other than an older cool convertible. It would not draw much attention which was good for Gina.

Gina, or Eleanor as many now called her hardly recognized Jonas. He looked so different, having a taut black T-shirt that clung tightly to his biceps and chest but hung loose around his trim waist. His Flat Top and neatly trimmed goatee completely caught her off guard. They talked and they talked. She had become a big star, but Jonas wasn't so sure that she seemed as happy as that day they went chasing that Buffalo herd.

Since that day, Jonas had seen her in magazine articles and on the big screen. She had looked like a million dollars the way those Hollywood technicians could work their magic. Of course, Gina was always beautiful but with the floppy canvas hat she now wore and the dark sunglasses with no makeup she really did not look recognizable. They drove to Zuma Beach and parked the car along the highway and headed for the surf. They took off their shoes and walked toward Paradise Cove. The wet sand and the frothy cool ocean felt good on the pads of their feet. Seagulls screeched, squawked, glided, and hovered overhead in their familiar manner. Higher up, a flock of Pelicans with long outstretched wings flew swiftly by toward Point Conception. Occasionally, the two met other couples, joggers, or young families. There was a cool onshore breeze.

"For a long time I wondered what happened to you after that last time I saw you," said Jonas.

"Yes, I know. You probably saw that guy who came out of my apartment. Well I was working at the Café one night and that guy and his partner stopped at the café. He started telling me how much charisma I had, how pretty I was. Well that kind of stuff wasn't anything a girl hadn't heard before. Then he starts talking about people he knew in the Hollywood business. That he could set me up with someone who could get me a screen test for commercials. Sure sounded like more of the same garbage girls have to listen to. Well he gave me a phone number and I took a chance. I happened along just when they were looking for someone like me for a part. If it wasn't for that guy, I might still be waiting tables."

Thinking, Jonas didn't respond. There was a short silence.

"Are you happy?" he asked.

"Yes, as much as can be expected. They expect a lot, and you have to come through for them."

"I know I can't do this forever, right?" she blurted.

"I think that would be sensible thinking. Is anything forever?" he asked.

"Maybe the waves," she answered, looking at the sea.

"Invest your money."

"I'm doing the best I can. At this point I really haven't made that much yet. Hard to know who you can trust. There probably is money skimmed from me."

"Yeah," blurted Jonas.

"I guess that boy ruined your singing career," remarked Gina.

"A good bet. I mean, yeah, looks like it. He's just a kid. God, I was a kid once and remember a few terrible things I wish I never did."

The two looking down as they talked and not paying any attention got hit by a rogue wave which quickly slid up on shore and caught them around the thighs. The two laughed as they tried to gain ground.

"I never doubted your innocence, Jonas."

"I really don't blame Tommy. He's just a kid. He felt left out. He was as a matter of fact. I have added him to my group, my orphan family."

Gina only knew about the orphan kids he was helping because of the media exposure surrounding his trial.

"To tell you the truth Jonas I wasn't in a hurry to see you again right after I talked with you at the charity dinner."

"Don't have to say anything Gina, I understand. The whole trial fiasco ruined my singing career. It doesn't need to hurt yours too, or anyone else's."

"That's the part that really sucks, Jonas. Even when you're innocent, it's like some bad odor that taints you and it lingers and won't readily go away," she remarked.

"What are you going to do now?" Gina asked.

"I'm going to play baseball."

"Baseball?" she said, as if she didn't hear him right.

"Yeah, I signed up for the county leagues. You know, where you play different cities and stuff."

"I guess that will be fun, but it doesn't provide an income, does it?" she remarked.

"Probably just a small one for the coaches," Jonas grinned.

"What team are you on?"

"The Inglewood Raven's."

"Well, I'll bet you'll do well, Jonas."

"We'll see."

Another impressive wave came up and Jonas saw a spot where bubbles were rising in the sand. He started frantically digging with his hands. Gina looked on in surprise. He pulled out a sand crab. It was quite normal, about the size of a half dollar. He felt its back. It was soft. Only about one in twenty have soft backs, most of them being hard shelled. It all had to do with molt timing. The crabs having the soft shelled backs were the most prized by marauding surf fish looking for something to eat. Local fishing tackle stores paid industrious kids who spent a morning catching them a tidy amount to place them in their live bait section.

"Bingo! It's a soft shell!"

"Oh?" responded Gina, not knowing what he met but they both laughed again as he tossed it back into the sea.

It was amazing how on such a day and place as that before them, beneath a deep azure sky such a vigorous appreciation for life could persist in ones bodily core. Here along that frothy ensemble of wave after wave countless people had come through out the ages to contemplate their thoughts or just find some peace within their souls. This was just such a place where life met the sea.

"You know what Jonas? You know what I would like us to do again, someday soon?" she asked.

He was silent, giving her a quizzical look as the pairs eyes met.

"I would like us two to go see my grandfather again and..." Jonas interrupted.

"So, he is still alive?"

"Sure, but he's hired people for assistance. He can't do everything anymore. Anyway, wouldn't it be fun to do that Jeep ride again?" she asked.

"It might be at that, but maybe I should do the driving," he responded, the two laughing.

They walked for several hours talking about all kinds of things. There seemed to be a chemistry between them. Then they decided they were hungry, but Jonas didn't think it a good idea for the two to go into an establishment, at least not while she might be recognized with him.

They drove to a drive-through and got a couple of burgers, some fries, and a couple of drinks. They stopped at a place near the beach, ate and watched the waves as they talked. Then they drove down to the pier and took a walk before Jonas drove by his place and showed Gina where he lived. Then he dropped her off by her car. He got out of his car to look at her new imported convertible. Then they gave each other a friendly kiss.

"If you ever need a shoulder, or a friendly ear, just call or drop by anytime," said Jonas.

"Thank you Jonas. We'll meet up again soon, I'm sure," responded Eleanor with a smile. Jonas got back in his car and drove the short distance back to his house.

Once inside, Jonas sat at his favorite place at the kitchen table. Jonas felt a little anxiety and disappointment about the way life could evolve sometimes. It could certainly have its share of complications.

"You know, Marilyn, sometimes when you meet someone new or get a chance to rekindle an old flame it seems like you could be taking the first step of a beautiful thing. Then you wake up and it seems like it's just another dream," said Jonas looking at her.

Within that beautiful face a pair of sad looking eyes peered back at Jonas as he spoke. Jonas could always count on Marilyn. It seemed no one could ever possess her. She was anyone's friend who had a good soul and who chose to show an interest. Truly, for Jonas, a good person to pour over ones alchemy of thoughts.

Jonas thought about Gina and wondered what she would say or how she would respond to his cardboard friend.

"She would probably take one look at it and think me crazy," thought Jonas.

"I suppose I'm no crazier than the rest of the world."

TWENTY EIGHT

Primordial Things

Six weeks had passed since Jonas came to his first practice session with the Ravens. There had been two practice games followed by four league games. So far the ravens had not lost a game. At the first day of batting practice when Theo asked Jonas if he was, 'just having a good day,' and Jonas answered with a 'maybe,' it was a question Theo wouldn't ask again. Jonas seemed to be always having a good day when it came to hitting. Seems the facts were saying he was just having a typical day. Jonas had been up to bat 15 times in the last four games, and got 11 hits, five home runs, a triple, two doubles, and three base hits. The other four at bats were outs via caught foul and fly balls. So far this season Jonas was carrying a .510 batting average. Theo was very thorough with his coaching position, keeping records on all his star players, including batting averages. After the seasons fourth game Theo ran some numbers.

"Let's see, Angel .310, Alvin .277, Leon .340, Adolfo .328, Benny .340, Jose .330, Ramon .360, Devan .300, and Jon .510."

With that Theo threw his computation tablet across his kitchen table.

"510! Man, that can't be right!"

Theo picked up his pencil and did the math again.

"Yeah, that's right. Well, it's still early in the season. We'll see what it is next month?"

There were all kinds of them, chubby ones, tall and lean, heavy, lanky, sinewy, but it was rare that any of the pitchers struck out Jonas based solely on pitching. There were the usual fly caught outs and the line drive grounders that got him, but there wasn't much even the best pitchers could boast about when it came to a no hit situation. Theo was right though, two months later Jonas's batting average dropped to .480, after coming up against a formidable host of talents. So far, they had played the Hawthorne Pirates, the Culver City Giants, and the South Gate Eagles and beat every one of those teams. They played Gardena, Rosemead, West Hollywood, Los Angeles, Downey, and Torrance. They had two cities left to play, Paramount and Lynwood.

Normally, when the Friday night sports segment of the five o'clock news aired it was common for the sports news caster to give a rundown on pro teams, college, and even high school scores. There usually wasn't any effort given towards results for the county parks leagues because of the nature of those games. They were usually open to practically anyone of any age group within a wide parameter of skill levels. Things had changed though, and some teams had coaches like Theo Scott that sought out the extreme talented players. Now that the Inglewood Ravens were tied with the Lynwood Cardinals, the team that had won the league playoffs for the last four years there was cause to take notice. Word spread of the gifted hitter that played for the Ravens, a county parks team.

"Who's this Jon Miles that carries a .480 batting average?" was a commonly asked question throughout the local community.

When such a batting average for a parks and recreation team gets broadcast through the nightly news it can catch the attention of all kinds of people. One might think professional organizations don't bother to check out the players of such teams, but they couldn't be more wrong.

The news piece did get the attention of professional baseball and for the final two games the Inglewood Ravens and their opponents would have a special audience of pro scouts. Even the Associated Press got a hold of the news bit. Jonas's batting average was broadcast nationwide. When the ninth inning was finally over in their next to last game, the Ravens beat the Paramount Pirates six to three. The Ravens only had one more game to win to take the title away from the Cardinals. They had a week to prepare and every evening after work the Raven players showed up for two hours of practice hitting, pitching, throwing, catching, and stealing bases. The team had twenty eight people on their roster, but of course Theo wanted his nine best out on the field. Sure everyone wanted to be the number one pick to start the game, but it wasn't possible. It really was like Theo said on that first day of practice. All the players would get to play, but only the best would be in the playoffs.

Finally, when the big game arrived on a Friday night they were scheduled to play on a Pasadena College field. While Jonas was out on the field practicing, two guys walked up to him. It was his two old friends, Jose and Kim. They had been following his progress ever since he hit the newspapers. They were proud to have known Jonas, to have called him a friend. They spent a while talking and wanting to know the latest news of the orphan children, and then they shook each other's hands and his two old friends left.

Once the game was underway the innings went quickly. By the end of the third inning the Cardinals were leading three to one. By the end of the seventh it was tied, five to five. With the Ravens up to bat in the bottom of the ninth inning, Jonas hit a home run with two guys on base that finalized the score at nine to six, the Ravens.

The game was a real adrenalin kicker with both teams leaving the field with sweat soaked shirts, but of course only one team left feeling good. It was the first year Theo and the Ravens took first place. This added a coveted award to Theo's trophy collection room.

After the game, for some of the players to try and reach the parking lot was like trying to cut a path through a jungle. Jonas was followed by a dozen major league team scouts. Just as soon as one scout was trying to whisk him off another scout grabbed him by the arm and was trying to lead him in another direction. The same scenario was repeated by other scouts to other players until Theo showed up. He put a stop to the whole shenanigans.

"Okay guys. I think I can speak for these men when I say they're very appreciative in your interest of them. I know they want a chance to talk to all of you, but...."

The truth was, Jonas was the one they wanted most. Theo knew the last thing Jon needed was to be herded into one particular organization without a chance of a practical and educated approach. Jonas didn't understand the rules, the criteria, the protocol and probably not baseball contracts. It was 1976. The average baseball player was getting about fifty grand a year. In the following year things would change with the free agent system where bidding on players would drive their salaries into the millions.

"Please take your pens out gentlemen and write down my phone number."

Theo gave him his office phone number and told them when to call.

"I will schedule an appointment with all interested parties and I promise you, Jon will not make any decisions until he has heard from each and every one of you," said Theo.

So with the help of Theo, the unruly chaos came to an amicable end. In the following days Jonas met with more than a dozen teams. During those meetings Theo sat in with Jonas's permission as an intermediary. After all, Theo had experience with major league baseball. All the offers and contracts were gathered up and organized for Jonas's review. The Yankee's wanted him, the Cardinals, as well as the Dodgers, Pirates, Angels, Red Sox, and others.

The ravens pitcher, Angel Smith, outfielder Ramon Norreiga, first baseman, Rocky Folmer, and short stop Devan Childs, were also seen being taken aside by scouts. Theo had most likely lost some of his best players that last game night to the professional ball clubs. The following night Theo took the whole team to dinner at Dillon's, a place he often went to for their ice cold mug beer and baby back ribs.

Theo thought about quitting after losing many of his best guys. He would have a championship trophy to brag about, but at 49 he was too young to quit. So he would continue with his job coaching as long as he loved what he was doing. Besides, who could know if maybe there weren't more guys out there who were really good and needed a break. As far as the guys he lost, what a great thing it turned out to be for them. Theo would be helping them and watching closely until every one of them made it out of the minors and moved up to the majors.

Jonas found it very difficult to turn down the historically prestigious Yankee ball club. In times past they had harbored some of the nation's most famous sports heroes. In terms of money, they didn't offer the most, but not the least either. Their offer was on par with many of the others, but it wasn't just about money for Jonas. In the end it wasn't too hard for Jonas to come to a decision. It was narrowed down to two teams, the Dodgers, or the Angels. There was too much to let go of here in the Los Angeles area where his home was. Besides the orphan children, his home was here, the factory building and the cars, and finally this place that he had called home for all his life, Southern California. It was the place he loved with all its famous beaches, beautiful mountains and clandestine deserts.

Perhaps if Jonas had been in his twenties then he would have chosen differently, had other options but as it were he and his father had always favored the Angels. They were the team they both always rooted for so Jonas's decision was an easy one. He would accept the deal as offered by the 'Angels'. How ironic he would wind up playing for the team his father had followed season after season. It would all begin the next year as Jonas would have to first put in his time with one of the AAA minor league teams. Jonas's future was looking up again. The final two months of the year came quickly and it was Christmas 76, marking the end of the American Bicentennial year. The past

July there had been much gala and many special events arranged for the occasion that occurred across the nation and it spilled over into the Christmas Holidays. It was a time of shared thanksgiving, planned activities, and historical colonial re-enactments. There were such things as special Fireworks and extravagant holiday lighting along city streets which helped to ease most people into a sense of patriotic thankfulness.

Jonas also had five young people on his mind. For each of these five kids, Tommy, Connie, Matt, Wanda, and Fred, whom he considered family he presented each with the same gift. He went to his bank and opened a savings account for each child and deposited five hundred dollars into each one. He also bought five wood chests the size of a small loaf of bread. They resembled miniature Pirates chests each having an ornamental pad lock. Inside Jonas placed the savings deposit booklets for each child. To celebrate his recent good fortune he also gave $2500.00 to the orphanage to spend on presents. It was a very giving and joyous year for all, as there had been much charitable giving by many wealthy people. Grover Samuelson, Kay's husband, one of the major benefactors of the home also gave double his usual amount as well. Indeed, the home seemed to be financially secure at least for the next several years.

About a week before New Year's Day Jonas received a phone call from his mom. She had wanted to tell him that Oliver called. He was one of his cousins whom he hadn't seen in a long time. Oliver was the younger of the two sons of Colin Miles, who was the brother of Jonas's dad, George. Years ago, when Jonas was a boy they had all gone on outdoor sporting events together and now Oliver had an offer he thought Jonas might be interested in.

Oliver had started a farm equipment dealership in Temecula, California. It was a very small community of mostly farmers, ranchers, and some local Indian tribes that sat in a serene valley near the Cleveland National Forest. Temecula was not a city, it was so small you could hardly call it a town. There were few businesses there, a small bank, a general store, a grocery store, a post office, a small western style hotel, a school, and a tractor dealership. The popular mountain recreational area of Idyllwild lay to the northeast and the seaside resort of San Clemente was just due west, on the other side of the coastal mountain range. Temecula and the nearby communities from Lake Elsinore and Perris to Murrieta, and south to Escondido were largely vast open undeveloped private ranches and government land holdings.

After Jonas's mom hung up Jonas dialed the number she had given him.

"Hey Cousin Oliver, this is Jonas calling. Long time no see. How are you?"

"Hey Jonas, I'm fine. How are you?"

"Well, can't complain - wouldn't do any good."

"Ha, ha, you're probably right."

"I hear you're down in the Temecula area?" queried Jonas.

"Yep, sure am. I like it down here, got clean air and not too far from everything."

"Yeah, I've been through there a lot," added Jonas.

"Swell, anyway Jonas I was thinking of you a few weeks ago when I got this letter size envelope in the mail."

"Is that so? What might that be about?"

"Do you still like to go bird hunting?"

"Wow, it's been a long time but you know I love it."

"Well yeah, I thought you would. To make a long story short, I met this guy named Frank Burroughs at a party several months back. Turns out he's some big shot publisher that lives over on the coast somewhere. Anyway, when I told him where I live and my line of work he sounded interested. There's this huge ranch out here called the Vail Ranch. Well, they recently sold out to this conglomerate of business people. It's now called, 'Rancho California'."

"Oh, yeah, I've heard of it," interjected Jonas.

"I guess the Vail's own another ranch by the same name over near Tucson. Anyhow, one thing led to another and soon we were talking about hunting and fishing, that sort of thing."

"Okay, you're getting my interest up real quick now," responded Jonas.

"Uh huh, thought I would. Anyhow, it turns out Frank Burroughs knows these ranch owners. He said he would see if he could get me on the ranch for hunting. Well, I never dreamed he would really follow through with the effort, but he sure did. I received this written letter on Rancho California stationary that gives me and three guest's permission to hunt the ranch. What a swell guy."

"Yeah, I'd say," Jonas responded.

"It looks to me like the Vail people are still working the ranch. As near as I can tell the ranch hands are still using the bunk quarters. It's a hunter's paradise, got duck ponds all over the place, with dove and quail so thick they fly through your arm pits."

"Wow!"

"Yeah, anyhow, I thought I would check it out a few times before I called you to make sure it was as good as I heard it was."

"I'm betting you checked it out real good," said Jonas.

"Well, you'd be right. As a matter of fact I may have been checking it out much more than necessary."

Jonas laughs.

I have even been doing some frog gigging there," replied Oliver.

"You devil."

"Yeah, anyhow, if you like to eat big tender batter fried frog legs, plump quail, and enjoy brazed duck and dove breasts, you might want to head over this way soon."

"I don't need any more coaxing."

"I didn't think so."

"I also got hooked up with this 'Butterfield Country,' company that owns Vail Lake down the road. There are record sized Canadian Geese that come in on that lake. We can hunt and fish that as well."

"How soon do you want to do this?" asked Jonas.

"How about next weekend? Bring your boys if you want."

"Don't know if you heard Oliver, but I got a divorce some years back."

"Yeah, sorry, I thought I heard something about that."

"Don't see much of the boys, but actually I have been taking some orphan kids under my wing. Maybe you heard about that? " said Jonas.

"Yeah, I did as a matter of fact. That's good of you to care about those little guys."

"Yeah, anyhow I'd like to bring these boys along but they have never handled a shotgun and this wouldn't be the time to teach them."

"Of course, and I agree. You better get to work with them. If they have the fire in them for the sport, fine, if not, well?"

"That's right."

"Well I'll plan on seeing you next weekend then. Like to be at the ranch bunk house before sunrise," said Oliver.

"I wouldn't like it any other way," responded Jonas.

"We'll all pile in my Jeep Wagoneer. I have another buddy going with us," stated Oliver. We don't really need four wheel drive where we're going, but I got it just the same."

"Sound's great."

"Okay Jonas, I'll see you Saturday morning."

"Yep, sure will," said Jonas, thanking Oliver.

Ever since Homosapiens could throw a rock, learned how to fashion tools, or launch sharpened stone tipped spears, humans have never totally relinquished their true nature as hunter gatherers. In a way, even going down to the local farmers market to buy produce, fish, and meat is an indirect way of affirming ones needs for basic food procurement. If our ancient ancestors didn't hunt for meat, dig for tubers, pick nuts and harvest grain, they would have starved. As time evolved, finding a place to hunt in many countries was nigh impossible for many classes of citizens. Hunting became a sport reserved for nobleman, or wealthy landowners even though for countless centuries hunting was how humans sustained their existence. Often, in parts of Europe ever since medieval times trespassers were severely prosecuted and poachers could be imprisoned or put to death.

One of the reasons the American colonists migrated to the New World as it was often referred to was to escape repression and gain opportunity. The New World was a hunter's paradise. The wildlife was so thick in numbers the colonists and their crude weaponry of single shot firearms were incapable of making a dent in the numbers of upland game birds, waterfowl, or antlered game animals.

Things changed rapidly after the early colonial times with the advent of repeating rifles and shotguns when market hunters slaughtered wildlife on a mass scale. It was an easy way to make a buck and in a short time the relentless massacre on wildlife became a scourge to all including the Native Americans who practiced a great sense of respect for wildlife. They as a rule never wasted any part of an animal. Today, in the last quarter of the twentieth century one out of every three Americans who live in a city still hunt some type of game. Seventy percent of all males who live in rural areas will take to the field. Most of these Americans have a great respect for the outdoors, for the quarry, for the sport, and for the camaraderie of those who share their love of hunting. Unfortunately, there are also those who carelessly kill game without any intent of benefit from it, except for some form of selfish gratification and these kinds of people are not true meat hunting sportsman.

There's something that excites an outdoorsman's senses with the changing colors of fall and the seasons bite of cool air whether within the aura of a high mountain glade, a high desert canyon, or a tall grassy field. What can be more basic than a crackling campfire within the midst of a pine covered mountain meadow cooking up a batch of fresh caught trout. For others, maybe it's the sensation of the lingering smoky resonance of a fired smoothbore that has put great tasting wild game meat on the dining table that excites them. In time, as the years go by it will be the memories of some sitting next to a cold night's warm camp fire just as our ancestors had done two hundred years ago, or even two thousand that will once again unite them with their primordial past.

The days went by quickly. Jonas had left his home for Oliver's place long before sunrise. He was in his VW Bus headed south on I-5. He would connect with the 91 heading east through Corona and then exit onto the 15 south. Once on the 15 there was far less traffic. After passing Lake Elsinore at such an early hour a car was rarely seen on the road. Outside the closed windows of the VW Bus it was pitch black and the moonless night rendered the vast open landscape invisible as the vehicle occasionally passed marshes, old withering corrals, or a lone distant ranch house. The outside air was very cold and its scent was filled of sage, various types of chaparral and the poignant scents of the dew laden earth. All the while the steady hum of the low powered boxer engine drummed on through the darkness.

The faint light of the vehicles no frills dash board was just enough to faintly see the shadows of the things that were inside the vehicle. Jonas wore blue denim jeans, lace up Red Wing hunting boots and a blue rip stop nylon navy flight jacket that kept him warm. The induction heater seemed to struggle to keep the large space inside heated. The radio was on low. He had been listening to a talk show about the Apollo Space program, but he changed the channel to a country western music channel. A Marty Robbins song had started. It was, 'El Paso.'

Within a short time Jonas found the gravel road driveway that led to Oliver's house. Oliver's home was closer to the town of Murrieta, which was not far from Temecula. Because it was pitch black outside the bus's headlights barely found the wooden sign near a mail box that simply read, 'The Miles.' When Jonas drove onto the gravel road that left the highway, he had wondered if somehow he had made a mistake but in a short time he saw a porch light on a distant house. As Jonas got close to the home, there was a vehicle out front with its engine running and parking lights on and in the cold air the heated exhaust fumes came out of the muffler pipes as wispy veils. There was a man walking amongst the vehicles, in fact making hurried trips between an old truck and Oliver's Jeep. He appeared to be busy loading things into the rear of the Jeep. When Jonas got nearer he could see that it was someone he wasn't sure he knew. Then when Jonas was parking his car another man came out of the home. It looked to be his cousin, Oliver. Running up ahead of him was a Black Labrador retriever with his tail wagging energetically. It seemed happy to see the new stranger as he ran up to Jonas and started sniffing his boots.

"Otis, get back here. Sit," commanded the man coming out of the house.

"Is that you Oliver?" said Jonas, looking at the man that walked from the house in a heavy jacket wearing a dark fatigued looking felt type cowboy hat.

"Jonas! I guess the last time we saw each other we were kids and now look at us. We got big didn't we?" said Oliver grinning.

"Jonas, this is Mitch Taylor. He works for me at the dealership."

"Hi Mitch," said Jonas offering his handshake which was readily accepted.

"Hi Jonas, Good to meet you," responded the stranger.

"Mitch is a valley native Jonas. He probably knows every fence post, tree, or spring for a hundred miles. Besides being a good tractor mechanic he's a good friend of mine."

Mitch shrugged his shoulders seeming to disfavor all the praise.

"Well I don't know about every tree," Mitch responded, drawing some laughs.

Jonas looked at Mitch and smiled. Mitch's mom was half Luiseno Indian. His dad was Irish. Mitch had his father's blue eyes. His sun burnt skin gave a false impression of his true skin color and his forty plus years of hard outdoor work made him look older then he was. A good part of his head was stuffed into a used up straw Stetson hat which had the maroon and white barred breast feathers of a mountain quail wedged behind his hatband. His faded blue denim Levi jacket was buttoned up tight over a beige and black plaid Pendleton wool shirt. Dark Levi 501 jeans hugged his narrow waist held taught by a wide natural tooled cowhide belt and cowboy style buckle. A sheathed stag handled hunting knife hung from his belt and round toed rough-out boots covered his feet.

As Oliver talked Mitch took a pack of Camel cigarettes out of his jacket breast pocket. He removed a cigarette before replacing the pack. He stuck the two and a half inch long unfiltered smoke between his lips. He then took out a wood match stick from his other pocket and holding the match in the cuff of his right hand struck it on fire with a snap of his thumb. He lit his smoke. He tossed the expired match stick before rubbing it out in the dirt with his boot.

"Ollie says you're a good wing shot," said Mitch looking at Jonas with a friendly gaze.

Many people called Oliver, 'Ollie.'

"I guess I'm no better or worse than most." answered Jonas.

"Nothing like a batch of nice smoked mountain meadow venison chops cooked just right sitting on your plate. You know though, I think I'll take a brace of properly fried quail just about any day of the week. Not much more fun than a good bird hunt," said the cowboy with a slow definitive deep drawl of a voice.

"Well, I have to agree," responded Jonas, as Oliver was busy finishing up with loading a few things in the Jeep. The tailgate was down and the top hatch was still open. Jonas grabbed all his gear and put it in the Jeep.

"Okay Otis, get in," ordered his owner as the Lab jumped into the truck. The dog was so excited it could hardly sit still. He knew where he was going.

The sky was getting lighter now but still hard to make out the countryside as the three men left in a dash for the highway. Mitch didn't watch a lot of TV but he had seen enough to know who Oliver's brother was. That is, 'Glen Miles,' the singer even if Jonas didn't look much like Glenn now. Mitch actually liked several of his songs enough so that he bought a couple of his singles. He also knew all about the fiasco on TV, about the orphan kid that had made certain claims. Even though he didn't know Jonas, Mitch had no reason to believe he was guilty, especially since the results of the trial had vindicated him. One just never could tell for sure about what was true or false about people. Certainly throughout history probably plenty of innocent people had been hung, and guilty let go.

There were a lot of things that Mitch couldn't forecast but before days end he would at least discover that Jonas was no slouch when it came to shooting fast flying birds. Jonas was not one to ramble on when it came to talking but he entirely enjoyed the busy talk of the other two men inside the vehicle. Oliver did a lot of talking about childhood times, with Jonas throwing in a lot of agreeing nods and verbal acknowledgments. There was much talk about the outdoors of places been and places to go and such things that needed to be revisited. There was talk of politics, football, boxing, and baseball, which led Oliver to ask a question.

"Hey, I saw this news bit about this guy who had a .480 batting average somewhere in L A. Said his name was Jon Miles. I was wondering if that might be you?" asked Oliver looking at Jonas. Oliver didn't know that Jonas had been picked up by the pros yet, and Jonas probably wouldn't make mention of it.

There was a long pause before Jonas said anything.

"Well yeah, maybe, it might have been about me, I guess," he answered just looking ahead down the road.

"Damn Jonas, how do you do it? Every time our mothers talk there's news about you and your good fortune in life. You inherit all this stuff, you become a famous singer, know these famous celebrities. I see photo's of you mingling with these gorgeous movie actresses. Don't get me wrong, I'm not Jealous," remarked Oliver.

Mitch was sitting in the back seat and his ears were wide open taking in all the words spoken with great interest. There was a pause after Oliver asked that question. Jonas was thinking.

"Well, I don't know Ollie. I don't get up in the morning and think I'm any different than anyone else. After that court trial, things have changed a bit. I'll say this, opportunity doesn't have to come along, people can make it come along if they will just get off their duffs and get out there and go get theirs."

Then, Jonas had a sort of afterthought, he was thinking about how strangely everything seemed to change in his life after the Marilyn cardboard object arrived at his door. He did not feel inclined to divulge much about that at the moment. Other people could easily misunderstand such things.

"I think part of it is being at the right place at the right time. You know, when I want something worthwhile I put a lot of work in it just like everybody else. I'm sure you know what I mean, you have your own business. Lots of work, right? You get out of life what you put into it. And failure is not an option."

"Amen to that," said Mitch.

After passing Temecula they turned east onto another highway where they would only go a short ways before turning off onto a dirt road.

"Yeah sure, whatever it is keep it up Jonas, because it seems to work for yuh," remarked Oliver.

"Hey, here's the road," exclaimed Oliver as he slowed down to turn. After driving in about a half mile there was a short row of eucalyptus trees and then a few scattered wood sided ranch houses. There was also a large barn, some other smaller buildings, a few tractors and other various implements that one could imagine seeing on a working ranch.

Oliver had been here several times before and was quite familiar with the process of getting the keys from the foreman to unlock the gate. It was a darn right unpleasant process but Oliver didn't have any other remedy for the predicament. It wasn't in his power. This would be the third time that Oliver would pound on the door to wake up the foreman for the keys.

"Somebody go up there and wake the dude up. Just tell him we need somebody to unlock the gate," said Oliver.

"If these guys are asleep maybe you better wake them up. They know you, right?" responded Jonas.

"Okay, can you get them up, Mitch?" asked Oliver.

"Not me Boss. I know a lot of these guys and I want to stay friends."

Gruffly, not getting any volunteers Oliver got out and walked over to the door and knocked. Nothing happened, than he knocked again. Finally, he had to bang on the door until he heard an angry man saying some choice words in Spanish coming to the door. The man jerked the door open. Looking like his eyes needed a few seconds to adjust until they focused on the man at the door. He finally recognized Oliver.

"Senor, porfavor."

The man looked like he had either worked too hard the day before or was trying to sleep off a Friday nights tequila binge, probably both.

"I'm sorry Raul to do this, but we have no other way to unlock the gate."

"Okay, Senor Miles this is what I'm going to do for you, and me!"

Then, Oliver espied a double barrel shotgun leaning against the wall by the door. The thought entered Ollie's head that hopefully the gun would not be Raul's solution to the problem standing in the doorway. Not really knowing Oliver's direct relationship with the landowners, Raul most certainly refrained from giving Oliver his piece of mind.

"You see that large rock over by the gate post, Mr. Miles? I'm going to start leaving the key under that rock in a can, OK. Just open the gate and put the key back in the can, under that rock," said the ranch hand, trying to maintain a measure of congeniality.

"Okay, I gotcha Raul, I'm really very sorry to have waked you, again," responded Oliver as Raul handed over the keys to the heavy metal framed gate that gave access to thousands of acres of ranch land that was a hunters paradise.

As Raul closed the door and headed back toward his bed he was thinking with any luck he would never have to see or talk to the man at the door again.

"Poor guy, I don't blame him for being peeved," said Oliver. "Yeah, sorry any of us had to do that but what are you going to do? Him sleeping is not more important than us going hunting, right," responded Mitch.

"We got it worked out now so we don't have to wake him anymore."

"Oh, is that right?"

"Yeah."

The men drove the short drive to the gate and let themselves through, making sure to close the gate. The sun had cleared the peaks of the hills and mountains casting enough light to see the features of the land. The road ran through a cold heavily dewed pasture and along the bottom of a ridge covered with chaparral that extended down from the highlands. The tops of Cattail reeds could be seen in various spots on the nearby low ridge. Oliver was quite familiar with what lay next to the cattails out of sight of the vehicle. There were a series of creek fed ponds that ran down alongside the road. In the winter they most always were full of ducks. Lying about near the ponds on the eastern flank of the narrow dirt road where the chaparral lay one could easily manage to stumble into large coveys of valley quail. Their incessant calling would always give their position away. An abundance of various plants such as thistle provided wild seed for game birds which served to lure in flocks of mourning dove as well.

Oliver parked his Jeep just off the road and they all very silently got out to retrieve their gear. It was about ninety-five percent certain that the surface of the ponds were full of some variety of ducks. Once ready they stealthily approached the peaks of the berms that held the water ahead of them placing themselves equally spaced out around the body of water. Their guns were loaded with high power six shot or larger. Once ready, they all jumped the pond in unison. The surface of the water exploded with Bluebills and Mallards. The birds shot straight up into the air like rising rockets, slow at first then quickly gaining momentum. The men took aim and fired all the shots their guns were legal to hold. Birds were falling out of the sky back into the water or hitting the ground with a thud. At Oliver's command, Otis the Lab retrieved all the ducks from the pond.

"Let's get the other birds and head up to the next pond!" stated Oliver.

There were two more ponds up the road all holding a variety of ducks. The men continued driving up the road. They would get out, jump shoot more ducks and then drive on. Meanwhile, quail could be heard calling in various places on the hillsides. The men were anxious and after hitting the last pond for ducks they went back to the vehicle to deposit their take of waterfowl. Between the three of them they all had their legal limits of ducks. Quickly changing out their ammo to low base number eight shot they headed for the hills that were close by pursuing quail. The ranch was like a hunter's paradise apparently not having any hunting pressure. At least, not that anyone could tell. The three men had limited out on quail in less than an hour as well as picking off some late season dove.

"Wow, this may have been the best hunt I ever had," remarked Jonas, as the three got back to the Jeep. Mitch unloaded his old side by side Ithaca while Jonas checked his Winchester 101. At the same time, Oliver unloaded his custom Model 12 and they put their guns back in their cases.

"Unreal ain't it?" said Olie.

"I'm just not use to getting everything at the same place on the same hunt in less than a few hours to boot. You know what I mean, but you got it all here like a one stop grocery store," remarked Jonas.

"Yeah, it's a nice set up. There are still good places to hunt in southern California if you know the right people. We may be the only people who have a letter granting permission to hunt this ranch. We can thank Mr. Burroughs for that," added Mitch.

"Yeah, I'll say," said Oliver.

They all got in the Jeep wagon and drove away. They went back out through the gate and locked it. Oliver put the key under the rock where Raul told him and they drove on.

"Mitch here has a drinking buddy who works for SCE, you know the electric company. He's got a key that opens the gate that gets us up on top to the high country that runs along the coast. It's beautiful up there just a flat high plateau full of oak trees and grass that runs for miles all the way to the Ortega highway. We'll have to take you with us next time. It's a great drive and you don't see a soul up there.

"Wow, sounds like you guys have all the necessary contacts," said Jonas.

"I believe we do," responded Oliver.

The men were back to Oliver's place before 10am. Jonas never got a good look at the place in the dark but now under daylight it was quite an interesting piece of real estate. The home was a modest white stucco Spanish hacienda style home with a red clay tiled roof. The grounds were fairly large, possibly ten acres or more. Oliver and his wife Karen had been lucky when inquiring at a Real Estate office about local homes while on a weekend country drive. When they saw the place it was love at first site. The owner, an elderly woman had a husband who had passed away. Her children didn't think it good for her to be alone. They decided to sell the place and take their mother with them back to San Francisco. It was a striking but older three bedroom home with a den, a living room, and a small study room.

The majority of the acreage was untouched and in a natural state. There was a creek running through the back side of the lot that was bordered by large sycamores and cottonwoods. There were Jeep trails cavorting around the property here and there to quaint spots that had been given a little extra attention. One place had a small very old looking chapel with a bench and a statue of the Virgin Mary. There was another spot that had various types of bird feeders and another place that had a bench in a park like setting under a large cottonwood.

"Looks like you've been at the right place at the right time as well cousin?" stated Jonas, with Oliver looking a little perplexed.

"Oh, you mean the property?" he asked.

"Yes, it's a gorgeous place," stated Jonas.

"Yes, we love it here. Will probably die here," he answered.

The three cleaned their birds trying to keep Otis's nose out of the feathers. They were going to do the same routine the following morning but were going to go up the road to Vail Lake instead which was a little further up the same highway as the ranch. It was a good sized lake that had plenty of ducks and flocks of geese. The adjoining foothills around the lake were also full of quail and small game. There was a boat house there with a plank dock. They had a small fleet of motor powered boats that were rented out on a reserve basis.

The three men had even made plans for the upcoming deer season in the mountains at nearby Idyllwild. They would rent a cabin at Mama Lee's cabin camp. Jonas wanted to make sure he went back home with enough wild game bird meat to last him a few decent meals before he came back for another hunt. After finishing with cleaning the birds of that first day's take Mitch bid them ado until the following morning when they would do it all over again.

TWENTY NINE

Vile Vermin & Blood Sport

In the interim since Jonas's hunting trip with his cousin, months had passed. Jonas found himself playing for the, 'Raptors', a AAA minor league team. Just about everyone was sure the management would draft Jon up to the majors as soon as possible. So far, Jonas's batting skills were everything his parent organization had hoped for to say the least. He had hit three home runs in five games and his batting average was well above .400. He was shaping up to be one of their star hitters.

As the weeks passed no one seemed to realize that Jon Miles was Glenn Miles, why should they, Jon Miles the hitter didn't look much like Glenn Miles the singer. Jonas knew it was just a matter of time before his past caught up with him. However, for the time being he wanted his past to remain separate from the present, at least until he could secure a new legacy for himself in baseball. Jonas had the children from the orphanage brought to all the home games. Thus far in the minors Jonas had batted against the Albuquerque Dukes, the San Jose Buffalos, the Hawaiian Islanders, the Spokane Bears, the Salt Lake City Gulls, and today they were going against the Phoenix Giants.

When the game started it was a lucky first inning for the Giants as they had two men on base when Rick Sanders hit a home run. In the second inning Glen Brighton of Jonas's team got a base hit. The Giants pitcher Tommy Thompson struck out two batters and then a fly to center field was caught finishing the inning. No one scored the next three innings but the Giants loaded the bases on top of the sixth. There was one out when Don Haight hit a grounder between first and second base bringing in another run. Then Skip Roberts hit a grounder to the second baseman enabling Wendell Fisher to throw for a double play. That left the score at four to nothing, Giants. At the bottom of the sixth, Rick Smith hit a line drive for the Raptor's and made it to second base. Then Jonas came up and hit a solid fly ball over the third baseman's head for a double enabling Rick to score. Then Bill Putnam hit a wild fly to right field that bounced off the steel mesh fence post allowing Bill to run to second, which brought Jonas on in to score. Next up to bat, Alex

Kamoto hit a grounder to the short stop allowing the Giants to make a double play to end the sixth with a score of two to four, the Giants. Eddie Shank finished the last three innings as pitcher for the Giants with Lou Parker closing the eighth and ninth for Jonas's team. Then the Raptors brought in three more runs in the eighth with Jonas getting a home run over left fielder Rob Harper's leaping glove and the ten foot mesh fence. The ninth inning brought no runs for either team.

Little did Jonas realize that even as the game was in progress a number of important men hundreds of miles away were in discussion of a number of issues concerning their baseball organization. These men were in conference about drafting a number of players because their skills and time had merited a draft move. Also, to a team manager's consternation they had been given some news about their Jon Miles, and they weren't quite sure what to do about it.

A Los Angeles Times reporter had crossed paths at a luncheon with a prior Angels manager by the name of Phil Rignold. The reporter in a liquor induced stupor had spilled the beans when he filled Rignold's ear with some startling information. It seemed he was going to write an article the next day to hand into his news agency stating that a certain popular minor league team's new slugger was actually the former singer, Glenn Miles. Regardless by what source the ball club management had received such privileged information, whether it was via Rignold or someone else, they now knew their Jon Miles was Glenn Miles, the singer. They weren't sure why it should be a problem.

He had signed the contract as Jonathan Miles, but no one ever made the connection that he was Glenn Miles, the singer. After much discussion they really wanted to draft Jonas immediately to the majors, but couldn't because he hadn't fulfilled his four year requirement. Also, he wasn't getting any younger. They would just let him ride the minors for the time being and if any ill begotten publicity should come forth they would deal with it then, while he was still in the minors.

Jonas didn't know it yet, but he would never make it beyond the next eleven consecutive games. It was only through luck that he would make it that far. That Times reporter who had the hot news lead about who Jon Miles was had gotten a bad cold that same evening which quickly turned to pneumonia. He wouldn't make it back to his news desk for some time, and he wasn't going to let one of his comrades take the credit for the story. He decided to keep the story under his hat until he returned to work.

Most people could care less about Glen Miles the singer playing baseball. However, some people do get paid to take pride in their ability to get a new twist going on sensitive news issues, regardless of the effects it has on their victims. It seems they seek out those whose hard work has paid off with success. Some of these column writers can be relentless in their search for news tidbits. Their goals might be compared to the tools of prospectors, such as ore rockers and screen shakers. They can work just as frantically as the arm that shakes that rocker to find those few gleaming glows of pay dirt. Perhaps if they are vain enough, they can even destroy their subjects. Truth or not, it can be what gets read or ushered into one's ear that prevails. Unfortunately for Jonas, it would come to be that there would be some media critics who would resurrect his past, question it again as if they had a right to a media blitz retrial. The write ups though only suggestive in nature would serve to be great fodder for the fans of the opposing teams. They would turn Jonas's new passion for a baseball career into a living hell.

However, there had been no news as of yet about Jon Miles alias Glenn Miles the minor league player who already had his free ticket to the majors. That is, he already had it in the bag unless something drastically changed. Drastic changes could and often did happen in sports. The Raptors next game was against the, 'Coyotes', followed by the, 'Badgers', and the 'Seals'. The Raptors beat every one of those teams. In the next six games the Raptors would win four and lose two. Jonas hit two home runs in one game, then four home runs out of four games, two triples, three doubles, and seven base hits out of twenty two at bats.

On the evening of game eleven, Jonas would bat against the Seattle Cubs. Sandra Steinman was bringing all five of the kids from the orphanage to watch the game. As fate would have it, Eleanor Marore was aware that Jonas was the big slugger in a western division minor team. She had heard about all his home runs and success with the Raptors. Kay Lincoln, now Kay Samuelson, would also be there with her husband Grover, to watch the game.

Of course, if it hadn't been for Grover, Jonas's good name would never have been tarnished. The Almighty himself only knew the true reason Grover ran with an unsubstantiated tale, dragging Jonas's good name through the mud. After all, he could have started by asking Jonas himself about the accusation. Perhaps it was his intent from the start to forever quash any feelings Kay may have had for Jonas by destroying his reputation, or maybe it was nothing so sinister, who could know?

So now, the Raptors had just gotten into their fourth week of games. They were coming out of six straight years of poor results and the management was hoping that with the new talent they picked up could get things turned around. This evening's game was at home and Jonas had been busy all day. In fact, he had been so busy he never even had time to see that the morning paper had his name all over it. He was even on the front page of an Orange County newspaper with the headline, 'Ball Player Jon Miles is Singer Glenn Miles?' Then, it went on to say that Glen, alias Jon was the new regional rookie that had been written up several months prior in the papers for his five hundred plus batting average, playing with the county parks and recreation leagues. It further stated that no one realized until recently that Jon Miles was actually Glen Miles, and that previously the courts concluded he had been found innocent of any charges.

It didn't take Jonas long to find out once he had showed up in the locker room that something was up. All the players were talking loud and joking around, than things turned as quiet as a church mouse when Jonas walked in. He didn't know why at first. He thought maybe because he had just been too good or too lucky at his hitting. Jonas didn't waste any time getting out on the field. Soon, the game had started and nothing was out of the ordinary during the game until the third inning when Jonas came up to bat, and the Raptors were ahead four to one.

"Hey Child Petter!" came one heckler from the opposing team's bleachers.

"It's seven o'clock. Do you know where your kids are?" shot out another.

The pitcher for the Cubs was Tom Houston. The first pitch was inside for a strike.

"Hey little girl you want a candy bar?" came another jeer, followed by noticeable laughter.

The Raptors had one man on base and the second pitch was a ball. Now it was fairly evident to Jonas that his suspicions were correct. His defacto name was out of the bag. He could see a change on the faces of his team mates in the dugout, and the loose grins of the players out on the field.

"Ball", shouted the umpire.

"Hey Freak, You ought to try a grown woman for a change," came a snide jeer from the visiting team bleachers..

Jonas stood his ground, doing his best to maintain his composure even though feelings of anger were beginning to overtake his good nature. Now, Tommy Roscoe was sitting in the grand stands feeling Jonas's pain. Tears were flowing out of the corners of his eyes. He blamed himself. The grief stricken faces of all the children as well as Jonas's friends could not go without notice. Connie, Matt, Fred, and Wanda watched on in such despair wanting to shout out at the hecklers, but knew it was pointless.

Both Eleanor Marore and Kay Samuelson, though sitting far apart felt very sad about what the crowd was doing to Jonas. They both knew that Jonas would be one of the last people who would have ever done what some of the mean spirited fans were insinuating.

The fourth pitch was somewhere over the middle of the plate between Jonas's knee and elbow. That was all he needed as the loud crack of the bat pounding the ball skyward brought a moment of silence as it sailed over the right field wall. It served to momentarily shut off the insults and wise cracks while raising some excitement in the Raptors dugout. The score was now five to one. The game continued through the next seven innings, with the same types of insults and sarcasm whenever Jonas came up to bat. The final score was seven to one, the Raptors.

After the game Sandra Steinman and the kids met Jonas in the parking lot. Everyone had teary eyes they tried to hide. Sandra knew how he must have felt. She wanted to have everyone be together this evening. It would be good therapy for Jonas. He wanted to go home but she insisted they go with her to a special place she knew. Sometimes fate places the right kinds of people in one's life. Sandra was an only child, and her father had perhaps had some influence on her outdoorsy nature. Perhaps a sort of a blessing for some gals who found themselves appreciating the wilds of nature and enjoying the pastimes in life that attracted men. Consequently, she learned about all those outdoor things that young boys do with their fathers, like camping and fishing, even hunting.

Finding Jonas's VW Bus they left it where Jonas parked it. They locked it up and then they all climbed inside Sandra's 1966 four wheel drive GMC Carryall.

Sandra drove straight to her house, loaded up a camp barbecue, charcoal, a large ice box, a tent, sleeping bags and some other things. She put some food items in the ice box and they were off. No one else had to get out of the vehicle. It was Friday night and there were a lot of vehicles driving about, but the closer

Sandra got to her secret place the less traffic there was. She pulled up onto a dirt road at the base of some foothills near Malibu. The 327 Chevy engine seemed to have amazing power for its size as it carried the bunch over hillside inclines and through ravines until they peaked out on a point high above coast highway. Far down below were the lights of many distant scattered homes. The light of the full moon cast its brilliance across the great span of the sea and in the distance the silhouette of Catalina stood out in its prominence.

"Isn't it beautiful?" remarked Sandra, as they all just sat there in the vehicle staring out across the ocean. No one knew what was on the others' minds but Sandra was trying to do her best to get Jonas thinking about other things. They were all perhaps behaving differently than they would have under normal circumstances because they were all thinking about Jonas.

Then Sandra got out of the truck and opened the rear doors for the kids to get out and they helped her to set up camp on the flat escarpment. They threw out a ground tarp and set up a couple of tents. Then they got a fire going in a hollowed out boulder that was surrounded by rocks. She brought hamburger, hot dogs, beer, soda, and all the necessary condiments. Then they dislodged the low spirited Jonas out of the truck and sat him in a fold up chair and then they all got around him and put their arms around him and hugged him. Jonas looked at Tommy who was crying and then tears welled up in Jonas's eyes as well. In their own way they all felt hurt for Jonas. The moonlight was ample enough to light up the hillsides that were covered with wild shrubs and scattered trees. So now, here was Jonas a man who never wanted to be seen in such a way, sullen and teary eyed.

Surely, there were times when even the strongest had a right to such sensitive moments. It seemed the more Jonas's eyes flushed with tears the more the people near him hugged him. Then, Jonas ran all out of tears and stopped. Failure when one was deservedly at fault was one thing, but when hard earned success was ripped away from one by another due to malice and forethought was another. Jonas didn't blame Tommy for the bad things that had happened in his life, he blamed Grover Samuelson. Tommy's life was a bad deal from out of the deck on day one. As for Jonas, he thought about one of Sinatra's songs that he had often sung so many times, 'That's Life.' So now in a sometimes harsh world love can heal and overcome many things.

"I love you all very much," exclaimed Jonas. The children were more than friends now, thay were like family. At the moment they were the only family he had. Jonas could tell that Tommy needed a hug more than him so he reached out his hand to him.

"Come Tommy," said Jonas, as Tommy slowly came forward, ravaged with feelings of guilt. Jonas took his hand and he looked into his watery eyes and then as he held Tommy's hand he said something to comfort him.

"Remember what I told you before, Tommy. I have done things I deeply regretted. We all have. You're still a boy. Plenty of time left to become proud when you are a man. We must forget this day. But I will never forget this evening. You all being here with me now is a great comfort. I love you all," added an emotional Jonas.

After that, Sandra threw a grill over the fire and they cooked hamburgers and hot dogs. Jonas and Sandra drank beer and watched the moon climb high into the midnight blue heavens. They pointed out shooting stars as they all huddled close together. On the distant horizon could be seen the cabin lights of occasional passing yachts under the moonlit ambiance of the night sky. Soon the charcoal burned out, and as the day had been emotionally exhausting they all quickly fell asleep. When morning came the sun peaked over the eastern foothills. Jonas's group slowly rose out of bed one by one, packed up the truck and left for their homes.

When Monday morning arrived just as Jonas suspected the great dream of playing professional baseball was over for him. The management called him in and though greatly sympathizing with him, could not afford to have a rookie ripe for ridicule being humiliated in their ball club. They felt controlling spectators yelling expletives out at the playing field would be a job too difficult to control. They also did not need any media frenzy geared against any players who were on their minors list. The team management verbally demonstrated their complete confidence in Jon's innocence just as the facts of the trial proved, but the ball club could not do anything to control the behavior of the paying spectators. They also reiterated the likelihood of the sports writers continuing with their negative mind set upon him whenever it was advantageous to them. Therefore, the organization released him from his contract letting him keep one seasons salary. Jonas was through with playing baseball. In all reality the whole debacle that Grover Samuelson had dragged Jonas through in court had greatly limited Jonas's options in life within the public arena.

Two weeks later, Jonas sat at his kitchen table to write a letter. It took him a good hour to write it. When finished he slapped a 13 cent Carl Sandberg postage stamp on the envelope, applied the recipients address, and wrote his name and city in the left hand corner. Then he inserted the letter in the envelope and sealed it. He would deposit it in the following day's mail.

THIRTY

The Letter

Many months had passed since Jonas left the professional baseball organization. He still had his, 'Glenn Miles', fan mail post office box, even though that mail had dwindled down to practically nothing. Some of that mail was in regards to his baseball activities. There was still a minute amount of the public who were writing disparaging and mean things in their letters toward him. However, most of the letters were sympathetic in nature as they praised him for taking the time to help out with orphan children. The few friends Jonas had that he confided in encouraged him to ignore the people who chose to think the worst. His friends referred to them as simpletons. There were many of his fans who wrote letters wishing him to return to singing and to come out with more original hits. Some had begged him to at least perform at that famous Tahoe Resort, the Cal Neva, and sing Sinatra songs again. That was something Jonas was considering. He didn't need Anniston Conroy to book him for that job.

When the news had hit the paper that Jon Miles the hitter, was really Glenn Miles the singer there was a large percentage of the populace who respected him even more. Jonas gave a good amount of thought to his future. For the time being for whatever reason, a small boost in sales with his old single releases slightly spiked his royalty payments. Occasionally, he was called on for interviews by magazine publishers, television, and radio shows. It was unfortunate that Jonas had at least two proven talents that were no longer significantly marketable at a sustainable level. He wished he could have stayed with baseball. He was sure he could have had a good run. Maybe another five years before he was too old to compete. There was also another thing that he wanted to have time for, his painting, his art. He never lost the desire to paint. His new interest in life from this point on would assume a much lower public profile.

Fortunately, in the privacy of his own home there had never been any necessity to confess to the public or anyone really, those mystical elements of his personal existence relative to a flimsy cardboard cutout. He felt that somehow the reality was that her spiritual force was sporadically present within the confines of his home. He never ceased his relationship to her as a friend nor her to him as the comrade she seemed to be. Jonas simply reasoned that the supernatural may affix themselves to things physically tangible, to accommodate a mortals visionary perception.

In the weeks to follow, Jonas began his oil painting projects as he began buying large stretched canvasses on which to paint. Whenever he found an exceptional photo of Marilyn that he liked from the thousands taken of her, he would paint it. He realized if the first painting was not great he would keep improving. He did not know how many paintings he would paint of her or of anything else, he just wanted to paint beautiful paintings.

Meanwhile, as Jonas was busy painting, Kay Samuelson had written a letter to her brother in Maine. She had ran out of postage stamps and decided to look in her husband's desk. While looking through his drawer and moving things around to find stamps there was a number of opened envelopes mostly from business associates, and then one in particular caught her eye. It had a Carl Sandburg stamp on it and it was addressed by Jonas Miles. She removed the envelope from the drawer. It was addressed to Grover. Surprised and curious she removed the letter and began to read it.

September, 1977
From: Mr. Jonathan Miles

To Mr. Grover Samuelson

Mr. Samuelson Sir, I'm sure you know who I am. Of course, how could you not? The first time I saw you, you stood in the entry hall of the Orphans Home as you proceeded to steal away from me the attentions of the woman I loved. Your relentless offerings and vigilance behind my back succeeded to claim her. I will not nourish any harsh feelings in regards to her decisions; one must know what is best for them as that was Kay's decision.

I have been thinking a lot about you lately. To be honest, it's impossible for me not to think about you as if anyone couldn't whose life's ambitions, career, and lively hood have been destroyed, ruined by either callous intentions, or complete disregard for others happiness. We could have gotten to the bottom of any questions, certainly the truth of any orphanage accusations concerning me in house, at the orphanage. However, at the height of my career you chose to drag my good name through the courts. It was hard to think that you would suggest that I could be guilty of such a charge. I have to assume because of your stature within the community you are not a dumb person, and must have been fully aware of what the consequences were going to be for me. Since I fail to see in an obvious way why one human being would choose to be so cruel to another, then that only leaves me to the obvious of my imaginings. I will leave it at that.

While saying all that I have said, in my life I have been blessed with many good things. However, I know that place we all call the orphanage is the real place where unhappiness arrives upon the feet of our deserted youth. Hopefully, with devoted people and the right amount of compassion we can all at least help ease that which will forever taunt children, the feeling of not being wanted or loved by anyone. Easing their pain was my full intention when I went there, but now I wonder who has helped whom. Many times they have eased my pains. I believe all that I did or achieved in my life, I did trying to show them that people can do anything when they put their mind to it. I think they know that now, and I will help them to find that confidence and belief in themselves that I worked so hard at to find in myself, so that one day they too might find that same pride in themselves.

In my own life, I will find something else I love to do. I'm lucky to live in a country that allows me to do so.

Jonathan Miles

After reading the letter under watery eyes, tears began running down Kay's cheeks. When finished, she folded the letter and put it back into the envelope before placing it back into the drawer. She would have to think about how to react to her find. She was glad for the discovery. Perhaps, some day the consequences of the discovery would not be in Grover's favor.

There is a melody, a song in fact that was once quite popularly played on a piano in a famous movie. It could still be said to carry its share of admirers. It's called, 'As Time Goes By.' Just as the implication of the tune suggests, time does go by very quickly, as it did for Jonas. The weeks became months, and the months stretched into years. His new passion for painting never ceased. His paintings were limited to western cowboy and stagecoach scenes, and also original Marilyn Monroe depictions. With each painting his work improved and he did get quicker but he never became a fast painter. There were literally thousands of photos taken of Marilyn Monroe. When Jonas was ready to paint another picture of her he would spend a whole day searching archives for the one that stood out to him. It would usually be one not familiar with the public that projected her sparkle and energy. Some were a reflection of her fame, and some were more personal. Jonas felt he understood her a little better than many. There would never ever again be a Marilyn Monroe. She had a mysteriousness about her which was bold, childlike, glamorous and secretive. To the camera lens, she knew how to throw out that intoxicating look that left the viewer wondering what was next and wanting more. In her youth she was cunning and ambitious. During her reign she was meticulous and a perfectionist. In the end she was used, but then, she was always used until she really didn't know what truth was or who her friends were. Jonas would keep his finished paintings locked up in a closet at his Industrial building.

One day, when Jonas was driving down Olympic Boulevard he saw a vehicle that had a 'For Sale', sign on it. It was a 1970 Toyota Land Cruiser FJ-40. He had just pulled up next to it at a red light. The driver was gunning the engine and Jonas could tell that this one had the echo of a mean and healthy V-8 motor in it. He quickly wrote down the phone number, than shouted at the driver that he was interested. He followed the driver to a close by parking lot and two days later Jonas owned it. There probably was never a tougher off road vehicle built for the general public. Compared to an American built CJ-Jeep it was much stronger and heavier than a Kaiser CJ Jeep. So this tough off road vehicle had the brand new and popular Gates Commando XT off road tires on double welded wheels. Toyota was already ahead of the game when they began delivering these vehicles to the marketplace in a slightly more toned down version. The stock power plant was an inline straight six engine, a sort of GM copy. A V-8 retro fit was a simple enough task for the do it yourself mechanic.

THIRTY ONE

The Last Cruise

With the passing of the years not only had Jonas grown older so had the children that became a big part of his life. It was 1987, and not only had all them left the orphanage and graduated from high school, Matt and Wanda finished college. Tommy was in his third year of college majoring in Business. Jonas had promised his bunch of fast growing adolescents that he would pay for their entire education as long as they were serious about it.

One day to Jonas's surprise he went out to the mail box and there was an envelope from Grover Samuelson. It was a sympathetic letter of sorts perhaps meant to be an apology. The letter would not go so far as to admit to accepting responsibility for the demise of any of Jonas's careers, but he did want to try to make some kind of offering of an apology. He wrote that he and Kay had watched Jonas play in several baseball games. Kay even asked Grover to go with her to watch several of Jonas's singing engagements. Grover admitted he was somewhat jealous of Jonas's multi-talented abilities. Whether it was at the demands of Grover's wife Kay or indeed his own conscience, enclosed within the envelope was another envelope. When Jonas opened it up there was a note and check enclosed for one hundred thousand dollars. The note read:

Mr. Miles,

I'm very well aware that Wanda and Matt finished college, and now Tommy is attending. They will be an inspiration to all those who now live at the orphanage. I would suppose they have you to thank for that far more than I who simply tries my best to keep the institution going. Please accept this check as an apology that I know doesn't begin to fix the harm I have brought on you. Money can never be a substitute for one's passions in life. I only hope it may be put to use for further worthy desires of these children, whom you have so skillfully guided to a better life than many whom have gone before them.

Most Cordially,
Grover Samuelson

In life, we are taught to try to forgive those who transgress us as best we can. That was what Jonas tried to do. It wasn't easy forgiving Grover Samuelson for taking Kay from him or being responsible for ruining his life's pursuits. However, all that was in the past now and he had only to think about the future.

The money that Jonas received from Grover would be kept to further the sensible ambitions of his adopted family. In fact, in that same year the last names of the orphaned kids were changed to 'Miles', because Jonas wanted it and they wanted it. With Grover's money, Jonas was able to fund Connie's desire to start a mail order business comprised of worldwide offerings of unique products. Fred moved south to Orange County and began a chain dry cleaning business in Corona Del Mar, Newport, and Costa Mesa. He took flying lessons and got his commercial pilot's license. For extra income he got work as a charter pilot flying people in and out of various airports throughout the southland.

Wanda, with the help of an older printer she dragged out of retirement set up shop in a corner of Jonas's factory building. She began using those old printing presses that Jonas's father once used with some other acquired machines and started her own edition of a Hollywood magazine which was drawing much attention. She vowed it would never become a character assassination tabloid but focus on constructive interviews of current stars. It would feature a new talent section of Hollywood hopefuls, young stars who had made an impression in the business.

In the immediate years following Jonas's dismissal from baseball, he had enjoyed taking some night classes at UCLA. He had never enrolled in any drama classes in High School and had regretted that he had never done a lot of things he wanted due to his once shy personality. Jonas was committing himself to accept new challenges in his life. He wanted to know how movies were made from the beginning to end. He took some cinematography classes, a writing class, movie editing, and even some basic acting classes. He found all of these classes very interesting and met new people whom shared the same interests as himself. Of course, it didn't take long for many of his classmates to realize who he was, even from the first day of class. Jonas entertained the thought of possibly finding a job with a movie production company or someday spinning off his own film company. One could never know how far they could go unless they tried and trying was something Jonas never give up on.

On a calm and beautiful warm Friday in May, Jonas was about to meet up with some of his old High School friends. The plan was they would all go on a weekend camping trip out to a local desert near Lancaster in Jonas's Toyota Land Cruiser. He removed the vehicles hard top and attached a soft vinyl roof that would serve to keep the sun off of them. Whenever desired, it could be removed in an instant. Once they got out in the desert he planned on folding the front windshield down on the hood. The rush of the oncoming air over oneself within a fast moving vehicle could be exhilarating. There was also a back seat so the rig could transport all three of his old high school friends, Tim, Oscar, and Dean. He would pull a small utility trailer that had all the camping equipment they would need. It had been a long time since they saw each other.

The following morning when the three met it took only a short while until they were making jokes about one another or talking about old times. Tim and Oscar were still married to the same women Jonas had remembered meeting long ago, before they lost track of one another. Dean had married but now was single again. Once they got out into the desert they found a good spot and quickly set up camp before going four wheeling. They brought some treasure finder metal detectors to try out by an old ghost town. They had great fun that day exploring and visiting old places they had never been. They made it back to camp just before nightfall. They got a roaring camp fire going with firewood they had brought. When the fire died down they threw some steaks on the grill. Then they decided it was time to break out their own spirits, be it beer, bourbon, or rum. By early evening they were all pretty well sloshed. There seemed to be a million stars out that night in the vast desert sky. Dean kept urging Jonas to head out for a midnight ride. He had some wild idea about cavorting around under the light of a half moon to see how many coyotes they could count. The idea didn't sound that interesting to Jonas, but finally he gave in and the four climbed into the off road vehicle and set off in a drunken stupor. Dean wanted to drive the vehicle which Jonas wasn't so keen on but finally relented. Besides, it wasn't that often that Jonas got to leave the driving to someone else.

Dean was an ex midget race car driver. Sometimes he would do the unexpected when one wasn't ready to anticipate his next crazy move. Like most race car drivers, he seemed to have a need for speed as they say. He liked to push vehicles to their limit. Perhaps that was why Jonas even though drunk, hesitated when Dean wanted to drive.

These guys knew all about Jonas's life, his career ups and downs and how he could surprise the hell out of them at times. However, of course they didn't know anything about his actual personal life except that he was single and the orphans he took in. They didn't know about any of his personal relationships, his inherited wealth, or other matters. Jonas kept much to himself.

Now Dean was barreling down a dirt road that went to God knows where near fifty miles an hour. The vehicle at times hit a rise in the road that left the vehicle momentarily air borne. The song, 'Peace Train ', by Cat Stevens was blaring out of Jonas's 8 track tape deck. They had been drinking for some time. The alcohol served to deny some of them their normal degree of common sense. They chose not to recognize what they had become, but what they once were; those long ago rambunctious kids just out of high school.

The fast moving throaty vehicle that carried them on their night's journey would return to them a glimpse of a dreamy nostalgia, one that served up their pasts and they would not give it up. Tomorrow it would all be over, perhaps never to live again. Now this boisterous quartet of delusional knights became hurled through the starry nights rushing wind, which pinned the hair back against their ears. A coyote crossed the road in the distance. Suddenly Dean turned off the radio.

"Hey Joni, sing us some Sinatra," said Dean.

Jonas grinned, not sure it was possible in his state of inebriation.

"Yeah Jonas, sing some Sinatra!" bellowed Tim.

"OK, so I'm a jute box now, huh? What's your pleasure then?" he asked.

"Sing, 'Drinking Again'" laughed Dean followed by the others laughing.

"Hey Dean, take a hit on this," yelled out one of the voices from the back seat. It was a joint, marijuana. The two front seat occupants turned around to look at what was being offered. The gesture came as a complete surprise to the two. As Dean and Jonas were looking at Oscar and Tim in the back, they noticed an immediate change within their faces. There was a complete loss of composure on the back seat occupants as their faces changed from expressions of devilish grins, to a state of panic stricken horror.

"Watch out," the two yelled from the back seat.

By the time Dean and Jonas turned their heads back around toward the road again, it was too late. Just feet in from of them was a telephone pole coming at them in excess of 45 mph. The two guys in the back seat had earlier independently fastened their seat belts because they had been bouncing around so much. Their precautionary considerations would spare their lives. Their bodies would remain in the vehicle. Even Dean himself had fastened his belt but Jonas never had as he was just holding onto the dash mounted handle like a bucking bronco rider, whenever the vehicle leapt up off the ground. It was just like he had done in Gina's Jeep.

If the vehicle they were in had been any other type of car or truck there could have been worse consequences. However, the heavy steel frame construction of the Toyota, its weighty V-8 engine, and strong protruding front bumper had delivered a blow similar to a black belt's karate chop. On impact the telephone pole became completely severed at the junction of where the bumper met it and the stout wooden pole rolled backward right over the top of the roll bar before falling off to the side of the road. Because the front windshield had been down the only place that had been badly damaged was the front bumper and hood. When the vehicle stopped there were severed live electrical wires hissing and sparking all about. The three people remaining in the vehicle looked at each other in a dazed like drunken stupor. They were in complete shock. Jonas was gone. He was no longer in the vehicle. The engine was still running as ugly as everything looked.

"Where's Jonas?" asked Tim.

"I don't know." replied Oscar.

The vehicles headlights were not facing down the road but out into the desert.

"Will the thing still drive?" asked Oscar.

Putting it in first gear Dean let out the clutch and it lurched forward.

"It still drives, so far" said Tim.

Tim climbed over the front seat and got in where Jonas was.

"Let's drive around slowly. We have got to find Jonas," said Tim.

Tim found a flashlight in the glove box. He turned it on and pointed it out toward the open desert.

"Is everybody okay?" asked Dean.

Oscars head struck the roll bar. There was blood running down the side of his face.

"I think everyone's okay, except we got to find Jonas. Let's hurry. We have to find him," yelled Tim.

While trying to stay out of the way of the electrical wires they searched for Jonas. They finally found him about eighty feet down the side of the road. His body lay still, deformed, bloodied, and seemingly lifeless. He was lying on his chest with his face in the dirt. They carefully rolled him over. His eyes were open, but still. The boys, the men, were gravely frightened. They feared the worse, and unfortunately their assumptions were correct. Jonathan Miles had tragically died that night with his old high school chums. He began some of the best years of his life with them and with them spent his last. The same ones he had shared a good part of his most memorable teenage days on long ago whims of fancy. They were the people one never forgot through the good and bad, right and wrong, scorn and praise. They were lifelong friends. It would be a night none of them would ever forget. They all blamed themselves. They cried and they cried, especially Dean. He would forever blame himself. That night would forever haunt him. If only he hadn't persisted in going out four wheeling. If only he had watched the road. If only he had done this or done that. Could Jonas have lived if it didn't happen so far away from home? If they had a big car maybe they could have taken him somewhere. They quit making up excuses, they all knew Jonas was gone. They picked him up and draped his lifeless body upon the knees of Dean and Tim in the back seat as Oscar drove to the nearest town.

THIRTY TWO

Thanks for the Kiss

When the news of Jonas's death hit the papers it was on the back side of the front page in a six by two inch column. The short headline just read,' Glenn Miles Dead at 43.' It went on to mention his singing career and his short lived baseball excursion. There were a few words about his former marriage and his sons. As for the Los Angeles Orphans home, the article only stated that he had helped out with orphan children. The article really did not have any praise to offer him, it just stated a series of facts that surrounded his life.

To say the least Jonas's mother was devastated over his death. His sister Elizabeth had to make the funeral arrangements. She remembered that not too long ago members of the family were discussing how they wanted to be disposed of upon death. Jonas had said that he thought that the Westwood cemetery was a peaceful place.

"I think Westwood is small, quaint, and peaceful. It lay's like a lost green oasis in the midst of fortress like buildings. It's a place where birds sing and the leaves of tall limbs dance within spring and autumns cool breeze," was how Jonas phrased it. After giving some considerable thought about her brother and the circumstances of his public life she thought it best to place him in a mausoleum as he wished. He would be at Westwood and she would have an appropriate bronze plaque made. The plaque would have musical notes, a baseball bat and an emblem of five children holding hands at arm's length. Under that would be, Jonas Miles, Our Beloved – A Life of Fancy, January 27, 1944 - May 12, 1987.

She also would hire auctioneers to go into the house to sell off Jonas's furniture and belongings. Elizabeth never expected more than a handful of people to show on the day of the funeral. The reality was that no one had any idea that so many people would show up at the chapel in his honor. They were mostly all the people who ever had any association with Jonas while he was singing, playing baseball and many others from the orphanage. Grover and Kay Samuelson and Eleanor Marore was there. Of course, Matt, Fred, Connie,

Tommy, Wanda, and Sandra Steinman were there. Anniston Conroy was there. It was shocking to many that even Frank Sinatra made a brief appearance for Jonas.

Another very passionate and good friend was there. He was asked to give the eulogy by Jonas's sister. His name was Theo Scott and he happily accepted. He didn't bring any written words, all his words were just memories from the heart. He started off by saying how that first day of baseball practice he watched this carefree, angular, limber guy walk toward a group of people made up of color of whom some were probably just as biased and prejudiced as some white people. Nobody there would have bet a plug nickel that Jonas was going to want to stay there longer than a few days. He went on to say;

.....well just by the nature of his character,
I couldn't see how anyone could not like Jonas.
Jonas was color blind. I think most of the guys figured that out. You can pretend to be colorblind but that's something you can see. Jonas was a gifted man. As I got to know him and share a few beers with him over a kitchen table I began to realize he was a solitary person. I don't think he felt lonely. He told me he was going to introduce me to someone that was really special which he did that day after we shared a six pack of beer. It was just after he got picked up to play the minors. I'm not going to say anything more about who he introduced me to, but I have to tell you it was then I realized how diverse the minds are of each of us. When I left the house I drove around the corner and parked so I could cry, or think, or just wonder how stupid, or smart, each of us is. In retrospect, I'm not sure Jonas was alone or lonely at all. Sometimes many of us just don't understand others, or why they are the way they are. Maybe it's beyond our comprehension. I do believe if Jonas just could have played a few more years of baseball I think he would have earned quite a name for himself in that sport, more than he already had. I feel a need to say a few more things. Injustice takes all forms and shapes, but if any man ever tries to suggest to me that Jonas was anything but the best of character, or cares to repeat what some of those drunken ignorant fans yelled out to him on the ball field, crushing his dreams, I will forget that I'm supposed to live in a

civilized world. Jonas didn't leave this world without leaving his footprints in the sand. There are five special people here today who know exactly what I'm talking about. God bless them. I know that wherever it is Jonas is right now, he's in the company of giants.

Theo left the lectern with teary eyes. Jonas's old school friends, Tim, Oscar, Dean, and Derek had been his pallbearers. It was a sad day that finally came to an end for Jonas's family and friends. Strangely, it had only been the preceding few months that Jonas had a living trust drawn up leaving all his assets to his mother, his sister, and his five adopted children.

Less than two weeks later a small freight truck pulled up to Jonas's home in Santa Monica. It was the estate auction company that Elizabeth had hired to liquidate Jonas's belongings. Elizabeth had gone into the home prior to that day and removed things that she thought she or her mother would like to have. Two guys got out of the truck. Their job was to make the home look presentable for the auctioneer on the day of the auction. That meant to get rid of any stuff that might be classified as junk or unsalable items. The sun room off the kitchen where Jonas painted was a mess. Besides his large heavy easel there were paint tubes, brushes, and all kinds of things one might use in painting scattered about on a small table. The auction people decided they could probably sell those things to an artist. They placed all the loose items in a box and put all the painting things in a corner and attached a catalog tag to the easel. They attached a tag to all the furniture items. Then they started the process of throwing out all those things that were personal in nature, with no value. One of the workers was a new hire, Christos, and the other guy was a nephew of the auctioneer. His name was Marty. Marty was the guy to ask that day about what to keep or throw out.

"Hey Marty, should I throw this Monroe cardboard thing out?" asked Christos.

"Yeah."

"Go get another trash barrel out of the garage. This one is about filled up," he added.

When he came back he folded Marilyn up and put her on the bottom of the container and then he went to look for more stuff to throw out. When he returned, Marilyn had strangely stood herself back up again, towering over the top. Christos just looked at her and shook his head.

"Okay, Marilyn, I don't blame you," commented the man as he started throwing stuff all around the bottom of the container until it piled up about Marilyn's torso. Marty was placing blankets in a box of which they would donate to a local shelter.

"Hey Marty, looks like I found some autographed photos," yelled out Christos."

"I'll take a look at them in a second," responded Marty.

When he came into the room he looked at the photos.

"Let's see, you got a Frank Sinatra photo done with what's supposed to look like a Sharpie autograph. That's fake, or just a copy. Hah, of course Marilyn fan worshipers always have a copy of a signed photo and this one has got a kiss stuck to it. I've never seen a Marilyn signature like that. See the way they signed the M's in Marilyn and Monroe. Doesn't have those smooth swirls like she does it, and the down stroke on the 'L' is all wrong. You can have them if you like fake stuff, but I'd toss 'em."

"Are you sure? Toss it?" asked Christos.

Marty just looked at him for a second, making a face.

"Yeah, they're both fake. I went through all this when I first got into this work. Keeping everything like that I found and taking them downtown only to be told fake, time after time," stated Marty, dropping them into the can.

"Where did you find them, anyway?" asked Marty.

"Just for the heck of it I ran my hand over the top of the book case. That's where I found them, up there."

The spot was where Jonas always placed the photos when he left town.

"Yeah, it's amazing the places people put stuff," responded Marty.

"Hmm," responded the other man.

"Fact is, there are hundreds of fans wished they had an authentic Marilyn autograph. Most all of them are just fake copies," repeated Marty.

"That lipstick mark, she might do that for someone special like Joe DiMaggio, or a close friend."

"Who the heck is this guy who lived here anyways?" asked Christos, the new hire. It seemed like a sensible question.

"I don't know. Let me see," says Marty taking a work order slip out of his pocket.

"Ticket says Jonas L Mills, residence." The two looked at each other and shrugged their shoulders. Even though the last named was misspelled, it probably wouldn't had made any difference if it wasn't.

By lunchtime, they had the home cleaned up and everything was tagged for the auction that was to take place on the following Monday. They set the trash cans out by curbside and left the job with only one thing on their minds; hunger pains, which they would soon take care of.

That same afternoon Mrs. Masters, Jonas's neighbor, was out watering her lawn. When she heard the news of what happened to Jonas she felt very sad for him because she learned what a good person he had been toward the orphan children. She was one of those at his funeral. At about 2:15 pm, she could hear the trash truck coming down the street. She usually waved to the driver if she was outside. She watched the truck park alongside her container. Then this big mechanical arm came out, picked up her trash container and dumped all within into the back of the truck just like always and then set it back down. She watched and thought it somewhat amusing to see a Marilyn Monroe cardboard figure sticking out of the top of Jonas's container. After dumping Mrs. Master's trash the truck was full and it was time to compact the trash. So before the truck pulled forward to Jonas's container the operator began the compact cycle to make more room for trash. It was just then that what looked like a brand new Ferrari was driving down the street. When the expensive vehicle got alongside Jonas's house it stopped just ahead of the trash truck. Then a woman got out of the car and ran toward the trash container, grabbed Marilyn, folded her up and put her in the back of her car and sped off. It was Kay Samuelson, the only other person besides Theo that Jonas had introduced to his cardboard Marilyn standup.

She thought of a better place for the time being to put the item than the local dump. Thinking back to that day she was in Jonas's home she had occasionally thought about that cardboard figure that Jonas seemed a bit protective of. Strangely, Kay had fantasized about some unique mysteriousness about the face of the caricature that seemed larger than life. Her husband might not like it, but she was going to find a place at the orphanage for her.

As for Elizabeth and Ariane Miles there was no immediate urgency to sell Jonas's house. Also, Jonas had brought the orphan kids over to his mother's home many times. Arianne had become attached to them and had a special appreciation for them considering what they had met to her son.

No one knew that Jonas had been doing any paintings until Elizabeth had went into his home and saw the easel, half used tubes of paint and those other things associated with artist equipment. She looked around everywhere for finished paintings but could not find any in the home. Elizabeth asked the orphan children if they knew anything about them. None of them seemed to know anything, except Wanda. She often saw Jonas bring large square items wrapped in brown paper and put them in a closet that he kept locked at the industrial building while she tended to her publication business. The following Saturday, Wanda, Elizabeth, and her mother Ariane went down to the industrial building. Strangely, neither Jonas's mother nor his sister had ever seen the building before, but now they owned it and all those things inside. Only Jonas's dad had seen the building and what was inside, that being a nice tidy tally in collector cars.

They had a bundle of keys with them and started trying all them on the lock to Jonas's closet. Eventually they found the right one and opened the door. Inside were several dozen large individually wrapped rectangular forms which they concluded were probably paintings. Nearly all of them had a side at least four feet in length. They talked it over about what they should do with them. No one had ever seen any of Jonas's paintings. They might be terrible, or on the other hand they might be good. No one knew what he painted; whether landscapes, portraits, modern, or what, so they took them all away to Arianne's home.

When they got them back to Jonas's mother's house, they removed the paper covering from one of the paintings. What they discovered was a beautiful full face close- up of Marilyn Monroe that was done from a Bert Stern photograph. She had her hands on her face as if she was looking into her mirror. They all looked at the painting and they found it breathtaking, in that Marilyn's pose seemed to consume your attention. It was like the viewer was her mirror. The painting was nothing short of magnificent. Wondering what the other paintings might be they removed the covering from one more. It was another Marilyn painting. This one was done from a George Barris photo. It was just as wonderful as the first. There were paintings done based on many of the famous photographers who photographed her. It was then they decided to just take the paintings down to a professional gallery.

The surprises that week were one after the other for Elizabeth and her mother. Jonas's two actual children, Calvin and Charles who were now grown men had sent them a letter stating that they were going to have an attorney challenge the beneficiaries of his estate. It was kind of comical that all of a sudden there was an interest in Jonas from that other family, but Ariane concluded it was all of his ex-wife, Lynn's doing.

Funny how, even in death, elements were in the works to ruin Jonas's final wishes. All it would amount to though would be an attempt that would never amount to any success. The Miles testimony and other documents could prove that Jonas was basically ostracized from the new family Lynn created. Jonas transferred his assets via a living trust, not a will which could have possibly been challenged. There was a letter enclosed with the trust that asserted his feelings that he had been excluded from his sons via his ex wife's psychological conditioning upon them. He went on to say how sorry and emotionally affected he became when his birth children seemed to express no interest in wanting to visit, or see him. No doubt, he thought it had something to do with the wealth of their new step father.

As for the classic cars, what were the two Miles women going to do with them? After all, there were more important things that the money could be used for, like new shoes and clothes. Well, that was only partially true, as some of the orphans who were of course now grown adults had successfully persuaded the two to keep most of them. After taking a closer look at the cars, Elizabeth concluded she would like to personally drive some of them on occasion, so selling the lot was postponed for now. She wanted Jonas's 1958 Chevy that he drove. She could never sell his 23 window, VW bus, she certainly wanted to keep that. None of Jonas's adopted kids would ever forgive her if she sold that. It was what transported them around when Jonas first met them and took them everywhere. They thought the best choice for Ariane would be the 60 Ford Starliner. When it came down to really putting the finger on which ones had to go, the number became less and less. Finally the ones they were letting go were a La Salle, a VW bug, and an Oldsmobile.

Other than the sadness that the loss of Jonas brought to the seven close people in his life, life went on for the new Miles family. They took care of each other, especially the new younger additions to the family, helping Ariane with things around the house. It was what Jonas would have wished for. In the years following the passing of Jonas, though Tommy never became a doctor he majored in business and landed a good paying job as store manager of a major department store. Fred's dry cleaning business took off and he bought himself a house two blocks from shore, in Corona Del Mar.

Connie's mail order business out earned her orphan siblings annual earnings by a long shot. She could not keep up with demand in the current strong economy. Needing more room it was perfectly all right with Ariane and Elizabeth for Connie to move into the Industrial building with Wanda. Both their incomes would make it easier to pay the buildings taxes.

Wanda was so busy trying to stay on top of her new Hollywood events publication that she rarely even had time for herself, but she liked being busy that way. As for Matt, after a few years with local police work he was successful in gaining employment with the IRS, investigating corporations and large 401k investment firms.

Meanwhile, a few days later a young and somewhat poor lad who worked as an Auction House prep helper, named Christos, came home from work one evening to his one room apartment in South Central Los Angeles. It was already dark out as he turned on a light. He had a Mexican takeout meal in a bag he brought home and set it on his small two person dining table. He walked over to a second hand entertainment table he had bought at the Salvation Army and turned on his 19 inch Zenith color TV to watch a ball game. Next to the TV were two glass framed pictures, one was of Frank Sinatra and the other of Marilyn Monroe. Monroe's photo had an imprint of a red lipstick kiss. They both had writing on them and were signed. Whether the writing was real or not did not preoccupy the young man's thinking. He had other things to think about. Christos didn't care what Marty had told him. He didn't care that they were fake. He took them out of the can after Marty went back to the other room to work. He liked the way Frank sang. He liked Marilyn Monroe very much. He thought that they were nice pictures of them both. Christos ate his dinner slowly savoring every bite as he watched the, Rams play the Browns. Tomorrow was another work day, but right now he was on his time. He looked content and happy as he ate, drank a beer and watched the game. He also brought home the newspaper that he bought that morning. He had thrown it on the other chair of the dining table. Maybe he would read it and maybe he wouldn't. On the front page the headline read, 'Hoard of Marilyn Monroe Paintings Found'. The story went on to say some Saudi Sheiks had expressed a great interest in them. For the time being the lot would be on display at a local museum.

THIRTY THREE

A Gathering of Souls

Many years had passed after Jonas's death. It was a very foggy late night evening in West Los Angeles. The fog was so thick one could hardly see across the length of a car. Through the fog came John Jeffrey Majors as he was walking along Glendon Avenue toward Wilshire. As he walked he was mumbling to himself his words not discernible. If he had any friends they would have called him JJ or John J, because that was what he told everyone his name was, JJ. However, JJ really didn't have any friends, at least not any real friends. He used to at one time years ago. He even used to have a wife and a kid and a successful hardware business. Once he took to drinking he just never could get his life straightened out again. Now he mostly hung out around the beach.

In a way it wasn't his fault that the big box stores moved into his neighborhood and drove him out of business. It happened to a lot of mom and pop businesses. It seemed like the only businesses that survived were specialty stores or cafes and restaurants that served up good food. Now it was sad he had to ask people on the street for money even though at another time in his life he freely gave to charities.

So along came John J, just like he always had before making his way toward Wilshire, down one street or another to get there. There was a place near Wilshire where he often could make a profitable nights sum with the pan handling. It was a place where people gathered who really didn't have anything left of the basic things in life, like a roof to call one's own. He was stumbling a little and the closer he got to Wilshire the more he seemed to stumble. Probably because he had already drank more than usual. He finally made it to what looked like an alley and ducked in a ways until he could carry himself a little better. He almost fell and put his hand out against a wall to keep from falling. When he looked up he could barely make out a plaque that read, 'Westwood Memorial Park Cemetery.' There was a place there where he decided to sit it out for a while so he sat down back in from the street. It was quiet except for every once in a while a car would slowly drive by through the fog on Glendon Avenue. No one would have a reason to turn into that very short and brief alley off of Glendon, except maybe another homeless person like JJ. The cemetery was closed and there was a tall wrought iron gate there that was locked after hours.

As the minutes passed, suddenly John J thought he could hear something like voices or a distant faint singing. Maybe it was someone's car radio. The voices seemed to be getting closer and a little bit louder. Even though his vision wasn't at its peak it seemed like in his current condition his hearing became superfluous. There was a conglomeration of notes, words, and voices. The bits and pieces of songs that were being intercepted seemed quite familiar to him. After all, he had lived in Los Angeles his whole life. There must have been a group of people coming his way but he could not see much through the thick fog. One by one he began identifying the voices of each individual. He thought he heard Dean Martin's voice.

"Volare, woh-woh-woh-woh," came a quickly sung series of vocalizations.

"Your voice has a twang in it, Dean," said someone with an unfamiliar voice.

"A twang, Is that good or bad?" asked another's voice that reminded JJ of someone famous.

"Well, for Dean it's good. If Frankie had a twang that might be a problem and it's a good thing Marilyn's voice doesn't have a twang. I don't think that would be good either," said a familiar woman's voice that sounded like Eve Arden.

"I can't imagine anyone but Dean having a twang in his voice," added the opinion of a new resident who had recently moved into that prestigious neighborhood of deceased celebrities. Again, it was another voice that John J was not familiar with.

There seemed to be only two distinct female voices, the one of Eve Arden and the other individual who had been called Marilyn. John J could not conclude for certain who the one called Marilyn was. There were many Marilyn's but Eve Arden's voice is very unique and couldn't be mistaken. The group was slowly getting closer to John J and louder.

One might not have a precise estimation of how logically conclusive or coherent an overly intoxicated mind could become, but John J knew he was in Los Angeles. Here, anything was possible, a city where impersonators and ambitious people roam.

"You know it should fog up like this more often. It's nice to give the old duds a little workout," said a voice that reminded John J of Rodney Dangerfield. Rodney was another person whose voice was unforgettable.

"Hey baby, come to Daddy," shot out Rodney's voice. John J wasn't sure to whom the statement was directed.

"Why are you walking with that mutt when you can walk with me?" echoed Dangerfield's voice again.

The one that was called Marilyn was with one of the men whom had an unfamiliar voice that sounded a little like Frank's. Those two were following up the rear. She was the woman whom Rodney had been speaking to.

"You mean come back to Grandpa, fella," came one of the voices that JJ now thought sounded like Sinatra.

"Jonas will kick your ass, Rodney," said Dean.

"He hasn't got it in him. He's too nice," said Rodney.

"You should try being nice sometime Rodney. It would give you a whole new look on life," came Eve's voice.

"Oh honey, you know I'm nice," responded Rodney.

"Sure Rodney, your nice, except it's hard to tell the difference between you and Don Rickles with the jokes," responded Eve.

Suddenly, the approaching voices were now making another noise, the sound of footsteps. Primarily the sound of a woman's high heels on pavement coming at a casual pace.

"Where we going anyway, would love to go into a night club," said Dean.

"Don't tell me you still crave booze?" remarked a person named Jonas.

"Hey, Kid, who said you could speak," blurted Frank.

"When are you going to start calling him Jonas?" demanded Marilyn.

"Never, I'll call him Glenn though, not Jonas. He's a Glenn."

"Hey! It's our night off, right? We spooks only get foggy nights off," said Rodney, with Marilyn laughing.

"I think they made it clear we're not spooks. We're creatures of the higher worlds now," said Dean, his leather soled shoes barely making a sound compared to Marilyn's heels as they walked along the alley.

"You know, we could just about go anywhere unnoticed if Marilyn wasn't wearing those heels," said Rodney.

"Sorry, but these are what I was given at my funeral," said Marilyn.

"Just joking darling, don't take me seriously. I'm trying to learn how to be nice, remember," Rodney laughed.

John J's head was still a buzz. He was far from sober but not crazy. He hadn't taken a drink since he first heard the voices. The group's voices were now quite close, nearly upon him. He was certain they wouldn't see him in the fog and he was sitting out of sight. Surely the gate must be locked. How could they have gotten through it?

"One thing about this crazy town, you can look just about like anyone and not get a second look," interjected Rodney.

"That's right, unless they're trying to look like you, Rodney," said Frank.

"Always coming with the punches, huh Frank," responded Rodney.

"You know, I've been nice to you but you haven't been especially nice to me," said Rodney.

"Oh, come on. You're with friends now, Rodney. Just don't piss Frank off. He'll put a contract on yuh," said Dean.

"Contract, I'm already dead for Christ's sake. Oops, I'm not supposed to say that word, am I?" responded Rodney.

"Okay guys, can you cool your selves off a bit. Were getting close to civilization," said Eve.

"Where's Marilyn?" asked Frank, looking around toward the rear of the ensemble.

"She's back there in deep conversation with your friend, Glenn," spoke up Rodney.

"By the way Frank, how's things over in your neighborhood?" asked Rodney.

"Fine, but I wanted to come over to see Marilyn for a change. Looks like I got competition with the kid," Rodney laughed.

"No, you will only have competition if Joe shows up," said Dean.

Now they were right in front of John J, as they were passing by. He could make out their moving shoes near the ground, even a portion of their clothes. He saw the intermittent dim outline of their moving figures, even their faces at times through the changing viscosity of the fog. Then he heard something he thought he would never hear.

"Hey, there's JJ! Hi John J," said Marilyn, everyone looking.

"Hi John," said everyone. John J was well hidden, but they knew who he was.

While looking at them with his head held low and his eyes poking through the top of his eyelids, JJ felt fear and a sense of inescapable vulnerability at that moment.

"I remember long ago when my first husband and I stopped at John J's hardware store to buy a garden hose for my aunt's yard," said Marilyn.

"Yeah, I was in there several times myself," responded Dean.

"Too bad about what happened to a lot of folks' family businesses," said Dean.

John J could plainly hear what they were saying now. It didn't matter to them. They knew no one else was around. He could also intermittently see them, but not in any long lasting definitive manner. John J was a privileged mortal that night. At times the fog cleared enough to allow him to see the obscured features of their faces. Those faces matched the voices of the departed celebrities he had imagined they were.

"Poor guy reminds me of a song," said Frank.

"Please don't say, 'Drinking Again,'" interjected Jonas.

"No, "My Kind of Town," answered Frank. So Frank sang a few chords of that song.

"Very Good Frank, What else, can you sing?" asked Eve.

"Well, if Marilyn Monroe would get her butt up here, I might sing something like, oh, say, 'The Way You Look Tonight'."

"Hey, I love that one," said Eve.

"Then I'll sing it for you doll," said Frank, as he began to sing a few chords.

"Hey, that was pretty good for no twang in the voice," said Marilyn, they all laughing.

"Sing us something, Deano," asked Frank.

As they reached Glendon Avenue and were turning to walk around the corner of the building headed toward Wilshire, John J heard Dean singing, 'Welcome to My World.' It was a particularly stimulating song with a noticeable twang in his voice that set him off from the others.

The last thing JJ heard was Marilyn laughing. She could project a very memorable carefree lively laugh when she found humor in something. Then their voices drifted away into obscurity until there was complete silence for several minutes followed by the noise of a passing car.

That night's experience would never lose itself from John J's conscience, not even his sober one. The following evening John J took himself down and joined the closest Alcoholics Anonymous meeting place. Something that night near the cemetery had awoken something in him that wasn't alive for years. He was so drunk he couldn't swear if anything he witnessed was real, imagined, or acted out perhaps by a bunch of crazies. Whatever it was, it changed something in him. Why did it take some foggy night's hallucination or whatever it was to wake up his senses? He didn't have the answers yet but he would find a way to get back to living a normal human existence. He would take back his life. Maybe he wouldn't get rich but John J would find some pride in himself again.

When a still and damp morning finally arrived the sun was just cresting the mountain peaks and it would still have the previous evening's fog to contend with. The sunlight came slowly as it dribbled in with increasing intensity within the climbing path of the sun. By noon, the sun had burned off any remnants of any remaining fog where the sea met land. There was a small flock of gulls coming in toward the Santa Monica pier as they were descending toward the beach. There was some squawking and screeching going on between some of the birds as if they had something worthwhile to say. The summer months had not fully arrived yet. There were very few people on the beach but there was a noticeably rather young, fit and shapely blonde jogging slowly down along the surf zone, just far enough into the water to get her feet wet.

The birds came in low with their wings set catching the air currents as they seemed to hover overhead near the pier. Most of the birds landed in a group on the sand in a scattered arrangement. There, they remained motionless except for their heads which turned when something caught their attention, usually people. They were making out like perfect observers as if they were waiting for something to happen. Some of the birds landed on stumps or whatever else caught their fancy. There were very few people on the pier. One person who was walking out on the pier was a lonely and lanky elderly man whose wife had passed away a few years prior. When she had been alive the two had always walked out on the pier together. It was still an everyday occurrence for him. He lived in a nearby condo that his wife's parents had left to them.

Halfway out, he stopped and peered over the side facing south. Just then a gull came in and landed on a railing post about six feet from the man. Looking out below over the railing the man watched the woman jogger as she slowly made her way down the beach. Suddenly, she broke her run and went to a walk. The man studied her. She left petite footsteps in the hard packed sand. Meanwhile, the gull seemed to be looking for something as it looked about. The man looked at the gull as the gull seemed to look at the man. The man had some thoughts about his observations of the bird. It wasn't the first time he looked at one of these creatures with a degree of suspicion. He often wondered about them. Perhaps they knew more then they let on.

"What are you looking for, gull?" asked the man with short gray hair and worn clothes. His button up plaid shirt was wrinkled but neatly tucked in his trousers behind the taut belt of a slim waist.

Meanwhile below on the wet sand the early afternoon's incoming waves lapped away a bite at a time at the impressions of the woman's footprints. The man was thinking about this. He wondered how many waves it would take before there was nothing left of her footprint. It seemed it depended entirely on the fierceness of the waves. However, the waves were presently quite gentle. The waves were not so powerful this day. Soon the woman had gotten to be quite far down the beach.

The man didn't know it but the bird had answered his question.

"How did you know we were looking for someone," answered the gull exercising his beak.

The man was still watching the gentle waves come ashore. The sand was firm and the footprints were not eroding as fast as one might imagine. The man looked at the bird again as the bird seemed to return the gesture.

"How old are you, bird?" asked the man.

"I'm older then you might imagine," replied the bird as he once again seemed to chatter. The man kept looking at the footprints in the sand.

"What do you know? Tell me what you know?" asked the man, believing the bird really knew something important. Very few people had been walking by, just a few tourists and some locals. It seemed the birds beak was now really busy in motion.

"Hah, humans can't know what we know. We're usually looking for one of your kind whom we think are really special. Once in a great while what we are looking for just comes along and then we take to the air, hover overhead and do a lot of screeching, squawking and soaring. I'm afraid it doesn't happen that often," replied the bird resting its beak.

The man looking down, reached into his shirt pocket and brought out a locket. He opened it to view a picture of his deceased wife. He gazed at it for a short while. Then the man looked at the bird again.

"Why do you birds just sit around looking at people," asked the man.

"Well not for the same reasons your kind just sits around staring and talking to us," answered the bird.

The man had no idea what the birds moving beak met or if it was even saying anything.

The woman's footprints were soon gone, eroded away by the time of the waves. There was only smooth sand remaining. From the time of the beginning to the end was not long, rather short really. Then the man stood up, looked at the bird and left. The bird's beak moved a bit, but one couldn't be sure what it was saying.

Author's note

I feel fortunate to have grown up at a wonderful place and time. Some of my life's experiences helped me to assimilate ideas and events into the body of this novel. I personally think that there are significant icons in any nations past that can serve to infuse a sense of pride in that country, be those icons statesman, sports figures, national heroes, patriots, scientists, or performers in art. Shouldn't it be the purpose of each of us in life to strive to be the very best that we can become. Fame may not be what we all wish for, but famous personalities have shown that a person can come from the very bottom and rise up through the crust to embellish a name that becomes immortal. A fiction writer may write from one's own experiences, from ones imagination, or what the writer has researched. Jonas began his life as an average person like most, struggling in their youth to make it somewhere. I think Jonas caught his wave and lived his dream as best he could. However, no amount of fame was as important as was his resolve to help others. We can't all be world famous stars and the reality is no one leads a perfect life. We should all be glad to be alive, to pursue our dreams and perhaps make a difference in our world by using our own god given abilities. To anything specific in the story that you may question I leave to your imagination. Isn't it imagination that makes us grow and makes our world a better place.

www.ingramcontent.com/pod-product-compliance
Lightning Source LLC
Chambersburg PA
CBHW022210241025
34508CB00053B/1800